Table of

The Designer People

Space Colony Journals - Book 5

Gail Daley

About This Book

L ucinda worked hard to earn a place among Vensoog's law enforcement community.

On her first assignment, compassion impels her to protect an alien mother and daughter fleeing off-planet bounty hunters. To ensure their safety, she must defeat a deadly Soturi warrior in hand-to-hand combat. Can she do it?

Then she rescues a 'designer child' who is a younger double for herself from a sex trafficking ring. Can she solve this case and rescue the other children trapped by those same criminals? To do so she needs to catch a vicious Thieves Guild assassin. But even with the help of the best private eye on Vensoog, these are tough cases for a rookie cop.

Signature Page

Dedication

To the readers of my books who give me the inspiration to keep writing, and to my husband and my son who never gave up on me.

Acknowledgments

I would like to thank my son, Andrew S. Daley, my number one beta reader, who listens patiently to my plot ideas and points out the errors in my fight scenes.

Sister, Sister

I T WAS MIDNIGHT and Lucinda nursed a cup of Cafka as she waited for the time to report in for her first shift on Port Recovery's Security forces. Agra, her Dactyl, snuggled with her littermate Saura in the fur-lined nest made especially for them. Dactyls were six-limbed flying mammals native to Vensoog. They came in all sizes, from creatures large enough to hunt the Water Dragons living in the rivers and along the channels between the Equator Islands, to miniatures like Agra and Saura who were tiny enough to hold in your hand. Although tiny, they possessed all the characteristics of their species: limitless curiosity about the world around them, wings covered with long lint-like hair, a fluffy, down-coated body, talons on the rear feet, and arms with hand-like paws. Humans fell in love with them because of their soft coats, large ears, big dark eyes and pointed noses.

In the wild, Dactyls depended on their lightning fast flight speed to escape from predators. Like the Quirka, another native pet adopted by the settlers, Dactyls were empathic, bonding in love with their chosen humans.

Domesticated dactyls were rare; they were shy and seldom tamed unless taken as kits. Several years ago, Lucinda and her foster brother Rupert had been on a plant foraging expedition and found four orphaned, hungry Dactyl kits and adopted them into the family. The two males had bonded with the girl's foster brothers, Roderick and Rupert.

Because she intended to keep Agra with her while on duty, Lucinda and the dactyl had undergone specialized training as to how the dactyl should behave during the times when she accompanied Lucinda to work.

Lucinda was not yet a full-fledged officer in the planetary police force; all cadets had to do a three-month stint under a trainer before transitioning to a qualified officer. Cadets like Lucinda, and Agra in this case, remained on probation until their trainer was satisfied with their on-the-job performance.

Lucinda was excited to begin, although she let none of her anticipation show in her face, not even to her sister Juliette, sitting across from her in a night robe. The sisters looked nothing alike. Juliette was tiny, with a thin body, green eyes and a long, curly mane of red hair, while Lucinda was tall and full-bodied. Her white-blond hair, cut to chin length, fluffed around a heart-shaped face with red, cupid bow lips, a short nose and light grey eyes.

When Juliette and Lucinda were twelve and their younger sister Violet was ten, Lady Katherine and Lord Zack had come to the center looking for Lord Zack's orphaned nephews Rupert and Roderick.

Discovering the illegal nature of Grouter's operation, the couple had made sure Grouter was arrested for his part in the child sex trade. They adopted Lucinda, Juliette, and Violet as well as Zack's nephews. Although the three girls considered themselves sisters, they were 'designer children' who had been ordered to specifications. They had been born in a laboratory on one of the moons of Fenris and later lived on Fenris in a child placement center run by Hans Grouter. Grouter hid his identity as a lieutenant in the local Thieves Guild by posing as a dedicated government official, existing in an uneasy alliance with Jerry Van Doyle, who ran the Guilds prostitution business. Over Grouter's protests, Van Doyle recruited much of his "new meat" for the child prostitution arm from the Fenris Child Placement center.

Grouter had plans of his own for the girls, so he protected them from being used by Van Doyle. However, their life was by no means an easy one. From the first day they arrived, they had been subjected to harsh training methods to enable them to utilize their programed genetics for the Guild's criminal purposes. By the time Lady Katherine and her husband had rescued them, the girls were already an accomplished team of thieves who raided the rich of Fenris at Grouter's request.

Five years after coming to Vensoog, Juliette and Lucinda were just a few months away from receiving their Match Lists. Under Vensoog law, receiving your first List made you a full adult. The Match Lists had been created to help preserve the biological diversity of the human population. Traditionally they were issued by the Makers and given to all young people who came of age during Festivals in the spring and fall of each year. Varying opinions as the usefulness of the lists abounded among natives to Vensoog. Some like Laird Genevieve thought them simply useless, others believed you always found your true love on your List. But that was for the future; right now Lucinda was more concerned with her present situation.

For the next three months she would be on her own in the apartment because Juliette was leaving later that morning on an expedition to the largely unexplored northern continent of Kitzingen.

As Lady Katherine's First Daughter and direct heir, Juliette was learning her trade by shadowing her mother when Parliament was in session. Juliette was destined to be heavily involved in politics; Lady Katherine wasn't only the next in line to rule Veiled Isle, she was Clan O'Teague's Parliamentary Representative. However, Parliament only met three times per year, and Juliette was taking advantage of the free time to go out with one of the exploring expeditions to Kitingzen, the closest of the four largely unexplored continents.

"There is just one *tiny* favor I need you to do while I'm gone," Juliette said.

Lucinda eyed her suspiciously. Juliette's designed genetics made her naturally manipulative, and while Lucinda's had given her genius level intelligence, as a child she had more than once been tricked by her sister into doing something she hadn't intended to do.

"What kind of favor?" she asked.

"I got tapped for helping with the plans for the Harvest Festival and I need you to stand in for me." Seeing the refusal in her sister's face, she rushed on, "it's not a big deal; I'm not in charge of anything. It's mostly showing up at a few meetings to vote on what the committee decides and going to the reception for the Free Traders when their delegation arrives. Please?"

Lucinda scowled at her. "I might be on duty when they have their meetings. Police work isn't like a regular job; there's a lot of unscheduled overtime."

Juliette smiled winningly at her. "It's okay if you have to miss a couple of meetings because of work. I cleared that with Duchesse St. Vyre, the head of the committee. She won't mind, as long as you let her know."

"What about this reception? Is it formal?"

"Well, yes, but you have that lovely new dress you got for Jayla's wedding. It's a shame to let it sit in the closet."

Trapped, Lucinda gave in. "Oh, alright, just let me know when these meetings take place. You owe me though."

Her sister jumped up and gave her a big hug. "I already uploaded everything to your calendar. You are the absolute, *best* sister. Anything you want, I promise."

"I'm the best patsy, you mean," Lucinda snorted.

The house alarm chimed, signaling her it was time to leave for her shift. She hugged Juliette again and stood up to put on her jacket. "C'mon, Agra, it's time to go," she told the Dactyl, who reluctantly left the warm nest and fluttered over to her shoulder, yawning.

Knowing Juliette would have left for Kitingzen when she came back from work, Lucinda stopped and looked at her. "You be careful out there, okay?"

"I promise," her sister said. "Besides, thanks to Dad, I've got Bridge and Terrence Mann along as minders, remember?"

Lucinda laughed, hugged her again, and left. She opened the garage section attached to their apartment and rolled out her air sled. Agra obediently settled into a made-to-order Quirka Seat attached to the dash. With so many Vensoogers having Quirka, the Quirka Seats, which resembled an upside-down helmet with a glass faceplate, had become popular.

Agra, being about the same size as a Quirka, fit into the seat just fine, her wings taking up the same space as a Quirka's plumy tail. Mini Dactyls such as Agra and Saura came in all colors. Agra's fur was a mixture of pale green, red and yellow, the skin on her face, feet and hands was a pale tan, shading to a darker shade outlining her eyes and on her nose. Dactyls were magpies and loved glittering jewelry, which Agra usually wore in the form of a bracelet around her neck. Tonight, Agra's neck adornment was a braided tan and brown leather collar to match Lucinda's Security uniform. Although plain, Lucinda had added several shiny flat metal bars etched with her badge number.

Settlers had adopted the Dactyls and Quirkas because both animals were small, affectionate and avid hunters of household vermin, which crept into human dwellings despite the best efforts of modern technology. The Quirka's and Dactyls had returned the favor because humans provided a mutually satisfactory love bond, and a ready source of edible goodies.

Lucinda threw a leg over the seat, strapped on her own helmet and fired up the sled. There was still some traffic out because Port Recovery, the capital of Vensoog, never really slept, but this section of the city was quiet as most residents who lived in the girl's neighborhood were in bed.

The apartment was located over a shop near their cousin Jayla's in a high-end merchant section of town. The two-story domed buildings, a necessity because of Vensoog's seasonal hurricane winds, were mostly dark because of the late hour but as she neared the center of town more lights showed in the windows. As she moved toward the core of the island where the city government offices were located, she could see the tips of shuttle noses at the spaceport peeking over the tops of the large government buildings.

When the Clans first landed on Vensoog, the huge city domes had been used as shelters. As the Clans moved to their permanent territories, the domes had been converted to government and commercial uses.

Lucinda parked her sled in the security employees parking lot, showing her brand-new ID to the gate guard, who nodded, grinning at her, and she and Agra went inside for roll call.

There was a mixed assortment of officers waiting in the roll call room: young, old, male and female. Lucinda took a seat by her trainer, Sgt. Mira Forest. She knew she had been lucky to draw Mira, a twenty-year veteran of the streets with a reputation as the best trainer in Port Recovery. One look at Mira and people immediately knew she was a cop from her short pepper and salt hair, tough, blocky build and most of all, the look in her eyes. She was a dead shot with both a pulsar rifle and pistol. Mira had been offered promotions to detective grade numerous times and refused. She preferred to stay on the streets and train young recruits.

Although she was the only one with a Dactyl, Lucinda was relieved to see that about a third of her fellow officers had a Quirka perched on a shoulder. About the size of a human fist, Quirka's faces resembled an Old Earth hedgehog. Quirkas had a squirrel-like body, hand-like paws and feet, a pointed nose and small upstanding ears. Their primary defense against predators in the wild, venom tipped quills, ran along their spine from their shoulders to their plumy tails. Like the small Dactyls, they were omnivores.

Lucinda had been a little worried Agra's presence might cause issues. Officers who were accompanied by Quirka or Dactyls were required to take special courses with them in how the animals should behave while on duty. She had been relieved when Agra easily passed the course. If she had failed, she wouldn't have been able to join Lucinda on duty until she passed.

Lucinda glanced at her mini-porta-tab to ensure she had received the list of the latest B.O.L.O. (Be On The Lookout) updates. A rash of break-ins along the waterfront shops had been happening, some vandalism by persons unknown in a couple of commercial sled parks, there was a list of stolen air sleds, and a peeper had been reported in a couple of neighborhoods.

When she joined Mira in the locker-room, she found the older woman frowning at her own porta-tab.

"Is something wrong?"

Mira tossed her a crystal DNA key for her official sled. "That is for your sled. If you've got one of those fancy Quirka seats for—Agra, is it? You can snap it into place. I'm afraid you'll have to use your personal one. Command hasn't gotten around to issuing them for the rank and file yet."

Lucinda caught the key easily and pulled the Quirka seat out of her locker. Tucking it under her arm, she followed her trainer out to the sled park.

"Why were you frowning just now?"

Mira shrugged. "Nothing really, I heard a few rumors there is some smuggling near the docks."

"Isn't that our area?"

"Uh-huh. This is your first night, so stick close. Don't go chasing off when you see something without telling me first. I'll do the same for you."

Lucinda activated the key and pushed it into the waiting slot on the dash of her sled. The DNA encoding meant that from now on, she would be the only one who could start it. When she gripped the handlebars the sled purred into life. She followed Mira out the gate of the secure lot and the pair of them rode side by side toward the docks and warehouses. There were few homes in this area, just manufacturing, small shops serving the offices and the warehouses who needed access to the ships bringing in meats, fish, harvested crops, and other raw materials from the outer islands.

Lucinda and Mira stopped their sleds at the edge of the district and dismounted, parking the sleds in the designated area saved for official vehicles.

"A map of our patrol area should have been downloaded to your sled controls. Set the monitor to meet us at the warehouses in an hour," Mira instructed.

Several storefronts selling paper, tools and a few all-night eateries serving simple, fast food and Cafka lined both sides of the street leading down to the docks.

"We do a foot patrol from here," Mira told her. "Keep your eyes open for anything unusual."

"That one looks as if there are workers inside," Lucinda said, gesturing to a lighted warehouse with its own attached dock.

Mira consulted her tab. "That belongs to Medford textile. They are supposed to be getting in a shipment of dragon silk to ship off world. We'll swing by there on our beat. We start here; we each take one side of the street. Check the windows and test the shop doors. If you find one open, tag me."

Domestic Disturbance

The street was quiet. At first, Lucinda had been a little nervous, but her nerves soon smoothed out. At least until she found the open door on a shop specializing in small hand tools.

She tapped her shoulder com. "Mira, I've got an unlocked door here."

"Okay, wait for me before you go in," Mira instructed, calling it in as she crossed the street.

Once there, she shone her light on the lock. "Doesn't seem to have been forced," she said. "Okay rookie, this is how it goes down. Draw your weapon. We enter and check each side of the store for someone who shouldn't be there. I'm going in high, you go in low. Try not to shoot any shop owners who just forgot to lock up."

They were moving cautiously through aisles of small tools when they heard the hullabaloo start at the back of the store.

"You cheating bastard! I come down to bring you dinner because you're working late, and I find you boinking this slut!" A woman's voice shouted, and there was a splat as if something messy hit a solid object.

Lucinda turned the corner of an aisle in time to see a man with his trousers partially undone wiping the remains of a messy take-out box dripping sauce and noodles off his face. Just as she arrived, the woman who had obviously thrown it jumped on another woman sitting half-dressed on the low counter. The two went over backwards, pulling hair, kicking and biting.

'Hey, no!" the man cried, and jumped in to separate them.

"PRS! Freeze!" Lucinda shouted. Seeing this had no effect, she holstered her gun and grabbed the nearest combatant, who happened to be the man, and pulled him out of the fight.

In the meantime, Mira had arrived and dived into the roiling mass of flying fists and kicks behind the counter. She separated the half-dressed woman from the pile, dragging her around the display case where there was more room to handcuff her. Climbing over the countertop the wife leaped to attack again, landing on Mira to reach her prisoner. The three careened around the area between the sales counter and a tool display, slipping in the spilled sauce and noodles, as they knocked over stands of products.

Mira ended up on her butt underneath the fighting women. The wife had the advantage now because of the younger woman's cuffed hands, and she used it mercilessly, landing several fist blows and kicks on the other woman's face and breast. She also managed to raise a lump over Mira's eye when she missed her target and got Mira instead.

Shoving the husband down in a seated position against a wall, Lucinda told him sternly, "Stay there," and rushed to help her trainer.

She grabbed the wife by the back of her hair and heaved her off Mira and her captive. She forced the woman down on her belly and pulled her hands behind her to apply restraints.

Disobeying Lucinda's order to stay where he was, the husband got up to help his girlfriend. Agra flew at his face, talons on her hind feet extended. He ducked Agra's charge, but he needed to get by Lucinda to reach Mira and her captive. Her hands busy restraining his cursing wife, Lucinda used her boot to shove him away. He slipped in the spilled dinner again, and ended up on his rump covered in sauce and noodles.

"I told you to stay where I put you! Go sit down!" Lucinda yelled.

Agra flew in his face again, this time hissing a threat.

Eying the Dactyl warily, the man dropped back down.

"You okay?" Lucinda asked Mira, who had staggered to her feet, dragging her captive with her.

"Just dandy," Mira said, swiping a smear of sauce off her chin and then wiping her hand on her captive's still undone blouse. "Welcome to patrol work, rookie." She looked down at the sauce and noodles spattered on her uniform and scowled. "I ought to charge the three of you for my cleaning bill."

"What do we do with them?" Lucinda asked.

Mira studied the three combatants. "Depends if they want to press charges or not."

"I do!" the half-naked one said. "She assaulted me!"

Mira sighed. "Okay, that's one. Anybody else?"

"Yes! I want to exercise *Code Duello!*" the wife snapped. "She's attempting to break up my home."

"*Code Duello* is a civil matter," Mira told her firmly. "You'll have to file that with your Clan Liaison." She looked over at Lucinda. "Call it in rookie."

Lucinda swallowed, and tapped her com, trying frantically to remember the codes for a domestic disturbance and assault.

The rest of the night was uneventful; sort of. They arrested three half-lit tourists serenading what one of them mistakenly thought was the home of a pretty girl he had met in a bar. They couldn't carry a tune between them and the din roused the neighbors as well as the homeowner and his wife. The justifiably annoyed homeowners had called in the disturbance and the irate husband had dumped a bucket of water on them. The neighbors had come out to watch.

"Call the wagon," Mira told her as they rode up, "and then shut them up." She indicated the trio of drunken singers. "I've got the homeowners."

"He didn't need to call you guys; we didn't know she was married," the first singer protested, when Lucinda identified herself to them.

"I don't think that's her," one of his friends whispered loudly.

"Yeah," the third drunk opined. "Where did she change her clothes?" He pointed at Lucinda. "That looks like a uniform."

"You're lucky you didn't get shot," Lucinda told them in disgust while Mira calmed the irate husband. "This neighborhood has reported a peeper these last few nights. Sit on the curb and we'll arrange a ride for you."

"Just go back to bed, sir," Mira told the husband. "We'll handle it from here."

"I hope they lock you up and throw away the key," he yelled, before he slammed his window shut.

Apparently losing interest in the couple, the first singer complained, "I'm hungry. How come you smell like Chinese noodles?"

"We broke up a fight. One of the weapons was a box of take-out," Mira said dryly.

"Hey, I'm hungry too. Can we stop on the way and pick some up?" asked one of his buddies.

"No," Mira replied.

"Hey, where are we going anyway?" the third one asked. "What kind of party are you girls taking us to?"

"Oh, you'll like it," Mira said. "There's lots of people in your condition there."

"You guys are keeping us busy tonight," Kneckie the Patrol sled driver, told Lucinda as they pulled up in front of the dome.

When he opened the door to the sled, the aroma of noodles and sauce wafted out, along with the miasma of vomit and sour booze.

"Don't you ever wash this thing out?" Mira demanded, as she helped Lucinda herd the three drunks inside.

"Why? We don't have to smell it. It's sealed off," the driver retorted. "What have you got for us Sarge?"

"Drunk and disorderly, disturbing the peace. The homeowner and his wife will be in tomorrow morning to sign a complaint. In the meantime, throw 'em in the drunk tank."

"Sure thing. There you go, upsy-daisy," he told the last man, as he boosted him up into the sled. When the drunks sat down, the sled's bench cuffs snapped into place. "See you back at headquarters, Sarge."

Mira rolled her neck. "Sure thing Kneckie. C'mon rookie, we've got reports to write."

Returning home, Lucinda parked her sled in the unused storage space on the ground floor. She glanced at the empty storefront, wondering who Jake Reynolds, their new landlord and cousin Jayla's husband, intended to rent it to. Because the girls were upstairs, he was being very picky about the tenants.

Opening the upstairs door to the apartment, she was struck by a sense of loss, as she realized she was going to be spending her first ever night alone. At Grouters, and later in Lady Katherine and Lord Zack's home one of her sisters had always been near.

Agra chirped comfortingly in her ear, and rubbed her cheek against Lucinda's, emitting reassurance and love.

Lucinda reached up and stroked the Dactyl, who purred at her. "Just us tonight sweetie. Let me get out of this smelly uniform and you and I'll take a shower and get something to eat."

Stripping off her uniform, which gave off a faint odor of soy sauce, she examined it for stains. Programing the clothes fresher for stain and odor removal as well as cleaning and pressing, she tossed in her uniform.

She had no fear of the stains not coming out; as a housewarming present, Jayla had sent Martha, her house-bot over to set up the house comp, which included programming the clothes fresher. Looking at the menu in the Robo-Chef, Lucinda realized the ever-efficient Martha had not only stocked it, but loaded it up with her recipes, which were far superior to the standard ones it came with.

Afterwards, Lucinda did a quick clean-up of the kitchen. The apartment came with a weekly cleaning service, but she hated the smell of dirty dishes. She and Agra tumbled into bed and slept dreamlessly.

It was late afternoon when she woke to the sound of her com chiming. Looking at the display, she saw calls from both her sisters. Setting up for a multi-vid call, she slipped on a robe and wandered out to the kitchen to program a pot of Cafka for herself.

"How was your first day?" Violet asked. That far south, the sun was just coming up over the horizon. She and Jelli, her sand dragon, were on the cliffs above the Dragon nests on Talker's Isle. Lucinda heard the ocean waves crashing on the rocks in the background.

"You look like we woke you up," Juliette commented. She was sitting outside her pop-up dome on Kitingzen, with Saura sleeping on her lap.

"You did," Lucinda laughed. "It was different. We broke up a fight over a man, got slopped with Chinese noodles and arrested three drunken tourists. How was your trip?"

"A bit crowded, and Jorge isn't happy to have me here. I think Dad must have threatened him if something happened to me."

Violet nodded. "He did that at Jayla's wedding. He was in full protective papa mode that night. I saw him talking with Tom Draycott too, and I know he laid down the law to poor Silas Crawford. It was kind of sweet really."

Juliette snorted. "He thinks Jorge is a risk taker. That's why Bridge and Terrence are getting a vacation on Kitingzen."

"*Is* Jorge reckless?" Lucinda asked, frowning.

Juliette shrugged. "I don't have a way to judge. We haven't really gotten started yet."

"I thought you would be mapping the area outside the new village," Violet remarked.

"Originally, we were going to do that, but apparently, Jorge saw something resembling buildings further along that mountain range on the vids the first-in scout made. He thinks it's an old city, and the council gave permission to go and look, so that is where we are heading."

"Did Mom and Dad know about this?" Lucinda asked.

"I don't know. I just heard about it in the shuttle on the way over to our first base camp. Today we unloaded our stuff out of the shuttles and set up for the night. Tomorrow most of us will spend the day going through our equipment to make sure we have everything we are supposed to have is here and organizing it for the trail. Jorge will be taking our mapmaker and the geologist up into the hills to try to scout out the easiest path to that old road he thinks he saw. When he returns we head up the trail into unexplored territory. We will be out of com touch a lot of the time, and we could encounter anything."

"Well, you be careful," Lucinda said.

"I could set it up through the link for all of us to know if one of us is in trouble," Violet offered.

"Judging by last night, mine could show trouble a lot though," Lucinda protested. "Violet, I can't have you two panicking whenever I have to chase someone or break up a fight."

"It can be fixed so we can talk to each other through the link," Violet promised.

"Okay, I guess," Lucinda agreed. "If Juliette is going to be out of com reach we need it."

"What are you going to be doing the rest of the day?" Violet asked Juliette.

Juliette made a face. "I've been told we will have a camp meeting after supper to arrange camp chores and go over the route and safety rules."

"That doesn't sound as if Jorge is taking unnecessary chances," Violet remarked.

"I doubt if he is as careful as Mom on the trail though," Juliette replied, and all three girls laughed. Lady Katherine had justly earned her reputation as an over-protective mother; she had once been tried for killing a woman who had threatened one of her children. The subsequent Clan trial had declared it a justifiable homicide, of course. Any attempt to harm children was taken very seriously on Vensoog.

"We do have a real greenhorn with us this time," Juliette admitted. "Our map-maker, Isaac Jordan has never even been camping. I had to help him with his pop-up dome, and those things practically set themselves up."

Picking up something in Juliette's voice, Lucinda asked her, "Is he cute?"

"How old is he?" Violet seconded.

Juliette's fair skin flushed a little. "He is about our age. A year older than Luce and me."

"You didn't say if he's cute or not," Lucinda pressed.

"Oh, there's the dinner gong," Juliette said hastily. "I've got to go. Later guys." She dropped out of the link.

"She didn't answer you," Violet said.

"I noticed that," Lucinda agreed. "She likes him though."

"Attracted," Violet corrected. "Couldn't you feel it through the link?"

"I felt something," Lucinda admitted. "Did you manage to do that while we were talking? You are getting really good with this link stuff."

Violet nodded. "Drusilla is a good teacher. I've learned so much since I've been studying with her."

Home Alone

WHEN LUCINDA turned off the vid com, she was feeling restless. Looking at the time, she decided her cousin Jayla was probably getting ready to close her shop about now. "C'mon Agra," she told the Dactyl. "Let's take a walk over to Whimsical."

Wayne, Jayla's sales-bot was up on the lift changing a light crystal when Lucinda entered. The sales-bot had been designed with a slim, toned body, light hazel eyes, and medium shaded brown hair. Wayne's costume today was a black and white striped skin suit topped with a soft flat cap of brilliant red. He was always a hoot and had a wide variety of costumes he wore in the shop. Jayla allowed it because she claimed the bizarre outfits helped him make sales.

Lucinda found Jayla in the back room of the shop, checking inventory. Ghost, her white Quirka, bounced over to Lucinda, chirping happily, before she and Agra went into a complicated dance routine as they greeted each other.

"Did you get Wayne a new outfit?" Lucinda asked. "I don't think I've seen that one before."

Jayla grinned at her. "I told him to pick three out of the catalog. We did so well on sales this last month I could afford it. How was your first shift?"

Lucinda laughed. "Crazy, tiring, and fun. I talked to Juliette and Violet this afternoon. It turns out Juliette is going to be off the grid most of the summer. The Leader, Jorge Carmody talked the Exploration Committee into allowing them to try and reach the ruins of a city he found on one of the First-In Scout vids."

"It sounds as if your dad knew what he was doing when he sent bodyguards out with her."

"Yes, it does. We don't like not being able to reach each other though so Violet set up a special link with the three of us, that way we will all know if one of us runs into trouble."

"A sensible precaution," Jayla agreed. "I don't know much about this link thing. How does it work?"

"It's a little like a combined *Push/Pull*," Lucinda said. "Drusilla and Lucas discovered it when they opened a channel into that stone his grandfather gave him."

"But you can talk to each other through it?"

"Violet says so, and she usually knows what she's talking about."

"Would have been handy to have when that idiot from Aphrodite kidnapped me," Jayla said wryly.

"It sure would," Lucinda agreed, remembering the panic that had ensued when Jayla disappeared on her way home from the last Harvest Festival.

"Would you like to stay for dinner? I think Jake should be home shortly."

"Thanks, I will. I guess you can see I was feeling a little lonely when I got home; the apartment felt empty today," she said ruefully.

When they arrived upstairs, the enticing smell of baked Ostamu wafted toward Lucinda. Ostamu were the large flightless birds bred by the Clans as a food source. "Umm, that smells good," Lucinda said. "Hi Jake," she said to Jayla's new husband.

"Hey kid, how was your first day?" he asked, as he came over and kissed his wife hello. Shade, his Quirka, immediately bounced over to Ghost, joining in the greeting ritual. Unlike Ghost who was almost pure white, Shade was all shades of brown and grey.

"Tom was reporting to Uncle Max when I got there, so I brought him home for dinner," he told his wife, indicating Tom Draycott, the Duc d'Orleans top investigator. Draycott was around Jake's age, a little taller than Lucinda, with a hard-bodied, powerful build. He had dark brown hair and cynical brown eyes in a wedge-shaped face. A blaster scar ran across one cheek.

"And as you can see, I took him at his word," Tom said. "I don't live in the compound on Versailles Isle anymore, so I don't get home cooking much."

"As long as you don't expect me to be the one who cooks it," Jayla replied, laughing. "That is why we have Martha."

"Jake said you were reporting to the Duc," Lucinda remarked. "Can you tell us about the case?"

Draycott shrugged. "It isn't a secret. Max thinks there is some smuggling going on. I spent the last five days working on the docks. If smuggling is going on, I didn't find out who was doing it. I'll move on to the spaceport workers next."

"What if someone from the docks recognizes you?" Jayla asked.

He grinned at her. "I wore a disguise on the docks. My own mother wouldn't have recognized me."

"Do you always wear a disguise when you go undercover?" Lucinda asked.

"Most of the time. A couple of years ago I spent some time establishing some unsavory cover identities. They come in handy for undercover investigations."

Lucinda was fascinated. "How many do you use on a single case?"

"As many as I need. Want to learn how to set one up?"

"Yes, I do. It sounds like a lot of fun."

The four of them spent a pleasant evening talking over old times. When it turned nine o'clock, Lucinda noticed Jayla yawning.

"Guess I'd better let you get some sleep," she told her cousin as she got up. "I forget not everyone is on the same schedule I am."

"Me too," Draycott agreed. "Why don't I give you a ride? I've got my sled here."

Lucinda collected a sleepy Agra who had snuggled into Shade and Ghost's nest, tucking her inside her windbreaker before mounting behind Tom on his sled.

When he dropped her off, they arranged for him to stop by and give Lucinda the basics of creating a disguise.

Makee-Learnee

U nlike a few of the more technological oriented societies that made up the Confederated Worlds, the Clans of Vensoog preferred to teach their children a profession by having them apprentice under a more knowledgeable mentor. Lucinda spent most of her first month on the job on patrol and answering calls under Mira's supervision.

"We switch shifts next week," Mira told her after she had been on the job a month. "Starting tomorrow, we will trade areas with Sargent Murtaugh and his trainee. Philps, I think is his name."

"Oh," Lucinda said. She had begun to feel proprietary about the area near the docks and was surprised at her reluctance to switch. "What area do we get?" Lucinda asked her.

"We've got the spaceport. Sorry I know it's going to disrupt your sleep cycle after you've just begun to settle in it, but we switch times too; They have Swing Shift. Things are slow right now," Mira told her. "We need to take advantage of it to get you rookies as familiar with every part of the city that we can before the Harvest Festival starts and we get swamped with drunken tourists. During the Festivals, we get almost 100,000 extra tourists coming in to celebrate with us, plus the visiting merchants and Free Traders."

The Planting and Harvest Festivals were held each Spring and Fall, and everyone who could get free usually tried to attend. During the festivals, some events like the Introductory Balls, where newly recognized adults received Match Lists, were only open to the Clans, but there was plenty of other entertainment for visitors. Port Recovery, because of the spaceport, was thrown wide open to off-planet visitors and merchants and the city took steps to entertain them royally. The Clans brought in native-made goods and Free Traders from all over the Confederation came to buy and sell their wares.

Lucinda rolled her eyes. "We can barely keep up now," she protested. "How do we handle that many extra people?"

Mira shrugged. "A lot of us work double shifts; or extra half shifts. The Clans send a portion of their home security forces to help out as well."

Dawn was breaking, and the sky had started to lighten when Lucinda heard the screaming.

"I think it's coming from down by the boats," she told Mira, and the pair took off running. Agra fluttered over Lucinda's head, making excited noises. Even tiny Dactyls like Agra could fly faster than a human could run, but she kept by Lucinda as she had been taught.

Mira had turned on her headlamp and used it to look around. "PRS!" she shouted. "Where are you?"

It was still dark enough that the moored boats cast dark shadows on the wharf. Long plastacrete ramps extended out over the channel. Agra's acute eyesight spotted something at the base of the farthest ramp, and she gave a shrill keen and dove toward it.

"Over here Mira!" Lucinda called.

When she arrived at the ramp, she found Agra hovering over the body of a woman. "Good girl," she praised the Dactyl, who preened in response, perching herself on her mistress's shoulder and looking down with interest. Dactyls were inherently curious, and part of the training she and Lucinda were given had included not touching a body without permission. Lucinda ran her Porta-tab over the body, scanning for life signs. She found none.

"She's dead," she reported looking up at Mira.

"Damn!" the other woman said. "Well, call in our sleds, and let's get this crime scene sealed off. Then we should inspect the area around the body while we wait for the coroner to get here. Document anything you find that looks as if it doesn't belong, but don't move it."

Their sleds arrived just as Mira finished calling in to report the body. Agra watched as Lucinda opened the side of her sled and pulled out the compressed privacy screens. Jamming one end into the ground near the ramp, she pulled on the loose end and made a wide circle around the body as the screens decompressed and grew to full size.

It was about a half hour before sunrise but they had drawn a few spectators from a nearby warehouse.

"Hey, what's going on kid?" An older man with an air of authority asked.

"What is your name?" Lucinda asked him.

"I'm Jesse Sanders. I'm the supervisor over at Maclin enterprises," he said, gesturing to the only lit-up warehouse in the area.

"I'm Officer Lucinda O'Teague," Lucinda told him. "Did you or any of your workers see or hear any noises out here tonight?"

"I sure didn't," Sanders answered. "It's pretty noisy inside though. We wouldn't have noticed if Dori hadn't stepped outside for some fresh air. She came running back in, screaming about dead people. Took me a while to calm her down. Do you want me to ask my men?"

"Thanks for the offer," Mira answered him, "But I'm afraid we have to do it."

"What happened?" he demanded again. "Dori ran into the warehouse yelling about dead bodies."

"Yes, there has been a death. Would you mind going with Officer O'Teague to see if you recognize the body? In the meantime, I'll need to start interviews with your people."

"Uh—well, okay," he said, reluctantly.

When he saw the state of the body, he turned green, and covered his mouth with his hand. Recognizing the signs, Lucinda hastily got him away from the immediate area around the body before he barfed, and held out an evidence bag for him to up-chunk into.

Handing him a wipe for his mouth, she waited until he had settled a bit before asking, "Do you know her?"

"No," he said, swallowing. He looked around for somewhere to dispose of the wipe, and she held out the open evidence bag.

"Thanks," he said. "It looked like she was wearing a ships uniform of some kind. What was left of it."

"Did you recognize it? Do you know what ship?"

He shook his head and swallowed again. "Can we move further away? I can still smell–"

"Sure. Why don't you come and sit down over here? The detectives may have more questions," she suggested.

The detectives arrived at the same time as the coroner's big sled.

Lucinda was glad to note that this time Gorsling wasn't one of them. When she had been interning in the Coroners' office, he had investigated the murder of Sara Lipski and there had been an unpleasant encounter, ending with Dr. Ivanov throwing him out of her lab.

"I'm Detective Jeness, and this is my partner, Detective Wilson. What do you have for us? It's officer O'Teague, isn't it?" The elder of the two, a tall, full-bodied woman with dark, curling grey hair asked.

"Yes," Lucinda answered the first question. "This is Jesse Sanders. He's the foreman in charge of the warehouse. One of his crew went out for a break, and came back in screaming about dead bodies, so he came out to investigate. My partner Mira and I heard the screams and were already on site by the time he came out."

"How did you locate the body?" Wilson asked.

Lucinda smiled. "Agra did that. A dactyl's smell and night vision are much better than a humans, you know."

"Ummn," Wilson looked Agra over speculatively. "Did she touch the body?"

"Of course not," Lucinda said, offended on her pet's behalf.

The Dactyl made the small snorting noise Lucinda knew meant she was irritated, and Lucinda reached up and stroked her soothingly. When the Coroner's sled pulled up she was surprised to see Doctor Ivanov hop out. She turned to her with relief. "Hey, since when do you work the night shift?" she asked.

"Lucinda! It's good to see you again." The Coroner gave the girl a hug. The doctor was a short, dumpy little woman, the top of her head barely reaching Lucinda's shoulder.

When Agra fluttered over to her, demanding her share of the attention, Dr. Ivanov laughed. "Yes, Agra it's good to see you as well. Your new collar and badge look very good on you. Dr. Glassen called in sick," she responded to Lucinda's question. "One of his kids is running a fever and he's quarantined his house until they figure out what it is. We've missed you in the lab. The cadet who replaced you isn't nearly as good. How are you liking your first weeks on the job?"

"It's been interesting," Lucinda admitted.

"Do you need her for anything else?" Dr. Ivanov asked the detectives. "If not, she can come and help me with the body. I'm short-handed tonight."

Wilson made a shooing motion with his hands. "By all means go with her officer."

Lucinda followed her, and while the Doctor was checking time of death, she bagged the hands under Agra's critical gaze.

"Humm," Ivanov was talking to herself. Lucinda knew the spoken notes would be logged on her department recorder, and given for transcription to the hapless cadet who had taken her place in the lab.

"Female, lying face down, approximate age late twenties, with multiple lacerations on her upper torso. Clothes are partially shredded, looks like the remains of a ship's uniform. DNA sample running through the Planetary database for ID. Mixed Race, thin, scan shows bones typical of someone who spends a lot of time off-planet. Death approximately four hours ago. Corpse is just going into rigor. Help me roll her Lucinda."

They turned the body over. "Same lacerations on her front. Lacerations would have hurt, but none of them are deep enough to cause death," Dr. Ivanov continued. "Death most likely was caused by the garrote around her neck. I'll know more when I get her on my table. I see you bagged her hands. Good girl. You're always thinking ahead. Get the body bag out of the sled, please."

When she returned, Lucinda lowered a specially made lift, shaped in a rectangle with rounded edges and straps to hold the body bag. She helped Dr. Ivanov move the body into it. She fastened the straps to hold it in place and towed it behind her to the Doctor's sled. Agra perched like a small gargoyle on top of the bag during the ride. Once inside the sled, she snapped the fasteners holding the lift in place.

"C'mon Agra, get off there. I need to turn on the stasis," she told her pet, holding out a small treat. Spying the cookie, Agra flew off the bag and eagerly took it. "You did great tonight girl," Lucinda crooned to her.

"You always talk to her like that?" inquired Wilson. "Like she's a person?"

"She is a person," Lucinda told him, her voice cool. "Not human so she can't speak our language, but she understands it very well. She can pick up feelings from me, but my tone of voice reinforces it."

"I've never worked with a Dactyl," Wilson observed, "but I've worked with detectives who had Quirkas. They didn't take to me, the Quirkas, I mean."

"I see," Lucinda nodded politely.

"You don't seem surprised," Wilson said. "Why is that?"

Lucinda hesitated, then said, "Quirkas and Dactyls read emotions the way a Dragon Talker does. They probably sensed that you don't really like them."

She was relieved when Dr. Ivanov returned to the sled with her kit. "Mira's looking for you, Lucinda."

"Thanks, Doctor Ivanov," she said. "C'mon Agra. We need to get back to work."

"Wilson giving you a hard time?" Mira asked when she returned.

"Not exactly; he had a lot of questions about Quirkas and Dactyls. Lab protocol says I couldn't leave the body unattended until Doctor Ivanov got back to the sled anyway. Sorry, I didn't get back sooner."

Mira nodded understandably, "One of the penalties of being uniform, I'm afraid; everybody and his brother gives us orders. Now our next job is to try to get names and addresses from everyone in the crowd for the detectives."

Lucinda had just about finished her share of this chore when she thought she recognized Tom's familiar stance on one of the men watching the crowd. She was so surprised she stopped and stared,

Tom, if it was him, was wearing one of the disguises he'd told her about. The man in question had black, slicked back hair, and a neatly trimmed beard. He was also wearing a black skin-suit and high heeled black boots.

"Something the matter?" Mira asked, joining her.

Lucinda jumped in surprise. "Not really. I just thought I saw someone I knew over there. He's gone now though."

The Sun was well up by the time they finished getting ID information from the warehouse crew. Lucinda dictated her report into her com on the way back to headquarters. When they arrived, she read through it, initialed her DNA signature, made two copies, one for her personal file and one that she sent on to the detectives after Mira looked through it.

Agra had fallen asleep in her Dactyl seat when Lucinda drove into her storage area. Gently she pried the little creature out of it and carried her upstairs where she set her in her comfy sleep basket. Stripping off her uniform and Agra's collar, she tossed them into the clothing recycler before slipping into a loose shirt and shorts. She tumbled into bed already half asleep.

She had set her alarm to wake up a little early, so she was up, dressed and enjoying a second cup of Cafka while Agra sulked over her breakfast of chopped nuts, fruit and fish flake, when Tom knocked on the door.

"Let him in," she told the House Comp getting another cup out of the cupboard.

"Cafka?" She asked, holding up the cup.

"I'd love some," he told her. "I've been up all night. Good morning, girl," he said to Agra, who ignored him. "What's wrong with her?"

"She's missing Saura, her littermate," Lucinda explained. "Saura went out to Kitingzen with Juliette."

"Do you have sweetener?" He asked. "I need the boost."

"Well at least you've taken off that lounge lizard disguise," Lucinda remarked, handing him the sugar bowl.

"You *did* recognize me. I thought you might have. What gave me away?"

She lifted her shoulders. "It was a good disguise, but I recognized the way you stand. You always stand like you're ready for a fight."

He stared at her, and slowly sat down in a chair. "I fooled both the Duc and Jake with that one once. You're going to make a damn good cop someday."

"Thanks," Lucinda felt her face blushing. "I bet you haven't had anything to eat either, have you? I'll dial up one of Martha's specialties."

He caught her hand and kissed it. "Bless you, I'm starving."

Lucinda watched, amused as Tom inhaled her food. "Don't think you are going to get away without telling me why you were there," she said. "I'm assuming this is a part of your investigation. How is that going by the way?"

He poured another cup of Cafka and sipped it before he answered. "Not as well as I hoped," he admitted. "Did you identify her?"

"Not yet, but the Doc thinks she spent a lot of time in a ship and not on-planet. Why?"

He sighed. "If she is who I think she is, she was my first real lead in this case."

She frowned at him. "What kind of information? Is the Duc running one of his private investigations again?"

"Him and the rest of the Security Council. After Jayla's kidnapping, they decided they needed to do something about Thieves Guild activities in Clan territories. Max has several other operatives besides me working on this. All we've found out so far is that something worth big credits is being brought in and smuggled onto Free Traders here in port."

"Do you know what it is?"

"Not a clue," he said in disgust. "Jora was my first real lead. She was supposed to give me the names of the ships and captains who are a part of it."

"Jora? You know her name?"

"Jora Loman off the Free Trader Saucy Suzie. She went into the Guild as a young girl and she wants—wanted out. The Council agreed to help her, give her a new identity and stuff."

"Does Port Recovery Security know the Council is poking it's nose into this?"

He shook his head. "Nope, and we'd prefer it not be spread around. We think we cleaned out all the cops on the Local Mob's payroll, but we can't be sure."

"But Tom," she protested, " Her folks need to be notified; I need to tell them who she is at least."

"Can't you just say it was a rumor?"

She frowned thoughtfully. "I suppose I could say I heard about a missing crewman off that particular ship."

By this time Agra had imbibed enough Cafka to recover from her sulks and fluttered over to Tom's shoulder and nuzzled his ear.

"Oh, so now you're talking to me?" he asked the Dactyl.

"She likes you for some reason," Lucinda said. "Usually she's a little more standoffish."

He handed Agra a wedge of fruit he hadn't eaten, and she gobbled the wedge of melon with delicate greed. "That's because she knows she can bum food, isn't it, cutie?"

The fruit Tom gave her had been very juicy. Since Dactyls were not nearly as fastidious as Quirka's, Agra had managed to smear it liberally all over her face. She transferred the stickiness to Tom by nudging his jaw with her messy nose when she finished.

He got up and put his dishes in the recycler, wiping his face with his napkin.

"Thanks again for breakfast," he said. "Do you think you could let me know if it turns out it is Jora?"

"I suppose," she answered.

You Can Run

A FTER ROLL call on Monday, she and Mira drove to the Spaceport, parking their sleds in front of joined offices of the Interplanetary Patrol (IPP), SpacePort Security Forces (SSF) and Port Recovery Security (PRS). "From now on, we will be attending roll call here," Mira told her.

The Spaceport was more than a hub of incoming and outgoing commerce. It also held the only hospital in Port Recovery. Originally placed near to the landing field to be close to troop transports bringing in injured Confederation fighters, the Joint Clan Council had seen no reason to change the hospital's location.

The Spaceport remained the planetary headquarters for the Space Patrol who graciously shared their office space with the locals. Since neither the Patrol nor SSF had jurisdiction immediately outside the Spaceport, PRS was treated as an auxiliary precinct whose chief responsibility was handling calls in the immediate area. No patrols generated out of the Precinct, but calls from the surrounding area were brought in.

The office was neatly divided into thirds with several desks and a file cabinet in each Section surrounding a common reception area. Six holding cells shared by the three agencies, could be seen behind a reinforced plexi-glass wall. When they entered, they were met by a short, whip-thin, middle aged woman in the brown and tan PRS uniform, who introduced herself as Officer Georgia Gannet, the day shift supervisor.

"I'm Sargent Mira Forest, and this is Officer Lucinda O'Teague and her Dactyl Agra. How are things today?"

"It's pretty quiet. We've got three ships taking on some cargo in the warehouse, and four of the Free Trade Ships are already here to negotiate the contracts for the Harvest Festival. I'm dropping you the information about all of them," Gannet said.

Lucinda's porta-tab chirped, and she pulled it out to accept the sent data.

"I've never worked around a Dactyl before. How is she with loud noises and aliens?" Gannet asked.

"She's fine with it, aren't you girl?" Lucinda responded. "Hold out your hand and I'll introduce you."

When Gannet complied, Agra sniffed her hand and then chirped inquiringly at Lucinda. "Work friend," Lucinda told her. "Be polite." She turned back to Gannett. "You can pet her if you like, but only with one finger. Dactyls don't react well to being grabbed."

"If it's slow today, I'd like to show Lucinda around, so she can get a feel for where things are," Mira interrupted.

"Sure," Gannet replied. "You can meet our Patrol counter parts later. Jonah, the IPP supervisor, and Twilya went on lunch break," she explained, gesturing to the empty third section."

"Patrol only has two officers stationed here?" Mira inquired. "I thought the minimum was three per shift for each section."

Gannett shrugged. "Actually they have three, two per shift, and a supervisor, but when your senior tells you 'let's go to lunch' you go to lunch. The other duty officer in my section Debra, is down at the warehouse, coordinating with our opposite numbers in SpacePort Security to check out those shipments I mentioned earlier. Right now there is only us since Lieutenant Sorbo got promoted to Homicide."

Spaceport duty was certainly livelier than the warehouse district had been. First time visitors were required to check in with Space-Port Security Forces before they could leave the spaceport grounds. Visitors were scanned for contraband, DNA was recorded for ID purposes, and a short vid about planetary customs and laws was shown before visitors were free to enter Port Recovery.

The com let out a shrill squeal, and Agra and Lucinda both jumped.

When Gannet walked over to the communication station and tapped it the sound quit. "Spaceport Security, Gannet speaking. How can I help you?"

A petite redhead appeared on the screen. "Georgia, I'm sending over a couple of tourists who claim they were robbed while they were in town."

"PRS afternoon shift just checked in. We'll handle it."

"Looks like you won't get that tour just yet. Since the crime took place in Port Recovery City, this one falls under our jurisdiction. Ah, here comes the wagon now." She pointed to a small runabout sled entering the dome. The sled was on automatic and without a driver. A middle-aged man and woman perched nervously on the side-facing seats.

"They are Fenriki," Lucinda observed. "I recognize the clothes."

"Let's go and introduce ourselves," Mira said, stepping forward to help the woman alight.

As Mira introduced Lucinda and herself, Lucinda noticed the woman kept glancing nervously at Agra. Trying to put her at ease, she crouched down in front of her. "Dama Miller, I'm Officer O'Teague, and this is Special Operative Agra. Agra is a Dactyl. She has been fully trained. You don't need to be nervous of her."

Agra chirped in agreement.

"Does she bite?" the woman asked?

"No, I assure you, she won't hurt you."

"I thought they had poison quills or something like that." Damon Miller, the man with her said, eyeing Agra warily.

"I think you must be thinking of our Quirkas," Lucinda said. "Dactyls don't have the quills. In most cases you needn't be concerned about a Quirka either; the quills are their primary defense against predators. The ones you see accompanying a person wouldn't hurt you unless you attacked them or their human."

"Can I touch her?"

Lucinda smiled. "Of course. Hold out a finger and offer it to her to sniff."

Tentatively, Dama Miller did so, and Agra purred for her. "Why, that sounds like a cat purring!" she exclaimed.

"She likes you," Lucinda said. "Now just using one finger, you can stroke her. Small animals like Agra are often prey for larger ones, and if a hand swoops at them even if its friendly, they become frightened."

After taking a description of the girl who snatched their travel documents and the woman's purse, Mira and Lucinda turned them over to the Planetary Tourist Liaison who would assist them in filing the necessary forms for reimbursement of their stolen property and arrange for them to be taken to their hotel.

Later that day during the tour of the spaceport, Lucinda noticed a medium sized man with lank, badly cut blond hair and a scraggly beard that did a good job covering the scar along his jaw, loading crates for transfer to a ship.

Did the man never sleep? she wondered. She was debating whether to mention Tom's presence to Mira, when the choice was taken out of her hands.

"Is that the same person you saw last night at the warehouse Officer O'Teague?" Mira asked her.

"Yeah," she said. "His real name is Tom Draycott. He's an investigator for the Duc d'Orleans."

"Do you know what he's investigating?"

Lucinda shook her head. "Not really. Some kind of smuggling, I think."

Mira frowned, "Smuggling, humm, maybe someone made a complaint. If they did, a case record will be in the station files. We'll check them just as soon as we finish up here."

Later that day as dusk was falling, they finally made it out to the tarmac where the shuttles were located. The ships themselves were too large and required too much power even using the Azorite crystals, to land and take off from a planet's surface. Instead they landed shuttles loaded with cargo or passengers. Almost sixty percent of Port Recovery Island was devoted to landing spaces for these shuttles. The shuttles were widely spread to ensure that they didn't cause problems for their neighbors when they took off or landed. Each area assigned to a ship was reached by carefully marked lanes restricted to cargo-bot traffic. Pedestrians were strictly forbidden on the tarmac, unless they were doing repairs on a stranded cargo-bot.

"We need to pick up our sleds, before we tour that area," Mira explained.

"I thought the cargo-bots are equipped with safety sensors to keep them from running down pedestrians," Lucinda said, frowning.

"Well, they are, but not all of them have working sensors."

"I would have thought that would be a high priority."

"It should be," Mira agreed. "Unfortunately, this place," she made an expansive gesture at the Port, "runs off fees collected from visiting ships. During the war, there weren't any ships in orbit except the Patrol, and they weren't bringing in cargo, so they didn't pay much. So—no fees—no money for repairs, etc." She shrugged. "It's getting better, but there are still an awful lot of the cargo-bots needing upgrades."

They had taken a wide swing around the perimeter of the field. Out toward the edge of the tarmac, Lucinda spotted the markers for the force field to keep thrill seekers out.

"One of the force field pole stands is down," Lucinda told Mira, pointing to a stake that tilted off center. "Does that mean it isn't working?"

"It means somebody has been monkeying with it," Mira said grimly. She tapped her com and reported the downed pole to the base.

"It looks as if whoever it was, uprooted the pole and crawled under it," Lucinda remarked, wiggling the pole.

"In that case, they must have approached on foot," Mira muttered. "That hole doesn't look recent either. We'll finish our swing but keep an eye out for anyone on foot."

About half-way back to the dome, Agra spotted the small figures near one of the marked lanes. She chirped inquiringly at Lucinda.

"I think Agra just found our trespassers," Lucinda called to Mira. "They look like kids to me."

"Dammit!" Mira swore. "Those idiots are playing Tag with the cargo-bots!" She gunned her sled and raced toward the group of mixed species teenagers. Lucinda did the same.

As they got closer, Lucinda could see that part of the group was holding back, while a Trellyan girl danced in the lane, taunting them. She could also see the cargo-bot bearing inexorably down on her.

Lucinda increased her speed, passing Mira who had maneuvered her sled between the kids hanging back and the marked path, leaving one child, the Trellyan girl, dancing in the lane.

Dodging to the side, Lucinda grabbed the girl by the back of her shirt, dragging her out of the path of the bot just in time to avoid being crushed as it continued serenely on its way.

The girl cursed her in Trellyan, fighting to get free. Several swings from her small, hard fists and feet made painful contact with Lucinda. She held the girl out at arm's length with the grip on her shirt and gave her a shake. "Knock it off, or I'll stun you!" she told the girl.

Agra dodged in behind the miscreant, nipping her sharply on her buttocks.

"*Oww!*" the girl yelled, still fighting. "You'll pay for that! My mother is High Priestess of the Mother of Fire! You'd better let me go!"

Lucinda heaved the girl across her lap and drew her force wand. She brought it down with a sharp *smack!* Across the girl's rump. "If you don't behave, I will pull out your eyes and present them to the Mother of Many as an offering!" she told her in perfect Trellyan.

The girl stopped fighting and looked up at her in astonishment. "You speak the language," she exclaimed. "How?"

Lucinda re-holstered the wand and held out her hand, fist closed so the girl could see the back of it and willed the tattoo to appear.

"What's your name kid," she asked in basic.

"Sesuna s'Klam'y," the girl sniffed. "You wouldn't really do that?"

"Maybe not," Lucinda said. "You got a hard punch for a kid."

"Thanks," Sesuna said grinning.

"You going to behave if I let you up?"

"Guess I'd better," Sesuna said. "I don't want to offend a Soturi."

Lucinda set her back on her feet, just as Mira herded the rest of the gang across the path to join them. One of them, a boy, was a Lupun, one wore the distinctive free trade ship suit, and the other pair, a girl and a boy, wore Fenriki dress. They all looked to be about thirteen or so.

"Everything okay?"

"Sure, we're fine," Lucinda said. "Do we make these little thrill seekers walk to the dome, or call for a passenger-bot to take them back?"

"It's coming," Mira pointed at the passenger-bot trundling toward them. When the bot had ground to a halt, Mira told the children to get on it. Once they were seated, she reached out and tapped a code into the control panel. She gave them a feral smile.

"Just so you know, I've programed your transpo for maximum child safety. That means you can't get off it until the order is rescinded by another officer. After all, we wouldn't want you children to fall off and get hurt, now would we?"

Lucinda bit her lip to keep from laughing. When the bot had lumbered out of hearing, she let herself laugh.

"C'mon, we have to follow them and write this up. Thank Goddess they'll be an SSF problem and not ours."

It turned out that was not exactly true. Upon learning they were all visitors, SSF had turned the miscreant children over to the Patrol. Lucinda and Mira were just going off shift when they heard a commotion from the Patrol Section. The children's parents had arrived to bail them out.

Lucinda strolled over to look through the arch separating the Patrol Office from the lobby. One of the parents was wearing what Lucinda knew was standard for most Free Traders: a tight shipsuit in bright colors (more visibility for crew in case their shipmates needed to search for them in unknown territory). He was male, and he had hold of his son. He was standing quietly behind the other three parents who were yelling at the duty officer.

As she watched, the Lupun nudged the woman in Fenriki dress aside which caused her to turn her wrath on him.

Sesuna's mother was a tall full-bodied woman, in a long, pleated gown, with an ornate headdress. Sesuna had buried her head on her mother's breast and was sobbing loudly, over her mother's yelling as she berated Twilya, the hapless officer attempting to pacify her.

Hands on her hips, Lucinda surveyed the scene in disgust. "Who was the fool who assigned that girl to deal with them?" she demanded.

"That is the way the Patrol does things," Jonah, the Patrol general supervisor, said pompously. "We've found that it's better to have a member of their own race explain planetary laws on alien worlds."

"You're a fool," Lucinda told him. "That woman is a Priestess of one of the Mothers. She has a higher status than Twilya. Don't you know anything about Trellyans? The Priestess is high caste. Twilya isn't even full blood Trellyan. She doesn't have the authority she needs to deal with her."

"Patrol ranks everyone. Officer Kinski needs to learn that," he began.

Exasperated, Lucinda strode forward and put herself between Sesuna's mother and Twilya. "Quiet!" she yelled.

All four parents glared at her. Lucinda pointed at the chairs off to the side. "You three, go sit over there and wait your turn," she ordered. "Don't make me arrest you for disturbing the peace." The two humans recognized the Port Recovery Security uniform and sat down. The Lupun glared at her, but sullenly did as he had been told.

Lucinda turned to the Priestess. She spoke one short blistering phrase in Trellyan. Sesuna's mother drew back in surprise then snarled back. Sesuna, tugged on her arm, whispering urgently. Her mother looked again at Lucinda, who stood there with her hands on her hips.

"Your pardon, Soturi," the Priestess said. "My worry for my child allowed me to become overwrought."

Lucinda acknowledged the apology with a regal nod of her head. "It isn't me you need to apologize to, its Officer Kinski here. Such behavior ill becomes you. Playing tag with cargo bots is foolish and dangerous. The child could have been killed or badly hurt, my lady. She was lucky I was there. She fights well, but no person is a match for those mechanized behemoths."

Ispone Klam'y turned to Twilya and nodded. "My apologies, Officer. I assure you I will ensure such an incident doesn't happen again. My thanks, Soturi. I am glad she listened. She fought well, you said?"

Lucinda grinned at her. "I'll have a few bruises."

"Come, Sesuna, we need to talk. I told you to stay in the spaceport while I looked at the records," Priestess Klam'y said as they walked away.

"But the landing field is a part of the Spaceport," Sesuna protested.

"You know very well I was referring to these buildings!" her mother retorted.

Lucinda turned to Twilya. "Can you handle the other three?"

Twilya stood up straighter, "Yes, Soturi."

"Want a piece of advice? Arrange to take the Ritual Of Fire And Water; it will help you to not roll over and play dead when you need to confront someone of higher status," Lucinda suggested.

"I will think about what you said, Soturi."

Jonah was still standing in the archway when Lucinda rejoined Mira.

"What did you say to her?" he demanded.

"None of your business," she told him. "If you want to know, ask the Priestess and Twilya."

"It's probably not my business either," Mira remarked as they left the building, "but I would like to know what it was you said to that Trellyan woman."

Lucinda shrugged. "My sisters and I were trained in how to deal with other races when we were living on Fenris. Like Humans, the Trellyans and the Lupuns are predatory species. I told Priestess Klam'y to shut up and stop acting like a fool."

"Why did she listen to you when she ignored the Patrol officer?"

"I have status. Twilya is of mixed race, which pretty much puts her on the bottom of the totem pole in Trellyan society. Juliette, Violet and I all passed through the ritual of Fire and Water. It gives me status as a Soturi, or warrior. Status is of prime importance to Trellyans."

Mira eyed her curiously. "How many languages do you speak?"

"Besides Basic, I speak seven others. My sister Juliette can do ten well, and three others not so well. Violet can only do about five, but she makes up for it with her empathy skills."

High Tea & Politics

SINCE THE head of the committee for developing the agreement with the Free Trade ships who would visit Vensoog during the next Harvest Festival belonged to L'Roux Clan, the welcome reception was being held on Versailles, the L'Roux Island in Port Recovery. Lucinda had heard about the fabulous interior from her mother and her cousin Jayla, and seen glimpses of it on vids, but that was a far cry from seeing the lovely recreation of the Versailles Hall of Mirrors in person.

Juliette was going to be sorry she had missed this, she thought.

"It's very beautiful, isn't it?" remarked the tall man in the uniform of a ship's Captain standing next to the stairs leading up to the Clan's private quarters.

"Yes, it is," she agreed. Remembering she was supposed to be making them welcome, she held out her hand. "Welcome to Vensoog, Captain. I'm Lady Lucinda of O'Teague Clan."

"Thank you," he replied, shaking hands. "I am Talon Delgado, off the Silver Samurai."

Lucinda tugged on her hand, which he had continued to hold long past good manners decreed.

Reluctantly, he released her. "O'Teague, did you say? I would have thought it might be Lister, or maybe Grouter."

Inwardly, Lucinda stiffened. The sixth sense for danger that had kept her alive and unharmed in the cesspit that had been Grouter's Child Placement Center on Fenris abruptly kicked into play. She blinked, and when she raised her lids, she wore what her trainer in the center had called 'the bimbo expression'.

"Sorry to disappoint you," she said with a puzzled smile. "Are those people you know? I'm afraid I don't recognize the names."

He frowned at her. "You don't come from Fenris?"

She continued to look puzzled. "Yes, I do, but I don't know how you would know that. I was adopted from a child placement center there just after the war ended. Who are Lister and Grouter?"

He seemed taken aback. "Oh, just some people I knew there. You look quite a bit like Lister, that's all."

"Really? That's funny." She slipped a hand under his arm, strolling toward the refreshment buffet. "It must be exciting visiting a new planet every few months. Do you like it?"

"It can be very interesting," he agreed. "Perhaps you would like to come aboard for a tour of my ship."

"I'd like that," Lucinda agreed, blinking wide eyes at him.

While part of her mind made flirty small talk, another part was analyzing what he had just told her. Grouter and Lister had both been Thieves Guild operatives. Lister had followed them to Vensoog and been killed by Lady Katherine in a raid on Veiled Isle, Lucinda's home island. The fact that Delgado knew both names must mean he had connections to the Thieves Guild himself. It was interesting he thought she resembled Lister. That was something that would bear future investigation.

When Madame Ilya St. Vyre, the head of Vensoog's committee for Trade claimed his attention, Lucinda stepped into a shadowy hall leading back into the keep, carefully looking over the other delegates. She fully intended to run all the names of the Trade delegation through the police files after shift tomorrow. If one of them had ties to the Guild, the others might also.

"What the Hell do you think you're doing?" Tom Draycott's voice hissed at her. He grabbed her arm and pulled her further back into the alcove.

Lucinda glared at him. "What do you think *you're* doing? How did you get in here?" she demanded, jerking her arm free.

He was a good friend of Jakes and a favorite of the Duc, but she knew Madame St. Vyre hadn't wanted any personnel at the tea party who weren't directly connected to the committee; that told Lucinda he was probably here indulging his curiosity bump.

She had met Tom for the first time earlier in the year when he had been investigating racketeering by Miles Standish for the Duc d'Orleans, Clan L'Roux's Head Of Security. Tom was built like a wall, with a tough blocky body. His dark face might have been handsome if it hadn't been for the blaster burn across one jaw. Most of the men this afternoon wore dress clothes, Tom wore them too, but the elegant clothes only accented the air of danger around him, which despite herself, Lucinda found oddly attractive. He looked like a highly paid bodyguard, not a guest.

When they first met, there had been an immediate physical attraction between them, but she had been under the age to receive a Match List, so her father had warned him off.

When a native of Vensoog turned seventeen, the Matchmakers gave them a list of names with suitable biological matches, and introduced them to each other during the annual Planting and Harvest Festivals. It was a way of keeping the genetic mix of the humans on the planet from developing issues with in-breeding.

When she had asked her father what he had said to Tom, Lord Zack had grinned at her. "Man stuff," he said.

"Dad!" she had protested. "I have a right to know."

Lord Zack had relented. "I told him if he didn't drop that chip on his shoulder, you'd kick his ass."

"You like him," she had realized with surprise.

"Well, he's not afraid of me, so that's a plus for him. It remains to be seen if he's good enough to court my daughter."

She had felt herself flushing. "There's no question of that," she protested.

Her father gave her an old-fashioned look. "You keep thinking that. But he'd better remember you're underage, or *I* might kick his ass."

The memory had distracted her. She was abruptly jerked back to the present when Tom glanced over her shoulder into the ballroom, then pushed her further back along the hallway. "Don't be such a little fool," he said. "Delgado is bad news. You and your cousins don't need to be playing cops and robbers with the likes of him."

"I am a cop," she retorted. "And I probably know more about him than you do. I think he's Guild."

"All the more reason you should leave mucking around with him to the experts."

"Meaning you, I suppose," she snapped.

"Yes," he said arrogantly. He wasn't enough taller than her to look down his nose at her, but he might as well have.

Lucinda wanted to hit him, but then she had wanted to do that sooner or later every time she ran into him. First, he kissed her senseless and then the next time they met he totally ignored that it had happened.

"It's none of your business what I do," she snapped.

"Someone's got to keep you from behaving like an idiot," he retorted. "What was that business of smiling and batting your eyes at him? You were acting like a love-struck teenager, for Void's sake!"

Lucinda did hit him then. She caught him unawares, and it was a nice flush hit with her fist. His head rocked back with the blow, but he didn't move.

He reached out and yanked her up against him. "Why the Hell do you do this to me?" he muttered, before fastening his mouth fiercely on hers.

A strong shock of desire ran through her. Despite her anger, she found her body softening against him. Just as suddenly, he let her go, and she staggered.

"Stay away from Delgado," he ordered, turning and walking away, leaving her unsatisfied and furious.

Tom stalked down the corridor and went outside the keep into the Princessee's softly scented gardens, more furious with himself than with Lucinda. His sense of honor was offended at his own behavior. He had no business kissing an underage girl like Lucinda. When he had first met her, she had been with her cousin Jayla who was old enough to receive a second list that year. Mistakenly, he had assumed Jayla and Lucinda were of an age, because Lucinda didn't look or act like the young girl he now knew her to be. Her behavior didn't excuse his own though, and he knew it.

After his warning from Lord Zack at Jake and Jayla's wedding, he had done some research into Lucinda's background, trying to figure out why she affected him the way she did. All he had discovered was that she had been raised in a Child Placement center on Fenris, whose head had later turned out to be a Thieves Guild operative. Much of her background and that of her sisters was shrouded in mystery, and his inner investigative voice told him the public information available was a lie. He was sure her real history must have been sealed.

When he overheard Lucinda's conversation with Talon, he decided to look up what the Clan records said about Darla Lister. The woman had to be connected to Lucinda someway. He needed a go at the archives. He had a vague memory of Lady Katherine going on trial several years ago for killing Lister after she tried to murder a child. Lucinda's mother had been cleared of course, but there *had* been mention of the Thieves Guild at the trial. Later that year at Gregor Ivanov's trial, he remembered mention of it as well. He had been just starting a career as an investigator, and the Duc had suggested he use the case to train on, so he had followed it.

Lucinda glared at Tom's back as she watched him stalk off down the corridor. She touched her fingers to her still tingling lips.

"Wow," said a voice from behind her. It was Odette, Duchesse Ilya St. Vyre's First Daughter, a tall, willowy girl with light brown hair and eyes. "That was some kiss."

"What? Oh. He's a Big jerk. He left before I could kick his ass."

Odette sighed. "I wish I had a boyfriend to fight with like that. You better go fix your lip dye before you go back in."

"He's not—never mind. Where is the lady's room?"

"C'mon, I'll show you. We're going to be good friends, I can tell."

Her good mood partially restored by the other girl's cheerful friendliness, Lucinda followed her. Odette was fun. As a First Daughter she knew almost all the younger delegates and First Daughters, and she happily introduced Lucinda to them. Hearing about Delgado's invitation to tour his ship, Odette immediately decided to make it a group activity, and during dinner, Delgado somehow found himself maneuvered into agreeing to the notion.

Lucinda was still upset about the nasty encounter with Tom when she got home. Odette and her friends had driven away the irritation while she was with them, but she knew she had used their company to avoid thinking about him.

She had developed the habit of taking a short nap when she had a few hours before her shift, but tonight she was too wound up to relax enough to do it. On impulse, she sat down at her comp and dialed her mother on Veiled Isle. There was an eight-hour time difference; it would be very early there, but Lady Katherine was an early riser.

As she had expected, Lady Katherine and Lord Zack were enjoying an early breakfast on their private Terrace. "Good morning, darling," said Katherine with a big smile when she recognized Lucinda. "Oh, but it's still night there, isn't it?"

"Yes, but I knew you two would be awake. Until I get off the night shift, I'm afraid this is how we will have to talk to each other. How is everyone?"

"Violet will be heading your way soon. The new Talker students need to be registered into the archive. Drusilla thinks Carolyn is too young to travel yet; apparently, she's teething and with her powerful *Push* it's giving everyone who can't block her a toothache, so Drusilla's sending Violet in her stead. Will your landlord mind if she and Jelli stay with you?"

Lucinda grinned. "My landlord is Jake, Mom. I think he'll be fine with it. When is she due to arrive?"

"She's stopping here to pick up a ride on the weekly shuttle into Port Recovery, so it won't be for a couple of weeks."

"Making a weekly run into Port Recovery sure increased the revenue coming into those bed and breakfast places," her father said with satisfaction. "It's gotten so popular we may have to start making a run twice a week and charging fares."

"Corrine has almost finished her colonial history, so she's letting it cook while she and Vernal go sailing around the islands," Katherine added. "Wasn't that reception for the Free Trader delegation tonight? How did that go?"

"Okay, I guess, but I think one of the captains has ties to the Thieves Guild."

Her father looked up sharply. "Why do you say that?"

"When we met, he said he expected my last name to be Grouter or Lister. When I asked why, he said I looked like Darla Lister."

Katherine frowned. "It's possible I suppose. Lister was Guild too. Grouter could have used some of Lister's DNA in your design."

Lucinda made a face. "Kind of gives me the creeps to think I look like her though."

Katherine, who knew her daughter, was struck by a sudden suspicion. "Lucinda O'Teague, please tell me you aren't planning to investigate this Captain because of a half-baked resemblance to that bitch. Those people are dangerous."

"I don't have time for any off the books investigating Mom, my trainer keeps me too busy. I thought that maybe Dad could pass on the information to Lord Gideon..."

"I'll do that," Lord Zack said. "Your Mom is right though hon; you don't want to get the reputation of taking off on maverick investigations. It would be detrimental in the long run to your career."

"I'll be good," Lucinda promised. "I'm going to try and get a nap now. Love you guys."

She hadn't told her parents she had already agreed to take a tour of Delgado's ship. It would only worry them.

Lady Katherine closed the com and looked over at her husband. "I don't like it," she said. "You know she's going to dig into this. Likely as not she'll drag Juliette and Violet into it with her. The boys too."

Zack sighed. "I think you are probably right. Rupert and Roderick are busy with their new design program, but that won't stop her pulling them in. Do you want to go into town to keep an eye on her?"

Katherine shook her head. "We can't, not with Corrine and Vernal off on that cruise. Maybe we can talk to Violet about it when she arrives."

"I think I'll give Jake a call," her husband said thoughtfully. "He's in a better position than we are to keep an eye on her."

Katherine looked relieved. "That is a good idea. Thank you, love."

Karma Is A Bitch

RIGHT AFTER lunch, Lucinda had a visitor. It had been a slow day and she was filing reports on the complaints the office had received this week. It was amazing how much time it took to document the scads of petty complaints accumulated. They ranged from a food fight in the canteen (handled by SSF since it concerned spaceport workers, but a copy still needed to be logged in the records) to the more serious attempted vandalism to one of the business offices of a company attached to the spaceport. Each of the data crystals had to be marked and cataloged. She was pouring another cup of Cafka to take back to her desk when Detective Jeness came in.

"Detective Jeness," she said with a smile. "How nice to see you again. I don't know if you remember me?"

The detective's solemn face lit up with a grin. "I sure do, it's Officer O'Teague, isn't it? I heard you were going to be permanently posted here. Congratulations. You'll be one of the first to get a permanent assignment. Dr. Ivanov was ticked that Mira jumped ahead of her in the new cadet choices."

"Thank you. This is an interesting post. I hope I do get it. There's always something new going on. But I know you didn't come all the way out here just to pass gossip to me. How can I help you?"

"Any Cafka left in that pot?"

"Sure, help yourself. How is your investigation into Jora Loman's murder coming?"

The detective sank back into one of the comfortable visitor's chairs. "Not so good. Dr. Ivanov did find some DNA under her fingernails, but it isn't in the planetary database. One of my snitches said he saw another woman in a ship suit following her the night she was killed. I'm hoping I can talk someone in the Patrol into letting me run a match through the Free Trade Registry."

By treaty, the Free Trade Registry was maintained by the Free Traders Association. It was a private database that they reluctantly shared with the Patrol in return for assistance in fighting Space Pirates. Local planetary law enforcement had to put in a request to view the database if they wanted access.

"You do know the Saucy Suzie left port the day after Loman was killed, don't you? If the killer was from her own ship, it's going to be hard to catch her."

"Yes, I know it. I doubt if the budget will pay for someone from our department to planet hop trying to catch up with the Suzie. I'm hoping the killer was from a ship still in port. That's why I want to check out the Free Trade Registry."

"I'll see if I can talk Officer Twilya into helping you. Nova Cohen isn't happy with me. I'm afraid I expressed my opinion of the Patrol's training methods on how to deal with Trellyan's a little too freely. C'mon, let's go across the hall."

They were lucky to find only Twilya manning the station. Lucinda poked her head in and asked, "Are you alone?"

Twilya laughed. "Yeah, Ciciereli and Abdul are doing the mid shift change over report so you're safe. Did you want something?"

"Twilya, this is Detective Jeness. Detective, Patrol Officer Twilya Kinski."

The two shook hands, looking each other over.

"Will Cohen squawk if you let Detective Jeness run a match through the Free Trade Registry?"

"I doubt it; just yesterday he was spouting off about interplanetary cooperation. C'mon ahead, Detective. Let's get the paperwork started and I'll open up the Registry for you."

"We got a match," Jeness said with satisfaction several hours later. "The Patrol is requesting she be sent dirtside for questioning."

"Who was it?"

"Someone named Lorian Thayer. She's listed as an assistant engineer on the Silver Samurai, and according to the Patrol it's still in port. Have you heard of them?"

"Yes, I'm supposed to go up with the Free Trade Reception Committee later this week to tour the ship. Do you want me to arrest her?"

Jeness shook her head. "No. The Registry lists the Silver Samurai as her permanent berth, so she isn't going anywhere until it warps out of orbit. We'll wait for the warrant."

"Suit yourself."

You Aren't My Father!

THE MORNING the group from the reception was to tour the Silver Samurai, Tom invited himself to breakfast again. He was developing a habit of visiting her around breakfast time. It would have been flattering if she could have believed he was making excuses to see her, but she suspected his motives. He probably wanted information about the police investigation into Jora Loman's murder. Yesterday she had overheard him arguing with the warehouse supervisor about sending a crew to repair the downed power pole she and Mira had found. Tom wanted to send a crew, but the supervisor didn't want to waste the manpower. She was sure Tom really wanted an excuse to check out the area for smuggler activity.

Agra was just finishing off her morning breakfast of nuts, breadfruit, chopped vegetables and meat, and chirped a messy welcome when Lucinda opened the door. Since she was acting in Juliette's place with the tour group, Lucinda was dressed like a diplomat's daughter this morning. Instead of casual clothes, she wore a soft blue, cowl-neck blouse of Dragonest silk and darker blue vest and trousers with grey half boots. Agra had donned one of her jeweled collars. Lucinda's uniform was folded and hung in a bag behind the pantry door. She planned to put it in her locker at work and change after the tour.

"Good morning," Tom said. "Wow, you look good. Going somewhere special?"

She gave him a scorching glance. "Oh, and I look bad if I don't make a special effort?"

"No, that isn't what I meant. I just—you're all dressed up today," he said. "Can I have a shovel to dig myself out of this hole?"

"Maybe. Depends on why you're here." Lucinda took a filled plate from the Robo-chef and set it down in front of Tom with a cup of steaming Cafka.

"I don't want to take yours," he protested.

"You aren't. I've finished," she informed him. "Somehow, I just knew you'd be coming by this morning to try to get information about the downed power pole from me—*Whoops!*" she caught Agra, still dripping breadfruit juice, as the dactyl tried to leap onto Tom's shoulder.

"Let me wipe your muzzle before you get Tom as messy as you are," she scolded, wiping down the Dactyl's face and paws.

"But in answer to your question, I dressed especially nice because the home greeting committee is taking a tour of the Silver Samurai today and I'm representing Mom and Juliette," she told him. "I'll change for work afterward."

He frowned. "Isn't that Delgado's ship?"

"Yes, it is, and a group of us are going. I don't want to hear any smart remarks about it."

He held up his hands in surrender. "Don't shoot. I was just wondering if I could tag along," he said, with his best winning smile.

"If you promise not to do anything to embarrass me you can come, but I doubt if we will be shown what you're looking for," she warned him.

"What am I looking for?" he asked blandly.

Lucinda snorted. "Evidence of smuggling? Listen, I don't mind if you're discreet about poking around on the tour, but this is an honor for Juliette to be included on this committee and I don't want to mess it up for her by causing a ruckus if you get caught with your nose somewhere they don't want it."

"I'll be good," he promised, scraping his plate into the recycler and putting it into the dishwasher. "What time does the tour leave?"

"You've got an hour. We're meeting at the Spaceport. I won't wait for you so be there on time."

Agra hummed happily when he dropped a kiss on Lucinda's mouth before dashing out the door.

"Don't bet on it," Lucinda told her. "We're just useful to him, that's all it is."

Agra snorted.

Lucinda put her uniform in her work locker when she arrived at the Spaceport offices. She didn't recognize the two PRS night-shift officers on duty. Knowing they would be curious why she was there so early, she stopped to pass the time of day with them.

They were nattering about the latest gossip when she heard Sesuna's shrill voice and Priestess Ispone Klam'y's deeper one getting louder as she protested to the Patrol duty officer.

"Sorry, got to take care of this. I'll catch you guys later."

Lucinda turned and went quickly to the arch separating the Patrol offices from PRS. This time it wasn't Twilya on duty, but a tall, dark-haired woman in the black and red Patrol Uniform who was holding a plastia sheet and stabbing it with a finger for emphasis.

Lucinda leaned against the arch with her arms crossed, watching the show. Sesuna looked up and immediately ran over to her.

"Soturi O'Teague can you help us? That woman won't let mother have her medicine. She says it's contr—Contra—"

"Contra-banned?" Lucinda asked.

The girl nodded vigorously, dragging Lucinda over to the desk. "Tell her!" she said. "It's for the baby!"

Ignoring the Officer glaring at her, Lucinda turned to the Priestess. "My Lady is there something I can help you with?" She was shocked to see that Priestess Klam'y's soft grey skin had acquired a shiny, greenish cast, and her black eyes were red rimmed.

"This is Patrol business. It doesn't matter what this woman says young lady," the officer, whose name tag read 'Abdul', snapped, pointing at Lucinda. "This item isn't allowed. It's on the restricted list, and I'm confiscating it."

Still ignoring her, Lucinda put a supporting hand under the Priestess's elbow. "Sesuna, get your mother a chair so she can sit down," she ordered.

Easing Ispone into the chair the girl brought, she knelt in front of Ispone, holding her hands. "My lady, in your condition you must take better care of yourself. Will you let me help you?"

Ispone Klam'y nodded. "Thank you," she whispered, leaning back and closing her eyes.

Lucinda stood up and held out her hand for the vial the Patrol officer had seized. Reluctantly, the woman showed her the label. "They've given it a different name, but the chemical compounds are the same as these," she said, showing Lucinda the plastia.

Lucinda frowned at her. "That is quite true, however, a combination of these *are* proscribed in diluted form for some pregnant Trellyan women. That bottle has a physician's symbol. Did you check with her doctor?"

The officer gave her a look of pure dislike. "I don't need to; it's on the list! Who are you anyway? What business is this of yours?"

"I am Lady Lucinda O'Teague, daughter of Lady Katherine of Veiled Isle, Clan O'Teague. I am a friend of Priestess Klam'y and her daughter. I strongly suggest you get a healer out here to tend to Lady Ispone as soon as possible. She isn't well."

Still scowling, the Patrol Officer put in a call to the Spaceport Healer. Dr. Worthy, a brisk, bright-eyed little man arrived several minutes later with six student healers trailing him.

"Oh, my. Yes indeed," he exclaimed, taking in Ispone's situation after a brief examination. "You should not have traveled off world in your condition. You there!" he pointed at two of his students, "Help me get her onto a Medi-lift." Spying the bottle still clutched in the Patrol Officer's hand, he snatched it away from her. "Is this hers?"

"Yes," Lucinda replied.

"Hey!" Abdul said, "Give that back!"

The doctor ignored her, stuffing it into one of his commodious pockets, and turned to give instructions to his students about not jostling the patient.

Before they took her to the infirmary, Ispone caught at Lucinda's hand. "The child, I don't want Sesuna to see if—"

"Why don't I keep her with me today? We're going to tour one of the Free Trade ships."

"Thank you," Ispone whispered.

"What possessed you to come off planet without your physician?" The doctor demanded as they left.

Lucinda put a hand on Sesuna's shoulder. "They'll take good care of her," she promised.

"Yes, Soturi," the girl sereptiously wiped her eyes. Pretending not to see, Lucinda handed her a box of tissues.

"I'm reporting this," the Patrol Officer announced. "That woman tried to smuggle in illegal drugs! I'm reporting you too! I don't care who your mother is!"

Sesuna whirled around, fists clenched, a snarl on her mouth. "My mother isn't—" she began furiously.

Lucinda checked her. She pulled out her badge and thrust it at the officer. "Here," she said brightly, "I wouldn't want you to not have all the information for your report."

"This say's you're a cop!" Abdul exclaimed. "Do you realize you are aiding and abetting a smuggler? Your superiors aren't going to like this!"

"Aren't going to like her promoting interplanetary relations by showing compassion to a woman who is ill?" inquired Odette, drawn by the loud voices. She entered the room followed by half a dozen other Clansmen and another woman in the Patrol's black and red uniform.

"Officer Abdul, may I speak to you privately in my office?" inquired the older woman. After a glance at her, the Officer turned on her heel and left.

"I'm Nova Cicereli," she said. "Is there something I can help you with?"

"You might explain to Officer Abdul the difference between smuggling contraband and carrying drugs proscribed for you by your doctor," Lucinda said dryly.

She turned to Odette, "Hope you don't mind, but we've got an extra on the tour. This is Lady Sesuna Klam'y, daughter of Fire Priestess Ispone."

"How do you do, Lady Sesuna?" Odette smiled a welcome to her.

"Very well, thank you," Sesuna replied politely.

"We've got another addition as well," Odette whispered to Lucinda. "Your boyfriend showed up and asked me if he could join the tour and I said yes. I think he's jealous of Delgado."

Lucinda felt her face heating up when she met Tom's eyes. He had apparently gone home and changed his clothes. He was good at blending, she thought. Today, he looked like any other young aristocrat. She had the urge to deny the relationship, but she realized if he got caught snooping, blaming Tom's jealousy of Delgado would cause less comment and kept her mouth shut.

"Who are you?" Sesuna demanded suspiciously of Tom when he sat beside them on the robo-tram taking the group out to the Silver Samurai's shuttle.

"I'm Tom Draycott," he told her. "I'm a friend of Lucinda's too. How did you meet her?"

"I stopped her playing tag with the cargo-bots," Lucinda said. "I warn you," she added, "if you get caught snooping you had better be willing for the Duc to say you asked me to get you on this tour."

Agra, of course, fluttered over to Tom and purred a welcome in his ear. Lucinda gave her pet a disgusted glance, and muttered, "cream pot love," under her breath.

Sesuna giggled. "Which ship are we going to see?" she asked.

"The Silver Samurai," Lucinda replied.

"Too bad it isn't the Queen of the Stars," Sesuna said. "I might have been able to see Jokan again."

Lucinda snorted. "Considering what you got up to the last time you were with him, I'm just glad it isn't!"

"I take it Jokan was a part of the game to tag the cargo-bot? How did you meet him?" Tom inquired.

"Yes," Sesuna admitted. "Oh, the four of us, Lacy, Boorkin, Jace, Lerys and I met in the canteen. Jokan was hanging around outside and he came over to talk to us."

Lucinda frowned. She hadn't previously thought much about how the children had happened to be outside on the Tarmac. She knew of course that Ispone had been accessing the records from during the war, looking for a transmission from any ships that might have crashed on Vensoog, hoping to find a record of the one carrying her older daughter. It hadn't occurred to her how unlikely it was that a Free Trader's child had come to joint Sesuna's merry band of teenage troublemakers.

"If Jokan is from a Free Trader, how did he get down on Vensoog?" she asked.

"I think he stowed away on a shuttle bringing down a load for the warehouse, but I'm not really sure," Sesuna admitted.

"And no one noticed him?" Lucinda demanded.

"If they did they didn't say anything."

"Wasn't he afraid he would get stranded on the planet?" Tom asked.

The girl shrugged. "He said there was going to be a shuttle picking up stuff to be loaded after dark, so he wasn't worried about it."

"That's interesting," Tom said thoughtfully.

Lucinda eyed him suspiciously. "You think there may be more than one Guild Trader in port?"

He shrugged. "Maybe. I need to check some stuff in the warehouse records."

Delgado hadn't been especially pleased when Odette had converted his tête-à-tête with Lucinda into a group tour, but he met them at the door to the shuttle, every inch the gracious host.

Silver Samurai's shuttle wasn't really outfitted to carry fifteen people. Like most of the Free Trade shuttles used to land on a planet, it was designed for carrying goods and cargo, not passengers. To save room, Delgado was doing his own piloting.

Once aboard, Lucinda admitted to herself the tour was interesting. The Silver Samurai was smaller and more compact than Captain Heidelberg's ship the Dancing Gryphon, the one they rode on the trip out to Vensoog from Fenris.

"We were lucky," Delgado boasted. "We weren't large enough to carry military troops, so we were able to continue our trade route without being confiscated by the navy."

"Where did your route take you?" Odette asked innocently.

Delgado shook a playful finger at her. "Now pretty lady, that would be telling trade secrets! If I told you, it might get to some of our competitors, and they might jump our Trade line."

"Is it really that competitive?" Lucinda asked. "I thought the Patrol prevented trade wars."

He shrugged. "Oh, they try, but some Free Trade routes take a ship outside Confederation Territory."

"The Karamine sector, for instance?" Lucinda innocently suggested, watching his face.

She caught a flash of anger before he smiled blandly at her question. "No, not before the war and certainly not while it was taking place; Karamines are much too aggressive for a single ship to attempt to land on one of their worlds. Besides the official patrols there is always the possibility of Karamine rebels attempting to steal or slow down any visiting ships."

"I wasn't aware the Karamines had rebel troubles," Odette remarked.

Realizing he might have said more than he intended, he quickly went on, "This is our control room; as you can see, it isn't large," he said as the tour group each poked a head into the small pilot area.

"Now here is where the off-duty crew spends most of their time," he gestured down the hall and they entered what was obviously one of the largest common areas of the ship; a combination recreation and eating area.

Just then, a crewman approached the group. "Excuse me, Captain but the doctor would like to see you in the infirmary. Jacobsen sprained his foot again on the exercise machine."

He frowned a little, "Of course, please excuse me ladies and gentlemen. Officer Tenako will continue the tour. The engine room next Tenako, then join me back in the lounge."

Tenako, a short, rotund man with laugh lines around his eyes stepped forward. "This way please. I'm afraid we will need to enter the engine room a few at a time; like our control center it is stripped to bare necessities."

When she stopped in the doorway of the small circular room, Lucinda saw Tom slip away. *Dammit! she thought.* She was even more exasperated to see Sesuna following him. Knowing there was nothing she could do about either Tom or Sesuna, she forced herself to pay attention to the tour.

The engine room was round, lined with various control panels and screens. In the center a large quartz lattice made its way from floor to ceiling. This was the actual engine, powered by a dozen Azorite crystals. To Lucinda's untutored eye, the crystals looked oversized for the ship. Just now the matrix was dim, because a tech with a fat mane of glossy red hair tied back, had a panel partway open working on it.

"As you can see, we are only running on minimal power, Tenako explained. "Engines occasionally need cleaning and fine tuning because the crystals will get dirty. Will Thayer, our chief engineer says an engine is only as good as it's Maintence."

"How's it going Will?" Tenako asked.

The thin, blond man who had been entering information on a data cube, looked up and smiled. "We'll be ready by the time the Captain orders lift off. Lorian is almost finished with the cleaning."

Lucinda took note of Lorian; this must be the woman Jeness wanted the warrant for. Lucinda was almost the last one to take the tour. She had never been in a ship's engine room before; It had been off limits to passengers on the Dancing Gryphon.

Thayer caught her eye as she thanked the crew for their time. He followed her into the corridor. "Miss? Excuse me Miss, could I speak to you a moment?"

She stopped and looked at him. "Well I can't lag too far behind the tour, but I have a minute while everyone is using the sanitary facilities. How can I help you, Engineer Thayer?"

"Are you—is it possible you are from Fenris?" he asked.

Her eyebrows rose. "Yes, I was in a placement center on Fenris before I was adopted by Lord Zack and Lady Katherine."

"Was your mother Darla Lister? Because if she was, I think I might be your father."

Lucinda stiffened. In fact, she had been one of Grouter's 'designer' children, and had no idea who if any, her biological ancestors might be.

"As far as I know," she said icily, "I am no relation to that cold-hearted bitch. If I were you, I wouldn't claim too close an acquaintance with her; she was a thief and a murderer."

"She was brave and beautiful!" he said. "I loved her! I was almost sure she was carrying a child when she left me. I—"

"If Darla Lister had gotten herself with child," Lucinda interrupted brutally, "she would have rid herself of it at the first opportunity."

"I knew it!" Lorian Thayer had appeared in the doorway, her entire body quivering with anger.

"I'll deal with you later!" she told her husband. She turned on Lucinda. "You're the daughter of that bitch Lister, aren't you? Well she didn't get my husband, and I won't have any whelp of hers hanging around—You get me?"

Lucinda looked her up and down. "Certainly, I understood you. Half the quadrant must have heard that screech. As I just told your husband—Lady Katherine and Lord Zack are my parents. I don't need or want any interlopers. You might be surprised to learn that—"

What else she was about to say was lost as Lorian Thayer, with a snarl of rage, leaped at her with her fingers turning into claws. Agra squawked in anger and started to dive at Lorian in Lucinda's defense.

"No!" Lucinda automatically sent at the Dactyl, who aborted her attack. Lucinda half-stepped to the side, grabbed one of Thayer's wrists, and using the woman's own momentum, tossed her over her hip. She let go at the height of the toss, and Thayer flew several feet down the narrow hallway before she landed hard on her back and slid into the wall with an audible thump.

WHEN TOM HAD TAKEN advantage of the engine room tour to slip away he headed for the locked cargo bay. It was too good a chance to miss getting inside it to see what the Samurai carried.

He was bent over, using his code cracker on the door, when Sesuna whispered, "What are you doing?"

He jumped. "What the Void are *you* doing here? Did anyone see you?"

She shrugged. "I followed you. Nobody saw us. Why are you breaking in there?"

He scowled at her. "I'm an investigator. I want to take a few vids of their cargo bay."

He got the door open, and after checking the interior, he yanked Sesuna in with him. "Don't touch anything," he ordered, taking out a small vid-cam and snapping vid stills.

Sesuna was bored. She had thought this would be exciting, but all he had done was take vid scenes. Suddenly, she felt a trickle of hunger, cold and pain at the edge of her psyche. Curious to know where it was coming from, she looked around. There, over against the back wall were a series of animal cages. All but one of the animals were in stasis. When she got closer, she discovered it was a Trellyan Fire Indri. The stasis cube lay in a broken mess below the cage. It was obvious it had been broken while loading the cargo. The Indri was exhausted, dehydrated, and close to dying. She was also starting to whelp.

"Oh, you poor darling!" Sesuna whispered. "Let me get you out of there." She bent and undid the clasp holding the cage closed. Shifting her hands under the animal, she was struck by how cold the little body was. "Stupid Traders!" she said. "Don't they know you need to be extra warm during delivery?" Hastily, unbuttoning her blouse, she stuffed the Indri into her shirt and re-buttoned it. The animal fit because the blouse was a little too big for her; it had belonged to her older sister Eloyoni, who had been taken in a Jack raid while waiting for her betrothed to 'kidnap' her as a part of the bridal ceremony. Sesuna wore it to remind her of her lost sister.

"You have to be very quiet," she told the Indri softly, rubbing its back. The little creature made a helpless burrowing movement, shivering against her.

"I told you not to touch anything!" Tom had come up behind her.

"I wasn't going to!" Sesuna snapped. "This is a Trellyan Indri. It's forbidden to sell it off-world. Besides, another few hours and she would have died. They haven't fed her or given her water, and she's cold and about to whelp!"

"You mean she's going to have a baby? Right *now*? Oh, Hell," he said, pulling off his jacket. "Here put this on and keep it wrapped around you. If anyone asks, you're cold, and I gave you my jacket."

He opened the door cautiously and looked out. "It's still empty. C'mon, we need to get back to the others."

They arrived back at the group just in time to see Lucinda throw Lorian Thayer across the room.

Lucinda had been totally focused on Lorian's attack. She jumped when Tom clapped.

"Wow! Can you teach me to do that?" Sesuna asked, excitedly.

Lucinda noticed the girl was wearing Tom's jacket and seemed to have something wiggly tucked into her shirt. *I just hope nobody but me spots it,* she thought grimly, as Tom and Sesuna followed her back to the shuttle bay for the trip back to the port. Behind them, she could hear Thayer fussing at his wife and calling for a medic.

"What is going on here?" Delgado demanded, stepping out of his office.

"Sorry," Lucinda told him. "I think your Engineer Tech needs a medic. She jumped me, I dodged, and she ended up a casualty."

"Why would she jump you?" he asked, frowning.

"She accused Lady Lucinda of being someone named Darla Lister's daughter," Odette had joined the conversation.

"See here Talon," Lucinda told him. "I don't have a clue who my biological parents were, and I don't care. As far as I'm concerned, Lady Katherine and Lord Zack *are* my parents. Darla Lister is the last person I would want for a parent. She made herself a nasty name when Lewiston sent her to invade my home. Lister went after my sister Juliette, and Mom killed her. So as far as being related to her—No Thanks!"

"My apologies," Delgado told Odette. "I am very sorry your tour ended on such a bad note. How can I make it up to you?"

Odette slipped her arm through his, "Let's talk about that," she purred, giving Lucinda a wink over her shoulder.

"You hang around when we get back," Lucinda told Tom grimly, when they were once more seated in the shuttle. Agra fluttered over to Sesuna and sniffed the front of Tom's jacket. She crooned softly in comfort and extended a wing over Sesuna's chest.

As soon as she could reasonably get rid of Odette and her crew, Lucinda hauled both Tom and Sesuna into the employee lounge, which fortunately was empty.

"Did you find anything?" she asked Tom.

"I took some vid stills. I will need to go through them to check for anything illegal being shipped," he told her.

"I want a copy," Lucinda said.

"Sure," Tom agreed.

She glanced at the girl's worried face and turned her attention to her.

"Alright, what did you steal?" she asked, eyeing the front of Sesuna's blouse which was moving. Slowly the girl undid a couple of buttons and lifted out a small animal. It was about half again as big as Agra, four legged, with a round head and a pug nose. It was covered in soft fuzz, with a feathery plume of a tail. It was obviously still cold, because it shivered when Sesuna uncovered it.

"It's a Fire Indri," the girl said. "I couldn't leave her there! She's hungry and cold and about to whelp. They were killing her!"

"Fire Indri's are also illegal to export for sale off Trellya," Tom interjected.

Lucinda sighed, "Of course you couldn't leave her there," she told Sesuna. There had been a few times lately when she had really wished Katherine were here to advise her, but her mother was eight hours away on Veiled Isle. Well Lucinda would just have to muddle along on her own. She pulled out her com and contacted Glass Manor on O'Teague Island.

When they answered, Lucinda asked to be put through to the animal husbandry chief.

"Karen," she told her, "I've got a pregnant Fire Indri from Trellya here who is about to whelp. She's hungry, cold, and I would guess dehydrated. Can you help?"

"Oh, my goodness!" the woman exclaimed. "Well give her some water and wrap her up good. I'll see what I can find out about them. Are you at the spaceport?"

"Yes, but I'm thinking of sending them over to my apartment."

"It will take me about twenty minutes to get there. Let me know where to meet you."

Inheritance Politics

A FTER SOME thought, Lucinda came to a decision. "Tom, I need you to take Sesuna and—what is her name?"

"I'm calling her Solare," Sesuna said. She pronounced it Sool-aara, with a short a. "It means bright spot."

"Take Sesuna and Solare over to my apartment and stay with them until Karen arrives. Get her whatever she needs."

"What's the rush?" he asked her.

"There might not be any," she admitted, "but after today's little display I'm damn sure the Silver Samurai is a Guild ship. I don't want Sesuna or her mother to be even a blip on their screens. You hear that Sesuna? Don't go near that ship, and don't bring Solare back to the spaceport. If you get in their way, the Guild will slaughter you and your mother without even blinking. Promise me."

"Okay," the girl said.

"It would be simpler to just go across the hall and tell the Patrol the ship is carrying cargo on the banned list," Tom suggested.

Lucinda caught the brief flicker of fear in the girl's eyes. "No," she said calmly. "Then we would have to explain how we knew about it."

"Okay, it's your party. Let me find a place to borrow or rent a sled," Tom said, standing up. "I'll be back as soon as I can."

Lucinda tagged Karen and told her to meet them at her apartment instead of coming to the spaceport.

She turned to Sesuna who eyed her warily. "Let me guess, you don't want to talk to the Patrol because your visit to Vensoog wasn't sanctioned by the Supreme Priestess of the Fire Mother was it?"

"No," the girl admitted. "But it's just a lot of politics. Some of the Priestesses didn't like how Mother went about arranging Eloyoni's marriage. I think she pretty much forced them to release some of our funds for Eloyoni's dowry. After Eloyoni was taken in the raid, Priestess Jokoti, got the ear of the Mother of our house, and talked her into 'not wasting the money on a lost hope', so the Supreme Mother refused to authorize the money to look for my sister."

"The Magistra has control of Ispone's money?"

Sesuna nodded. "Yes, Mother was angry about that and other things. You see, every third daughter becomes a Priestess of one of the Mothers and they get control of all her credits. She isn't supposed to spend anything without their permission, and they refused to pay for someone to look for my sister. Then they found out about the pregnancy and forbade us to leave the planet. Mother defied them, and she booked us passage on a Free Trader under a false name. We went to Fenris first, because that's where our money is."

Lucinda nodded. "A lot of planets bank there because of the banking laws."

"Mother was able to get some of our funds sent here before they realized what she was doing and locked her out of the account. We came to Vensoog because Mother heard a rumor that a Guild ship was brought down by the Karamines near here and a lifeboat crashed on Kitingzen. She thinks those people are who took my sister," she said.

"Is there a wanted notice or a bounty on you and your mother?"

The girl shook her head. "I don't think so, but—you see because mother took the money without the Priestess's permission, she is afraid they might send a couple of warriors after us. It's *our* money, but when mother entered the Magistra, they took control of it, but they couldn't deny Eloyoni a dowry. When Eloyoni disappeared, her dowry went back to them. I guess they don't want to let it go."

"How long ago was your sister taken?"

"Three years ago. Eloyoni was on her bridal journey. Mother had arranged a good match for her. His family is old-fashioned though; they still adhere to the 'capture' part of the marriage ceremony. Eloyoni was supposed to wait on the outpost for her betrothed to land a sled and pick her up. Only when he got there the place had been raided, and Eloyoni had disappeared."

"No body was found?"

"No, that's why mother still hopes she might be alive."

"Why wait until now when Ispone is carrying another baby to come here? She had to know travel was dangerous."

Sesuna nodded. "She does, but Eloyoni's name has been called six times during the Fire Ceremony. If she is called a seventh time without answering or being declared dead, we all become Ubah, unclean for seven years and we forfeit all our land and money. Mother had started the ritual to have Eloyoni called as gone beyond the final screen, but then she heard about the crash on Vensoog."

"That's what she was doing in the Port records? Looking up transmissions from when she thinks the ship came down?"

"Yes, we came nearly every day."

"Where have you been staying?"

"We rented rooms within walking distance of the Spaceport," Sesuna admitted. "Mother deposited what credits she had into a Vensoog bank, but I don't have access because I'm underage."

"Well, you won't need much money while you stay with me, but you are going to need your clothes. Give me the codes and the address where you've been staying, and I'll stop by after work and pick up some of your things."

"Can you help us find the downed ship?"

Lucinda frowned thoughtfully. "Maybe. If Ispone found any record of the ships last transmissions, there might be a transponder still active. I need to talk to Ispone and get more details though.

Lucinda's com beeped. She looked at it, "Okay, that's Tom. He's outside. I'm going to put his jacket around you and walk you out."

Sesuna looked up at her. "Will mother be alright?"

"I'll ask the doctor for an update as soon as I can. I'll let you know." She put the girl into the airsled and shut the door. Tom was driving. "My shift starts in a few minutes. I'm going to go by Sesuna's rooms and pick her up some clothes on the way home. Tell everyone to help themselves to the Robo-chef," she told him, reflecting she was going to need to go food shopping soon.

Lucinda and Mira were about to take a lunch break when Twilya notified them that a body had been found on the Tamarac.

They arrived to find the SSF officers had cordoned off the area, and Dr. Worthy, the doctor who had attended Ispone, bending over the body.

"What happened to his clothes?" Lucinda asked.

"Have you identified the victim?" Mira asked at the same time.

"Not found," Gannett informed Lucinda.

"No ID yet," Debra added. "That makes me think he's newly arrived off a ship out there," she gestured to the shuttles parked in the distance. "He must have been stripped to delay identification."

"Any luck Doctor?" Mira asked.

"Nope," he replied. "DNA's not in the system, and he doesn't have any fingerprints because his fingertips have been burnt off. Probably done after he was dead. Somebody sure didn't want us to find out who he was anytime soon. He's human or at least part-human. I'm thinking some mixed blood because of the triple-jointed toes and fingers."

"How did he die?" Mira asked.

Dr. Worthy shrugged. "He's been in a fight, but nothing to kill him from what I can see. I'm going to contact Dr. Ivanov and ask her to do a complete autopsy. She has better equipment than I do."

"Why dump him here?" Lucinda said. "If he came off a ship in orbit, it would have been simpler to dump the body before they made planetfall."

"That is a good question," Gannett admitted. She turned to the newly arrived Patrol Officers. "Jonah, do you have any ideas?"

He knelt by the body, holding a small scanner over it. "I need to roll the body," he said. "Okay with you doctor?"

"Go ahead."

Lucinda came and knelt by the feet. "Let me help you," she offered. "I used to do this with Dr. Ivanov."

They rolled the dead man onto his stomach. Lucinda made a face, as Jonah spread the man's scrotum and scanned again. This time the scanner burped, and a name popped up.

"Damn!" Jonah ejaculated. "He's one of ours. His name is Okar Joisih. I'll have to check our database to find out what he was working on. I can't do that outside a secured area."

"Does that mean you are assuming jurisdiction?" inquired Mira.

"We don't have the facilities you guys have," Jonah admitted. "I'd like to make this a joint op, if that's okay with everyone."

Mira took out her com and called her boss. "Lieutenant Margrove is okay with it," she reported. "Doctor Ivanov will be here in about half an hour. Faster if she doesn't need to go through the main building first."

"Tell her to come straight here," Gannett said. "I'll see she's cleared for it."

"I was in the middle of rounds," Dr. Worthy said, "I left Dr. Johnson in charge, but he's pretty green. I need to get back. Have Doris call me when she gets here, will you?"

He turned and started toward where the sleds were parked.

"Just a moment, Dr. Worthy if you don't mind," Lucinda called.

He turned frowning. "Yes?"

"I'd like to check on Ispone Klam'ys condition if you have an up-date."

"Who are you again?"

"I'm Lady Lucinda O'Teague," she reminded him. "Ispone's daughter is staying with me while she is in the hospital."

"Oh, yes, I suppose the girl wants to see her mother."

"Yes, she does."

"Priestess Ispone is experiencing premature labor," he told her. "Even with the medicines she was proscribed, it's going to be touch and go. I'm hoping I can slow down the labor enough that both she and the baby survive."

"Ispone didn't want Sesuna to see her lose the baby," Lucinda said.

"Bring her in late this evening, after you go off shift," he said. "The meds are having some effect, so I'm hopeful she will be well enough to see her daughter by then."

Dr. Ivanov and her entourage arrived a few minutes later. Lucinda's replacement was a thin, nervous young man, plainly afraid of his brisk, bright-eyed superior. He tripped getting out of the coroner's shuttle and the Doctor rolled her eyes.

Lucinda bit her lip, trying not to giggle. "Here, let me help you," she told him. "I'm Lucinda, I did a stint in your job. Dr. Ivanov's a good egg, you don't have to be nervous around her, you know."

"She scares me," he admitted. "She's so good at what she does. I'm hoping to specialize in forensics, and I won't get in without an okay from her."

"She doesn't expect you to be perfect at this stage," Lucinda said, helping him to slide the body onto the lift, and fastening the belt at her end. "That's too loose; you need to tighten it." She pointed to the strap crossing the dead man's chest.

She and Mira were about to sit down for a delayed lunch when one of Doctor Worthy's students caught her. "Priestess Ispone wants to see you, Lady Lucinda," the girl said breathlessly. "Right now. She's getting agitated and she needs to be calm."

"Okay with you if I'm gone for a while, Sarge?" Lucinda asked Mira.

"Go ahead. I'm going to have another go at the files. I'll tag you if something comes up."

Lucinda stuffed the rest of her burrito into her mouth and rose to follow the messenger.

She found Ispone in an frantic state when she arrived. She entered the hospital room in time to see her slap away the medication a nurse was attempting to administer to her.

"I'm here," Lucinda told her, taking her clutching hands. "C'mon now, you have to let them help you. You don't want to lose this baby, do you?"

"It will make me sleep," Ispone said. "I must make sure my girls will be safe. Please, Soturi."

Lucinda nodded at the nurse, who slipped in to press an air syringe against Ispone's arm. Immediately, she began to breathe easier.

"Sesuna is at my apartment with our Clan's vet tech, helping her Fire Indri to whelp," she said reassuringly.

Ispone looked puzzled but nodded gamely. "I need to see a legal person. I must assign the guardianship of my daughters to you, so the Mothers can't take them."

"Do they know you are on Vensoog?" Lucinda asked.

"By now they must. I was forced to join them even though I wanted to espouse a young man from a neighboring estate. It was because I was a 3rd daughter, you see. I don't want that for my girls. I was determined to break from the church even before they refused to help me find Eloyoni."

"Clan O'Teague has a good lawyer here in Port Recovery. Why don't I call her and ask her to come here? You will need to pay her fees," she warned.

Ispone nodded. "Thank you. Will you act as guardians of my daughters, Soturi?

"I won't legally come of age until after the Fall Festival," Lucinda warned her, "but I will call my mother and ask permission to assume guardianship if something happens to you," she promised. "I will bring Sesuna to you late this evening. She misses you very much."

"Thank you," Ispone whispered again. Her eyes closed, and she drifted off to sleep.

Lucinda sat down in the chair beside the bed and called Jess Braydon, who agreed to make time for Ispone this evening. Then she called Lady Katherine.

Lady Katherine was in the village along the cliffs, inspecting one of the new bed and breakfast inns. When Lucinda's face showed on the com, she excused herself and walked toward the cliffs overlooking the ocean. She listened quietly as Lucinda told her the whole story.

After a moment's thought, Katherine said, "Because Ispone is a citizen of a Confederation ally who think they have a claim on her, we can't just adopt her and her girls out of hand; we need to run this by Genevieve before I can give you a go ahead on it."

Initiating a conference call, she found Laird Genevieve alone in her office doing paperwork.

"My goodness!" Genevieve exclaimed, seeing Lucinda hooked into the call. "This looks serious. How can I help you?"

Katherine rapidly explained the situation and a frown gathered on her sister's brow. "Humm," Genevieve said, tapping her fingers on the desk. "I actually think it will be simpler if this Ispone and her family simply become Clan members. That way the Mothers' of Trellya would no longer have a legal claim on them and Lucinda being under age won't come in to the matter. I suppose there isn't a problem genetically?"

"Genetically Trellyans are compatible with humans," Katherine admitted. "The dowry won't be an issue either. According to what the daughter told Lucinda, Ispone has plenty of money; she was the sole heir after her family was killed in the war. The only issue will be getting it out of the Mothers' hands."

"I had an idea about that," Lucinda interjected. "When we were on Fenris before you rescued us, Grouter used Roderick's computer skills to tap into the banking system and siphon off some credits and wash them, so they didn't look stolen. I was thinking about asking him if he could free up Ispone and Sesuna's funds the same way. The Mothers moved them to Fenris when the war started."

"Are you taking Sesuna to see her mother tonight?" Genevieve asked.

Lucinda nodded. "The doctor thought she would be well enough by then. I also arranged to have Jess Braydon visit her. That's okay isn't it?"

"It's fine. When you get there tonight, call us so I can make the offer in person," Genevieve directed.

After lunch, Mira told Lucinda to begin a search on the DB's DNA signature Jonah had reluctantly furnished. "I want to know when he really arrived here," Mira said. "Be careful though, we don't want to trip up any investigations the Patrol has going."

"If he ever came through the entry screen, it's been erased," she told Mira at the end of her shift. "The Patrol is good, but you see this marker on the entry ledger? It's an erasure. Of course I can't tell if it was our Vic without a lot of digging that might draw attention to the Patrol's investigation, so I don't know for sure."

Mira made a disgusted sound. "Okay, you tried. I need to talk to the Lieutenant about the block. Go home Rookie. You did good today."

When a tired Lucinda with a sleepy Agra draped over her shoulder, arrived back at her apartment with Sesuna's clothes, she found Karen getting ready to leave.

"Everything go okay?" Lucinda asked.

"Of course," Karen said, rubbing her nails on her shirt and blowing on them. "I'm good. This was a brand-new species for me. It's going to look great on my records. I am going to leave the Vet-Bot here for a while; the kit will need round-the-clock feeding for the first few days, and I want the mom to get some rest and recover her strength. We set up the whelping nest in Juliette's room. I increased the ambient temp in there to ninety degrees and upped the humidity."

"Thanks Karen, "you've been a godsend," Lucinda told her.

She handed Sesuna a backpack full of clothes and other items. "Here's your stuff. I promised your mom I'd bring you by tonight after shift, so why don't you hop in the fresher and put on some clean clothes while I see what's in the Robo-Chef for dinner."

Troubling Records

Both Ispone and Sesuna shed tears when the girl walked into the hospital room. Jess Braydon had set up her portable workstation in the corner and was busily keying in a document. She looked up and smiled when she saw Lucinda.

Lucinda gave the mother and daughter time to reassure each other both were doing well (although she suspected Ispone was fudging for her daughter's sake), before she interrupted them.

"I spoke to my mother and to the Laird, Ispone," she said. "The Laird would like to speak to you in person. May I initiate the com?"

Ispone nodded, her eyes wary. However, her guardedness soon dropped away under the Laird's warm greeting.

Genevieve smiled at her from the screen. "How are you feeling Lady Ispone?" she asked. "I was sorry to hear your pregnancy was not going as well as it could. Does your doctor think he can keep your baby from coming too early?"

Sesuna gasped, her face paling. Lucinda put a hand on her shoulder reassuringly.

"He has hopes," Ispone told her. "We must take one day at a time."

Genevieve nodded. "That is so. Rest assured we will do whatever we can to ease the situation. I understand you want Lucinda to assume guardianship of your children in the event something happens to keep you from caring for them yourself?"

"When they find me, they will send Hyati-Soturi after me to force me back so they can keep my inheritance."

"Are you sure you want to permanently break with them?" Genevieve eyed her shrewdly.

Ispone's mouth set. "Oh yes. The church was never my free choice, but custom and tradition decreed I become one of them."

"I am concerned that Lucinda being underage might provide a legal issue they could use to challenge the guardianship," Genevieve said frankly, "However, there is another solution."

"I see," Ispone said slowly. "She is Soturi, so I assumed she would be in command of her actions no matter her actual age."

"Soturi?" Genevieve asked.

"Warrior," a male voice outside the com area supplied. "It means Lucinda has passed the Trellyan Warrior Rituals."

"Fascinating," Genevieve muttered. "Lucinda passed those rituals before she entered puberty? Amazing. However, her fighting ability makes no difference on Vensoog; she is still underage until she gets her first List, but as I said, I do have another solution. I wish to formally invite yourself and your family to join Clan O'Teague as full Clan members."

"I don't understand," Ispone faltered. "What does that mean?"

"As a full Clan member, the Mothers or their agents can't legally force you or your children to return to Trellya. As Laird of O'Teague, I can make a formal demand that any of your property or funds be returned to you. I expect you would like more information on our laws and customs before you decide. Jess will provide you with the information you need, and in the meantime, to protect you while you decide, I will ensure the intent to adopt is registered in the archives. It is late, and I see you are tired. Please feel free to com me at any time you feel the need, Lady Ispone."

Genevieve's image faded, and Lady Katherine's became more prominent.

"Lady Ispone, this is my mother Lady Katherine of Veiled Isle," Lucinda told her.

"Welcome to O'Teague, Lady Ispone," Katherine said. "My daughter has told me a great deal about you."

While Lucinda was dealing with the dead body on the Tarmac, Tom decided to have a look through the official records in the archives for any reported discrepancies between what the Clans claimed was brought to the port and what went out.

The Archives were set up with three separate areas: Research, Data Entry and Storage. The storage area was underground; it was packed with data crystals and old plastia sheets. The area most commonly used was the one set up for straight data entry. Clan personnel brought in data crystals containing records of events such as births, deaths, land sales, crop records, etc. that took place throughout the year. It was most heavily used before and directly after the Festivals. A space for research took up most of the floor above the storage areas. Each research area was large enough for ten or fifteen people to sit at the computer modems as well as extra blank crystals for copying records.

The clerk assigned to assist Tom in his search was named Isiah Jordan, a thin young man with melting brown eyes and dark curly hair. Isaiah led Tom to one of the larger research areas, which fortunately was empty. He located the records Tom wanted to see easily, although he seemed puzzled. Finally he asked, "Your search seems a little random. If I knew what you are looking for, I might be able to help you better."

Tom looked up at him ruefully. "The trouble is I'm not exactly sure. I'm looking for a pattern of some kind in the outgoing shipments; differences between what the Clans turn into the warehouses and what goes out."

"Are you looking for thefts?"

"That's a part of it. Has anyone complained about not getting paid for their goods, or not as much as they expected?"

Isiah studied him, wondering if he could trust him. "Who are you working for?"

Tom turned away from the screen and studied him in return. "I'm a private investigator, but I do a lot of work for the Duc d'Orleans."

He waited patiently while Isiah made up his mind. His brows rose when Isiah went over to the door and locked it. "Yeah, I've found stuff, some discrepancies. When I reported it, I was told to forget about it. That it was none of our business."

Tom flashed him a grin. "Isiah, my boy I think you're just what I've been looking for. Do you still have the records?"

"I made copies to turn in with my report. A few days later, I found the original records had disappeared."

"Damn! I don't suppose you kept your own copies?"

Isiah shrugged. "After the ones I turned in disappeared, I started keeping copies whenever I found a discrepancy. A lot of these guys are poor farmers and fishermen, and it made me mad to see them cheated."

"Did you come from a farming community?"

"Saramon's main industry was historical research, but there were lots of farms and ranches. My mom did bookkeeping, and my dad's study of the ancient city sites brought him into contact with a lot of the ranchers in the area. Dad was an archeologist. He had promised to take Isaac and me with him on his next trip, but the war happened, and we got evacuated to the displaced citizen center on Camelot."

Are your parents still alive?"

He shook his head. "Dad was killed on Cymry in one of the battles when they still thought they could hold it. Mom died last year after Isaac and I graduated. Isaac is a mapmaker. He's out on Kitingzen with a team now."

Tom nodded. "My folks are gone as well. Mom didn't make it here, and Dad died on Taprion, fighting a rear-guard action to help families get off the planet. He never made it out—"

The door knob rattled, and someone pounded on the door. It sounded as if it was being kicked as well.

"Open this door before I break it in!" someone shouted.

When Isiah opened it, he was thrust rudely back into the room by a big bruiser with a broken nose, who in turn was shoved out of the way by another man who might have been his twin.

"I don't know how it got locked," Isiah said, picking himself up off the floor. "What can I help you find?"

"We got a message for Isiah Jorden," the first man growled, looking from Tom to Isiah, obviously not sure which of them was his target.

Isiah stepped forward. "I'm Isiah. How can I help you?"

His answer was a powerful blow to his stomach that doubled him over. A second blow caught him across the cheekbone, splitting it open. Isiah stumbled and fell backward into a chair at the closest workstation, breaking it.

Tom got up from his chair and moved to help Isiah, coming in on the left and putting the two thugs between him and Isiah.

When the second man moved in to the fallen Isiah as he struggled to get back up, Tom kidney punched him, and followed it up with a kick in the same spot and he doubled over in agony.

The other man turned to face Tom with a scowl. "You ought to mind your own business, mister," he growled. "Same as this clerk needs to. He's been poking his nose where it don't belong, see? Back off or you'll get what he's getting."

"I don't like two-to-one odds," Tom grinned at him.

"Thanks Tom, but this is my fight," Isiah said. He doubled his fists and assumed a boxing stance. "You caught me by surprise earlier, but I'm not afraid of you."

The man on the floor started to get up. Tom kicked him again, this time in the head, and he slumped down.

"Who told you to come here?" Tom asked softly.

The thug still standing pulled a knife out of his belt. "You want to play rough? Let's dance with this."

Tom laughed. "Isiah, download those records so we can take them when we go. Me and dummy here have a dance to attend."

"His beef is with me, not you," Isiah pointed out.

"Me first," Tom retorted. "You aren't even armed.

"All the same," Isiah began. The man on the floor stirred and started to rise. Isiah picked up the broken chair leg and whacked him behind his ear. This time the thug stayed down. Shrugging, Isiah backed off to watch. It was plain his new friend and his attacker were already so engaged in their 'dance', that neither one heard him.

Tom dodged when his opponent slashed at him with the blade. "Before you pull a knife, you should learn how to use one," he said with contempt, pulling a rolled leather strap about a yard long out of a pocket. Tom popped the strap open and caught the man's next thrust with the end, jerking the knife loose. The knife fell free when he followed up by rapid-fire snapping and popping the short whip at the man's face body and legs. His opponent tried to grab it, but Tom was working the leather strap at top speed, and the razor sharp stones imbedded in the ends of the strap made grabbing it not only tough but painful.

Isiah downloaded a crystal and shoved it in a pocket. "I've got it."

"Get behind me as I move toward the door," Tom instructed. He drove his foe backward into the room, saving one last hard snap with his weapon to the man's temple, leaving a bloody slash. When his opponent stumbled, Tom exited the door behind Isiah.

"Grab the end of that bench," he told the other man. Together they blocked the door into the room with the heavy bench that had been sitting against the wall of the building.

"It won't hold them long, but we should have time to get out of here," Tom said, rewinding the leather strap.

"Where are we going?" Isiah inquired. "Shouldn't we report this to the police?"

"Do you know who they were or who sent them?"

"No, I guess I don't," Isiah acknowledged. "I can't believe my boss sent them after me. She isn't a criminal."

"Well someone sent them," Tom pointed out. "Guys like that are hired, they don't just wake up one day and decide to whip on innocent archive clerks."

"No, I guess not," Isiah admitted. "I thought I could defend myself okay, but it's obvious I need more training. Can you teach me that trick with the strap?"

"It's Wikamor whip fighting, adapted for humans," Tom said, referring to an avian Confederation ally. "One of the teachers was also a Taprion refugee. I learned it from her. It takes years to become really skilled at it, but I can show you the basics."

Isiah frowned. "What about reporting it? Someone is sure to notice them. That one guy was out cold."

"We will make a police report, but first we see the Duc, and then we ask if you can stay at the Palace tonight. If those two know where you work, they probably know where you live too. Do you live with anyone?"

"I share an apartment with my twin Isaac, but like I said earlier, he's out on Kitzingen. It's an apartment complex though. Do you think I ought to warn the manager? He's just a bot, but—"

"Better have him notify whoever does security for your building anyway."

He took Isiah out to Versailles, L'Roux's ambassadorial seat in Port Recovery. The Duc probably wouldn't be there; when the security council wasn't meeting, he spent most of his time at home on Anjou, the Clan's main Isle territory, but as the Duc's top investigator, Tom had an office there with a cot. He also had two apartments in town, one he owned under his own name, and the other under an alias. Supposedly it was a flop for one of his disguises, and occasionally he hid clients or witnesses he needed to protect there. Isiah wasn't exactly a client, so he pulled out a spare cot and made up the beds for the night in his office.

When he commed Port Recovery Security, Tom found the fight had already been reported, and he and Isiah were listed as 'persons of interest'.

Arriving at Tom's office on Versailles, Detective Jim Gorsling frowned at him. He and Tom had a troubled history. Both men were L'Roux clan and had been competing against each other for several years. Gorsling was an ambitious young man with a strict belief in obeying the rules and a deep admiration for those in power. Tom Draycott was a rule breaker by instinct and inclination and held absolutely no respect for rank or power. It was quite natural that they should come in conflict; even more so because they worked in the investigative business.

When Gorsling had chosen Security as a career, he had hoped to be picked as an investigator on the Duc d'Orleans, L'Roux's head of Clan security's personal staff. After all, He had good family connections, and good reports on his work. Instead, the old man had chosen a troublemaker like Draycott for that position. In consequence, he resented Tom. Switching over to Port Security had seemed a good decision, and Gorsling's career star had been rising, but last year, Gorsling and his partner, June Sipowitz had been assigned to investigate the murder of a shopkeeper. Sara Lipski had ties to the local mob and the Thieves Guild. He had been sure the new owner of Lipski's shop was connected somehow, but that turned out to have been a mistake. When Lady Jayla was kidnapped, the Duc's nephew Lord

Jake Reynolds had accused Gorsling of taking a payoff from the actual murderer and wasting time investigating his wife. While Gorsling and his partner had been cleared of anything except developing target fixation, his behavior during the investigation had earned him a blistering reprimand from the Duc and from his superiors at PRS.

To make matters worse, Tom had been instrumental in capturing the actual murderer. Gorsling wanted to recover his standing in the Clan, so he was being very careful not to irritate the Clan's chief investigator.

When Tom called in, Sipowitz agreed to come out and take the report in person. While he and Isiah were grabbing dinner out of Tom's robo-chef, the two detectives arrived on Versailles and were shown into Tom's office.

"Thank you for coming," Tom said. "Did you guys get dinner?"

"No, we haven't had a chance," Sipowitz said.

"Please, help yourselves," Tom invited. "I'm afraid I don't run to much besides sandwiches and Cafka, but there's plenty of that."

"Thanks, but we will get something back at headquarters," Sipowitz said, deflecting the attempt to put the interview on a friendly basis.

"We've interviewed the other two men involved in the fracas, Monsieur Draycott. Now we'd like your side of the story."

She turned to Isiah. "I understand you were the clerk on duty at the time?"

"Yes."

"Please state your name for the record."

"Isiah Jordan, Clan Caldwalder."

"Please walk us through the events."

"I was helping Tom with some research, when someone started pounding and kicking on the door. I realized that the latch must have slipped (it does that occasionally). When I opened the door, one of the men shoved me to the floor. He demanded to know which of us was Isiah Jordan. When I identified myself, he punched me, saying I'd been poking my nose where it didn't belong. Tom helped me fight them off, and we ran, managing to block the door so we could get away. Then we came here and called you."

Gorsling turned to Tom. "Is that what happened, Draycott?"

"More or less."

Gorsling opened his mouth, but Sipowitz cut him off. "What stuff were they referring to?"

Isiah shrugged. "I assume it was the discrepancies in the records I reported to my superior several days ago."

"What kind of discrepancies?"

"There seemed to be a difference in the amounts of some goods being turned in at the warehouses for shipment and the amounts being sold. No disposition of the extra goods was accounted for. My supervisor told me to ignore it."

"I take it you didn't?"

"No, I didn't," Isiah said defiantly, "but from then on, I kept my own records of each discrepancy."

"What kind of goods?"

"Ah—building supplies, preserved foods, clothing, stuff like that. The missing amounts might have been a clerical error, but the quantities were just too large to account for it that way.

"We will need copies of those discrepancies."

"Alright. I will send you copies of what I have."

"Why didn't you call security after you were attacked?"

"We wanted out of there and to find out who sent them," Tom said.

"That's our job," Gorsling snapped. "We don't need any smart-ass P.I.'s horning in on our investigation."

"Like you have such a great track record Gorsling when it comes to investigating the local mob," Tom sneered.

"What reason do you have for saying the discrepancies are mob related?" Sipowitz hastily interjected before Gorsling could turn the interrogation into a personal fight.

Tom snorted. "Who else sends thugs to beat up on a clerk for reporting missing goods? The farmers or fishermen wouldn't have complained directly to Isiah for reporting it, they'd have gone to their Clan Liaison first." He gave Gorsling a contemptuous look. "Of course, you wouldn't pay attention to a mere farmer's complaint, now would you?"

Gorsling took a step forward, fists clenched. Tom's attitude always gave him an itch to smack him down. In addition, although he wouldn't admit it to himself, he resented the idea that Draycott was rumored to have a relationship with the young blond cop he'd been eyeing. Lucinda's family was highly connectable and he had been thinking of marriage to her as a possible way up the promotion ladder. Last year he had attempted to overawe her with his status during the investigation. He resented that she had apparently ignored his claims to her attention and teamed up with Tom to catch the real murderer.

"Jim," Sipowitz said quietly, intervening before trouble could erupt. "Thank you for your cooperation, gentlemen. We'll get in touch if we need anything else."

Money, Money, Who's Got The Money

ISPONE CONTACTED Genevieve two days after the offer to join the clan and accepted the invitation, and to thank her for her help.

"We'll hold the formal ceremony after you get out of the hospital," Genevieve told her, "but you and your daughters are legally citizens of Vensoog now."

"Thank you," Ispone told her.

That evening when Lucinda brought Sesuna to visit her, she told Lucinda, "Dame Braydon filed the formal request for the Mother's to return my inheritance, but they aren't going to part with it willingly."

"Are they that broke after the war?"

"Yes," Ispone said. "Like all the worlds, the funds were moved to Fenris for safekeeping, so they have very good records of any transactions, but the Mothers are counting every penny used for restoring the economy."

Lucinda nodded. "Yes, that might be a problem. Let me make a com."

She pulled out her com and punched in her foster brother's com sign. "Roderick, I need your help," she said when his image appeared.

Roderick, like his twin Rupert, was a slim, dark-featured man, grey eyed, with short, wiry black hair. His father Timon had been blood brother to Lucinda's adopted father, Lord Zack. Like Lucinda and her sisters, the boys had spent time in Grouter's placement center.

"What can I do for you, Trouble," he asked with a grin.

Lucinda made a face at him. "Is that fair? It isn't always me that causes trouble. This is Lady Ispone and her daughter Sesuna, our new Clan members."

"Welcome to the Clan, Lady Ispone, Lady Sesuna," he said with a smile.

"Lady Ispone has some funds tied up on Fenris by the Mothers of Trellya, and she thinks they may try to hide them. Jess Braydon filed papers requesting their return, but I was hoping you could locate the money and make sure it arrives safely on Vensoog."

"I'm going to need more info than that Luce," he reminded her. "You know, nasty things like account numbers and codes?"

She nodded. They were both remembering his skill with computers had been the reason Grouter had kept him and his brother from becoming a part of Van Doyle's 'stable' of kiddie porn stars.

"I can't promise anything until I see the accounts," he said. "Let me look around a little at the edges. In the meantime, perhaps you could bring me the codes and account numbers? I don't want the info going through the regular com channels."

She looked over at Ispone, who nodded. "I'll give them to Sesuna and she can bring them to you."

"I'll be at the office all day tomorrow," he said, and abruptly signed off.

"He doesn't mean to be rude, Lady Ispone," Lucinda apologized for the abrupt sign off. "Once he gets a focus, he sometimes forgets social niceties."

The older woman chuckled. "He's young and enthusiastic. I remember those days. Sesuna, why don't you go and get us a drink from the canteen? There are credit chips in the top drawer over there."

The girl rolled her eyes, guessing her mother had something to say to Lucinda she didn't want her daughter to hear, but she obediently got out the money and left the room.

"The Hyati-Soturi may still come for us," Ispone said. "The Mothers will think if they have me back they can make me refute the adoption to protect my children."

Lucinda looked thoughtful. The Hyati-Soturi were the enforcers of the Trellyan Theocracy; an elite group of warriors who answered directly to the Magistra. They had a reputation for ignoring laws on other planets. They were the best, most skilled of the Soturi's who passed the rituals. If they came they would be hard to defeat.

"I'll put out an alert to be notified if they arrive. If they come through regular channels we will know about it. I'm also going to ask O'Teagues local head of security to post guards in here just in case they slip through, but I don't know how much manpower they can spare for a vague threat like this. All the Clans' security forces are spread pretty thin during the festivals."

She started to com Ted Jorgensen, and then stopped. It was after eleven in the evening. "But I'd better wait until morning to call him," she said. "He's like Mom, gets up and goes to bed with the sun."

"All through with secrets now?" Sesuna asked, without rancor as she entered the room. She handed her mother a juice drink. She had gotten Cafka for Lucinda and herself.

"We need to get home," Lucinda told the girl. "I want to stop at the office to check something on the way out. Give your mother a kiss goodnight."

When she and Sesuna entered the PRS offices, Lucinda went straight to the arrival log. Although the screen showed several more ships in orbit besides the three Free Traders, none of them were Trellyan or showed Trellyan passengers.

"You're looking to see if any Hyati-Soturi came in, aren't you?"

"Yes," Lucinda admitted. Ispone hadn't wanted her daughter to be frightened by the idea they might still be in danger, but Lucinda didn't agree with the theory that children should be kept in the dark. If something was dangerous, a child needed information about it the same as an adult would. "I don't see anyone from Trellya on the legit passenger lists." She shrugged. "I think it's too early for the Hyati-Soturi to be sent; I doubt the Mothers will get desperate enough to get you back until they start getting hit with the formal demands to return your mom's inheritance. Even on a fast ship, it still takes a couple of weeks to get from Trellya to Vensoog. All the same, I think we need to get you into some of the weapons classes on O'Teague Isle."

While she was making arrangements for Sesuna to join the children's self-defense classes out at O'Teague Manor, Lucinda discovered that no one had heard from Jorge Carmody's exploration team in six weeks.

Frowning, she attempted without success to reach Juliette through the link Violet had established. Finally, she gave up and commed her sister. When Violet's face came into view, she demanded, "Have you heard from Juliette?"

"No, I haven't," Violet responded.

"What about through the link you set up?"

"Something was wrong yesterday, but this morning it feels back to normal. I intend to try this afternoon. I'll let you know what is going on, okay?"

"Alright," Lucinda agreed.

The Code Cracker

The offices owned by her foster brothers was impressive, Lucinda acknowledged. It was a triple decker dome with the company name R & R Security and Pharmaceuticals blazoned across its newly repainted face. They had obtained a good price on the building too. The top story was living quarters, somewhat spartan to be sure, but neither of the twins was much concerned with luxury, so they had moved in immediately. The second floor was devoted to offices and Roderick's computer design laboratory. The enormous attached greenhouse dome had been considered useless as storage by the prior owners, but it just suited Rupert's needs for cultivating the obscure plants he used in his concoctions. Rupert was gaining quite a reputation as a herbologist, combining plants native to Vensoog and others from Confederation allies into new and unique medicines and beauty creams. Rupert had a workstation on the second floor too, but he spent more of his time down in the laboratories working on applications for the stuff he grew.

When Lucinda and Sesuna entered, the receptionist, a very pretty brunette named Lina attempted to prevent them from going upstairs. Sesuna watched with interest when Lucinda put on her cop face and stared Lina down as she walked toward the lift, forcing the young woman to back away from her.

Roderick accepted the data crystal Sesuna handed him and popped it into his work comp. The kid was cute, he thought, she reminded him of Lucinda at that age, not in her coloring, but her expression had that same watchful look. Sesuna had bright maroon hair, cut short around her narrow, fine-boned face. Her soft, delicate gray skin had a pearly sheen setting off her onyx colored eyes. She was going to be a heartbreaker in a few years, he thought. Well Uncle Zack was going to need another young lady to protect about that time.

Roderick and Rupert were young for business tycoons, but the twins original design patent for security bracelets that doubled as coms had been immensely popular. Their Uncle Zack had negotiated fiercely with the other Clans on their behalf, all of whom wanted the new style security bracelets after they proved their effectiveness during the Kitingzen Incident.

The income from the sales had gained the boys enough credit to set up their laboratory in the warehouse district of Port Recovery last year.

"Where's Rupert?" Lucinda inquired, sitting on a corner of a dusty workstation.

Roderick shrugged. "He went down to the docks. Captain Smithers commed he'd managed to get in a shipment of those fish eggs Rupert wants and he lit out of here."

"Fish eggs? Yuck," Lucinda remarked.

Roderick grinned at her. "Yep; I hear he wants them for some kind of face cream."

"Remind me not to offer to test that one," Lucinda said, making a face.

"I'm back," Rupert announced. "Did you know Lina is bawling her eyes out?"

"She tried to stop us from coming up here," Lucinda said. "You need to explain to her about the consequences of interfering in Clan business."

"I'll explain who you are and give her a family tree," Rupert said resignedly. "But do try not to intimidate our staff please."

"Will you be able to use the codes?" Sesuna interrupted anxiously.

"These are the ones your mother used on Fenris?"

"Yes. We only got a small amount of credits transferred before someone discovered what we were doing. Mother is the sole living heir to her family's property and money, so there should have been lots more. One morning we got up and Security was at our door. The authorities on Fenris told us our tickets had been updated and escorted us up to Selene and put us on a ship headed for Vensoog," Sesuna told him.

Roderick and Lucinda exchanged glances. "In other words, they—er—ran you out of town on a rail?"

"Off planet on a ship," Sesuna corrected, and he hastily turned a laugh into a cough.

"Let me do some checking with the codes. I'll let you know in a couple of days if I need anything else," he told them.

Waterbaby

THREE WEEKS later Doctor Worthy commed Lucinda as her shift was ending.

Lucinda took one look at his expression and knew their time had run out. "What's the matter?" she demanded.

"The meds are not working. Lady Ispone has started labor. How much do you know about Trellyan birthing rituals?"

"You don't know?"

"I was a combat surgeon during the war. I treated Trellyans, but I have extremely limited experience with delivery. I do know there are specific rituals that need to be performed for a safe delivery."

"How much time do we have?"

"At most, a few hours before the child actually comes."

"Okay. I need to access the archives and talk to Sesuna. We'll be there as soon as we can."

After she signed off, the first thing Lucinda did was contact the healer at O'Teague Manor.

When Thomasina, the Chief Healer on the Isle, answered she was in the common room of the Manor. It was late so most of the resident staff and guests had retired for the night. Thomasina had obviously been on her way up to bed.

Lucinda was aware that healers were accustomed to being called out at odd hours, nevertheless, she apologized for calling so late at night.

Thomasina sat down in one of the comfortable, overstuffed chairs circling a round table. "What's up?" she asked, propping her elbows on the table and sipping her hot Cafka.

"How much do you know about Trellyan births?"

"I thought Lady Ispone isn't due for several more weeks," she said, frowning.

"Doctor Worthy says the meds are getting less effective. He thinks the baby is coming."

"Did you ask her daughter?"

Lucinda shook her head. "Not yet; hopefully she is in bed asleep. I don't want to scare her, and Ispone doesn't want her to be in the room if she loses the baby."

"I'm sorry, but we may need her advice to prevent that; she was raised in the temple, it's possible she observed the rituals."

Lucinda frowned at her. "What do you mean?"

"My records indicate birthing can be difficult for Trellyans; more-so than for a human woman. The rituals are a way to help her relax her body and allow the baby passage through the womb canal. Oh, here—I found a vid of a birthing chamber."

"I thought it was forbidden to take vids there. Something about betraying the myths of the Mothers?"

Thomasina nodded. "It is. However, this looks like it was done with a sneak vid-cam. It's a little grainy. I'm sending it to you."

"Thanks. I hope I can count on you to help?"

"Of course; Ispone is Clan now."

Lucinda commed Dr. Worthy. "I'm sending you a vid of a Trellyan birthing chamber. In the meantime, I'm told to increase the ambient heat in Ispone's room to about ten degrees over her body temperature, lower the lighting, and to bump up the moisture content in the air. I'm heading into town to collect her daughter. Our Clan Healer Thomasina should be there shortly. We're also going to need several types of teas for Ispone."

Lucinda found Sesuna still up when she arrived home.

"Why aren't you in bed asleep?" she demanded.

"Solare is very restless. I think it's Mother's time to give birth," the girl blurted out.

"Why would that make her restless?"

"The Fire Indris always know," Sesuna explained. "When a woman's time for birthing comes, they sit on her tummy and massage it to help the baby relax and not fight the birthing. We need to contact her doctor."

"No need. He is already getting a birthing chamber ready. Our Healer says Ispone needs some special teas. Do you know what she needs?"

Sesuna closed her eyes and recited, "She needs Twilight Walker for the beginning, made from fresh pulp and brewed on a coal fire to just under boiling then strained. 1 cup every 20 minutes. Then for the middle of the labor, some Ice Shield, to give her strength and ease the pain of the contractions. For the last, she must have Perfect Pearl, but only a tiny bit, and diluted with fruit from Heart's Lily."

"How do you know all this?"

"My mother was the Priestess in charge of the birthing chamber at the priory. I used to sneak in and watch the ceremonies. I also found her instruction booklet and read that," the girl explained.

"Kid, you're going to fit in just fine in this Clan." Lucinda showed her the vid. "This is what we've got. Is there anything missing?"

"Mother's tea pots, measuring spoons and the blessing bells are still at our old place."

"Okay, we'll stop there on our way and pick them up. You get Solare and her kit ready. I need to com my cousin."

"Geeze, Luce do you know what time it is?" Rupert groused, rubbing sleep out of his eyes when he answered his com.

"It's only eleven," she retorted. "Besides, this is Clan business. I need some special plants from Trellya for Ispone's labor. It's started."

"Which plants?"

"Um, Twilight Walker, Ice Shield, Perfect Pearl and Heart's Lilly."

"How much do you need?"

She turned to Sesuna. "What quantities do we need for the teas?"

The girl closed her eyes for a second. "About this much of the Twilight Walker, leaves only," she held out two cupped hands, "for the Ice Shield, about half that , but instead of leaves I need the pink bulbs under them, and only one leaf of Perfect Pearl. I also need about 5 ripe Heart's Lily Melons to make the juice."

Rupert made a rude noise. "It's a good thing you guys are family; do you know what these cost on the open market?"

"Quit griping," Lucinda ordered. "You can afford it; this is more important."

"Yeah, yeah," he replied. "Where do I send this stuff?"

"Bring it to the hospital," Lucinda ordered. "And hurry, please."

Lucinda approached the rooms rented by Ispone cautiously. It didn't look as if it was under watch, but something was causing an itch on her neck. Dismounting from the sled, she and Sesuna went inside. The rooms had a dusty, closed-in feel from being unoccupied. It also looked as if someone had searched it.

"Get what you need for the ritual," she told the girl, her eyes scanning the street out front.

Sesuna returned with a bulging bag. "I had to get Mom's tools as well," she explained. "I didn't think they would have them at the hospital."

When they left, Lucinda made the girl wait in the doorway while she scanned the area a second time for watchers. When she was sure it was clear, she nodded. Sesuna ran to her as the door to the room swung shut behind her. She jumped on the sled behind Lucinda and they took off for the hospital.

•

Behind them two big bruisers, one of them with a broken nose and the other with a newly healed whiplash scar on his temple, stood up.

"I think she knew we were here," Broken Nose said.

"Could be," Scar Face answered.

"So what do we tell him when he wants to know why we're watching this place instead of hunting for the archivist?"

Broken Nose shrugged. "He knows we take work from other guys. He may gripe about it, but he'll have to lump it. We weren't hired to grab anybody but that kid working in the archives," he reminded his co-hort. "Besides, the cop is connected to that guy who rescued the kid last time. I think if we follow the cop sooner or later we'll find the investigator who ran off with the kid."

"I vote we tell the boss only if he pays us for the stuff we've already done," Scar Face muttered.

"Yeah," agreed Broken Nose.

When Lucinda and Sesuna arrived at the hospital, Rupert was waiting out in the hall, holding a crate of aromatic plants, which he thrust at his cousin. "What are they *doing* in there?" he whispered. "I don't remember any of this stuff when Aunt Genevieve had Jeannine."

Lucinda leaned in and kissed his cheek. "Female stuff, cousin, just female stuff. You're a doll to bring these plants."

He cast a wary look over his shoulder. "Well, unless you need me for something else, I'm gone. Let me know how it comes out."

Lucinda grinned as he escaped down the hall. She nodded for Sesuna to open the door. She was relieved to see that Dr. Worthy had done the best he could setting up for a birthing ritual. He had darkened the room and raised the temperature to a steamy heat. Soothing music was being piped in. Simulated coal braziers set close to the walls. Ispone partially reclined in a water therapy bed with her eyes closed. Thomasina and six O'Teague Clan women sat around the bed in a semi-circle. A single nurse stood in the background.

Ispone's eyes opened when they entered the room. She frowned a little when she saw Sesuna, but relaxed when the girl placed the Fire Indri on her wide belly. Solare immediately began to knead it, humming. Sesuna put the Indri kitten into the bed prepared for the new baby.

The nurse started to object, but stepped back when she encountered a fierce glare from Sesuna.

Setting the tool bag on the bed, Sesuna removed carved sticks with small bells attached. She handed these to the six Clan women. "Shake like this every few minutes while a contraction is happening and say Bless This Child," she ordered, demonstrating the rhythm.

"Put the plants on that table," she directed Lucinda, getting out a large red teapot and filling it with water, which she set on the coals to warm.

"How can I help?" Lucinda asked her.

"You are Soturi," Sesuna said. "Your duty is to guard the room to make sure no one interferes with the birth."

She washed her hands at the room's sink and unwrapped a bowl and pestle. Pinching leaves off one of the plants, she began to grind them into a pulp. By the time she was satisfied with the amount, the water in the kettle had begun to steam. Sesuna eased the pulp into the water and closed the lid before taking the bowl and pestle to the sink where she washed and dried them.

"Now we wait?" Lucinda asked.

"Yes."

Lucinda's com chimed. She had turned it to privacy setting so only a family member could have gotten through. It was Roderick. She stepped outside the door before she answered him.

"I'm a little busy just now. Ispone has started labor and—"

"Sorry," he interrupted, "But I'm about to jump ship for Fenris and I wanted to let you know before I left."

"But that takes weeks!" she exclaimed in dismay. "You'll miss getting your List!"

"I'll be back in time," he assured her. "I'm catching a ride with the Patrol on a two-man shuttle; we should be there in three days and back in six."

"How did you manage to get the Patrol to give you a ride?"

He shrugged. "You remember Double Nova Jeffreys? I asked Uncle Zack to contact him. When I made the offer, they were practically dancing on the sky. They've been trying to get into the Guild's accounts for years, so they agreed, but they want an officer to be on hand when I crack open the banking system code. They've assured me I'll be back in time for the festival."

"Oh," she said a little uncertainly. "Be careful, okay?"

"You bet," he said with a grin before he shut down his com. Lucinda thoughtfully closed hers as well before stepping back into the room. She leaned back against the door, her thoughts in a turmoil. The true Fenris banking headquarters wasn't on Fenris, so why had Roderick said that was where he was going? Obviously, he had some tricky plan afoot, but it was almost as dangerous to play games with the Patrol as it was with the Thieves Guild.

Sesuna handed her mother a cup of the steaming tea and removed the tired Indri from her tummy. Placing the small creature in the crib with her kit and some restorative paste, Sesuna returned and began slowly stroking her mother's belly downward.

The nurse assigned by the hospital came bustling forward. "What are you doing now?"

Sesuna looked up. "Pretty much the same as the Indri was doing. On Trellya we usually have a team of six of them. Solare is tired. She needs to rest so I'm giving her a break. I'm sorry, I didn't catch your name."

"Rhoda, Clan Okoro. You are her daughter, aren't you?"

"Yes."

Thomasina leaned forward. "You will get tired too my lady. Can you show us how to do the massage, so we can share the burden?"

Sesuna looked up at her with a smile. "Thank you. Mother and I are not used to having someone besides ourselves to rely on."

"You are O'Teague now. You have us."

Ispone had finished the tea. Doris, one of the other Clanswomen came forward and took the empty cup from her. "Do you need more?" she asked Ispone.

"Thank you, but I need to rest for a few minutes," Ispone responded.

Doris took the cup to the sink and rinsed it out, setting it on the drying pad where the pestle had been placed.

Shalendra s'Klam'y was born just as the sun was rising. She came into the world with a dissatisfied yell, but quieted once she was placed on Ispone's tummy. Under her mother's quiet directions, Sesuna tied off and cut the umbilical cord. In the crib, Solare began whining and bouncing up and down.

"Hush now," Lucinda told her, lifting the tiny creature out of the crib. The Indri strained to reach Ispone, nearly wiggling out of Lucinda's grasp.

'It's alright, bring her over here," Sesuna told her.

Keeping a firm hold on the Indri, Lucinda let her sniff the baby. Solare leaned down and began to lick the birth film off Shalendra.

"Should she be doing that?" Thomasina asked.

"She is welcoming new life into the world and our family," Ispone said softly.

Although she joined them a little ahead of schedule, Shalendra was healthy, but the doctor decided to keep both mother and baby in the hospital until he was satisfied that there would be no complications from the early arrival.

Bankers Express

RODERICK FINISHED his conversation with Lucinda and shut down his com. He turned to the young officer the Patrol was sending with him. "Ready when you are," he said.

Officer Travis was a serious young lady of mixed Trellyan and human blood. Her slender, wiry frame was nearly six feet tall; big for a human woman, but short for a Trellyan. Her hair, in its tightly woven braid, was a muted red, and her delicate grey skin had a faint pink cast. Her fine-boned, oval face was offset by a wide, full lipped mouth over a determined chin. The most unusual thing about her was her different colored eyes. One was the pure Trellyan black, and the other a bright, human blue. She was examining Roderick as if he were a specimen under a microscope.

"Then let's not waste any more time," she said, striding to the sleek two-man shuttle waiting in the shuttle bay.

The craft had been stripped down to essentials; two pilot seats which would lay back and double as beds in the cockpit. Sanitary facilities and a minimal robo-kitchen sat atop the engine room, which took up most of the lower half of the ship.

"Sit there," officer Travis pointed to the seat on the left. Obediently, Roderick sat back and relaxed as she piloted the craft out the shuttle bay door. He could see his Uncle Zack on the observation deck with Roderick's Dactyl Rahjit sitting sulkily on his shoulder. The Dactyl was in a huff because he had been left behind. Roderick knew his uncle would wait until after the shuttle had left the bay to ask Double Nova Jefferies for a private word to explain their actual destination.

"Have you ever been to Fenris?" Roderick inquired.

"No," Travis admitted. "I'm looking forward to it. I understand you grew up there."

"Well, my brother and I spent several years there after we were evacuated from Moodon. How soon do we reach the edge of the solar system?"

"In about 20 minutes."

"Okay. I think I'd better use the facilities before we jump; land-lubbler you know," he added depreciatingly.

"Sure." Travis turned back to her console.

Rupert did use the facilities. However, he made sure he stumbled on the way back to his seat, catching himself on the back of Travis' chair.

"Sorry!" he said. "I guess I'm a little unsteady on my feet." As he spoke he accidently grabbed the girl's shoulder with his hand.

"Ouch!" she exclaimed, rubbing her arm.

"Sorry again," he said, "Did I hurt you? Guess I don't have my space legs yet." He turned his ring and slid the large gem back across its setting, hiding the needle he had jabbed her with.

"It's okay. I guess your ring pinched me," she said, pointing to the jewel on his hand.

"I'm so sorry. I don't usually wear rings, but this one was a present from Mom. One of the prongs seems to be bent a little." He pretended to push on the setting. "I guess I'll take it back to the jeweler when we get home."

He continued making light conversation until she slumped in the chair. Quickly, he took out the navigation crystal he'd preprogramed and exchanged it for the one in the console. As soon as the console showed it was engaged, he leaned over and shook his companion.

"Hey!" he exclaimed. "Did you fall asleep? Are we on course?"

Travis sat up with a jerk. "Wha—"

"You just looked like you fainted or something," Roderick told her.

"I *fainted*? Why would I do that?" hastily she checked the console, confirming the ship was on course. She turned to look at him suspiciously.

"Did you do something to me when you tripped?"

Roderick hesitated and then decided to go with the truth. "I had my orders too. Right now, my Uncle is explaining to your boss that we were afraid you might com back to the ship to double check the orders, so I put you out for a few minutes while I changed the destination."

"You *changed* the Destination? Are you out of your mind? You bet I would have checked! I stocked this ship myself. We only have enough air, water and food to get us to Fenris and back!"

"Relax. We *are* going to Fenris," he said, "At least we are going to one of the moons."

She frowned at him. "Why weren't we told the real destination?"

"You are being told now," he said. "Just not before the mission. Look, the Guild has ears everywhere. They bank on Fenris like everyone else. What do you think would happen if they found out a Patrol ship was going to Wasobi? I don't know about you, but I've got plans for the rest of my life. I'd like to keep my skin intact if you don't mind."

Travis glared at him. Roderick sighed and opened his porta-tab. It was going to be a long three days.

When they reached Wasobi Travis started to take over the controls.

"No, don't," Roderick said. "They will take us in on manual."

"How do you know this?" she asked suspiciously. It was the first thing she had said to him since he'd broken the news about the course change.

"I was brought here as a kid," he answered.

"I don't believe you! Who would bring a child here?"

"Somebody who wanted to use my code cracking abilities," he replied.

Their ship landed smoothly. "Okay wait for them to open the door before we exit."

"Why?"

"To make sure there is enough air to breathe," he snapped. He was getting tired of her attitude.

The door opened. "Me, first," he said.

She opened her mouth to ask why, and he cut her off. "Because there are protocols here too. These are robots. Just keep your mouth shut, and don't draw a weapon, okay?"

Travis snorted, but took her hand off her gun.

When they walked down the ramp, a ceiling scanner ran over them.

"Identify yourself," the guard in front of him requested. The robot-security guards were the same. As far as he knew they had no names and you couldn't tell them apart since they had been made from the same model.

Roderick held up a hand palm out, then turned it over and closed a fist twice.

When the scan moved to Travis, he said, "New employee. Please set up identity protocol."

"Come." The guard turned to leave, and Roderick followed, noting with relief that Travis was doing the same.

They followed the guard to a secondary room. Travis was instructed to stand on a white square while the machines recorded iris prints, fingerprints, DNA and a voice recording.

"Can they hear us?" she whispered when she exited the room.

"Everything we do and say here is recorded," Roderick told her.

They were taken to another room with several workstations. "Sit there," Roderick told his companion. He took out a data crystal and popped it into place. A virtual keyboard appeared in front of her. "Now lay your palms face down on the console."

A ripple ran over the keyboard. "You now have general access so go ahead and look around until you get familiar with how the system works. If you find any accounts you want a deeper look at, let me know."

He sat down beside her and repeated her actions. It didn't take him long to find Ispone's records and make the transfer to an account in her name. Once he had that, he simply linked the new account to her Vensoog one and set protections around both accounts to block access to them by the Mothers.

While he was there, Roderick checked on Grouter's accounts to see if there had been any recent activity, frowning when he discovered there had been. He set up a trace on it he could access later and pulled out of the system.

He turned to Travis, who was typing furiously on her keyboard. "Need any help?"

"No, I've got it. How much time do we have?"

"About ten minutes before they run a system check from Fenris. We need to be out of here by then."

Six days later Roderick stepped out of the shuttle onto the deck of the Patrol ship Ironsides. He wasn't surprised to find his uncle, accompanied by two husky patrolmen, waiting for him. Before he could get his mouth open to ask what was going on, Ranjit dived on him, scolding furiously for being left behind.

"Yes, alright I'm sorry for not taking you," he soothed. "But they shoot flying critters up there."

Travis had been given the go ahead by the patrolmen, and she dashed up the ramp leading to the command level.

When one of the Patrolmen made a 'follow me' gesture, Roderick fell in beside his uncle.

"Are we under arrest?" he asked.

Zack shrugged. "Not quite. Relax kid, and let the Clan system work."

They were shown to the officers' lounge. Their guards took up places on either side of the sliding door. Zack went over to the robo-chef and programmed in cups of Cafka for himself and Roderick, and a bowl of water for Ranjit. When he reached into a pocket for Dactyl treats, both the guards went on alert.

Zack grinned at them. "Relax, boys—I'm not carrying." He set the water and treats on the low table in front of his chair and sat back to sip his Cafka. Roderick imitated him.

He could see his uncle was enjoying poking at the guards. Like Roderick's father, Zack had been Force Re-con during the wars and he missed the edge he got from pushing the envelope. Nothing much intimidated him, not even his fiery wife.

A few minutes later they were shown into Double Nova Jeffrey's office. The Patrol commander was a stiff, whip thin man with a head of graying hair. Travis stood at attention next to the clear plastia sheeting behind his desk. The thick, clear plastia was as strong as a metal alloy and it allowed Jeffreys to see out into the cargo bay.

He didn't invite them to sit down, but Zack did so anyway, gesturing for Roderick to do the same.

Jeffrey's frowned. "See here Lord Zack, I gave your man a ride to Fenris in good faith. Travis here tells me he not only drugged her, but he used an unauthorized nav code for the trip."

Zack sipped his Cafka. "You bet he did. I told you why that was done. We might not have gone over your head if you had been amendable to taking the precautions I requested."

Jeffreys breathed through his nose. "Are you telling me your man's actions were authorized by the Vensoog government?"

"I'm telling you the actions were authorized by the joint Clan Security Council of Vensoog."

Zack looked around for a place to set his empty cup. Not finding one, he leaned forward and put it on Jeffreys highly polished desk. Jeffreys turned red with indignation.

There was a discreet knock and a cadet poked his head inside. "Beg pardon for the interruption, sir, but we've received a message from the Clan Liaison for O'Teague.

"That would be my wife Lady Katherine Double Nova. You remember Katherine, don't you?"

Jeffreys glared at them. "Get out of here. I expect you," he pointed at Roderick, "to make yourself available if we have questions."

Truth & Lies

TOM INVITED himself to breakfast a few days after Shalendra was born. He brought a data crystal with the vid stills from the Silver Samurai's Cargo hold.

"Thanks," Lucinda told him as she took it. "I'll turn this in to Mira saying a confidential informant gave it to me. I don't have to tell her your name. Oh, I thought you might be interested to know that the body dumped on the tarmac was an undercover patrol agent. Apparently, he was investigating the smuggling."

"Do you have a name?"

She shook her head. "No, I'm afraid the Patrol is being sticky about releasing the name he was working under, but his real name was Okar Joisih aka Tory Kinkade."

Sesuna came in, rubbing sleep out of her eyes. "Hi, Tom. How come you guys are up so early?"

"Mira got a request to check out a place Kincade rented under his real name. Since the body was dumped at the Spaceport, we get it because there aren't any detectives attached there. She wants to go by before our shift starts."

Sesuna sighed. "Oh. Could I come with you? It's pretty boring here all day."

"No you can't come with me when I'm on duty, but maybe you could take Solare and her baby out to Glass Manor for a check-up. There's a lot of things to do there, and I can be sure you are safe if the Hyati-Soturi show up."

"Great! I'll get them ready." Sesuna practically danced out of the room.

Tom's eyebrows rose. "You're expecting trouble from the Hyati-Soturi?"

She nodded. "They've had time to find out Ispone's money has been transferred here, and about the Clan adoption. It doesn't take a genius to figure out she's on planet. If they grabbed Sesuna, Ispone would fold up and do whatever they want."

"They couldn't get her off planet," he protested. "The Clans would be all over them."

"Not if they land a shuttle on one of the continents. They are pretty much unexplored territory. I need a favor too. Can you give her a ride out there? I'll warn security you're coming."

"Yeah, sure I can take her out to O'Teague Isle. We need to be able to talk though. How about we meet over dinner?"

She eyed him suspiciously. "What do you want to talk about?"

He grinned at her. "The case mostly, but some other stuff too."

"Okay. I get a lunch break about six. Do you mind eating in the canteen?"

"Well I was actually thinking about that new cafe Fire & Ice. It's right across from the Spaceport."

"Okay. I'll meet you there."

After seeing them off, Lucinda went back inside. On impulse she added her personal art evaluation kit to the field kit issued by the department. It was one of the few things she had taken with her from the placement center.

Kinkade's apartment was in an expensive part of town. When they drew up before the gate they had to show their badges before it was opened. She looked over at Mira. "IPP must pay their agents a lot more than we get. Isn't this place a little pricey on a cop's salary?"

"It is," Mira admitted. "Maybe he had family money."

The apartment itself was on the ground floor, with a meticulously groomed garden circled by a wrought iron fence.

"Alarmed force field on the fence," Mira observed. "That costs money too."

The apartment interior was elegant and tasteful, with designer leather furniture, art on the walls and a few sculptures set to be shown off on the display tables. However it showed no signs that someone actually lived there.

"You start in here," Mira instructed. "I'll take the bedrooms."

Lucinda set down her field kit and walked around the living room. She stopped at the fireplace and examined the painting hung over it, frowning. Opening her kit on the couch, she took out a specially programed spectrometer and scanned the painting.

"What are you doing?" Mira asked her from the doorway.

"Checking to see how valuable this painting is."

"With that?" Mira gestured to the instrument Lucinda was holding. "What is it? And where did you get it?"

Lucinda had prepared for this question. "It's an art spectrometer for evaluating art. It's a part of the kit given to me at the placement center."

"You were what? Twelve when you left? That looks like a pretty expensive tool to give to a child."

Lucinda shrugged. "Like I said before, the Center subscribed to the philosophy of 'Idle hands are the devil's playground'. We didn't have much recreation equipment and I had a talent for art, so they trained me for a career in it. I think the idea was for me to go to work in a gallery or a museum when I left the center."

"I see. Well, what does your fancy gadget say?"

"Judging from the readings, this is from Saramon, and it's very expensive."

"Saramon? Isn't that the planet where all those ancient ruins are located?"

Lucinda nodded. "Yes. This work is painted on a single slab of Saramon shale rock, sanded to make it smooth enough to take the pigment. It's an original, and it's about three to four thousand years old. Retail price at auction would run around eleven million. Black market about nine."

Mira looked at her in astonishment. "That little critter told you all that?"

Lucinda handed her the special tablet that was a part of the kit. "It's got an artifact database," she explained.

"This is fascinating," Mira muttered. "Any of the rest of this stuff like that painting?"

Lucinda pointed to a sculpture of a woman rising from the sea. "That is from Oceana, also about a thousand years old. If you look closely at it, you can tell the center figure isn't quite human, and the material is carved from the shell of a Pellagone Snail, coated with a mixture of the water-resistant varnish used to protect art on that planet."

Mira squatted and peered at the statue. "Yes, I think this is a Syrene. She is riding on some type of alien water horse."

"A Capella," Lucinda supplied.

"Okay. You catalog the art in here. I need to call this in, so this stuff can be taken into evidence."

She turned away to her communicator, reflecting that Lucinda was going to be a real asset to the force once she got her trained.

It took Lucinda all the afternoon to catalog the art in Kinkade's apartment, so she missed the tag that four Soturi had arrived on a Trader from Oceana.

"The kid will be a real asset once she's trained," Mira told her superior, Lieutenant Jerusha Margrove the next day. Jerusha oversaw recruit placement and she liked to keep an eye of all 'her' boys and girls by demanding regular reports from their trainers.

"Give me your evaluation of Officer O'Teague, Mira," her Lieutenant's shrewd dark eyes inspected her over a cup of Cafka. "I can tell you like the girl, but you asked for her specifically out of the new recruits, why?"

"I was curious," Mira admitted. "Doris Ivanov was very impressed by her, and you know as well as I how difficult it is to gain her approval."

They shared a look coupled of mingled amusement and commiseration about their colleague's idiosyncrasies.

Mira sat back and sipped her Cafka. "Ivanov admitted she would have kept her in Forensics if she could have; in fact, she still has hopes of getting her back when she finishes her training. But I think the spaceport is a better fit, if only because we don't have anyone on the force who knows as much as she does about alien cultures."

"You only have her word for how much she knows," the Lieutenant pointed out.

Mira shook her head. "I watched her with that Trellyan mother and daughter. She knew how to handle them, *and* she knew the woman was pregnant, which I couldn't tell—neither apparently could Patrol officer Abdul, who has gone through the Patrols Alien Training course."

"How do you know that?"

Mira shrugged. "I asked Abdul's Supervisor when she commed me about the incident."

The Lieutenant sipped her Cafka, alternately running a pencil up and down between her slim brown fingers. "I okayed your request to be her trainer because you have the best instincts I know for judging a young recruit. There *have* been rumors about her though, and yes, I do know they were partially started by Jim Gorsling out of spite and jealousy. *But* that placement center on Fenris where O'Teague and the other girls were raised was run by a Thieves Guild operative. How much credence do you place on the rumor she has ties to them?"

Mira made a rude noise. "Admittedly she seems to have been taught some unusual skills, but she was a child for Voids sake! I don't say that—what was his name? Grouter? Might not have been grooming her for something, but indications are he intended to use her in the art and antiques game, and we know he only had a few feelers out in that area when he was captured."

Lieutenant Margrove studied her thoughtfully. She had attempted numerous times to get Mira to accept a promotion to detective and been turned down. Now she saw a way to compel her subordinate to take the promotion.

"So you don't think there is any residual taint?"

"Not a chance, Lieutenant. She's clean, I'd take oath on it."

"Good enough. I'll lend my weight to her placement at the spaceport with you as Detective In Charge. With you filling in as a detective Sargent on staff, I can justify assigning Lucinda and yourself there permanently."

Mira eyed her superior, who grinned back at her, malovently. Margrove was an old friend; in fact Mira had trained her. She was justifiably proud of how her former trainee had turned out, but it annoyed her when Jerusha got the better of her.

Now she made a face. "You got me. You're a rat, Jerusha, you know that, right?"

Jerusha's white teeth gleamed against her dark skin. "I learned from the best," she replied. "I'll start the paperwork. I leave it up to you to tell Officer O'Teague."

"I'm making you primary on the murder at the spaceport," Jerusha continued. "Bring me up to speed on your investigation so far."

"Using Lucinda's art database, we determined that the art in the apartment is worth approximately six to seven billion credits. Granted the Vic was working undercover, so he might have been given art to support his background, but this stuff was in his private apartment, not the one he was using while he was undercover. Not that we've been given access to that one; the Patrol is being cagy about that. It seems they still have operatives working undercover and are afraid our investigation might jeopardize those operatives covers."

Jerusha nodded. "It's a valid concern. I'll see what I can do to get you access on the QT. I agree the expensive art collection is suspicious. In the meantime start checking out Kinkade's background and finances. It will be good experience for your recruit."

Lucinda was eyebrow deep in Kinkade's financial data when her com chimed. It was from Dr. Ivanov with a DNA report from the apartment, there was a deed attachment. Before she could open it, a second one arrived from the Archives. When Lucinda opened it, she stared in astonishment. It was an ID photo of Troy Kinkade. But the ID wasn't the face of the man on the Tarmac. After a moment's thought, she closed her screen and went to find Mira, who was dealing with the latest complaint; a member of a Free Trade crew had been involved in a dispute with a local merchant, and the merchant had come to demand the ship be impounded until the damages had been paid.

"I've requested the ship's Captain to come down to the office, ma'am," Mira's voice was soothing. "I'm sure we can settle this amicably."

"Amicably? That jerk broke three of my tables and two chairs! They were specially made for my bar! I want—"

"Have you filled out the complaint form ma'am?" Lucinda asked.

"Yes! I've filed ten of them! Why won't you go out there and arrest him?"

Mira closed her eyes. Lucinda brought the merchant a cup of Cafka. "Mistress Lenard is it? Why don't you sit here with this cup of Cafka while we take a ride out to the ship?" Lucinda suggested.

Although not completely pacified, the merchant consented to wait in the outer office for them.

"What's up?" Mira demanded. "We won't find the ship's captain out at the shuttle and you know it."

Lucinda nodded. 'Yes, but I wanted to talk where we wouldn't be heard. I think we're in trouble."

"In trouble? How?"

"Because I just got a copy of the DNA contract on the apartment from the Archives. The Troy Kinkade who is resident in that apartment we searched this morning, is *not* our DB. Doesn't that make the search illegal?"

"*Oh, Hell*," Mira muttered. "I got that address from Jerusha. She found it waiting in her comp this morning when she got to work."

Mira pulled out her com and tapped in her Lieutenant's code.

Jerusha listened to her in silence, her expression darkening. "Why those jerks! I bet this is a ploy to delay our investigation by tying us up with a wrongful search," she growled. "You're sure about the ID?"

"Lucinda is. She just got a fresh copy from the Archives."

"Send me everything you have," the Lieutenant ordered. "We'll see about this!"

"One more thing," Lucinda interjected before the irate Jerusha could sign off, "This Troy Kinkade also owns Kinkade Excavations, and they have permits to fly drones over both Kitingzen and Barisi. There was a note attached to the archive file cross-references something called the Dragon's Tear. What is that?"

Mira snorted. "An old legend. Supposedly one of the Clan ancestors brought it with them when they colonized Vensoog. It's supposed to hold a treasure map. I doubt if it has anything to do with this case, but go ahead and research it anyway."

Odds & Ends

LUCINDA WAS surprised when the restaurant where she was
to meet Tom for dinner was somewhere a man took a date. It
had subdued, romantic lighting, each table was covered with white
tablecloths, crystal glasses and flowered centerpieces. She hesitated
in the entryway, feeling out of place in her work uniform, but since
she needed to return to work after dinner she hadn't changed.

"Lady Lucinda?" asked the hostess, a trim woman in a blue velvet
suit.

"Uh—yes," Lucinda replied, realizing she was looking at the top
of the woman's neatly coiffed hair. She sighed, reminding herself that
her height was an asset in police work, even if it put her at a disad-
vantage on the social scene.

"Please come this way. Your party is already seated." She wove a
way through several tables of diners, some of whom were in casual
clothes, others in fancy dress.

Lucinda followed her to a private alcove where she discovered
Tom waiting for her, breathing a sigh of relief to discover he was
dressed casually.

"May I get you a beverage?" the hostess inquired.

"Just Cafka; I'm on duty," Lucinda replied.

"Ah, then perhaps one of our specialty Cafkas." She handed Lucinda a small menu which Lucinda scanned warily. There was a cinnamon flavored one. That seemed safe enough. "This one," she said
pointing, "And the same in a Quirka bowl for her," she indicated
Agra, who chirped happily.

"Wow," she said, when the waitress disappeared. "I'm glad you're not all dressed up, I was beginning to feel underdressed in my uniform."

He grinned at her. "The owner's a friend of mine. We did time in the Center on Camelot. I know it's not fancy like you're used to, but the food's good."

"Fancy?" she asked, puzzled. "You've seen my kitchen. Jake and Jayla made sure it had all the latest bells and whistles, but it isn't fancy."

"No, I meant at your home."

She looked at him, dumfounded, remembering arguing with her sisters and cousins as they cleaned the table after dinner. A dinner that had been programmed by whoever's turn it had been to cook that evening. At Veiled Isle, everyone in the family had taken a turn at cooking and cleaning up, even her father and Uncle Vernal. Although Lady Corrine had banned field rations after the first time Vernal had served it, claiming he was cheating.

She shook her head. "You have weird ideas of how we live," she said.

"Doesn't your family rule O'Teague?"

"I suppose so," she said, smiling her thanks at the waitress as she set a cup of cinnamon scented Cafka in front of her. "But that doesn't mean we sit down to fancy formal dinners and stuff; we don't have time. And ruling? It's a lot of work settling disputes, planning crops and decision making."

"Oh," he said. "At L'Roux they are very formal."

"They're French," she reminded him. "O'Teague is Scotts/Irish. We aren't exactly prim and proper. What are we going to eat?"

"Ah—I hope you don't mind, since I knew you wouldn't have a lot of time, I just asked Arno to give us tonight's special."

"That's great," she said. "Mira only gave me an hour."

She smiled as the waitress came back with servings of a rich stew and warm bread. She also sat a small bowl of the same down for Agra, who waited until Lucinda tapped it to begin eating.

"I know you came over to L'Roux from Camelot. Are your folks still around?"

"No, we originally came from Taprion. My dad was in the militia there. His unit was part of the troop protecting us when our shuttle lifted. I was around four, I guess. I had my mom before she caught Ironbark Syndrome in the camps and died. They put me in the creche for 'unparented' children. I started getting into trouble when I objected to being tagged as unparented. On Camelot, like on Aphrodite, 'unparented' meant you were a bastard. When I objected, they called me undisciplined. I stayed at the center because I had nowhere else to go until I was about twelve. That was when I started sneaking out at night."

"Didn't you get caught?"

He shrugged. "I don't think they cared as long as I wasn't causing trouble. I only showed up for classes. You and your sisters were in a Child Placement Center on Fenris weren't you? How was it?"

She hesitated, deciding how much to say. By policy, she and her sisters didn't talk about Grouters much except among themselves or to family members. "Different. Juliette and I were three and Violet was one when we were moved there. We didn't have much time to get into trouble. Grouter, the Center Head, believed in the maxim 'idle hands make mischief' so we weren't given much free time. We did a lot of training in different stuff. He was Thieves Guild," she added, watching Tom carefully. "After Mom and Dad rescued us, he was arrested."

Tom nodded slowly. "I did some reading on that center on Fenris," he admitted.

Her eyebrows rose, and she paused with a bite of stew halfway to her mouth. "Why? Checking up on me?"

"You—bother me. I wanted to see if there was anything in your background to account for it," he admitted.

Lucinda sat down her spoon and picked up her cup to give herself time to think. "I *bother* you? What does that mean?" she demanded.

"If I knew, I wouldn't be looking for answers," he snapped.

"Do you always kiss girls who bother you?" she asked.

He scowled at her. "No, dammit, I don't. And you—I usually react differently to underage girls. I don't go around making passes at them! When I met you I thought you were the same age as Jayla. It wasn't until Lord Zack warned me off that I realized how young you are."

"I see. Look, I don't usually talk about this, but you've been honest so—you may be reacting differently to me because my sisters and I are designed differently."

"Designed differently? What does that mean?"

"It means we were born in a lab. Grouter had the three of us designed to his specifications. We were given specialized training in certain fields, and he protected us from Van Doyle's kiddie parties."

"Kiddie parties?"

"Van Doyle handled prostitution for the Guild, including providing children for those whose sexual urges ran to kids. We used to see the rejects when they came back. They were—damaged—most of them. Whenever Van Doyle came to the center to recruit fresh meat, Grouter would send us to a hidden room."

His gut clenched as he had a brief vision of a smaller Lucinda huddled with other kids, hiding from a monster in a dark place. He opened his mouth to ask another question and changed his mind. That lovely rosebud mouth had set like iron, and her bright grey eyes had gone flat and shiny. She obviously wasn't prepared to say more, so he let it go.

"Ah—you were trained? Do you know what you were being trained for?"

She relaxed. "Sort of. I was given training in art and design and how to rate and value art. I was taught to draw an interior room from memory and I can give you the schematics of most electronic security systems. I suspect I was supposed to become a fence or an art thief."

"But it was different when you came here?"

She smiled. "Yes. Until we came to Vensoog, we never really had a childhood, or got to do normal childhood stuff. Lady Katherine and Lord Zack are the best thing that ever happened to us. No matter what anyone says, *they* are our real parents."

"You love them, don't you?"

"Yes, very much."

"I had my mom until I was about eight, and she told me lots of stuff about my father, but I understand what being on your own is like. After I ran away from the Center, I fell in with one of the youth gangs. They were mostly runaways from the displacement center or kids who grew up on the streets. They had taken over a lot of petty crimes in the City. I earned a place with them by fighting. I stayed in the gang until I met the Duc."

"How did you meet him?"

He laughed. "I was in the wrong area and I got swept up by one of the government work gangs, the job turned out to be working for the Duc. To this day, I don't know why he singled me out, but he did. He sort of rescued me from taking up a career as a thug. My first job for him was finding out who had beaten one of the immigrants, and I decided I liked being one of the good guys. When he got the offer to come to Vensoog, he asked me to join him and Jake."

Lucinda's com chimed. "Whoops! That's my cue to get back to work. Thanks for dinner."

She got up and dashed out the door, followed by Agra who unfortunately was dripping stew gravy as she flew.

"What did you say to run her off?" inquired a youngish man wearing a stained cooking apron.

"Nothing," Tom replied. "She was late for work. She takes her job pretty seriously."

"Did you find out what you wanted to know?"

"Sort of, Smart Ass," Tom said to his friend Arno. "At least I have a place to start."

Arno shook his head. "You don't fool me. This wasn't business. She's the one you've been mooning about for the past six months, isn't she?"

"I haven't been mooning over anyone!" Tom snapped.

Arno just grinned at him and began to bus the table.

It was obvious Lucinda wasn't telling him everything, Tom thought, but he was reasonable enough to recognize she didn't fully trust him yet. He wasn't telling her everything either, he ruefully admitted.

"It's boring staying inside all day," Sesuna complained the next morning.

Lucinda eyed her thoughtfully, remembering how much mischief bored teenagers could get into. "I have to attend another meeting of the Clan Festival Committee this morning," she said. "It is boring too, but it would get you out of the house..."

"Yes! Anything!"

"Well, go change into something besides those ragged sweats and comb your hair."

"Can I wear makeup?"

"Um—maybe. Would Ispone have let you wear it?"

"Sure, she bought it for me."

"Okay. Leaving in about fifteen minutes, so move it!"

Agra chirped at her. "I know, she's scamming me about the makeup," Lucinda admitted, slipping a wide gold band set with a single red stone over Agra's head and ears.

She added a matching bracelet of her own, and bent to fasten her clutch pistol to her ankle. She dropped a small palm sized gun into the cross-body purse she planned to wear, and slipped it over her head.

"Wow," Sesuna said. "Can I have one of those?"

"After your firearms instructor says you're ready," Lucinda said firmly, inspecting Sesuna's outfit.

The girl had put on a pair of red trousers and topped it with a pale yellow vest and a maroon blouse. "Do I pass inspection?"

"You look great," Lucinda told her.

"Will there be food?"

"Probably just finger foods, but afterwards we can stop on the way to see your Mom and pick up something. I imagine Ispone is tiring of hospital food by now."

"Wow! This place is mag!" Sesuna exclaimed when they entered the hall of Versailles on L'Roux Isle.

"It's beautiful, isn't it? I think it's supposed look like one of the French palaces on Old Earth," Lucinda told her.

Odette greeted them with a big smile and promptly introduced Sesuna to her younger sister Giselle, who was watching a vid in the common room. The two girls were soon munching popcorn and arguing about the singer talent.

"Whew!" Odette remarked, invoking a silencer on the doorway to the room. "Thank you for bringing Sesuna with you. Giselle was sulking because she wanted to go out to a vid club in the city and Mom wouldn't let her."

Lucinda laughed. "That makes two of us. I'm too busy to take Sesuna around much and I think she's too young to be let loose in the city without supervision, so she's been stuck in the apartment all day."

"How much longer will her mother be in the hospital?" Odette inquired.

"Not much longer, I hope. As soon as she's released, I'm supposed to take a few days off to escort the family out to Veiled Isle. They'll stay with Mom and Dad while their dome is being built."

"Is Tom going with you?" At Lucinda's blank look, she exclaimed, "you should invite him. If he comes, it will mean he's serious about you. It's always good to know these things."

"Maybe I will," Lucinda said thoughtfully.

She had no time to brood on Odette's suggestion, however. They had barely seated themselves before the Duchesse handed out a list of vendors who had requested booth spaces during the Festival.

"These are returning vendors from the Planting Festival," Antoinette pointed to the list, "showing how much space they allotted them last time. Again, we have so many applicants we will need to infringe on the spaceport area to make room for them."

The representative from Caldwalder asked, "Has that been okayed?"

"Yes, it's all in place."

As Juliette had predicted, all Lucinda needed to do was vote yes on accepting the spaces allotted to returning vendors.

As she was getting ready to collect Sesuna, Antoinette stopped her.

"If I could have a word, Lady Lucinda?"

"How can I help you?"

"This has nothing to do with the planning committee, but a proposal to move the older archive records to make space for newer ones will come up before Parliament at the next session. I was wondering what your mother felt about that?"

"I can ask her if you like."

"Yes, well, it would be great if you could also ask Reverend Mother Drusilla if we could put them on Talker's Isle."

"I'm sure mother will be fine with getting an opinion from Aunt Drusilla. Shall I have her call you about it?"

"Thank you."

While Lucinda was dealing with issues concerning the Free Trade Welcome Committee, Detective Jim Gorsling had been researching another aspect of the smuggling going on. Lacking Tom's connection with Isiah, all he had to go on were some complaints reported to the police. Sadly, he wasn't having much success there either.

The past six months hadn't been good ones for Jim Gorsling. Until the debacle with Lady Jayla and the Crown Jewels that ended in her being kidnapped, he had felt he was on the fast track with his career. He had been sure Jayla had ties to the Thieves Guild because of her prior involvement with Gregor Ivanov. She had been only fourteen, but he profoundly distrusted beautiful women, and Lady Jayla was a stunner. When their part of that case had ended with himself and his partner getting a big fat black eye, he had been furious. During the case he had decided what he needed was better connections higher up, and the quickest way to get that would be a good marriage into the higher Clan ranks.

Jayla's cousin Lucinda had been a cadet at the time. Gorsling had long since decided to improve his chances for advancement by marrying into a family with Clan power. Lucinda had met his requirements; he considered her good-looking, but not excessively beautiful, she was the daughter of the ruler of Veiled Isle, one of Clan

O'Teagues subsidiary islands, and she was planning a career in law enforcement. Hoping to impress her with his status as a detective, he had tried to interrogate her about her cousin, but the Coroner, Dr. Ivanov had gone all protective and threatened him if he bothered her. He still resented this because he felt he could have made a better showing solving the case if he hadn't been blocked from getting the information he needed.

He felt being assigned to investigate theft and smuggling at the Port was a step down from homicide, but the investigation had turned up some interesting data.

"What's that?" Sipowitz inquired, looking over his shoulder at his screen.

"A list of all the buyers who bought those missing plants in the past." He hesitated and pointed to one on the second row. "Recognize that one?"

'Humm,' Sipowitz said. "Lord Rupert O'Teague. Any relation to Lady Jayla?"

"Cousin."

"Well, he works with rare plants, so he has a legitimate reason to have bought them. What's the problem?"

"He spent time in that center on Fenris too," Gorsling said.

Sipowitz sighed. "Jim, let's not go there. All of them were *children*. Run the probabilities of who might be smuggling and work the case on the evidence. Please?"

"I see here a complaint that Lady Lucinda, blocked an official at the Spaceport from confiscating a banned substance. That's a connection."

Inwardly Sipowitz cursed to herself. "No, it isn't. That particular substance was legally proscribed medicine for a pregnant Trellyan woman."

"The O'Teagues have adopted that Trellyan woman into the Clan, and last year, the woman who got away was a Trellyan—that's another connection," he said, stubbornly.

"You're making connections out of thin air!" Sipowitz snapped, exasperated. "I warn you, we follow the evidence in this investigation, not your stupid hunches, or I'll go to the lieutenant and request a new partner! You hear me?"

"I hear you," he said, sullenly.

Murder Screams Out

THERE WAS a staff meeting scheduled for all three PRS shifts to formally announce Mira's promotion to Detective In Charge, so Lucinda arrived at work early that afternoon. She found most of her colleagues, SSF, and those of the Patrol clustered in the common lobby. A few were pretending not to listen to the shouting match going on in Nova Jonah Cohen's office between him and Mira, but the majority didn't even pretend they had work and were listening avidly.

"What's going on?" Lucinda asked Twilya.

Twilya grinned at her. "The shit hit the fan this morning when your boss confronted Nova Cohen about sending you guys off to search the Kinkade Expeditions apartment yesterday."

"What did I miss?"

"Well, at first he denied it, but she has proof. Her boss apparently tracked the bad info back to a comp in the Patrol Offices here. That's when they went into his office and closed the door."

"He started blustering about not wanting any ham-handed local yokels screwing up his investigation," Debra put in resentfully.

"That's when the *real* yelling started," Twilya added. "Your boss really went off on him."

Just then Mira came out of Cohen's office, slamming the door behind her. Her livid glance took in the audience, most of whom hastily found chores to do. Mira jerked her head at the PRS officers and they followed her into their section for the staff meeting.

Mira looked them over. "As some of you may have heard, I've been appointed Detective In Charge here at the Spaceport. I look forward to working with all of you. Incidentally, Officer O'Teague has been posted here permanently. Congratulations officer. For the time being, I'll continue to work a transition shift between Days and Swing, with occasional switches to Graveyard. Does anyone have any questions?"

Gannet spoke up. "So she finally got you, did she? Congratulations, Mira."

"Are we going to get a replacement for Swing or is Lucinda going to be working it solo?" asked Takeo.

"That's a good question, Sgt. Takeo. Lieutenant Margrove has assured me that three more officers are going to be assigned out here. Two of them will be permanent additions, the third is going to be assigned to help with the anticipated manpower shortage when tourists start arriving for the Harvest Festival. If you know of anyone who wants a chance to work here, they need to put in a request with the Lieutenant."

Takeo, who was an old hand at interagency politics, asked, "What about the DB on the tarmac? Did the Patrol really give us a bum steer?"

Mira nodded. "Oh, yeah. They suckered us good, and Officer O'Teague and I wasted an entire afternoon taking inventory of a private citizens home, under the mistaken impression he was our DB."

"Are we still cooperating with them?" demanded Gannett.

"As much as they are with us," Mira said, causing a few chortles to run through the room. "Copy them on our findings, but that's it. Officer O'Teague suggested we go through vid feeds from the cargo-bots and citizen transports. If we are lucky, we can spot whoever dumped the body. If you see something suspicious, take a close look at the bot's load. If we can figure out which shuttle it came from, we might be able to narrow our search. Dismissed."

Twilya, who had been listening from the archway, came in and gave Lucinda a hug. "Congratulations on your permanent posting. I'm so glad you're going to be here from now on. If you need help with the vid scans, I can probably arrange a time to do it. Nova Cohen doesn't want a black mark for not cooperating on his record, so he is going to be trying to mend fences with Vensoog security forces. I'm sure he'll okay it."

Lucinda yawned. "I had the comp sorting out all the relevant vid feeds when I left last night. They should be ready today. Pull up a chair and let's get started."

A few days later, Detective Jeness, this time accompanied by Detective Wilson, showed up again at the spaceport offices. Lucinda had been looking at vid feeds from the cargo-bots and she felt as if her eyes would start to bleed any moment.

"Hi," she greeted them, grateful for the interruption. "Did you get your warrant?"

The detective waved a sheet of plastia at her. "Formal request for the Patrol to issue an interplanetary warrant for Thayer, and to stop the Samurai from leaving Vensoog space until they turn her over."

"That's great, but when you get hold of her, you be careful; I know from personal experience she's got a hair-trigger temper, and she likes to mess it up hand-to-hand."

Jeness's eyebrows rose. "How do you know that?"

"I went up to tour the ship with a few members of the Free Trade Reception Committee. Her husband tried to tell me he was my father and when I told him to spin off, she jumped me. Apparently he had a fling with Darla Lister and I'm supposed to look a little like her."

"Lister? Wasn't she one of Lewiston's original crew?"

"Yes. She led the raid on Veiled Isle. Mom killed her when she went after Juliette."

"How much did you turn up when you did a background check on Thayer?"

Lucinda grinned. "Not a lot, but she's listed as a person of interest in several homicides on IPP's database. The local police of three planets on the Samurai's trade route would like to question her about suspicious deaths that happened when the Samurai was in Port. She isn't on IPPs known assassin's list though."

"How were the other victim's killed?"

"Shallow cuts to the front and back of the torso, then finished off with a garotte. Same as Loman and our body dump. Here, I'll copy the files to you." She pulled up the files and transferred them to Jeness's pad.

Jeness read through the information, frowning. "You've met this Captain Delgado. Think he'll surrender her to us?"

"I think he'll pretend to cooperate, but you won't get her without taking the ship. I'm sure he has Thieves Guild ties."

Jeness stood up. "Okay, thanks for the info. I'll keep it in mind. Partner, let's go get our warrant issued."

She headed for the archway leading into the Patrol section. She looked back over her shoulder. "Sorry, I should have asked, I guess. Do I need to go through your boss or can I just go in?"

Lucinda grinned at her. "Go ahead. Your timing is just about perfect. When Tom told the Duc about Nova Cohen giving us that bum steer on our body dump, The Duc went over his head and complained directly to the Patrol base on Selene. The scuttlebutt is Cohen got zinged for obstructing our investigation, so I think he'll be cooperative."

Jeness looked interested. "Is he just being a butt-head or is he really trying to block your investigation?"

Lucinda shrugged. "From what I can see, he's pretty territorial. He didn't like being told to share the case with us to begin with, and he seemed to have a thing about—what did he call it?"

"Local yokels sticking their noses into Patrol business," supplied Twilya from the doorway. "We just got an earful at the last staff meeting."

"Twilya, this is Detective Wilson, and you remember Detective Jeness?"

"Glad to be of help Detectives," Twilya gestured them into the Patrol section. "Just go right through this door. He's in his office."

After announcing them to her boss, Twilya came back into the PRS section.

"Is Cohen still going to let you help me go through the vid feeds?" Lucinda asked Twilya.

"Yes, he okayed it. I think he hopes it will *look* as if he's actually being cooperative without doing anything."

"Then he'll be sorry when we solve it, won't he?"

Stake Out

ISIAH SPENT the night after he was attacked in Versailles Palace on L'Roux's Isle, but he insisted on returning to work the next morning.

"What if they are waiting for you?" Tom asked reasonably.

"Then I call security," Isiah said stubbornly. "Look, I appreciate the help and advice, and yes, I know you have gobs more experience in this kind of stuff than I do, but I can't afford to miss work. I'm on probation for this job. If I don't show up, I can be fired."

Tom sighed. He knew what it was to be wholly dependent on a job. If a Clan member appealed to the Clan Liaison, his Clan would feed and house him but to an independent man it would be a blow to his pride. He decided he would ask the Duc to speak to Penteulu Richards, Caldwalder's head of security, about getting Isiah put on retainer and assigned to the investigative task force.

"Okay, but you aren't going to go to work naked. What kind of weapons do you own?"

"Ah, I have a force wand; I'm not very good with it, but I have one. And I can box."

"Can you shoot?"

"Yes, I took the classes."

"The same with a knife, I suppose?"

"I'm pretty good with a crossbow."

"Do you have one?"

"Well, no, but I was intending to option one my next payday."

Tom got up and went to his weapons safe on the back wall. He opened it to reveal a variety of weapons racked on the door and walls. His ammunition was stacked on shelves. "Okay, I'll lend you what you need for the time being. We'll go down to the range to see how good you are with them."

He pulled out a pulsar pistol, a seven inch knife in a sheath, and a hand-held crossbow, along with a utility belt to hang them on. He also got out ammunition boxes for the crossbow and the pulsar gun.

After twenty minutes under the amused eyes of the Range Master, Tom declared Isiah competent to handle the pistol and the crossbow. "Let's see how good you are with the knife," he told Isiah, drawing his own.

"I don't want to accidentally cut you," Isiah protested.

Lora deVillers, the Range Master, laughed. "I doubt if you can," she remarked. "Tom here is one of our best; he's our blade trainer."

On his mettle, Isiah drew his borrowed knife and waited. Tom eyed his stance: feet spread for good balance, the half-crouch, with the blade extended. He did a couple of easy feints which Isiah countered just as easily.

Abruptly, he sped up the attack and there was a brief clash of blades before Tom swept the younger man's feet out from under him. Isiah landed in an ungainly heap on the ground.

Tom extended his free hand and pulled Isiah back to his feet. "Not bad," he said. "You've been started right, but you need a lot more work. Knife fighting isn't just about the blade; a good blade man uses his head, his hands and arms, as well as his feet."

"Does that mean I keep the knife?"

"Yes, until we can get you one of your own. And if you show up here for weapons training when you don't have work. Deal?"

"Deal," Isiah said, shaking his hand.

Tom dropped Isiah off at the apartment he shared with his brother when Isaac was in town. Isaac's career path was to hire himself out as a mapmaker. He was on Kitingzen now with an exploratory team.

Isiah stopped dead when he came in the door. The apartment looked like a tornado had gone through it. Fists on hips, he looked around in disgust. He didn't have the time to do more than set the worst damage to rights before he was due at work, but he commed the apartment manager, registered a complaint about the break in, and arranged for a special clean from the weekly cleaning service. He hoped the trashed rooms meant his unwelcome visitors wouldn't come back; maybe they found what they were looking for. *I'd feel better if I knew what it was*, he thought ruefully, deciding to go over the discrepancies again with the idea of figuring out what the missing items could be used for.

When he arrived at work, Isiah decided to research the shipping anomalies again. He found a shipping manifest that had been skipped when the original files had disappeared. It showed a shipment of building materials, clothing and foodstuffs being sent to Barisi, the Southern Continent. The packing slip showed the stuff being signed for by someone in Kinkade Excavations. His curiosity whetted, he researched the company and discovered they had exploration permits allowing them to search for the Dragon's Tear and one of them was for Brisai, which technically wasn't open for exploration. Brisai was a long sinuous continent, mostly lowlands covered in jungle type vegetation with lots of sandy beaches. The Clans had ranked it low on exploration, preferring to concentrate on Kitzingen which had valuable mineral deposits.

"They had permits so why would someone want to hide a shipment of building materials," he wondered. When he researched Dragon's Tear, he found:

The Dragon's Tear is a legendary gem, purported to be over 10,000 years old. According to legend it was made by a race of humanoid 'dragon' people. Allegedly the Tear contains maps to all their colonies and to their storehouse of treasures. It first came to human attention about 500 years ago. Rumors of its location have been rampant, but no known location has ever been found. The last rumored location was to a planet answering Vensoog's description.

It was interesting, but he couldn't see a connection with the present problem. He filed the information away for future reference and returned to his research.

As Isiah was packing up to go home that evening he heard familiar voices outside the open windows. They were familiar even though he had only heard them once; the voices of men who knocked you down and threatened you made an indelible impression in your memory.

"Are you sure he went in that room?"

"Yes. What makes you think it's here at his work?"

"The Dragon's Tear wasn't at his house. It has to be here."

"Maybe he doesn't have it."

"Then he's found out where it is or how to find it. Besides, we need to make sure he isn't going to talk any more about those building materials and supplies going missing."

"I don't understand why that matters."

"It matters because the boss doesn't want anyone nosing about where the stuff was shipped. Barisi isn't open for settlement. If building supplies went out there the Clans will want to know why, and what or who is building something."

"Why should they care?"

His companion sighed. "Because the Clans *own* this planet; no one can even emigrate to Vensoog without their permission, and no one claims any land without their say so. The boss doesn't want their attention drawn to the lab on Brisai."

"Oh. Say, who do you figure did the guy out at the spaceport?"

"I heard it was some guy off the Free Trader, same as with that woman down by the docks."

"Why dump the body at the Spaceport?"

"Sending a message to somebody would be my guess. Look sharp, its quitting time. We want to catch this guy alone so we can make him talk."

Isiah had been so concentrated on the voices outside the open window that he jumped when the jovial voice of his co-worker Leo came from behind him. "Hey, 'Siah are you working late again?"

Isiah looked up, "No, I'm cutting out early. I may not be in for a few days, I just got a com from my doctor. They want me to come out to Pembroke for testing in case I have internal injuries after the attack."

"I didn't realize it was that bad," Leo exclaimed in surprise.

Isiah shrugged. "Could have been worse I suppose."

He joined the group of workers exiting the office. Off to the left, he saw the two men who had attacked him had retreated to a spot by the cafeteria door as the group passed them.

About fifty yards from where the two men waited, the group began to break up. Isiah darted off down an alley and across the busy street. Behind him he heard cursing and running feet.

"Hey what do you think you're doing?" Leo demanded.

A quick glance over his shoulder showed Isiah that Leo was helping one of the older women up off the ground after she was shoved out of the way of his two attackers.

He slipped into a cafe and moved quickly towards the back, going through a door saying "Kitchen – No Admittance" and hid behind an enormous industrial oven.

When the two thugs rushed into the kitchen, they were met by a large woman wielding a cleaver, yelling at them to get out of her kitchen.

When broken nose attempted to shove her out of the way, she took a swing at him with the meat cleaver. He ducked, slipped on a greasy spot on the floor, and fell back into his companion. Scarface pinwheeled, failed to catch his balance and catapulted back through the batwing doors separating the kitchen from the restaurant. When he landed, he smashed into a Server-Bot carrying a tray of dirty dishes. The dishes, the bot and Scarface all ended up in a heap in the floor with Broken Nose on top of them. The chef followed them, waving her meat cleaver.

Someone in the eating area screamed, and the subsequent melee enabled Isiah to slip out the back door without being noticed. He ran for about a mile, ending up down by the waterfront.

"I should have listened to your advice," he told Tom when he commed him.

"Did they come after you again?"

"Yeah. Listen, I want in on this investigation. I told my boss I wouldn't be in tomorrow. Where can I meet you?"

"I'll come get you."

"The Duc just let me know you've been temporarily assigned as a member of the task force," he told Isiah. "His assistant notified your boss. You've got a temporary leave of absence for the duration of the investigation."

"Wow," Isiah exclaimed. "This is going to sound crass, but do I get paid for this?"

Tom laughed. "Yes, you've been put on retainer. I don't know how much you usually draw as a salary, but the retainer is pretty good. Tonight I was planning to stake out a spot on the beach where I could watch the Traders shuttles. You'll need boots and some different clothes, those you are wearing are too light colored," Tom told Isiah over dinner in his office. "We'll take a look in stores. They'll probably have some stuff to fit you."

When Isiah rejoined him after changing into the clothes Tom had recommended, he looked him over. The L'Roux storage had an abundance of camo style clothing left over from the Karamine War. Military camouflage apparel for humans had changed little over the centuries. Tom had recommended outfits in two or more shades of brown, grey and green, and a pair of heavy boots. Isiah had also strapped on the knife and gun Tom had loaned him.

Tom considered wearing the right clothing was one of the main components when playing a part. He had discovered that using appropriate dress in his many disguises helped him get into character. It was remarkable how much the ex-military clothes made a man feel like a warrior, Tom reflected, watching with inner amusement as Isiah stood taller and looked more confident in the combat attire.

He resisted the urge to tease the younger man about the attitude change. Instead he handed Isiah his secondary pair of binocular vid goggles and showed him how to adjust the lighting for infrared vision at night.

"We won't take vids unless we find something worth recording," he explained. "I've already checked out two sleds from L'Roux security for us." He held up a small box. "This is a sound muffler, we'll use it when we get near the end of the Spaceport."

He called up a map of the tarmac near the end of the Island. "Here is where that power pole for the force screen was tampered with. There are only three shuttles close enough to make them viable destinations for smugglers trying to get something to them using that access: the Silver Samurai, The Queen of the Stars, and the Black Dragon. Thanks to Lucinda I searched the Silver Samurai. They had a few contraband animals in stasis, but I saw nothing like what we're looking for," he explained. "Most Free Traders skate the edge with a few banned items in their inventory, but usually it isn't enough to draw attention from IPP. The Queen made an after dark delivery when she didn't need to, so she's a possibility. The Black Dragon has a clean reputation at spaceports, but since it's within reach, we'll watch it too."

"Won't they see us?" Isiah asked.

Tom grinned and picked up what looked like a fist-sized gray rock. "This little beauty is a holo projector. I've programmed it to create rocks, kelp, seaweed and sand around us. It will fool the naked eye and most electronic scanners."

"Wow," Isiah said. "This will be fun."

Tom laughed and clapped him on the shoulder. "We'll see if you still feel the same at dawn tomorrow!"

Skirting the edge of the cordoned area around the eastern edge of the spaceport, Tom found a group of large boulders to hide the sleds. They dismounted and pulled a pile of kelp over them.

"Ooof!" Isiah tripped over a small rock and landed on his hands and knees. "Sorry," he whispered, Tom having already warned him to keep his voice low.

"Turn on your goggles," Tom suggested.

"Oh, I thought we weren't recording anything yet."

"You don't have to push the record button to enable the night vision," Tom replied.

He selected a point about fifty yards from the spot where the smugglers would go under the force-field. "This will be a good spot," he told his companion, setting the holo box down and turning it on. Immediately his program kicked into place. Out of his pocket, he took two small cubes and tapped them. Without more ado, two chairs inflated.

"Sit down and be comfortable," he suggested. "We're going to be here all night."

Isiah stared at them, "I thought we'd be lying on the ground or something."

"Well you can, but I prefer to be comfortable. It will be a long night."

"How come we can see through the holo?" Isiah asked.

"This holo is used in surveillance. It's like a one-way mirror in a police interrogation room," Tom explained. "We can see out, but no one can see in."

Throughout the rest of the night, several ships passed the end of the isle but didn't stop.

"What if nothing happens tonight?" Isiah asked.

"Then we do this tomorrow night. Any attempt to reach the shuttles will be soon because all the ships have logged departures with the spaceport in the next month."

"The next month, huh? Well, at least it will give me something to do at night besides read books," Isiah said ruefully.

"Sorry to ruin your social life," Tom told him.

Isiah shrugged. "Nothing to ruin; I don't have one at this point. But what about you? Isn't that cop Lucinda your girl?"

"Not yet," Tom replied. "She won't get her first Match List until the Harvest Festival, and her dad is one bad-ass dude. He reminded me at her cousin's wedding that she's under age and I don't want to start off on the wrong side of my new father-in-law."

"She's the one then?"

"Yeah. I didn't think I was ready to settle down, but when it happens, it happens."

Warrior vs Warrior

VENSOOG'S SUN was just creeping up over the horizon when Dr. Worthy arrived on his morning rounds to examine Ispone and her newborn daughter. He politely, but firmly booted Lucinda and Sesuna out of the room. "Go have breakfast or a cup of Cafka, or something," he said.

One of his satellites held the door open for their exit.

"Sure," Lucinda agreed, jerking her head at Sesuna who obeyed reluctantly. Agra snorted irritably in Lucinda's ear. "C'mon kid, we can get some wake-up juice in my office. Better stuff there than the canteen."

"Why did he make us leave?" Sesuna asked suspiciously.

"Too many people in the room, probably," Lucinda told her.

"But we came early to hear what he had to say. She's my mother; I have a right to know if something is wrong," Sesuna protested.

"I agree, and we will ask Ispone what he said when we get back," Lucinda told her, reflecting she could always put one of Roderick's listening buttons in Ispone's room if the former Fire Priestess wasn't forthcoming about her condition. The original buttons had been stolen from Grouter's office when they escaped from the Placement Center. Roderick had since modified them to record as well as listen to the sounds around them. But Sesuna didn't need to know that yet.

They were returning to Ispone's room along the deserted hospital corridor when Lucinda saw the Hyati-Soturi. The two women were standing with their backs to her while they questioned an unhappy orderly. Both were easily seven feet tall. Trellyans were slimmer than humans, making them look awkward for their height, but this pair

showed the well-developed ropy muscles of trained fighters. The older one had a knife scar across the bridge of her nose. They were
dressed for fighting on Trellya where the median temperature was a
few degrees warmer than Vensoog: heavy boots with reinforced-toes
rising to mid-thigh, armored gloves with wrist and elbow guards, and
a vest and short pants designed to deflect weapon blasts. The colors
depended on which religious house the Soturi owed allegiance to.

Quickly, Lucinda opened the door to Ispone's room and thrust
Sesuna inside. "Get in there and lock the door!" she ordered. "Don't
come out unless I say to!"

Looking around, she grabbed the closest hospital personnel she
could find. She flashed her badge at him and said, "I need this corridor cleared and a level 4 lockdown on it, STAT."

When he turned to run to the duty station, Lucinda commed the
PRS station on the Spaceport.

George Takeo the night shift senior answered. Lucinda identified herself and reported, "I'm off duty visiting a friend and I noticed
two Trellyan Hyati-Soturi armed with Photon Equalizers here in the
hospital."

He frowned at her. "Aren't those classed as Level 5? That's combat issue. It's banned for on-planet use on all the Confederation planets."

"These are Hyati-Soturi," Lucinda informed him. "They are the
elite combat and enforcement arm of the Mothers of Trellya. If they
are here it's to capture someone. They recognize no authority but the
Mothers. Regulations aren't likely to bother them. I happen to know
there is a Trellyan woman who has just delivered an infant here in
the hospital. She is a new member of Clan O'Teague. I think they are
here for her."

"Okay. We'll get there to back you up as soon as we can. You be careful. Sara!" he yelled. "Get on the com to PRS headquarters. Tell them we have a potential hostage situation at the Spaceport hospital with outlawed weapons. Ask for backup!"

He eyed Lucinda warily. "What are you going to do?"

"They've noticed the hall is on lockdown and are heading my way. I'm going to try and arrest them for carrying illegal weapons."

Ordering Agra to fly high and stay out of sight, she left her recorder on and stepped out to confront the two Soturi. She didn't draw a weapon, but she made sure both her force wand and her pistol were close enough to grab in a hurry.

"I'm officer Lucinda O'Teague," she told them when they stopped about twenty feet away from her. "You are carrying military grade, Level 5 weapons not allowed on the surface of Confederation planets. I must ask you to come with me to the precinct office here at the spaceport."

"Stand aside," one of them said. "I am Protector Ferine s'Rudin of the Hyati-Soturi and this is Exarch Tainte s'Maris. We are on official business of the Mothers of Trellya. Stand out of our way."

Lucinda didn't move. "I am a duly sworn officer of Port Recovery Security. You are carrying weapons banned on the surface of Vensoog and other Confederation planets. You must surrender them and come with me to the security offices. Requests from off-planet governments must be presented to the Clan Security Council who will decide if they can be honored."

Lucinda had been watching the Protector. If Agra had not screamed a warning, she wouldn't have noticed the Exarch drawing her weapon in time to counter the action. Reactions learned during the games her father played with them down in the caverns above Hidden Lake stood her in good stead. She tucked and rolled, coming up on one knee with her pistol in one hand and her force wand in the other.

The shot from the Exarch's Photon Equalizer buckled the hardened plastacrete wall behind Lucinda, leaving a stench of melted plastic. Chalk pebbles and dust dribbled down the wall.

Lucinda's return pulsar blast caught the woman's gun hand just as the Exarch fired again. The equalizer exploded, knocking the Trellyan unconscious and cracking the walls on either side of her.

The Protector had taken advantage of her subordinate's attack to charge Lucinda's position. Lucinda surged to her feet, stabbing out with the force wand's sharp blade. The Soturi jumped back out of the way, and Lucinda reversed the wand, powering it up to full strength. A full strength hit, designed to subdue a Water Dragon, would kill a human; she was unsure of the effect on a Trellyan.

The Protector had drawn an eighteen-inch combat knife favored by the Trellyans. She slashed at Lucinda with it, forcing her to jump back to avoid the other woman's longer reach.

It had been years since Lucinda had fought a Soturi battle, and as a young girl, she had the advantage of her smaller size to make it harder for a larger opponent to land a blow.

Unfortunately, this Soturi had come prepared to fight a human. Taking advantage of her height and faster reflexes, she employed the brutal Kali-Targ technique designed to disorient an opponent through fast feints with hands and feet. Lucinda ducked most of the blows, but the Protector managed to get a strike past Lucinda's defenses. The wallop from the armor-plated glove hit her in the face, knocking her to the ground. Desperately, Lucinda swung her force wand to sweep her opponent off her feet, but a hard kick in the ribs from the Protector's armored boot knocked the wind out of her. Lucinda could hear the sirens heralding the arrival of her backup, but it would be a few minutes before they found her.

The locked door to Ispone's room had splintered open when the Exarch's shot had hit the wall next to it. Sesuna had been peeking through the crack. Seeing Lucinda go down, she flew out the door and stabbed at the Protector with a small, sharp knife she had stolen from the canteen.

The Protector laughed. She grabbed the girl's wrist, twisting it painfully to make her drop the knife. Agra screamed in rage and dove at the Soturi's face with her outstretched talons, barely dodging a backhanded slap aimed at her.

Lucinda struggled to her feet. She had lost her pistol, but she still had her force wand. She spun it and aimed a blow at the Soturi's head and missed when the wand was slapped away.

Sesuna had been biting and clawing at the Protector's hold on her wrist. When the battle got too painful, the woman simply clouted the girl alongside the head with her armored glove, knocking the child unconscious.

Port Recovery Security forces charged into the corridor, yelling for the Soturi to release her captive.

"Tell Ispone to come to me," the Protector said, throwing the limp weight of Sesuna over her shoulder and racing down the corridor.

Agra screamed and dove after her. *"No! Don't attack! Follow!"* Lucinda sent the command and felt Agra's grudging agreement.

The Soturi fired twice at the wall, blasting out the clear sheet of Plastia meant to let in light, and leapt through the still smoking window. They could hear the roar of a sled taking off outside.

Ispone appeared in the doorway to her room, holding onto the door to keep from falling.

"My Lady, Please get back in bed," Lucinda told her. "Leave this to me. Shalendra needs you."

"I can't lose another daughter. You will get her back Soturi?" Ispone whispered.

"Yes," Lucinda said grimly. She turned to Takeo. "Lady Ispone will explain what just happened. My Dactyl Agra is following the Hyati-Soturi who kidnapped her daughter. I need to get on her trail before Agra tires out and loses them."

She ran to the window the Protector had used and climbed through it. Behind her, she could hear Takeo reporting the kidnapping to headquarters in Port Recovery and giving orders to get mounted and follow.

Lucinda's sled had come to her signal; she jumped aboard and gunned it, shooting skyward, following the tug of Agra's mind as the tiny dactyl chased Sesuna and her captor into the rising sun.

The Soturi had headed east across the tarmac where the shuttles were parked. If she had hoped to hide among them, that hope was unfulfilled. Lucinda had got on her trail too quickly. The sleds raced out across the channel between the islands toward open ocean.

Tom and Isiah had been in the blind all night watching the three shuttles with no results and both were tired.

The men came abruptly alert when they heard the commotion at the spaceport. It had been years since either had heard the distinctive sound and flash of a Photon Equalizer being fired, but once heard, it was never forgotten.

"That's the port!" Isiah exclaimed. "Are we being attacked?"

A few minutes later that question was answered as the Soturi, with her captive draped across her lap, crossed the power line. The weight of the two Trellyans made the sled sluggish, and they could hear the Azorite crystal motor straining to fly at top speed.

"That's Sesuna!" Tom exclaimed, jumping to his feet as he recognized the unconscious passenger. He knew Lucinda would expect him to help the girl. Besides, he liked the kid. He hesitated for the first time in his life torn between the job and his heart, and then told Isiah, "That was a Hyati-Soturi and it looks as if she's captured Sesuna. I have to follow them and see if I can rescue her. I'm leaving you in charge here. Remember, if the smugglers show up, just film it and get a good shot of whichever shuttle they approach so we can take it to the Duc and he can get warrants."

Not giving Isiah time to respond, Tom slid backward, and belly crawled out of sight of the shuttles over to where he had hidden the sleds under a pile of kelp and seaweed.

Careful not to draw attention to his sled and Isiah's position in the blind, he floated the sled out into the water, pulling it behind him until he was several hundred feet from Isiah's position.

He glanced upward when he felt Agra's fierce determination as she hunted her prey pass overhead. She was followed a few minutes later by a sled at full-throttle with Lucinda crouched behind the windshield.

Once he thought he was far enough away from Isiah, he mounted his own sled and started the engine. Behind him, he could hear the sirens from the Port Recovery Security sleds following Lucinda.

Lucinda had been off duty, so she had used her personal sled to take Sesuna to visit Ispone. It was faster and more maneuverable than the rental being used by the Trellyan. Lord Zack and his nephews had modified it for the speed racing contests held on Veiled Isle each summer. She knew she would be able to overtake the Soturi since the other woman's sled was carrying double the weight, but it was unlikely that no one would be hurt when she took Sesuna back. She contacted O'Teague security and asked for a medi-vac sled to follow her.

"Why?" Mara, the tech at the com demanded. "Are you hurt?"

"Not yet," Lucinda replied. "But I'm chasing a Hyati-Soturi who kidnapped Sesuna and we're out over open water. I'm sure she won't give her up without a fight."

Mara swore. Lucinda heard her shouting to scramble a medi-vac sled out to the east side of Port Recovery. Satisfied that help would be at hand if she needed it, Lucinda closed the com.

Even heading straight into the rising sun, her mental tie with Agra enabled Lucinda to locate the tired dactyl. When they came even, she reached out for the mid-air catch they had practiced back home. Agra dropped gratefully into her palm and then slid into the Quirka seat, exhausted.

"Good Girl," Lucinda cooed at her, feeling the dactyls contentment and pride at the praise. She popped open a panel in the sled and took out a small concentrated food/liquid tube for her pet. Rupert's clever designs had downsized the tubes so they were the right size for Quirka and small Dactyls. This was a prototype; the tip was digestible, so Agra bit it off, swallowed it and then sucked on the end.

Hearing another sled behind her, Lucinda glanced over her shoulder, hoping it wasn't another of the Hyati-Soturi. When she recognized Tom, a strange warmth started inside her. He and Isiah must have been out at the beach watching the three suspect shuttles again. He must have abandoned the untried Isiah at the stake-out to come watch her back. She knew how much his work meant to him. Maybe she was more than a useful friend after all.

Trusting he would handle any trouble coming up her backside, she returned to her pursuit. She was close enough now to see that Sesuna was still draped across the Soturi's lap. That must mean the girl was still unconscious and wouldn't be awake to help if Lucinda tried a mid-air snatch. She needed to disable the engine on the Soturi's sled. She reached down for the backup gun in her ankle holster. It wasn't as powerful as her service weapon, but it was accurate. She put the sled on auto-pilot, and resting her hand on the top of the curved windshield, she took careful aim and fired.

She missed because just as she fired, Sesuna woke up and started fighting. The other sled began to buck and weave. The Soturi was having difficulty managing the sled and keeping the fighting girl under restraint. Abruptly, the sled speared skyward, obviously out of control. Following them, Lucinda soon realized that both sleds were too high for a safe splash-down into the ocean. If Sesuna fell or jumped now she might be badly hurt.

She swore as Sesuna suddenly kicked free of her captor and dropped toward the water. Lucinda held her breath as Sesuna reversed her angle to try and convert the free fall plunge into a dive. She shoved her sled into a nose-dive, trying to intercept Sesuna's fall before the child hit the water. From this height it would be like landing on plastacrete. Hastily she snapped the safety closure on the sleeping dactyl's seat, so it wouldn't fill with water in case she missed and had to go underwater after the girl.

Lucinda caught the falling child barely above the water line. The impact from the catch knocked the wind out of both of them and smacked the sled down onto the water's surface, where it skipped and bounced like a rock skimming across a pond. Lucinda had all she could do to hang on to Sesuna and not let the sled overturn.

Sesuna helped by grabbing Lucinda around the waist and trying to scramble on behind her. In her Quirka seat, Agra came awake with an angry screech as she was doused with safety foam in response to the sled's violent antics.

When Tom caught up with them a few minutes later, Lucinda had brought the sled under control. Sesuna was no longer in danger of dropping off into the ocean, but when they came to a stop the girl was shaking like a leaf and clutched Lucinda like a vise.

"Wow," Tom said. "That was some terrific sled handling. You're good. Did you damage the bottom of the sled?"

"Thanks," Lucinda gasped out. She checked her position in the water. "It looks intact. At any rate we aren't sinking."

Agra was angrily beating on the inside of the Quirka window to be let out. Lucinda flipped the emergency switch to off and the acrylic partition slid up. Agra climbed out and dove into the water to clean off the foam. When Tom pulled up beside them, she climbed up his leg and shook salt water all over him, spitting foam in disgust and loudly complaining about her nap being interrupted.

Overhead, the security forces following the Trellyan passed, sirens still screaming. Takeo dropped out to check on Lucinda.

"Everyone okay here?" he asked.

Lucinda nodded. "Yes sir, we're okay."

He turned to look at Tom. "Who might you be?"

Tom pulled out his credentials. "I'm an investigator for the Duc d'Orleans. I was out on the beach and I saw the Soturi and the girl. I recognized her, and she didn't look like she was a willing passenger, so I followed them. Lucinda got here before I did. It was quite a rescue."

"I'll take Sesuna back to her mother before I file a report if you don't mind, sir," Lucinda said.

"Yes, do that. Those Soturi made quite a mess at the hospital. Suppose the Mothers will pay for it?"

"Right," Lucinda snorted. "Good luck with that one."

Takeo looked up as O'Teague's Medi-vac sled pulled up beside them. The sled had been designed for water as well as land rescue. A temporary docking bay slid out on one side with a counter weight on the other. The three sleds that had accompanied it landed in the water beside it.

"Let's get you guys checked out," Tomasina Harris, O'Teague's chief medic stood in the hatch doorway. Securing his sled to the dock, Tom tucked Agra into his shirt and stepped aboard. He handed the still wet and complaining dactyl off to the medic, and reached out to help Sesuna. The girl winced, holding her ribs when she stood up.

"Ummn, what happened here?" Tomasina asked.

"I was falling and Soturi Lucinda caught me," Sesuna said.

"Knocked the wind out of both of us. We got bounced around pretty good too," Lucinda told the medic, steadying herself with a hand on Tom's shoulder as she swung off her sled.

"You look it," Tomasina, running a diagnostic wand over the swelling cheeks they both sported. "You two are going to have matching black eyes as well. Did you tangle with the same buzz saw?"

"You could say that, it was a Hyati-Soturi named Ferine s'Rudin," Lucinda said wryly.

Tomasina dug out cold packs, activated them and handed them each one. "Here, hold that against your face. It will reduce the swelling."

The Medi-vac sled's communication center began to crackle, and Lady Katherine and Lord Zack appeared on the holo display.

"Are you alright? Violet said you were in trouble," Both parents asked simultaneously.

"We're fine, a little banged up because I almost wrecked the sled when I did a mid-air catch, but both of us will be okay. Sesuna needs to call her mom to let her know she's safe."

"Who hit you?" Lady Katherine demanded when she saw Lucinda's face.

"How the Void did you let that happen Draycott?" Lord Zack demanded, turning on Tom.

"It isn't Tom's fault," Lucinda defended him. "The Mothers sent some Hyati-Soturi after Ispone and her family. I had a fight with them at the hospital. That is who hit both of us. One of them got away with Sesuna, but I got her back. Tom wasn't even there."

"Well, maybe he should have been," Lord Zack growled.

He glanced over at the wide-eyed Sesuna and when Lady Katherine coughed and jabbed him with an elbow, said, "I'm glad you got away kid. We'd better quit tying up this line so you can call your mother. Lucinda we would appreciate a com tonight so you can give us the full story."

"Sure," she promised.

A Rose by Another Name

DUSK HAD fallen several hours ago and it was mid evening. Summer was winding down and the sweet, dry scent of it, a combination of dead grass, dry dirt and shuttle fuel, drifted in through the open doors of the Spaceport. It had been two weeks since Sesuna had been returned to Ispone, safe and sound if a trifle bruised. Exarch Tainte s'Maris was in the prison ward at the hospital. A Clan-wide alert was out on Protector Ferine s'Rudin and the others but so far no trace of them had been found.

Lucinda rubbed her eyes. She had spent the last few days watching vid feeds from cargo-bot cameras and it felt as if her eyes were starting to bleed. Twilya and Mira had helped with the task but it was tiresome, boring work.

She was taking her mid shift break when her world turned upside down. The child staggered into the lobby of the spaceport and collapsed. Lucinda set her cup of Cafka down on her desk and ran into the reception area. When she knelt to turn the girl over, she found herself looking into a white, waxy face and her stomach jerked. It was as if she looked at a vid of herself from ten years ago. The kid was breathing in fast shallow breaths and Lucinda could see the trip-hammer beat of her pulse in her throat. Grimly, she pushed up one of the girl's eyelids, noting the telltale, glassy edge on her iris.

"Is she hurt? What's wrong with her?" demanded Mira, who had followed Lucinda into the lobby.

"Call the EMTs and tell them we have a juvenile rape victim who has been given a heavy dose of Submit combined with an erotic booster," she told Mira grimly. "She will need doses of 1.5cc Wake Up every half an hour over the next three hours."

She heard Twilya's shocked gasp of "She was raped?" over her boss's sharp demand, "How do you know that?"

"I saw these symptoms at the Child Placement Center on Fenris." Lucinda hesitated and then added, "Some of the kids we got in the center on Fenris tried to kill themselves when they woke up. Submit has a memory inhibitor, so this girl may not remember much of what happened to her, but I don't want to chance it."

Since the hospital was attached to the spaceport, medics were there in a matter of minutes. Lucinda stood up to let them do their job.

"Doctor," Lucinda waited until the head medic looked at her. "She may have been sexually assaulted. Do a rape kit now, before she wakes up. She will come out from under the Submit screaming and fighting. The fear will be worse if she is being handled in her pubic area when she awakens. On no account give her any drugs to calm her down. If she was dosed with Submit and an Erotic, which I think she was, if you give her any other drugs you risk damaging her heart and nervous system."

The man nodded. "You said she was given Submit and an Erotic?"

Lucinda shrugged. "You'll have to run a tox screen to be sure, but it was probably a combination of Submit and an erotic, maybe Payome or a derivative of it."

He nodded. "We'll run a screen. Thanks for the heads up."

"Where did she come from?" Mira muttered.

The three women went to the entry and looked down the street in both directions. It was late. This time of night the shops and cafes that were open during the day had closed and no other activity showed.

Mira got on her com to headquarters. "Dispatch, this is Sargent Mira Forest. I need a tracking dog out at the spaceport. We have a possible child rape victim we need to backtrack."

"She can't have walked far in her condition," Twilya said. The young Patrol officer had been sharing break with them because she had been helping with the vid search.

"It will be a private pleasure house or a bed and breakfast combination requiring reservations," Lucinda offered.

Twilya looked at her in puzzlement. "How do you know so much about this stuff?"

"Fenris looks like a nice planet, and tourists can have a good time there, but it has a dark side. Sex trafficking of all ages goes on. Homeless, orphaned and abandoned children are easy prey for the procurers. Once their customers were done with them, the kids were usually dumped back out on the streets. Sooner or later they were picked up by the police and sent to the Center. A few had been treated by a hospital before being dumped with us, but a lot of the kids were still under the influence when they arrived." She smiled wryly. "My sister Juliette and I were three and Violet one when we were placed there. In a way, we were lucky; Grouter, the head of the center, had plans for us so he hid us from the traffickers when they came looking for fresh meat. He also believed that idle hands made mischief, so he didn't give those of us who lived permanently at the center much free time. When we got older, some of us worked in the medical unit. The Center didn't have a full time nurse, just a First Aid Bot, so we older kids had to learn how to take care of the patients in the infirmary. A lot of victims were like this girl when they came in."

When the PRS officers pulled up to the door, Lucinda sighed. It was Gorsling and Sipowitz, her least favorite detectives. Gorsling was short, with a square, bulldog face and dark hair in contrast to his partner, a tall, hazel-eyed woman with bronzed skin.

"Wonderful," she muttered to herself.

"What?" Twilya asked.

"Nothing, just Detective jerk-face there. He has about as much sensitivity as a bull Sand Dragon in Rut," Lucinda replied. "Not my first choice to question a traumatized child."

She and Mira turned their report over to the two detectives. "What makes you think she was raped?" Sipowitz asked.

Mira nodded at Lucinda. "Officer O'Teague here thinks the kid was given Submit mixed with Payome. Said she saw kids in the medical unit at the Child Placement Center on Fenris who had been dosed with that combination."

"The symptoms were very similar," Lucinda added. "Those kids on Fenris were all rape survivors. The medics are running a tox screen on her."

"You aren't a detective O'Teague," Gorsling snapped. "You are a rookie. I don't think you're qualified to make a judgement in this case. Or maybe your friends in low places taught you about child prostitution?"

"Detective!" Mira snapped. "That was uncalled for! As it happens, I agree with Officer O'Teague. Are you going to say *I'm* not qualified?"

Sipowitz rolled her eyes. "Knock it off Jim," she said.

"No, of course not Sargent," Gorsling said stiffly.

"You say the child was taken to the hospital?" Sipowitz asked.

"Yes," Lucinda replied.

"Then we'll head over there. Thank you for your hard work Officers."

"Whew!" Twilya said, watching them leave. "He sure doesn't like you."

"It's not just me," Lucinda replied. "It's my whole family that's on his shit list."

"Why?"

"It's a long story," Lucinda said. "I'll tell you about it when we have more time."

At the end of her shift, Lucinda stopped at the hospital to check on Ispone. She found her asleep, so she didn't wake her. She was about to leave her a note when she heard Gorsling and Sipowitz discussing the girl who had wandered in with a doctor.

"That young officer hit the mark on the head identifying the drugs this girl was given," Doctor Reisling, a tiny, green eyed woman, told the two detectives. The three of them were standing just outside one of the patient rooms. Realizing they must be talking about the child with her eyes, Lucinda moved to the door of Ispone's room so she could hear better.

"Were you able to identify her using the DNA base, Dr. Reisling?" Gorsling asked.

"No," the doctor's voice was compassionate. "Whoever she is, she didn't come through the gate; we don't have a record of DNA for a child this age, but—"

"But what?"

"I did find a match in the database. This girl's DNA is a copy of the DNA from one of the girls Lady Katherine O'Teague adopted from Fenris several years ago."

"A copy? What does that mean?" Sipowitz asked. "Are you saying she's a clone?"

"No, it's original DNA without cloning markers, so she isn't a clone. I would say she was created from the same embryonic material as the girl who came from Fenris with Lady Katherine. My guess would be she is a designer child."

"What is a designer child?" demanded Sipowitz, frowning.

"Designer children are specifically created to a buyer's specifications. A buyer puts in an order for what he wants, and an embryo is created and grown in an artificial womb. When gestation is complete, the buyer takes possession."

"Isn't that illegal?" Gorsling asked.

"Oh, yes, it's considered a form of slavery and it's been banned under interplanetary law for several hundred years, but it still happens."

"Since her DNA matches one of Lady Katherine's children, that means the girl belongs to the O'Teague Clan?"

"Technically, yes. I need to contact the Laird to find out her position about this child, but O'Teague has an excellent reputation in this area; if the child is O'Teague she will have the full protection of the Clan. In the meantime, you need to contact the child services representative assigned to her before you can question her."

Sipowitz nodded. "Alright, give us a call if she wakes up. She's still our victim. Let's go and see if those tracking dogs found where she came from Partner."

When the two detectives had disappeared around the corner, Lucinda stepped into the doorway of the child's room. The girl had been cleaned up and put into a hospital gown too big for her. She was breathing easier, and a medical monitor beeped steadily over the bed.

Dr. Reisling looked up as she entered. "Officer O'Teague?" she asked.

Lucinda turned to face her. "Yes?"

"You were on the mark with the tox screen. The information you gave us helped begin treatment immediately."

Lucinda nodded, watching the child.

Dr. Riesling hesitated, then continued, "I didn't tell those detectives it was your DNA that matched hers, just that it was one of Lady Katherine O'Teague's children," she said. "Will O'Teague take responsibility for this child?"

"Yes," Lucinda said. "I would do it immediately, but I'm not of age yet, so I need to contact my mother—"

The child started tossing and whimpering. Lucinda went to the bed and gathered her up. "Sshh, it's all right now," she said, cuddling, and stroking her hair the way Lady Katherine had done when one of them had a nightmare. Agra crooned to the girl, *pushing* love and calmness.

"She is beginning to wake up. If you have a Dragon Talker on staff, I suggest you call him or her in," Lucinda told the doctor, who called the nursing station.

"I need a Dragon Talker to room 701 STAT," she said.

The girl opened her eyes and Lucinda found herself staring into a mirror of her own: sharp, intelligent and calculating. She felt an instant bond of kinship, of blood calling to blood and saw the answering shock in the child's eyes; she felt it too. Lucinda and her sisters had a similar bond of love between them, born of risk and shared experiences, but this was different. The three of them, despite the two-year age difference with Violet, were equals. This was a child/adult bond so fierce it almost choked her.

Agra crooned encouragement.

"Who are you?" the child whispered.

"I am Lady Lucinda O'Teague, and I believe we are related. What is your name?"

"Rachel." The child's voice was rusty and hoarse. "My throat hurts."

Lucinda reached for a water carafe on the bedside table and poured some into a paper cup. She held it to the girl's lips while she took a couple of sips.

"If she is awake, the detectives asked to be called," the Doctor said.

"No!" Lucinda exclaimed. "Can you hold off calling them until my parents arrive? It will take about nine hours on the regular shuttle to get here from Veiled Isle. Please?"

"The Doctor hesitated, "I suppose so, but can't you stand in for them?"

"I won't get my first Match List until the Harvest Festival and that is still two weeks away," Lucinda explained. "Technically, I don't yet have the authority to act in Rachel's behalf."

"Rachel is her first name?"

"Lady Rachel O'Teague," Lucinda told her firmly.

"Lady Katherine O'Teague is your mother? And this child is her daughter?"

"Uh-huh."

"O—ka—ay, I'll think of something to stall Gorsling until she gets here," the doctor said, reflecting that she wouldn't want to be in Gorsling's place if it came to a clash with Lady Katherine. She and Lord Zack had well-earned formidable reputations.

"You sent for a Dragon Talker Doctor? I'm Brenda McWhorter, level three Dragon Talker," said a soft voice. The girl in the doorway was dressed in hospital scrubs, around five-ten with curly black hair, dark skin and kind brown eyes.

"Yes I did," the Doctor turned to her. "Dragon Talker McWhorter, we have a child here who has been brutally traumatized and overdosed with Submit and a derivative of Payome. I need you to put her to sleep and keep her calm so she can rest and heal. I don't dare give her any drugs to calm her until the stuff her attackers gave her is out of her system."

"Alright. Please bring me a more comfortable chair." She slid in front of Lucinda and gently took over holding the girl. Lucinda could feel the Talker's soothing *Push*. Reluctantly, she rose from the bed. Agra crooned comfortingly on her shoulder, rubbing her cheek against Lucinda's.

When the child had drifted back into sleep, Lucinda retreated to the employee lounge, empty this time of night, to contact her parents, waking Lady Katherine and Lord Zack when she commed them.

Her mother took one look at her face and sleep immediately disappeared from her eyes. "What happened?" she demanded, sitting up in bed. Lord Zack slid out of bed and disappeared from the vid feed.

They listened to her in silence as she told her story. Already dressed, her father took over the com while her mother dressed.

"We'll take an orbital approach with the shuttle," he said. "We should be there in four hours."

Katherine had tied her hair back in a long tail. "You think they used some of the leftover embryonic material from when they created you and your sisters for this girl, don't you?"

Lucinda's voice cracked. "Yes. Mom if they had leftovers from me, they might have the others as well—I—"

"Don't blame yourself for this darling. None of it is your fault." The smile her mother turned to her was feral. "Leave this to us. Rachel belongs to us now. You go home and get some sleep baby."

Ghosts

TOM FOUND Lucinda alone in the office where she had returned after talking to her parents. Mira had left for home when the shift ended, and Lucinda had stayed late looking up property records for the buildings around the spaceport. The night shift was out patrolling the area around the outside of the complex hoping they would spot someone looking for Rachel.

Like her mother, Tom spotted the shadows in Lucinda's eyes. He put a hand on her shoulder. "Are you alright?" He asked.

Instead of answering, she turned her face into his shoulder and burst into tears. His arms came up around her, giving comfort. Agra fluttered around chirping in distress.

After a few minutes Lucinda stepped back, wiping her eyes with her fingers. "Sorry, I didn't mean to blubber all over you."

"You don't need to be the tough girl all the time, especially not with me. I promise I won't go blabbing it around that you had a weak moment." He handed her a mostly clean bandanna.

Lucinda took it, wiped her eyes and blew her nose. "Thanks," she said, giving him a rueful, if damp smile. "I'll wash this for you before I give it back."

"Let's start over," he suggested. "I could tell something was bothering you when I came in. What's the matter?"

"it's a long story. Have you got time?"

He shrugged, "I only came in to go through the warehouse files when no one is there. They will keep."

"C'mon let's sit down." She moved to one of the interview chairs and he followed her, taking a seat opposite the one she had chosen.

"Tonight, a juvenile rape victim staggered into the lobby. She not only looks just like me, but she has my DNA."

He frowned, "Another sister?"

"I guess you could say that. She doesn't just have *some* of my DNA, *her* DNA is a close enough match that she could be me about seven years younger."

"What? How is that possible?"

"I told you I was a designer child, remember?"

"You think someone used the same specifications creating her that were used for you," he said, recognizing the implications.

"It looks that way. The thing is, Grouter is in jail, so it couldn't be him that ordered this girl be created."

"Is his genetic lab still running? Maybe he put in the order for her before they caught him."

"It's a possibility. Once VanDoyle found it, Grouter probably did move the lab to hide it from him. Someone else must be running it now though. If Grouter was still in charge, he wouldn't have allowed Rachel or any of his 'special' children to be used as prostitutes. I heard him tell VanDoyle once that he didn't want any of us mucked up with Submit. My sisters and I hated Grouter, but thanks to him, none of us had to endure what happened to Rachel. Seeing her close up and imagining what happened was almost as bad as if I had gone through it myself."

"This Submit, it has memory wipe properties doesn't it?"

"Yes. How much she remembers about the rape depends on how big the dose was and how long she was on the drug. She may not be able to tell the detectives much. I've sent for my parents. I'm still underage so I can't prevent Gorsling from questioning her, but they can."

"Why don't you want him to ask her questions?"

Lucinda snorted. "He's got about as much sensitivity as a Sand Dragon Bull in rut. She needs gentle handling."

"He might be better than you think. I don't like him because of some stuff in our past, but he is very single minded when closing a case. If Rachel needs to be handled gently, I would be willing to bet he will do just that."

Lucinda looked unconvinced, "Maybe. I wish Mom or Dad were here. Maybe I can find out who had her from this."

He looked at the list of properties she had generated. "All these are around the spaceport. You think one of them may be where they were keeping her?"

"She couldn't have walked very far, not in her condition. It has to be around here."

"How about I look into some of them for you, and you go home and get some sleep?"

"Okay," she said, surrendering the list without a fight.

When Lucinda arrived back at her apartment Sesuna was still up watching a vid and Solare was sneaking popcorn out of the bowl in her lap when she wasn't looking.

"You look terrible," the girl said frankly. "What happened to you? Looks like you've been crying."

"How nice of you to say so," Lucinda retorted.

She ordered an herbal tea to help her sleep and sat down on the couch beside Sesuna.

Solare belched loudly, emitting a pungent gust of methane gas.

"Gah!," Lucinda waved a hand in front of her face. "No more popcorn if it makes her let out stinks like that!"

"Sorry." Sesuna put the bowl down on the coffee table where Agra immediately investigated it's edible properties.

"You're right," Lucinda told her. "I was crying earlier."

"So what happened?" Sesuna demanded.

Lucinda told her story again.

"How awful! How old is Rachel?"

"About twelve maybe thirteen, I'd guess."

Sesuna shuddered. "Close to my age then. Girls my age in the temple sometimes joined in the fertility rituals, but Mother never wanted me to. In any case I would have needed to be a Novate Priestess to take part, and I didn't *want* to become a priestess."

"What do you want to become?"

Sesuna's chin lifted. "I'm going to work with plants and stuff."

"My cousin Rupert has a greenhouse here in the city and he's planning to put one on Veiled Isle. Maybe you can work with him."

"Great! The doctor was there when I commed Mom today so I didn't get to talk much. How was she?"

"She and the baby were asleep when I went by tonight. Would you like to come in with me tomorrow? You can visit with her and I'll introduce you to Rachel."

That same night on Veiled Isle, Lord Zack had come down to the shuttle bay in the underground lake cavern beneath the manor and discovered the shuttle's engine parts all over a workbench. It obviously wasn't going anywhere until it was in one piece again. Annoyed, he woke up the Isle's chief engineer. Mark Simpson, awakened out of a sound sleep blinked blearily at him.

"Is there a problem, My Lord?"

"Yes. Katherine and I have an emergency in Port Recovery we need to handle. I intended to use the shuttle, but it looks like you're still working on it. Can you put the engine back together so it's usable?"

Mark yawned. "Yes, but if you are in a hurry I wouldn't trust it for suborbital until I get the new crystal moderator installed."

Zack sighed. "Okay. I hate to ask this, but can you come down and get started now? We really need to get there as soon as we can."

"I'll be right down as soon as I get dressed. What happened?"

"It looks as if Katherine and I have gained a daughter and she's in trouble."

"What? Did you say something happened to one of your girls?"

"I'll tell you on the way. For now, just hurry and get this thing back together. Oh, Katherine suggests you pack for a trip out to Glass Manor on O'Teague Isle. You can finish working on the shuttle there."

Next, he commed Tom Draycott, who admitted he had been up all night. "You keep funny hours Draycott," he remarked.

"I had some stuff I needed to do that can only be done when no one is working in the spaceport warehouse. What's up?"

Zack quickly gave him a rundown on what he needed.

"Sure, send over the authorization and I'll handle it until you get here."

With the forms sent off, Katherine eyed her husband. 'You realize that by calling him in on this you virtually gave him our blessing to court Lucinda?"

"I know," he sighed. "He's alright. It's still going to be up to her to decide though and he'd better remember it."

If It Quacks Like A Duck

LUCINDA AND Sesuna arrived at the hospital about ten the next morning. Against Lucinda's better judgement, Sesuna had insisted on bringing the Indries with them.

"They need to be near Mom and the baby," the girl said.

"Why?"

"Solare will knead Mom's tummy muscles. It stimulates the stretched muscles to begin to tighten up again," Sesuna explained.

Lucinda suspected she was being snowed, but since she was no longer worried about someone from the Silver Samurai accusing Sesuna of stealing the Indri, she agreed. She had asked Roderick if he could quietly fudge the records to show Solare had arrived with Ispone and Sesuna. Two days ago, he told her it was done. If the Samurai filed a complaint, they wouldn't have a leg to stand on.

When they arrived, Ispone was sleeping with Shalendra cuddled against her breast. Sesuna allowed Solare to sniff the sleepers and then stepped back.

"Let's go and visit Rachel a while," Lucinda suggested. Maybe they will be awake when we come back."

They found Rachel moodily watching a vid when they came into her room. The Dragon Talker was gone. Dirty dishes and the remains of breakfast sat on the tray covering her lap. She looked up when Lucinda and Sesuna arrived.

"Who are you?" she asked.

"We met last night Rachel. I'm your sister Lucinda, and this is Lady Sesuna. She is staying with me while her mother recovers from childbirth. How do you feel?"

"Okay, I guess. What do you mean you're my sister?"

Lucinda sat down in one of the visitors' chairs. "How much do you know about your origins?"

"I know I'm a test-tube baby, so how can I have a sister?"

Lucinda made a wry face. "It's complicated. I said I am your sister because the same embryonic tissues and DNA used to create me also created you. Our design was specifically created to order. That's why some ignorant individuals will refer to us as 'designer' people."

The girl frowned at her. "Is a test-tube baby the same as a designer child?"

"Sort of. The genetic mix used to develop a designer child is very carefully selected for specific attributes rather than done by random choice as usually happens with a test-tube baby."

Rachel looked down at the blanket covering her legs while she digested this. "Oh. Were the other kids at the school made the same way?"

Absently she reached out to stroke Agra who had fluttered over to her.

Agra sneezed. The girl smelled like Lucinda, but different. Different enough to register as a separate entity to the Dactyl. She decided it was a good smell and allowed herself to be stroked.

"We won't know for sure until the Clans locate the lab. If Grouter followed pattern, I imagine some of them are designer kids like us. How many other children were there at your school?"

"It varied. Some, like Zahra and Patrice and I were born there. Others came later."

"I don't know about the latecomers, but I suspect anyone who was actually born at the school is one of us."

"That would mean Zahra, Patrice, Azalure and Meredia are also test tube babies?"

"Designer children, yes. Do you know how many of you were born there?"

"Well, there was me, Zahra and Patrice (we think we are mostly human but Patrice can do some odd stuff), and then Azalure and Meredia (they're part Syrene). A couple of others had some elf blood, but they weren't born at the school."

"When you were taken away how many children were there?"

"About—" she stopped abruptly, looking at the doorway.

Lucinda turned around to find Detectives Gorsling and Sipowitz scowling at them.

"May I remind you, Rookie, that you are not authorized to investigate this case?" Gorsling said.

"I beg your pardon, Detective, I was merely speaking to my sister about where she has been kept since she was born," Lucinda said stiffly.

"Well, you can get out. Detective Sipowitz and I need to question this girl about what happened to her."

"Do you have my parent's permission to talk to her?" Lucinda inquired.

"Come off it, Rookie. We know this girl isn't really your sister. You never met her until last night. Even if she *was* your sister, you're still a minor. You don't have the right to stop us questioning her, and if you don't quit butting into our investigation, I'll report you to your superiors for interference."

"Jim," June Sipowitz intervened quietly. "Let's not fight a battle we don't have to. Lady Lucinda, can you stand in for your parents while we ask—Lady Rachel is it, some questions about last night?"

Lucinda shrugged. "It depends on what questions you want to ask her. Rachel, would you be comfortable answering Detective Sipowitz's questions?"

"Do I have to?"

"Well, if you do, it might help us rescue your friends from the people who arranged for you to be hurt."

After a moment, the girl said, "Okay, I guess."

"What do you remember about last night, Lady Rachel?" Sipowitz kept her voice low and non-confrontational.

"I don't remember last night. I remember being taken into Cornhill's office and given some candy. When I woke up I wasn't at the school anymore. I was on the bed in a strange room. I don't know where I was. I got sick when I tried to stand up. I was afraid and I ran."

"Well," said Tom from the doorway. He was holding a carryout tray with four cups. "If I'd known we were having a party I would have brought more Cafka."

He nudged a scowling Gorsling aside and set the tray on the table holding the remains of her breakfast next to Rachel's bed. "Caramel and sugar for you," he handed Lucinda a cup, "Cinnamon and milk for you," to Sesuna. "I didn't know how you like yours Rachel, so I brought plain Cafka, some flavor packets, and cream and sugar." He picked up the last cup off the tray and looked around. "What did I miss?"

"This is none of your business Dragcote," Gorsling snapped, deliberately mispronouncing Tom's last name. "Get out."

Tom grinned at him, enjoying infuriating the other man. "Wrong boyo. I have here," he flourished a data crystal, which he handed off to Sipowitz, "permission to stand in for Lady Katherine and Lord Zack. They're still about two hours out," he explained to Lucinda. "They didn't get to leave Veiled Isle as soon as they hoped because someone had taken the shuttle engine down for maintence, so Zack commed me to stand in till they get here."

Sipowitz stuck the crystal into her port-a-tab. "Dammit," she said, showing it to her partner. "Do we have your permission to question Lady Rachel about what happened to her, M'seiur Draycott?"

"You can ask questions, but if I say stop, you stop, understand?"

"Absolutely. Lady Rachel, you mentioned going to Cornhill's office. Who is Cornhill?"

"He runs things."

"So, some kind of administrator then. What kind of a place is it?"

"It's sort of a school, but we live there."

"Do you know where it's located?"

Rachel's brow wrinkled. "Not really. We were in a fenced complex near the water. There was a forest around us. We were told to stay inside the fences because the wild animals outside would eat us."

"Did you ever see any of the animals?" Lucinda interjected. "Can you describe them?"

Rachel shrugged. "The five of us, Azalure, Meredia, Patrice, Zahra and I thought it was a trick because we only ever saw the Nessies down by the water and they eat plants not people."

"Was it warm or cold there?" Sipowitz asked, redirecting the questions.

"Yes, very warm, even during the rains."

"A southern Island or continent then," Sipowitz made a note on her tab.

"What does Cornhill look like?" Gorsling asked.

"He's an old man, like you," the girl answered, causing Gorsling to scowl.

Lucinda choked on her Cafka and Tom met her brimming eyes, coughing to cover a laugh.

"We'll have to get a sketch artist in here," Gorsling told Sipowitz.

"Why wait?" inquired Tom. "Lucinda is an excellent artist and she knows how to use the morphing materials."

"I'm tired," Rachel said, closing her eyes.

"I think we need to take a break," Tom said. "Lady Rachel is still recovering from her ordeal. Why don't you come back this afternoon?"

Scowling in frustration but mindful of the agreement, Sipowitz stood up. "We will be back this afternoon when you are rested Lady Rachel."

"How can she stand that guy? Smart Aleck P.I.," Gorsling groused as they left.

"How can who stand him?" Sipowitz asked, looking at him sideways. "Oh, you mean Officer O'Teague. You won't make much headway with her by trying to intimidate her, you know. Lady Katherine doesn't raise weak sisters."

"I never said—Never mind. Forget it. They deserve each other."

Sipowitz kept her thoughts to herself, wondering if Gorsling had really developed a romantic interest in the young blond cop. Since Lucinda plainly wasn't impressed by him either personally or professionally, her attitude of polite disdain would go far to explain his latent hostility. Gorsling was a good cop and he worked hard, but he had often pointed out how advantageous being married to a woman of high rank was in getting promotions. It was the worst thing she knew of him. He had already known who Lucinda was too, she remembered, because he had mentioned her during the Lipski case. Lady Lucinda certainly met his requirements of rank, but if he was setting his sights on her, he was aiming for a fall. Clan O'Teague hadn't been happy with the investigation of the Lipski murder and Lady Jayla's abduction. Lady Katherine and Lord Zack were unlikely to approve of her partner's courtship of their daughter. It was doubtful Lucinda would choose a man her parents disapproved of; while the woman could choose a marriage partner not approved by the Clan, most girls preferred to marry with parental approval. Even if Gorsling managed to get himself on Lucinda's Match List this fall, she didn't think much of his chances with the girl. It was obvious Lady Katherine and Lord Zack were already treating Draycott as family. They had Clan members in the city who could have stood for them to protect Rachel. Tom wouldn't have been representing them without their blessing to court their daughter.

Gorsling was young, ambitious and with more seasoning would make a good detective, His worst flaw as a detective was a tendency to develop target fixation in an investigation, and as senior partner, Sipowitz was having some luck training him to be more open-minded. He would get his promotions but not through nepotism.

Gorsling's peculiar methods of courtship never dawned on Lucinda. She had dropped Sesuna off in Ispone's room and was taking a quick nap in the Spaceport officer's lounge when a weary Katherine and Zack arrived.

"You look tired darling," Katherine said, cupping her palms around Lucinda's face. "Did you get any sleep?"

Instead of answering, Lucinda threw her arms around her mother and clung for a moment. Sooka, Katherine's Quirka and Agra immediately took up a soft croon, *pushing* comfort at the two women. Zack awkwardly patted his daughter and wife on the shoulder.

"I needed that," Lucinda stepped back. "Would you guys like some Cafka? The stuff in the robo-chef isn't bad."

"I'd love some." Katherine sank down on the sofa Lucinda had just vacated. Zack perched in a chair opposite her.

"Did Tom get here in time to help you this morning?"

"Yes." Lucinda handed her parents both a steaming cup and fixed a third one for herself. Agra chirped at her, and as an afterthought, she programmed two Quirka bowls for the Dactyl and Sooka. "Thank you for sending him. Gorsling tried to throw him out, but he had your authorization, so they had to let him stay. He got a kick out of deviling him. Tom did I mean."

Zack snorted. "Don't blame him. I wasn't much impressed by Gorsling either."

She set the bowls of chopped vegetables, nuts and fruit down on the coffee table between the couch and chairs and both pets fell on them as if starved.

"Is Sooka eating for more than one? Agra always acts like I starve her, but Sooka usually has better manners," Lucinda remarked.

"Yes," Katherine answered placidly. "She and Divit are expecting another litter after the Harvest Festival."

Katherine took a deep breath and brought up the subject they had all been avoiding. "How is Rachel?"

"Physically she's recovered from the Submit. Doctor Riesling doesn't think she was on it long enough to become addicted to it."

Katherine nodded. "How much does she remember about what happened to her?"

"Nothing of last night, thank the Goddess. The rape kit was positive though. Dr. Riesling says she might remember later but she might not—some people given Submit never recover the lost memories. Rachel remembers being taken into someone called Cornhill's office and given candy. She woke up alone in a dark room, up-chucked some stuff and ran."

"Was she followed here?"

"I didn't see anyone when we looked out into the streets in front of the Spaceport offices. Neither did Mira and Twilya."

"What did you tell Rachel about us?"

"I told her she was my little sister. She knows she's a designer child, but she called it being a test-tube baby. I was right; there are at least five other children like her at the school, so I'm betting on Juliette and Violet also having little sisters."

Katherine nodded. "Okay, come and introduce us to our new daughter. We can visit with Ispone too. I want to invite her and the children to make a home on Veiled Isle as well."

They found Sesuna back in Rachel's room. Sesuna had introduced the other girl to Solare and her baby. The Fire Indri was snuggling on Rachel's lap while the girl stroked her. 'She's so soft," Rachel said.

The kitten Indri woke and made a tiny mewling sound. "Koko is hungry. Would you like to hold them while Solare feeds her?"

"Sure. What do I do?"

Sesuna arranged the Indris on Rachel's lap.

"Can I pat her?"

"Sure, nothing an Indri likes better than attention," Sesuna said cheerfully.

"Good morning," Lucinda entered the room, followed by Katherine and Zack.

"Rachel, I'd like to introduce our parents to you, Lady Katherine O'Teague and her husband, Lord Zack," Lucinda said, gesturing to her parents who had followed her into the room.

Rachel eyed them suspiciously. "I don't have parents. Who are you?"

"I'm Lady Katherine, Lucinda's mother. Zack and I adopted Lucinda and her sisters when I found them on Fenris. Since you have the same DNA as Lucinda, the planetary base decided you are my daughter as well."

"Oh." The girl said nothing, obviously waiting for more. She was easier to read than Lucinda at that age, but then this girl hadn't had the intensive training in interrogation techniques Lucinda had suffered through.

Katherine smiled at her. "I can understand you might feel reluctant to regard me as your mother at this point; we are strangers after all. For now, do you think you could consider me a friend who has your best interest at heart?"

"What's in it for you?"

Lucinda made a protesting move, and Katherine lifted a hand to stop her making an objection. "That is a fair question Rachel. All I can tell you, is since I adopted Lucinda and her sisters I've had more joy come into my life than ever before. I'm prepared to love you too, if you allow it."

"I'll think about it."

"That's all I ask." Katherine took a small duffle out from under her chair and put it on the end of Rachel's bed. "I had to guess at your size. These are clothes Lucinda wore at your age. If you feel up to it, you can change into them. We can go shopping for new ones when they release you. In the meantime, Lord Zack and I are going down the hall to your mother's room Sesuna. When Solare has finished feeding KoKo, perhaps you'd like to join us."

If You Wake At Midnight

A S THEY manned their stake-out hide, Tom and Isiah could hear the peaceful noises of the night, the small rustlings of nocturnal animals hunting food, the buzz of insects feeding on the kelp washed up on the beach, and the hypnotic rhythm of waves lapping the shore. Somewhere out in the channel, a riverboat's horn tooted.

Isiah yawned. "You're sure it will be tonight?"

"As sure as I can be. It's the dark of the moons so there's less chance of someone from the other shuttles parked out here spotting them. Tomorrow, the moons start building back up, so the light will be worse."

"If we were waiting for the dark of the moons, why did we come out here on the other nights?"

"Because I could have been wrong," Tom said, grinning.

Isiah snorted. "Fat chance of that. By the way, thanks for getting me assigned to the investigative team. The Archive agreed to give me a leave of absence until the investigation is over."

"Sure. It's the least I could do. The team could use a good research coordinator."

Somewhere close there was a splash, and a faint cry.

"What's that?" Isiah whispered, excitement echoing in his voice. "Is it them?"

"Sshh!" Tom adjusted his night vision glasses for telescopic sight. Beside him, Isiah copied his action.

"There!" he whispered. "See that dark shape where the shoreline curves?"

"Yeah, but I can't see much else."

"That must be the smuggler's boat. They're coming this way. Turn on your vid camera and wait."

Tom touched a button and his chair softly collapsed. Isiah quickly copied him. The two men rolled over on their bellies, aiming their night sight goggles down the beach.

Two short flashes of light came from the dark ship. It was answered by a series of five from the tarmac. Five tall figures prodded a group of shorter outlines toward the damaged power pole.

"I don't get it," Isiah whispered. "They don't seem to be carrying anything."

"They aren't," Tom replied, his voice grim. "See how much smaller some of them are? Those are kids. They are the cargo."

"Kids? What do they want with kids?"

"Fodder for the sex trade," Tom answered.

He took out his com and enabled the cone of silence so those coming up the beach couldn't hear. None-the-less he kept his voice low. "Sir, the cargo is here. It's kids sir."

Offshore in a stealth shuttle with forty men trained in amphibious maneuvers, the Duc waited for Tom's signal. The Clans didn't intend to let the boat bringing in the cargo escape. At his gesture, half of his men glided down the cargo ramp and swam over to the ship that had brought the children. When they reached the boat anchored offshore, the Clan operatives shot padded grappling hooks over the top rail of the ship's deck. The hooks had been padded to reduce any noise made when they connected to the wooden rail. Silent as death, the men crept up the sides and swung aboard. The Thieves Guild crew was small; five had landed with the children, and they had left one man in the wheelhouse, one below in the engine room and a man out on deck to watch for danger. Unfortunately for him, he was looking toward the shore when the Duc's force came aboard. He only realized he was in trouble when he was seized from behind and a knife held under his chin.

"How many?" whispered a voice in his ear.

"What?" he gasped.

The knife nicked the skin under his chin, drawing a drop of blood. "How many of you are on board?"

"Just me, Jerry in the wheelhouse and Torigen in the engine room," the captive gulped.

Silently the Duc's man held up two fingers, then pointed up toward the wheelhouse and down toward the engine room. Four shadows slipped away. There was a brief flash of light in the wheelhouse. Five minutes later, the Clan had taken over the vessel and two bound captives were sitting against the wheelhouse, awaiting questioning by the Duc. The third, having unwisely attempted to pull a weapon on the Clansman sent to take him out, was dead.

As soon as he came aboard, the Duc, a medium sized man with light brown hair showing traces of grey, directed his best com expert to the wheelhouse to decipher the route taken by the ship to get to Port Recovery. "Our first priority is to locate their base," he told his man.

As Tom and Isiah watched from the beach, they were joined by the remainder of the Duc's forces. Their job was to prevent anyone escaping once the units on the tarmac made their move. One of the delivery men lifted the leaning power pole out of the ground, leaving about eighteen inches clear. A second smuggler crawled under it and stood up. As the first child approached, he was pushed down on his hands and knees and urged under the fence. Once clear, the child was pulled upright. Soon the children stood in a group over to the side.

"Why don't they run?" Isiah whispered.

"They've been drugged is my guess. Never mind that. We need to get a vid of which shuttle they approach."

Finally the last two smugglers crawled under the fence and stood up.

They herded the smaller figures toward a shuttle. Out on the Tarmac, Zack and a mixed team of officers waited for them to reach their destination. Zack was the only civilian. The rest of the team was a joint group from IPP, PRS and SSF. Zack had only been dissuaded from joining Tom and Isiah by allowing him to go with the team responsible for taking out the shuttle.

Back in Ispone's room, Lady Katherine, Rachel, Ispone and Sesuna waited impatiently for news of the raid.

"This is ridiculous," Lady Katherine declared. "C'mon everyone, I think we ought to be able to get a vid feed from the Tarmac in Lucinda's office."

When she got up, she was followed by Rachel and Sesuna.

"I need to finish feeding Shalendra. I will join you later," Ispone said.

The office was empty because everyone available was out with the team on the Tarmac. Their first obstacle was Lucinda's comp being password protected.

"Does that mean we can't see what is going on?" Rachel asked in disappointment.

"No, it's just a delay. I can crack this," Katherine said.

"I think I know what the code is," Sesuna offered.

"Okay, try it."

Sesuna took Katherine's place at the comp and typed in a code. The desk screen lit up. She scrolled down and found the outside vid feed. After a little fumbling, she managed to transfer the feed to the large plasma screen and then zoom in on the three shuttles.

"It's too dark," Rachel complained. "I can't see anything."

"There ought to be a night vision adjustment," Katherine told Sesuna.

"There! That's better," Sesuna exclaimed as the feed adjusted itself to low light conditions. "Can you see Lucinda Lady Katherine?"

As they watched, Lucinda and Zack crept up to either side of a darkened shuttle door. It was open, but no lights inside were on. Obviously, those handling the shuttle didn't want to draw attention by showing a light.

"Oh—Oh," Sesuna said, pointing to an insignia on the shuttle side. "That one is from the Silver Samurai."

Out on the tarmac, Zack glanced at his daughter and nodded. The two of them slunk silently inside the hatch door. By pre-agreement, Zack went for the pilot while Lucinda checked out the rear of the shuttle. When she returned, she found Talon Delgado, with his hands and feet tied and a tape gag across his mouth.

"Clear," Lucinda said softly. Talon glared up at her.

She crouched down, so his eyes were on a level with her own. "Captain Delgado, *this* is my father," she told him proudly, "Lord Zachery O'Teague *ni*-Jackson."

Talon couldn't speak because of the gag, but he glared malovently at her.

Zack and Lucinda took up positions on either side of the door. The plan was to allow the children to board so they would be out of the line of fire, and then the LEO's waiting outside would take down the delivery crew.

When the children reached the shuttle door they stopped. The man with them made an exasperated noise.

"Go up the steps and sit down," he told the red-headed girl in the lead.

She tripped on the step and went down. The man made an ugly growling noise, and reached down to yank her upright, twisting her arm and eliciting a gasp of pain from her. He dragged her up the steps and flung her inside. She stumbled again, and fell against the row of seats, partly blocking the doorway.

"Hela's Seven Hells!" the man swore, mounting the steps. "Get up, you stupid slut and sit in the chair."

When the child continued to stare at him, he came inside, reaching for her. The girl flinched back from him, and her body flickered, blending with the seats and the floor. Her eyes widened as Zack caught him around the neck in a headlock, jamming a force wand in his side. The man slumped unconscious. As Zack wanted him alive to answer questions his wand hadn't been on a lethal setting, but he had made the shock calibration as painful as possible. While Zack bound and gagged the second man, Lucinda went to the girl, gently helped her to rise to her feet and guided her to a chair.

"Lyle, what's the hold-up?" Another of the delivery crew, a woman with a shock of white crew cut hair, walked up, frowning. "Quit playing games with the kid! Toro saw a flash of light out at the ship. We need to complete delivery and get out of here."

When there was no answer, the woman cursed under her breath, and grabbed the next child, a boy this time, and told him to step up and enter the shuttle. When all five of the children were aboard, Lucinda shut the door, locking the woman outside.

"Hey!" she pounded on the door. "What's the big idea? Where's our money?"

Zack turned on the illuminations inside the shuttle, just as the tarmac outside was flooded with brightness from the portable spotlights brought by the LEO's.

"This is Port Recovery Security! Drop your weapons and get down on the ground!" Mira yelled. The command was repeated by the heads of the other security forces.

Inside the shuttle, Lucinda went to kneel in front of the little red-head. "Patrice?" she asked softly.

The girl looked up at her but didn't answer.

"It's alright honey, you're safe now," Zack said. He turned to Lucinda. "She looks just like Juliette did at that age."

Lucinda nodded. "Yes, she's one of us."

She tapped her com. "We're clear in here Mira. We're going to need the medics. We've got five children who've been dosed with Submit."

"On their way," Mira answered. "As soon as we get these guys locked down, we'll let them through. How many hostiles were inside?"

"We've got two in here under restraints. Unharmed except for bad temper."

As soon as Mira signed off, Lucinda commed her Mother. When Katherine's image appeared, Lucinda told her, "Mom, Patrice is here. Is Rachel with you?"

"Yes, she's here."

"It would help if she could identify the children. None of them are in any shape to give us information."

"Were they given Submit?"

"Yeah, I'm afraid so."

"I hope you beat the crap out of whoever did it," Lady Katherine said viciously, her maternal instincts aroused.

"Rachel, Lucinda needs you to identify the children they rescued."

When Rachel came up to the screen, Lucinda turned her com so that Rachel got a visual of the other children. "Can you give me some names Rachel?"

"The girl with red hair is Patrice. The boy next to her is named Mason, Tyson is next to him, Anita and Byrony are next, and the girl on the end is Azalure. She's one of us."

"Thank you Rachel." Lucinda signed off.

There was an outburst of yelling outside and a voice yelled "Officer down!"

Lucinda started for the door.

"Don't open it," Zack warned. He went to the control panel and turned on the outside feed, angling the view back toward the fence.

One of the smugglers had made an escape attempt.

When approached by Nova Jonah intending to put him in restraints, he jumped up and pulled out a Wickamor fighting whip. The whips weren't just leather strips; a true fighting whip had sharp stones imbedded in the lash to create maximum damage. He slashed at the Patrol officer, ripping a slit across Jonah's face before darting toward the beach. Blinded by the blood running in his eyes, Nova Jonah stumbled and went down. Several of the officers dashed after the escapee. Skidding to a halt when they saw the other team blocking the way to the power pole.

Twilya knelt by Jonah, rendering what first aid she could.

Tom and the Duc's men saw the slaver coming with the bloody whip still dangling from one hand.

By mutual consent, they stepped back, allowing Tom to handle the smuggler. Pulling out his own whip, Tom made a quick snap at the running man. The man slid to a halt, returning the blow with his own whip, hoping to yank Tom's away from him when the whips tangled.

Tom laughed, stepping in toward the man instead of back so the whips would loosen. As soon as they did, he spun around, cutting the man's face open with a backhanded strike. The man attempted to copy Tom's move and Tom spun in the opposite direction, this time aiming at the man's legs. The would-be whip fighter stumbled, and a strip of red began dripping down his leg.

He tried a frontal attack, but was driven back by Tom's snapping whip, suffering cuts to his arms and face as Tom's blows hit home. In retreating, he tripped and went down on his back. Knowing he was beaten, he dropped his whip and glared up at Tom, making rude comments about Tom's ancestry and sexual habits.

"A man who can't use a whip shouldn't try to fight with it," Tom commented. "Roll over, away from the whip," he instructed.

"Your young man can handle himself in a fight," Zack told his daughter, pleased with Tom's performance. "He doesn't have a mark on him."

"He isn't my young man," Lucinda protested.

"If he isn't, he will be soon," her father said. "Trust me, a man knows when someone is interested in his daughter."

Raid on Brisai

KATHERINE AND the two girls were waiting at the hospital when the rescued children were brought in. Rachel rushed forward and hugged Patrice and Azalure, who stood passively under her attentions.

"What's the matter with you?" she demanded, drawing back to look at them.

"It's the drug," Katherine told her. "As soon as it's out of their systems, they will be back to normal."

Rachel turned to look at her. "You said you wanted to be my mother. Are you going to take all of us?" she demanded.

Katherine met her eyes. This was a test, and she knew it. "Yes, you will all be welcome to me."

"Alright. I want to stay with Patrice and Azalure."

"We'll get more beds brought into your room," Katherine promised.

Dr. Riesling listened to Katherine's request in silence. "Putting them all together will certainly make it easier for a single Dragon Talker to control them," she agreed. "As soon as they've each been examined, we'll bring them to you. It may be necessary to move Rachel to a larger room to accommodate all six."

Returning from the raid, Zack and Lucinda found Katherine and Rachel waiting with a Dragon Talker for the rest of the children to be brought into the new accommodations.

He grinned at his wife. "All of them? You'd better com the Isle so they can get rooms ready. We don't know what we will find when we get out to Brisai."

"You located the lab then?"

"The Duc's men did. The ship that brought in the kids had a return course already laid in. I'm going out with the team on the raid." He cast a wary glance at his daughter. "Lucinda has duties here, but Tom and Isiah are coming as well."

Katherine flung her arms around his neck. "You're enjoying this aren't you? You be careful. If you get yourself shot, I'll kick your butt, you hear?"

"I hear," he said, giving her a thorough kiss. "Take care of our girls."

"We're getting boys too," she reminded him.

"Them too. Lucinda, Tom is waiting in your office if you want to say goodbye."

She gave her father a hug and dashed for the office.

"I've called Larry Jorgensen to send over some security officers."

"Thank you," Katherine nodded. "Ispone and Sesuna need it too. I wish I could just bundle all of them up and take them out to the Manor, but I suppose that will have to wait until the doctor clears everyone."

LUCINDA FOUND TOM WAITING in her office. She stopped and just looked. "I saw your fight. You're good," she said.

He flushed a little under her admiring gaze. "Not as good as I could be," he admitted. "That guy was an amateur compared to the Wickamor I trained with. Now *she* was tough."

"Dad says you're going on the Brisai raid."

"Yes, he and Isiah are going too."

"You will be careful? I—I wouldn't like it if you got hurt."

He held out a hand, and she put hers into it. A soft pull brought her into his arms. "I'll be careful," he said. "You and I have a date as soon as the Lists come out."

Lucinda took a deep breath and lifted her face to his. "What makes you so sure you're going to be on my List?"

He grinned down at her. "I'll bribe someone if I have to."

When he lowered his mouth to hers, she slid her arms around his neck, answering his passion with her own.

Isiah coughed from the doorway. "Hate to interrupt, but we need to get going. The Duc just commed me. Guess you forgot to turn your wrist com back on."

Lucinda stood watching them walk back out toward the tarmac for a long minute. Mira laid a hand on her shoulder, jerking her back to reality.

"We've got reports to fill out Rookie."

"Yes, just the stuff that happened tonight, right? The doctor says she doesn't want us to try to question any of the children until she can be sure they are off the Submit."

"Yes."

"I figured Gorsling and Sipowitz would be all over us by now. Isn't this still their case?"

Her boss shrugged. "Lieutenant Jerusha talked to his Lieutenant. This is now a joint investigation."

"Bet he's loving that," Lucinda remarked.

•

The Raid on Brisai as it came to be known was fubared from the get go. When the Clan transport arrived, they could see the burning buildings from the ship.

"Someone must have warned them we were coming," the Duc said harshly.

"It had to be someone at the spaceport," Zack agreed. "No official announcement about the capture was made in the media."

When they landed, they found the entire compound was deserted. The remains of flames guttered in the husks of buildings. In the remnants of what had once been the embryonic lab, some of the embryo's in their artificial wombs had been cooked by the heat from the fire. Hardened soldiers lost their stomach contents when they found the charred remains of children and adults in the buildings.

"This isn't all of them," Zack said harshly. "Rachel told us there were about twenty kids here. Keep looking."

It was Tom who found the opening in the fence on the jungle side of the compound. A piece of a shirt clung to the ragged edges of the hole, which looked as if it had been gnawed through rather than cut.

Zack laid a plasma cutter against the rest of the opening, enlarging it and smoothing out the sharp edges. "Wait," he held up a hand to stop anyone entering. "I need to check for tracks."

He squatted down on his haunches. The ground cover here was piled with half rotted vegetation, but small disturbances showed a faint trail. Carefully, so not to smudge any of the traces, he edged past the break in the fence.

"What do you see?" Tom asked.

"Someone, maybe several people light on their feet came through here."

"You think some children got away?" Isiah asked.

"Maybe. One of you go and report this to the Duc while I check this out."

"No need," Max Browning said. The Duc d'Orleans had come up behind them. "I knew there was a reason I brought you along Jackson: Your Recon skills."

Zack grunted. "Keep everyone but Tom and Isiah out of here in case I need to come back and start over."

"Why them?"

"Because they'll do what I tell them," Zack retorted. He stopped at the edge of the vines and carefully lifted one out of his way, ducking when sharpened wooden darts sprang out at him. Fortunately, Tom and Isiah had circled to the right of Zack's position and the darts missed them as well. One of the men with the Duc cursed when two of the darts buried themselves in his leg and arm.

"What sweet little kiddies," the Duc deadpanned. "If you don't come back Jackson, I'll have to figure you got taken out by kids."

"Ah shut up," Zack replied. "There you are, you little devil," he had spotted the trigger mechanism. "Clever, clever girl. You used the vines own elasticity. I bet you're one of mine. You were getting ready to run, weren't you?"

Isiah stared at him. "One of yours?"

Zack chuckled. "Yes. All my kids are too smart for their own good, and sneaky—oh boy. These kids were getting ready to run, and they set up traps behind them when they did. That little trick wasn't done on the spur of the moment. It took time and work. From here on out guys, watch for trip wires, traps and holes in the ground. Use your force wands to test the ground in front of you."

"Does he always talk to himself when he's following a trail?" Isiah asked.

"How would I know?" Tom answered.

As they made their way cautiously through the jungle, they found several more trip wired booby traps, and had to rescue Isiah out of a hole covered with broad leaf fronds. When the ground started to give way he was able to catch himself on the side of it, so he didn't impale himself on the sharpened stakes at the bottom.

After about an hour, they reached the edge of the jungle. A herd of dragons was feeding on the lush vegetation. Eight children were huddled on a large boulder in the center of the herd. Zack took out his field glasses and focused. He breathed a sigh of relief when he saw a younger girl who looked like Violet, sitting on the edge of the boulder watching the dragons.

Tom and Isiah eyed the animals warily. "Are those Nessies or Sandies?" Isiah asked. The animals were much larger than the Sand Dragons found on the islands and there were subtle differences in the way they were made. Obviously they were grass eaters because they were munching contentedly on the lush grass.

Zack glanced over at him and shrugged. "Kin to them at least," he said. "The big problem will be getting the kids to come to us."

"Isn't that dangerous? Shouldn't we go to them?"

Zack handed him the glasses. "See that little girl sitting on the edge of the boulder? The one with black hair? I'm betting that is Zahra, and she is a natural Dragon Talker like Violet. That's probably how the kids got through the herd to begin with."

"How do *you* plan to get through it old man?"

Zack grinned at them. "Easy. I got a safe word from Rachel. Hopefully, Zahra will recognize me as a friend. Watch my back and don't let one of those monsters step on me."

He stepped out into the clearing and several of the dragons shied away, snorting in challenge.

Cupping his hands around his mouth, he yelled, "Zahra! Can you hear me? Rachel and Patrice sent me."

The girl turned cold blue eyes on him. "Why should I believe you?"

"I'm supposed to tell you the moon is in the seventh house," he yelled.

Her eyebrows rose. "Oh, really? And I suppose you're the seventh son of a seventh son?"

"No," he called back, "but *you* are a daughter of the dragon."

She considered a minute and then turned to talk to the other children. After some discussion, she said, "We don't want to go back to the compound."

"Alright, we can come to you, if you can make us a path through the dragons."

"How do I do that?"

"Do you know what a *push is*?"

"Nope."

"Okay, first calm your mind. Then reach out until you can feel the dragons' emotions."

Frowning, she sat for a moment, then her face smoothed out. "Alright, I can feel them. What now?"

"*Push* at them a feeling that the line between us is bad. They should begin moving away and leave us a clear path to you."

Zahra watched in astonishment as the dragons began moving away from the path she had marked in her mind.

"Walk slow guys," Zack instructed. He had enough experience working with Violet to know how to behave around a herd of wild dragons.

Once they reached the rock, the children slid down and headed toward the beach where they traveled along the shore until Zack decided they were probably safe from the herd.

When they stopped, Zahra turned to him. "Okay, we trusted you. Now it's your turn. How do you know Rachel and Patrice?"

Zack sat down on the sand, motioning Tom and Isiah to do the same. He had learned early to explain things to his adopted children as if he were speaking to another adult. "Well, it all started on Fenris..."

The telling took about an hour, and at the end, Zack felt as if the children were passing judgment on him. The small group sat in silence for some time while the children digested what they had been told. In his turn he looked them over as well.

They were a good-looking bunch. Plainly, the Guild had chosen them with an eye to being able to utilize that beauty in the future. Aside from Zahra, whom he would have recognized because of her resemblance to Violet, and Meredia who was Azalure's twin, there were four boys, and girls. Meredia like Azalure, plainly showed her Syrene heritage. She had light copper colored skin which seemed to shine like a new penny in the sunlight, aquamarine colored hair, clipped short, and silver eyes. Byrony Selman the third girl was plainly of human stock, with light brown hair, a brown complexion and brown eyes. The fourth girl appeared to be part Trellyan like the Patrol officer who had gone with Roderick to the banking moon of Fenris. Selick s'Rudin had pinkish toned gray skin, lighter in shade than a full blood Trellyan, but she had the curly maroon colored hair. Her human heritage showed itself most clearly in her blue eyes.

Even to his untrained eyes, two of the boys showed definite signs of Elf blood. The other two boys, Kirt vanHuron and Taglen Jorkinski, both looked to be pure human, with long narrow faces, sandy colored hair and eyes an indeterminate shade of gray.

Finally, one of the boys he had identified as part Elf, asked a question. "So you're telling us that adults will still be telling us where to go and what to do?"

Zack nodded. "Unfortunately, until you are of age, that will happen where ever you go."

He studied the boy who had spoken thoughtfully. The boy had brilliant green eyes, straight blue-black hair, cut chin length, and delicate almost feminine features. If he were human, Zack would have guessed his age to be around ten, but the almost inhuman beauty of his face and body told Zack he had Elven blood. Elves were extremely long-lived compared to many of the races in the galaxy, and the species was famous for the unearthly beauty of their features. They didn't tolerate those of mixed elf blood well and Zack judged both of the boys to have some human or maybe Trellyan blood.

"I'm guessing that will come sooner for some than for others. What's your name?"

"Airen Philen," the boy replied. "And you are correct. In human years, I am sixteen."

"Pleased to meet you, Airen Philen. Am I correct in assuming you are at least part Elf?"

"My brothers and I have always thought so, but we were very young when we were brought here."

"You have brothers here?"

The boy looked down. "Not any more. Tasmylee was sold last year. I have vague memories of some others who were older, but I can't remember their names anymore."

"I'm sorry. We have resources to help you look, but I can't promise anything."

Airen nodded.

"May I be introduced to the rest of you?" Zack asked.

Zahra seemed to have nominated herself spokesperson for the group. "Yes, of course, but you knew my name."

"I told you I spoke to Rachel just before we left to come here. She described you and Meredia to me."

"What will happen to us?"

"Katherine and I hope to be able to bring all of you home with us to Veiled Isle. We have put in a request to adopt all of you. Zahra, Rachel, and Patrice, your DNA matches our older daughters, so you are already considered a part of O'Teague Clan, and there is no question about you coming home with us. Katherine is negotiating for the rest of you to be able to come with us as well, at least until a decision can be made about those of you who have ties to other worlds."

He turned to Airen, "You and Aymar are part Elven, so to stay with us, we will need to get a release from your relatives on Y'leneor. The same with Azalure and Meredia with Oceana."

Aymer, who had been silent until now laughed. "We're Halflings. They won't want us back, and even if they take us, it would be a miserable existence. I'd rather take my chances in the wild."

Zack shrugged. "I've heard that the part Elven don't fare well on your homeworld. I'm sure it's one of the arguments Katherine will use to get you transferred to our custody."

"What if they decide against us?" Meredia, asked softly.

Zack grinned at her. "The Joint Clan Council is a convenient form of government for negotiating with the Confederation and other planets, but they aren't all powerful inside Clan borders. If it looks as if they are going to decide against you, we can take you to Veiled Isle without their permission. I doubt if they will mount an offensive against a sovereign Clan to recover a few children."

"That will mean a lot of trouble for your Clan," Kirt vanHuron, one of the human boys spoke up. "Why would you be willing to do that?"

"Not as much trouble as you think. My wife is the Laird's sister, and she is a delegate to Parliament. Katherine gave Rachel her word we would stand as parents to all of you."

Tom snorted. "What he isn't telling you, is that Lady Katherine created the program that matches homeless settlers with the societies where they will most likely fit in. She tweaks it for each colony. If she wants something, she'll probably get it."

"And it won't cost the other planets anything, so why would they oppose it?" Isiah added.

The children held a silent communication. Finally Zahra turned back to Zack. "We will go with you, but not back through the camp."

Past / Present / Future

DOUBLE NOVA Jeffries had made it a practice to be in or around Vensoog during the Festivals. He had a theory that more than one of the ships that came for the Festival came to conduct Thieves Guild business. Until now, that theory while of interest to himself and his superiors, hadn't had much to support it. However, the capture of so many Thieves Guild operatives during the raid on the tarmac greatly interested the IPP. The ship and crew of the Silver Samurai were still in orbit around Vensoog. He hadn't moved against it yet because his superiors were negotiating the ship's status with the Free Trade Registry. The Registry had taken the position that despite the warrant out for its assistant engineer; the crew were innocent until proven guilty and that the ship itself belonged to them. If it was damaged in an attempt to board her, the Patrol would need to pay the crew reparations.

He felt that because so many of those rescued from the tarmac and later from Brisai were children it would make interrogations easier if they were aboard an IPP vessel. Though not actual operatives, the children might have heard things. He was eager to take them aboard his ship where they could be questioned properly.

Unfortunately for his plans, he soon realized the children had found a powerful protector in Lady Katherine. She had no intention of allowing him to remove any of the children from Vensoog. Since three of them shared DNA with three of her daughters, the Joint Clan Council had approved her request to stand as guardian for all of them. Being well aware of the lady's formidable reputation, he was wary of trying to use his authority to try to enforce his will on her.

He was unlikely to succeed and he knew it. He had first made Lady Katherine's acquaintance several years ago when he had come to Vensoog to speak to her daughter Juliette, who had been an informant in Hans Grouter's organization on Fenris. When he arrived, he found Juliette on the stand, testifying in her mother's trial for the unlawful death of a Guild operative named Darla Lister. The Clan judges had acquitted Lady Katherine.

"More Cafka Double Nova?" Lady Katherine inquired.

"Thank you Lady Katherine," he said, extending his cup for her to pour some of the dark, rich drink into it from the steaming pot. "Please understand that no harm will come to the children. It's merely that my ship has better facilities for caring for them and helping them to remember more about the operatives running that compound on Brisai. I know the Manor must be terribly crowded with the Festival so near."

Her finely arched eyebrows rose. Lady Katherine's delicate features assumed a gently concerned expression. "I'm sure you intend them no harm, but these children have been isolated on Brisai and need to be immersed in a more civilized human culture as soon as can be. They have developed very strong bonds with each other. My child care experts tell me that separating them before they can have time to become adjusted into our culture would dangerously interfere with their adjustment to society. I'm afraid I will have to insist that they remain here under my eye on Vensoog."

Jefferies controlled his exasperation. "With all due respect, some of these children may have relatives on other worlds who may want to reunite with them. Without knowing what they know, they may also have information into the Thieves Guild operations that will help us to stamp out this pernicious sex trade in children."

"I didn't say you couldn't ask them questions Double Nova, only that you must do it on this planet and confine your questioning to what is appropriate for children. I won't have them frightened or intimidated."

"They will stay at the hospital?"

"No, I feel the sooner they become introduced to their new family the better it will be. For the duration of the Festival, they will remain on O'Teague Isle. Afterwards, they will travel out to Veiled Isle with Zack and I."

"I would prefer they stay in the city for easier access my Lady."

"Nonsense! You have shuttles. It is just as easy for you to travel to Veiled Isle as it to come here. I assure you we will welcome you. There is plenty of room and we have a shuttle landing facility there."

That evening when Katherine paid a visit to Ispone, she found her up and dressed and changing Shalendra's diaper under the supervision of Solare.

"How do you feel?" Katherine asked her.

Ispone turned to her with a smile. "So well I think they will be glad to get rid of me."

"Would you like to come and stay at O'Teague Manor until the rest of the Hyati-Soturi are captured? I know you and Sesuna have your own apartment here in the city, but security is much better out at the Isle."

"Thank you. I would appreciate that. It would also give Sesuna time to enjoy the festival with girls of her own age."

"Excellent, I'll tell the house manager to expect you as soon as they discharge you and Shalendra."

Ispone had finished her daughter's toilette and lifted her to her shoulder, rubbing her back. Solare, her baby clinging to her with its tiny hands and feet, climbed up and laid across her other shoulder.

"I will be visiting the children next, perhaps you and Shalendra would like to come with me?"

"Yes, I would. Lucinda told me there is a Trellyan girl with them?"

Katherine nodded. "Selick s'Rudin. Do you know the family? Are they likely to be searching for her?"

Ispone frowned. "I heard a rumor several years ago that drunks off a Free Trader had attacked a girl of that family. It was hushed up, and the child she carried disappeared. The girl was found a husband who would accept her disgrace for a large dowry, but he didn't take the child. I doubt if the girl's family will want her back, and if she goes back, they'll treat her as Ubah, unclean. It's not a good life for those characterized thus, and without the support of her family..."

"I see," Katherine said. "Do you feel she is Ubah?"

Ispone snorted. "No, that is nothing but an outdated, morally repugnant belief. As if the girl could help being attacked! And as for her child—pah! I find my homeworld's caste system tiresome at best, and abhorrent at its worst." She hesitated. "I know you are eager to take them all under your wings, but perhaps Selick could spend time with Sesuna and myself?"

Katherine gave her a wide smile. "Thank you. I had hoped you would volunteer since you can explain so much more about Trellyan culture to her than I can. Are you sure it will not be too much for you with the new baby though?"

"I will manage," Ispone said serenely.

They found the children gathered in Rachel's room. It made quite a handful, with the eight from the compound added to the six already present.

Rachel looked up from her seat on the bed when Katherine entered. "Did you speak to the Patrol?" the girl asked anxiously.

Katherine smiled at her. She looked so much like Lucinda had at that age. "Yes, I did. I'm happy to report that Double Nova Jefferies has come around to my way of thinking. You will all be going out to O'Teague Manor with me until after the Harvest Festival."

"What did you use to blackmail him with?" inquired Patrice, and Katherine chuckled. So much like Juliette. That same shrewdness coupled with the ability to understand and judge people.

"Well, this isn't the first time I met him; he wasn't eager to come to blows with me." She gestured to Ispone. "This is one of our Clan, Lady Ispone and her daughter Shalendra. They will go with us to the Manor and then later out to Veiled Isle."

Selick had been staring at Ispone. "You look like me. Why?"

Ispone crossed over to her and sat down on one of the cots. "That is because we both have Trellyan blood."

The girl looked her over curiously. "What is that?" she asked, pointing at Solare, who sniffed at her experimentally from her position draped across Ispone's shoulder.

"This is Solare, a Fire Indri and my daughter Sesuna's pet. Fire Indris are fascinated by new babies." As she spoke, she laid Shalendra down on the cot between them. Solare promptly hopped down, purring at the baby and rubbing her cheeks against Shalendra's arms and hands. Sometimes stopping to give the skin a few licks with her tiny tongue.

"Is she trying to taste her?" Selick asked, horrified.

Rachel laughed. "No, silly. Sesuna told me that is an Indri's way of welcoming the new baby. She's absorbing her scent. She will do the same to you if you pet her."

"Can I?"

"Hold out your fingers for her to sniff and then rub gently along her back."

Dr. Riesling came looking for Ispone. "There you are," she exclaimed. "The discharge nurse is looking for you. Are you ready to go home?"

Ispone smiled. "Quite ready, I assure you."

The doctor turned to Katherine. "Lady Katherine, I understand the children are now in your charge?"

"Yes. I assume you have crystals for me to initial?"

"If you wouldn't mind. They are being released as well."

Where Lies The Heart

THE SHUTTLE bringing Juliette home from Kitzingen was due today. Katherine knew Lucinda would have wanted to be there to greet her sister after so long an absence, but Lucinda was working an extra shift to be able to have time off during the Introductory Ball, so she did the next best thing. She commed Lucinda when Juliette's shuttle touched down at the dock that afternoon.

Juliette ran down the ramp and threw her arms around her mother's neck, laughing while Saura flew around chirping happily.

"It's wonderful to have you back," Lady Katherine said. "I've missed you this summer."

"It's great to be back," Juliette told her.

"I have so much to tell you," Lady Katherine said, "Lucinda was sorry she couldn't be here to welcome you home, but I've got her on the com so she could greet you," Katherine said, returning the hug. She tapped her wrist com, and Lucinda's face appeared. "She's working an extra shift at the spaceport in exchange for allowing her the day of the ball off," she explained.

"Hi Sis," Lucinda said. "How was your trip out?"

"Pretty tiring," Juliette admitted. "Most of us slept on the way back. I brought home an unexpected visitor. The Trellyan girl I was telling you about—"

Their voices were drowned out when Sesuna screamed "Eloyoni!" and rushed toward Juliette's companion. Ispone gasped, and then she too rushed forward to envelop the Trellyan girl in weepy hugs and kisses.

"We were afraid you were dead," Sesuna said.

"I never gave up hope," Ispone declared, wiping her eyes. "I always knew you were out there somewhere."

"What happened to you?" Sesuna demanded.

"Ispone, why don't you take them up to your room, so you can have some family privacy to explain things to Eloyoni? I'll have the service bots send you up some Cafka, shall I?" Lady Katherine suggested.

Ispone took her eldest daughter's face between her hands. "Yes, I think that will be good. Thank you, Katherine. Selick, perhaps you'd like to join us?"

Selick cast a questioning look at Lady Katherine and receiving a smiling nod from her, took a deep breath and followed Ispone.

"Who is she?" Juliette asked.

"Lady Ispone is a new Clan member," Katherine told her. "Something which I felt she might want privacy to explain to her elder daughter. You see, when Eloyoni was taken, Ispone was a Fire Priestess on Trellya."

"Oh, wow," Juliette said. "I go away for the summer and the entire family gets turned upside down."

"There are other surprises as well." Lady Katherine gestured the girls forward, "Lucinda discovered that the three of you have younger sisters. This is Rachel, Zahra, Jessie, Meredia, Azalure, Byrony, and Patrice."

Juliette heard her, but the words didn't quite register. She was staring down at herself in miniature. The younger girl's green gaze met hers with a touch of defiance.

"Hello Patrice," Juliette said, stunned. "Mom?"

"It seems Grouter had not only ordered duplicates of you girls, but he also moved his embryonic lab to Brisai. I assume to hide it from VanDoyle. We found it when Rachel escaped."

"Kind of a shock, isn't it?" Lucinda said. "I felt the same way when I met Rachel for the first time."

"I don't know what to say," Juliette said, "except welcome to the clan."

"Thank you. It isn't just us," Zahra put in, "We have brothers as well." Juliette stared, finding herself confronting Violet as she had looked five years ago, but with a lot more assurance than Violet had displayed at that age.

"Come in and have some Cafka and I'll debrief you on what's been happening," Lady Katherine said.

"Well, I've got to go too," Lucinda said. "I've got someone here with a complaint. I'll see you tonight when I get home."

Lucinda discovered her sister asleep on the couch when she came home that evening. An old romantic comedy vid was running on the house comp. Quietly, she went into the kitchen to dial up two cups of Cafka.

At the sight of each other, Agra and Saura both gave out happy cries and began their greeting dance. This involved flying around the house with dizzying speed and a kind of chirping song. Their noise finally woke Juliette, who sat up, rubbing her eyes.

"Cafka?" offered Lucinda holding out a cup of the steaming beverage.

"Thanks," Juliette took the cup and sipped cautiously. "Wow, it's been ages since I had Cafka. We ran out weeks ago."

"We have plenty," Lucinda said. "How was it?"

"Different, exciting, and scary at times."

"I heard about the rock slide and the attack. I was having lunch with Tom and Isiah when his brother arrived."

"What's the brother like?"

"Isaac? You spent practically three months—"

"No, silly, I meant Isiah."

"Okay, I guess. Tom likes him, and I think he did okay on that raid on Brisai, well enough to pass with Dad anyway. But you aren't asking because you're interested in him. Something you want to tell me? About Isaac, maybe?"

Juliette grinned at her and petted Saura who had settled back down in her lap. "Pull up a chair sis, while I tell you a tale."

Homeward Bound

ELOYONI HAD been looking at the new baby and wondering what her own child would look like.

"This is Shalendra, your new sister," Ispone told her eldest daughter once they had arrived in Ispone's rooms.

"Greetings, Shalendra," Eloyoni told her new sister. Unconsciously she touched her stomach. "She will make a fine addition to the Magistra Mother."

"Oh, but she won't be a Priestess," Sesuna exclaimed. "Not unless she wants to. She won't be forced like Mother was."

"What do you mean?" Eloyoni demanded. "The third daughter is always destined to join the Magistra."

This statement was greeted by silence. "Mother?" Eloyoni asked.

Ispone sat down on a loveseat, opening her blouse to allow Shalendra to nurse. She gestured to Selick to come and sit beside her. "Much has happened in the two years you were gone daughter."

Just then, the serv-bot knocked on the door. Sesuna went to admit it, taking the tray of Cafka and finger foods and bringing it to the low table in front of the loveseat.

"Shall I pour Mother?" She asked.

"Thank you my dear." Ispone studied her eldest daughter while Sesuna and Selick poured cups and handed around small plates with tiny sandwiches. Selick settled back with Solare on her lap. The Indri investigated the sandwiches, while the girl petted her to hide her unease with the family situation. Koko pulled on Sesuna's pants leg to be picked up. Obeying the demand, Sesuna pinched off a small piece of sandwich for the kit to nibble on.

"I said there was much you didn't know Eloyoni. Please sit down and join us," Ispone said, waiting until Eloyoni sat down in one of the chairs, watching her mother.

"It is plain much has happened to you while you were away from us; it is so with us as well. I have broken with the Magistra Eloyoni. Sesuna, Shalendra and I are now members of Clan O'Teague. As my daughter, you too can be considered Clan, if you wish it."

Eloyoni looked down into her cup. "Why did you do this Mother?"

"Because it was time," Ispone said flatly. "When you disappeared, the Mothers refused to allow me to use my rightful credits to search for you. Also, the Church was never my free choice. I have decided to take command of my own destiny."

"What does Grandmother say?"

"She passed into the flames the year you disappeared. The house of s'Klam'y no longer exists except for us. I am free at last to do as *I* choose. You are full grown, and I see you carry a young one under your heart. I do not force you to abide by my choices. If you wish to return to Trellya, I will see that you have enough funds and property to support yourself. Do you want to contact your husband's family?"

"No," Eloyoni said curtly, "but I always assumed that if I escaped, I would return to Trellya."

Ispone nodded. "If you do return, you will have to make your own peace with the Magistra. When we left, we did not have their permission to go. Also, your name has been called six times at the Fire Ceremony. You may have been declared Ubah by now."

Eloyoni gasped. "Why would they do that?"

"As a way to force me to give back your dowry," Ispone said calmly.

"I see," Eloyoni said. "May I have time to think about this decision?"

"Of course you may," Ispone responded. She handed Shalendra to Sesuna, who took the now sleeping infant and laid her gently in the crib.

Eloyoni's eyes landed on Selick who was feeding the Indri's bits of sandwich. She frowned over at the girl. "Who are you?"

Selick's chin came up. "I am Selick O'Teague *ni* s'Rudin," she said.

Eloyoni ignored her reply, unconscious of the girl stiffening at being snubbed.

"Is this—Selick related to us as well?" she asked.

"*Lady Selick*," Sesuna corrected her, meeting her sister's eyes with a challenge in her own. Because of Ispone's ambivalence at serving as a Priestess, Sesuna had never felt completely at home in the Temple. It was different now; since joining the Clan, she felt welcome and accepted for the first time, and she had quickly adopted her new family's ideas about rank and judging someone by their birth. She stepped in to protect Selick from what she felt was a snub. "Selick is one of Lady Katherine's new daughters. She is spending time with us so she can learn about the Trellyan part of her heritage. She is *Clan*, like us."

An experienced mother, Ispone recognized a family fight in the making and hastily intervened. "Sesuna, please find that crystal Dame Braydon gave me about the Clan laws and customs. I think Eloyoni should read it before she makes her decision."

"Sure," Sesuna agreed. She removed the crystal from a drawer in the dresser and handed it to her sister.

"We are anxious to learn what happened to you as well daughter," Ispone sat back sipping her Cafka.

Eloyoni began, "As had been agreed, I walked out away from the house. When the shuttle landed..."

Crime & Punishment

I T WAS still two weeks until the Festival started, and ships had begun arriving loaded with tourists and traders as well as natives of Vensoog from the outer Islands eager to sell their wares. Landing traffic at the spaceport was so heavy that there was some danger of mid-air collisions, and SSF was swamped processing visitors.

PRS Central Command had put on two additional officers per shift to help handle the overload: Trace Microft, a quiet, mixed race veteran of the War from Clan Okoro, was assigned to Swing Shift. He was on loan from the Clan for the duration of the Festival. The other new Officer was Suze Kalimari from Clan Ivanov, Suze was going to be a permanent addition, bringing the number of officers per shift up to the required three. Kalimari had requested a transfer out of her other assignment. Her blue eyes contrasted sharply with her bronzed skin. She wore her short, blue-black hair in a buzz cut.

Mira looked them over and nodded. "Welcome to Port Recovery Spaceport," she told them. "This is Officer 2nd grade Lucinda O'Teague. We deal with a lot of visitors to our planet, some of them non-human with different customs. You are both new here, so until you get the hang of things, take your lead from myself or Officer O'Teague when dealing with our Confederation allies. We are an auxiliary precinct; we don't patrol, but patrol officers may bring offenders here or send us citizens who have a complaint. Roll call will be in ten minutes. Get your lockers set up and then report back here."

Mira had barely given her new assignees their desk assignments when the first call came in. It was the warehouse manager, Lester Jones, a middle-aged man with doughy features and a slight pot belly.

"Sargent Forest, I've got a couple of traders out here fighting over a sled. One of them is Lupun, and he looks like he's about to jump the other guy."

Mira nodded at Lucinda. "O'Teague, take Microft with you. Let me know if you need more backup."

"Lupun?" Microft asked. "Does that mean one of them is from Lupus?"

"Yes." Lucinda eyed him. "Ever dealt with a Lupun before?"

"No, we fought alongside a couple of units, but we didn't mix much off duty."

When they arrived, the warehouse manager pointed at the two men facing off in the loading zone. "Korgor and Van Rhyke," he said.

Korgor, the Lupun Trader, had vaguely wolf-like features, yellow eyes and a guttural voice. He snarled, "I optioned this sled. You get your stuff out of it or I'll rip you into pieces!"

"First come, first served," Van Rhyke, the other trader snapped back. He was a big barrel of a man with a red goatee, and obviously not intimidated.

"Alright, that's enough!" Lucinda barked, moving in between the two combatants. Overhead Agra's wings whirled rapidly as she got ready to dive at one of them if she needed to. "Nobody is ripping anybody into pieces." Both men turned, transferring their anger at each other onto her.

"He stole my sled!" Korgor yelled.

"I got here first!" Van Rhyke retorted. "I didn't see your name on it! First come, first served!"

"Shut up! You'll get your turn," Lucinda pointed a finger at van Rhyke.

"Korgor did you make prior arrangements with the sled driver?"

"Yes!" he growled.

She turned to the sled driver who had retreated from the argument, cravenly putting his sled between himself and the two men. "Is that true?"

He glanced nervously from one to the other. "Sort of. I mean my dispatcher told me to report here and pick up a guy to take him out to the Festival booths. I got here and he," he pointed to Van Rhyke, "started putting his stuff in my delivery sled. How was I to know he wasn't who I was supposed to pick up?"

Lucinda turned to Van Rhyke. "Well?"

"The sled was here so I took it. He didn't say he was booked," he said sulkily.

"Okay, you," she pointed at the driver. "Call your dispatcher and get another delivery sled out here pronto. Van Rhyke get your stuff out of this sled. When the next one gets here it's yours."

Korgor snarled at van Rhyke. "I want him arrested. I demand satisfaction. I want—"

Lucinda, who until now had appeared perfectly reasonable to Microft, turned on the Lupun. She seemed to grow about three feet and she made a sound markedly like an animal snarl, and spoke one short phrase in Lupunese. Agra made almost the same noise. Openmouthed, Microft stared at the dactyl who suddenly appeared to be twice her normal size as well.

To Microft's further astonishment, the Lupun trader ducked his head, saying, "I'm sorry. You are right officer. The matter is settled."

"It had better be. Now put your stuff in the sled and get out of here."

By this time another sled had arrived. She gestured to van Rhyke to start loading.

Microft eyed her as they returned to the office. "I see why Sargent Forest said to take a cue from you with off-worlders. You backed him down. I would have sworn he was ready to fight. How did you do that? And what did you say to him?"

"Lupuns are a pack culture. They are ruled by status and their ranking within their pack. Never let them get away with challenging you. If you respond by challenging back, usually it just ends with posturing."

"Always?"

"No. I would have needed to fight him if he hadn't yielded."

"So why did he yield?"

"I displayed Alpha behavior. My guess is he isn't an Alpha, so he knuckled under."

"How could you tell?"

She grinned at him. "You can't always, but chances are the captain wouldn't come down here to set up the trade booth himself, so I figured Korgor was crew. That means he isn't Alpha."

"Oh, I see. How did you and Agra do that thing making you seem larger than you are?"

Lucinda hesitated. She wasn't sure how much to tell him because she wasn't sure how much of the effect was learned and how much a part of her designed genetics. Instead she told him, "To learn to do that, I practiced feeling myself larger and more powerful. It's kind of an internal *push*."

"I see. Did you know she," he pointed at Agra who was flying a little in front of them, "Got bigger too?"

"Really?" Lucinda exclaimed, delighted. "I never knew that! I can't see myself you see. Aren't you a clever girl," she told the Dactyl, who had come back and was preening and doing a little air dance.

"Why is she doing that?" Microft appeared fascinated.

"That's her I'm proud of myself dance," Lucinda explained. "Dactyls do a lot of non-verbal communicating with each other. Agra considers me an honorary Dactyl."

That was just the first call of the day. When she and Microft got back into the office, the complaintents had stacked up. Patrol officers had hauled in three teenagers who had been caught painting graffiti on a sled parked outside a souvenir shop and the sleds irate owner who had caught them in the act. All of them looked a little worse for wear, and it was obvious the sled owner and one of the kids would soon be sporting black eyes. Mira was taking a statement from the owner and Kalimari had the kids.

Parked in one of the six temporary holding cells waiting to be booked were six people who had been involved in a drunken brawl in a nearby cafe. The Officer who had brought them in, was standing by the cell, keeping an eye on them in case the fight started over again. At Lucinda's signal, he opened the cell and motioned for two of the unhappy ex-fighters, a petite blond woman in a torn dress, and a big bruiser with a fat lip, to come out.

"Flip you a coin for who takes who?" Microft offered.

"Who calls the toss?"

He laughed. "I'll let you call it."

"Heads," she said.

"Don't trust him," Mira called out. "I heard about you and that coin Microft."

"Tails it is. I'll take the pretty blond."

"Fine. You," Lucinda pointed at the big bruiser who stared sullenly back at her. "Park it in that chair."

Lucinda was so busy over the next week that she found only spare tidbits of time to continue searching the vid cams for suspicious activity. During an all too brief lull in complaints, she seized the opportunity and called up the vid feed again.

"What are you looking for?" Suze Kalimari asked her.

"Someone dumping the DB on the tarmac, or any kind of suspicious activity around that time," Lucinda explained.

"Who is that talking to the warehouse manager?" Microft who had been listening in, asked.

"That's Talon Delgado," Lucinda exclaimed. "Mira when you get a chance, come look at what Microft spotted.

"Now, isn't that interesting," Mira said. "I think we'll just go and have a talk with him."

"Why don't we have him come here? That way he'll be on our turf," Lucinda suggested.

Mira nodded. "Good idea. In the meantime one of you run a background check on—what's his name?"

"Lester Jones," said Kalimari who had been running through the roster of Spaceport Employees. "Says here, he's married with two kids."

The PRS officers shared the interrogation rooms with both IPP and SSF. When Jones arrived, he was shown into the one with the observation window. Mira let him stew a little. The wait was supposed to make him nervous. Lucinda studied Jones through the window; he looked far too calm and collected to her, and from Agra, who was scanning him, she felt his wariness coupled with a smug feeling of superiority. There were many things she could have concluded from this, but memory brought up a whole different conclusion. Despite his milk-toast appearance, Jones had to be Guild.

"Mira," she said quietly, "if he's Guild he will have some training in resisting interrogation techniques."

"You don't trust him?" Kalimari asked.

Lucinda shrugged, "Agra says he's not afraid and feeling smug."

"You mean she can read him the way a Dragon Talker can?" Microft asked, staring at Agra, who preened and gave a sassy little wiggle.

Her lips twitching, Lucinda nodded. "Yes, Dactyls, like Quirkas can read emotions. It's a part of their survival in the wild."

Mira nodded. "Bring her in with us then. Kalimari, take our DBs DNA next door And ask Twilya to run it through the Free Trade Registry. I'm the bad cop," she informed Lucinda.

When they entered the room, Mira checked to make sure the vid-cam was working. "Interview with Jones, Lester, Warehouse manager at Vensoog Spaceport. Present: D.I.C. Mira Forest, Officer 2ndgrade Lucinda O'Teague, Special Operative Agra, a Dactyl and Lester Jones. Mister Jones, have you been given your rights under Vensoog law?"

"What? My rights? What is this? I thought this was about those two traders who fought over the sleds."

Mira sighed. "I'll repeat the question. Were you informed of your rights under Vensoog law?"

"Yes, I guess so."

"Do you wish to be represented by council during this interview?"

"Ah, no. Why would I need council?"

"Please note: Jones, Lester is declining to be represented by council during this interview."

As pre-arranged, Lucinda started off. "Mr. Jones, I see that you emigrated to Vensoog two years ago from Fenris?"

"Yes, I did."

"May I ask why?"

He looked uncomfortable. "It seemed like a good opportunity. The job openings on Fenris in my area of work were scarce."

"You must be good at your job to rise to warehouse manager so quickly," Lucinda said.

He blushed a little. "Well I don't like to brag. I've been very fortunate."

"I see you were given a waiver allowing you to by-pass the screening program. How did you manage that?" Mira asked.

"Well, I had a friend in the Fenriki emigration service who obtained it for me. Is there a problem with it?" he asked anxiously.

"It's unusual, certainly." Mira stared at him until he shifted uncomfortably in his chair. "We'll get back to that later." She then slapped a vid print showing Jones talking to Captain Delgado down in front of him. "We arrested this man last week because he was a part of a child sex trafficking ring with Guild ties. What were you talking about?"

Jones looked frightened. "It isn't what you think," he said desperately.

"Really? Someone here at the Spaceport had to be helping them. Convince me it wasn't you."

Lucinda discovered watching the interrogation through her link with Agra was disorienting. On the surface, Jones was simulating fear and worry, natural emotions for an innocent man suddenly faced with grilling. But superimposed over that, a canny predator was analyzing Mira's attack and devising a defense.

Jones looked even more frightened. "I can't!" he exclaimed, wringing his hands. "My family—he knows where I live. That devil showed me vids of them and what might happen to them if I didn't agree—"

"Agree to what?" Lucinda inquired. "What did he want you to do?"

He turned hopeful eyes on her. "It didn't hurt anyone. All I had to do was ignore a few things. Please, you have to protect my family!"

"Who threatened your family?"

"Delgado did. And that woman, she was worse. She's evil. She's the one who killed that man—that patrol agent dumped on the tarmac."

"I don't believe I mentioned a dead body. Why did you bring it up?" Mira said softly.

He looked confused and did more hand wringing. "I—I don't know what this about. If it's not about those traders fighting, what do you want?"

"You said there was a woman present during your talk with Captain Delgado. What was her name?"

"I don't remember. She had red hair." Jones hiccupped. "Could I have some water?"

At Mira's nod, Lucinda got up, left the room returning a few minutes later with a bottle of water. She showed it to Jones. "As you can see, the seal isn't broken."

She held her pad over it, and the tabs mechanical voice intoned, "Pure H_2O no minerals, free from other ingredients." This was in case Jones later accused them of drugging him during the interrogation.

He took the bottle and made a big play out of fumbling with the lid, spilling it when he finally got it open.

"Officer Microft is checking on your family Mr. Jones," Lucinda told him gently. "What kind of things did they want you to ignore?"

He swallowed some water and choked, coughing as it went down the wrong way. Lucinda handed him a napkin to wipe his mouth.

He hesitated, then said, "There is a mark on certain shipments. I was supposed to turn off the screening when they came in or went out so there wouldn't be a record of them."

"What does this mark look like?" Mira asked.

"It's an upright red triangle with an inverted yellow one inside it and a blue dot inside that."

"Mr. Jones we have been aware for some time that a smuggling ring has been operating on Vensoog. Our sources say it's been in operation for a couple of years. We need the name of the head operative."

"But that's Delgado," he said.

"No it isn't." Mira rapped out. "This is Delgado's first visit to Vensoog. He couldn't have set up an operation like this. Stop protecting your boss and give me a name, and I'll speak to the Accuser for you."

He flinched back. Through Agra, Lucinda could feel him getting ready to tell a big lie. "Alright, I'm not sure, but I think it's Max Browning, the Duc d'Orleans."

Agra sneezed. Lucinda shook her head. "Now you know that isn't true Lester."

"You can't know that."

Lucinda stroked the Dactyls back. "Agra can, and she can spot a lie by reading your emotions. You've had good training, but you can't fool her."

"That's illegal!" he snapped, and for the first time, some of his real persona showed through. "She doesn't talk. She can't testify in court."

"No, she can't," Mira agreed. "But Officer O'Teague can. Why do you think special mention was made of her for the record? Quirka's and Dactyls can read emotions, and their evidence, as sworn by their handlers is allowable in court under Vensoog law."

The two officers stood up. "By your own admission, you have participated in smuggling goods and services in and out of this port. Lester Jones, you are under arrest for smuggling. As we speak, my officers have obtained warrants to search any cargo still in the warehouse with triangle marks."

Microft entered and put Jones in handcuffs. He would be taken downtown to the Central Port Recovery Security lockup and kept under detention there until his trial.

The next morning before their shift started, Mira called a meeting that included Sipowitz, and Gorsling, to discuss the body dump on the tarmac.

When Twilya had asked permission to attend the meeting, Cohen had reluctantly agreed. "You seem to spend half your time over there anyway," he had told her.

"Have you all had a chance to review the interview with Lester Jones?" Mira asked.

At their nods, she continued, "It's my opinion that Jones is more than he seems. When I pressed him about the identity of his boss, he first tried to name, Talon Delgado from the Samurai and then he claimed it was the Duc d'Orleans. Delgado can't be the head smuggler because the Samurai wasn't on Vensoog two years ago when we think the smuggling went big time. Thanks to our Dactyl Special Operative Agra, we know both of those claims were lies."

Everyone except Lucinda stared at Agra, who flicked her tail and purred at all the attention.

"But—she's not a person," Gorsling protested.

Agra snorted.

"As I told Lester in the interview," Mira reminded him, "Vensoog discovered the usefulness of Quirka's, Dactyls, and tracking dogs in police work when the colony was first established. Their testimony can legally be used in criminal and civil cases if a qualified handler certifies it."

He frowned at Mira. "Is O'Teague certified?"

"Yes, Lucinda is an accredited Special Operative Handler."

Sipowitz glared at him and he shrugged, holding up his hands in surrender. "Don't shoot, I was just checking."

Mira held up a hand for silence. "I'm going to be handing out assignments so we can organize our investigation. Sipowitz, you and Gorsling check out the properties around the spaceport for possible ties to Jones. Kalimari, you'll continue to dig into Jones' finances and coordinate with Sipowitz and Gorsling. If he's Guild, Jones has hidden assets somewhere. Microft, co-ordinate with our colleagues in Space Port Security to check out those triangle shipments. Find out where they came from and where they're going. Twilya, I need you to find out what you can about Delgado's crew from the Free Trade Registry. Since you are Patrol, it shouldn't raise any flags if you look. Lucinda, keep going through those vids-cam feeds. The DB didn't just drop out of nowhere. There has to be a record of when he was dumped."

"What are you going to be doing Sarge?" asked Kalimari.

Mira made a face. "For my sins, I'll be downtown, updating the brass about our progress."

"Or lack of," Microft said under his breath. He could have sworn he heard Agra chuckle.

"What about our regular duties?" Lucinda asked.

Mira grinned evilly at them. "We still have to take care of our regular business, so you're going to investigate in your free time."

Kalimari sighed. "How did I know you were going to say that?"

As Mira had predicted, the influx of visitors from other planets caused clashes with each other and with Vensoog natives.

Lucinda was hoping to break free and meet Tom for lunch when a woman in a badly fitting dress came in. She had been crying and her make-up had smeared.

"How can I help you?" Lucinda, who was the only one free, asked.

"I want to report a crime," the woman announced.

Lucinda nodded. "I'm Officer O'Teague. Please sit here so I can get some information from you. May I ask your name?"

"Glory Mondi," the woman replied. She hesitated and then drew a deep breath. "I want you to arrest an elf for putting a spell on me."

At the next desk, Microft stifled a laugh. He looked up from keying in a report on a lost child who had been found hiding in the luggage compartment of a passenger tram, hastily turning the laugh into a coughing fit.

Lucinda shot him a glare as he rolled his eyes at her. "Yes Ms. Mondi? What kind of spell?"

"He made me fall in love with him, then he stole my credit out of my bag."

"What is his name?"

"Zandro Zylmyar," she said

"Where did you meet him?"

"The Unique Leaf. It's a bar."

"Give me a description of him please."

"He's tall and handsome, with black hair and blue eyes. He sent me a drink and then introduced himself when I thanked him." Lucinda sighed. Almost all the Elven even the halflings had pretty features. "Was his hair long or short?"

"Medium I guess, it came to his collar."

"How was he dressed?"

"A bluey-green shirt and pants. Black boots and belt."

"Okay, I'm going to send you to the Visitor Liaison here in the Spaceport. That office will arrange for some temporary credits and see that you get back to your hotel. In the meantime, we'll have Zylmyar picked up and brought in for you to identify."

After pointing the woman in the right direction, Lucinda reported to Mira and asked if a couple of uniforms could go by the Unique Leaf to pick up Zylmyar. "This sounds like he might have put something in her drink and used a *Push* on her. It was too practiced for this to be his first time. I'm betting that bar is a regular hunting ground for him," she explained. "They can pick up a copy of the security feeds and bring it when they deliver him."

While Mira called the dispatcher, Lucinda and Agra left to meet Tom at Arno's restaurant across the street. She still wasn't sure how it had become a regular thing for them to meet during her lunch break. When she came in, the hostess just waved her back to their regular booth. Without asking, the hostess, whose name was Mari, brought out two plates of the night's special, a Quirka dish of diced vegetables, meat and nuts and a bowl of water for Agra. Having figured out that Agra was a messy eater, Mari also brought out half a dozen extra napkins which she placed by the Dactyls spot on the table.

"You're a little late," Tom said. "Did you catch a case?"

"Yes," she sighed. "Some tourist claims an Elven man put a spell on her then robbed her. I'm having some uniforms pick him up."

"A spell?" he asked with raised eyebrows.

She shrugged. "A lot of humans still have misconceptions about the Elven. He bought her a drink, so he might have put something in it and then used a *Push* on her."

"I didn't know an Elven could do that."

"According to Violet, most of the humanoid races can *Push* if properly trained. If he's high enough on the EMPH scale, a *Push* from him could be mistaken for a spell, especially if whoever he's *Pushing* is helped along with a few illegal drugs."

"Sounds as if you have a handle on it," he remarked.

She shrugged. "Maybe. It's a nice theory, but I still have to prove it. I'm hoping the security vid from the bar will show him actually putting something in her drink. If not, it's her word against his, unless I find he's spent some of the credits she says he took while she was under the influence."

Love Me—Love My Family

W HEN LUCINDA got home that evening, she found Juliette and Saura were sitting up watching another vid.

"Making up for lost time?" Lucinda asked her, yawning.

"Well, I haven't watched a vid in three months," Juliette retorted. "Mom said to tell you she was sending a wake-up call for us. She's planning on breakfast at the manor before we go shopping. I understand the whole gang will be there."

"The gang?" Lucinda repeated.

"Yes, she intends to get new outfits and stuff for all her new daughters. Sesuna's coming as well."

Lucinda was counting on her fingers. "That means we're clothes shopping for eight—no nine, teenage girls?"

Juliette shrugged. "Eloyoni needs new clothes too, but she isn't coming. Ispone is taking her to a healer to check out her pregnancy."

"I thought we had an appointment at Dame Teryl's Closet tomorrow."

"We do. It's right before lunch. So we should have time to get it in before your shift starts."

Lady Katherine had originally planned on eating breakfast at a cafe in town, but discovered most breakfast cafes simply didn't have enough room to accommodate so large a group. It was two weeks before the Festival started and none of the food booths that would be available during it were open yet, and the town was rapidly filling up with tourists so the Port Recovery eating places were doing a booming business.

Lucinda noticed that except for Rachel, who sat close to her and Sesuna who sat on her other side, the girls were quiet, watching Lady Katherine, herself and Juliette for cues as to how they should act.

Juliette pointed at the group with her chin. "How careful they are around us. Remember those days? We were wary too right after Mom adopted us."

"What are they afraid of?" Sesuna asked.

Lucinda shrugged. "Everything. They aren't sure what to expect from Mom and Dad, or what will be expected of them. It's a matter of learning to trust and that takes time."

"You always had your mom," Juliette reminded her. "They have no idea how a mom acts. They'll learn. We did."

"What are the boys doing today?"

"Zack and Gideon organized some kind of game that involves a lot of running and hiding for all the visiting boys and young men," Katherine told them. "It's supposed to keep them occupied and out of the way while the manor staff are setting up for the Festival." She grinned at her daughters, "Tomorrow your father gets to take the boys shopping for festival clothes."

They stopped at a store specializing in teen and young adult clothing, accessories and decor items. The girls were very hesitant about picking out clothing at first. "We never got to choose what we wore before," Rachel told Lucinda.

"The school just issued stuff when ours wore out, or we out grew it," Patrice added.

Lucinda was mentally adding up the cost of all this new clothing for the girls as well as her and Juliette's dresses and it came to a lot of credit.

When she managed to get her mother alone for a few minutes, she told her, "Mom, I think I should pay for my dress for the Ball."

Her mother looked her over. "Worried about money?"

"Well, yes. I mean you just took on fourteen more children and that's got to be a big chunk of credit. I know you and Dad aren't rich, despite what some people think and—" she stopped because Katherine was smiling and shaking her head.

"Oh, honey, that is sweet of you, but I've been getting paid plenty for all those cultural compatibility programs I've been writing for the Confederation planets. Outfitting my new children and buying dresses for my girls won't break the bank. Please let me do this for you." Sooka, Lady Katherine's Quirka and constant companion, chirped in agreement.

Lucinda hugged her mother, not answering in words.

Lady Katherine hadn't asked for a security escort for her shopping trip, thinking the danger was over for the girls since the ground crew from the Silver Samurai were all under arrest. With only herself, Lucinda and Juliette along though it was difficult to keep track of everyone.

Engaged as she was in bonding with her new daughters, Katherine might not have been suspicious but Lucinda was rapidly developing a cop's sixth sense for when she was being watched. She had felt it outside Ispone's old apartment when she and Sesuna had gone there to pick up the birthing tools. She felt it now, reinforced by an uneasy feeling transmitted by Agra. Carefully she scanned the area, locating all the girls. As she watched, Azalure disappeared behind a display of purses that towered over her head. Lucinda nudged Juliette. "Watch everyone for me, I think I saw something that isn't right."

"What did you see?" Juliette demanded, but Lucinda was halfway to the display. Juliette hesitated, but she quickly called out, "Girls, come and look at these blouses and tell me what you think of them."

When Lucinda rounded the display, she realized she was just in time. Two men had grabbed Azalure despite her struggles. One man had a hand over her mouth, and the other had her by the feet.

Drawing her force wand, Lucinda shouted, "PRS Freeze!" and charged them. Agra dived at the one with his hand over Azalure's mouth making him duck away from her talons. Lucinda pressed the extend button on the wand and rotated the power jewel up so it would give a healthy stun to whoever it touched. The wand snapped out to its four-foot length, jabbing the man holding Azalure's feet in the stomach. He keeled over, falling half on the child, and half on a display of breakable vases that crashed to the floor with a clatter of shattering glass.

Azalure managed to drag down the hand covering her mouth so she could get her mouth open far enough to bite down hard.

The would-be kidnapper screamed as the girl's razor-sharp teeth cut the tendons in his hand. He dropped her and wheeled to run, dodging another dive by Agra. As he did so, he smacked into Lady Katherine, who hearing the ruckus, had come running with her wand out. Taking in the situation at a glance, she slapped him alongside his face with her wand. The stunner left a red mark across his cheek. Then she stuck out a foot to trip him when he stumbled away from her and Agra's combined attack.

He landed flat on his back, looking up at the blade end of her extended wand about an inch from his eyes. He gawked at her enraged expression, and lay perfectly still hoping she wouldn't stab him. Overhead, Agra watched him, picking up on Katherine's fierce maternal anger that one of her children had been threatened.

Lucinda finished securing the man she had stunned and took out her com to call in the attempted kidnapping. By this time Juliette and the other girls as well as a few spectators had gathered around.

"What did you want with my daughter?" Lady Katherine asked softly, and both Sooka and Agra hissed.

If he could have retreated from his prone position, the man would have done so. As it was, he flinched from the soft menace in her voice.

"We weren't going to hurt her," he stammered. "We were told she belongs to Delgado. We were just supposed to pick her up and return her for the bounty money. He wouldn't pay if she was damaged."

"Delgado is in jail; you won't be collecting any bounty from him," Lucinda informed him, taking her spare cuffs from her purse. "Roll over, so I can cuff you." When he hesitated, she added, "Or I can just let my mother 'accidentally' slip a little with her wand. You might live over it if the wagon gets here in time to put you in stasis until you can get med treatment."

He decided to cooperate and rolled over on his belly with his hands behind his back.

"*Is* there a bounty out on my daughters?" Katherine demanded.

"Not on the older three," he answered, "but on the young ones, yes. Delgado already shelled out a lot of credits for them. He wants his investment back."

Katherine hissed in anger and the girls drew together protectively.

Lucinda intervened. "Mom, I've got this. I think Azalure could use something to wipe her face. She has blood on her mouth."

To Lucinda's relief, Lady Katherine instantly morphed from a deadly virago to a tender, concerned mother. She took Azalure into a protective embrace, "Saying, oh honey, does it hurt?"

"Look what you've done to my store!" the manager howled, pointing at the broken glass and purses scattered all over. "I demand you leave at once!"

Lady Katherine glared at him. "Look at my daughter's face! How dare you let animals like that in here!"

"Yes, this is supposed to be a safe environment," Juliette chimed in, gathering all the other girls in close to her.

"Bring me a first aid kit at once," Lady Katherine ordered. "And some water, ice, antiseptic, and a soft cloth."

The irate store manager glared at her. "I should sue you for breaking my display," he declared.

"Mother I think we should report him to the Festival Committee. This store obviously caters to rougher elements like those kidnappers! It should be listed as unsafe for families," Juliette said.

The manager looked at her in patent horror. "My store is safe," he protested. "Those thugs must have followed you in here!"

Keeping one eye on the two cuffed men, Lucinda was amused to note that Patrice was watching Katherine and Juliette as if she was taking lessons. The girl blinked in surprise when Juliette winked at her. The other girls were just staring at Katherine in awe and the beginnings of hero worship. None of them had ever experienced an adult who rose so firmly and wholeheartedly to their defense.

By this time, the manager had taken in Juliette and Lady Katherine's fine clothing and decided he might not want to offend a high clan lady. He shut up and sent one of his sales-bots for a first aid kit, and told another to begin gathering the scattered totes.

Fortunately for the kidnappers, two patrol officers showed up and wanted to know what was going on. Lucinda identified herself, and began to explain, hampered by the store manager who was again complaining loudly about his ruined display.

Lady Katherine told Juliette to take the other girls and gather up the things they wanted and request the sales-bot to process the purchases. This successfully distracted the manager from complaining to the two officers and he hurried over to supervise.

"We'd like to ask your daughter what happened, if you don't mind Lady Katherine," the older of the two patrolmen said.

Keeping a protective arm around Azalure, Lady Katherine looked down at her. "Do you feel up to it dear?"

"Okay, I guess."

"Just start from when they grabbed you," Lucinda suggested.

"I saw a purse with really pretty feathers, and I wanted to look at it but it was on the other side of the display rack. When I went around, those two men grabbed me. I couldn't call for help because he," she pointed to the man with the bleeding hand, "put his hand over my mouth. I tried to kick him, and the other one grabbed my feet. Then Lucinda came and hit the second man with her force wand and I pulled the hand of the man who was holding me away far enough to bite him."

"You are pressing charges for kidnapping, Lady Katherine?"

"Yes. I will come in tomorrow to sign the official complaint."

The large order Katherine placed for clothing and other accessories reconciled the manager to the broken glass display (especially when he was told by Juliette to send her a bill for the broken vases). By the time they left the store, he was calling Lady Katherine my dear lady and bowing over her hand. The patrol hauled the two would-be kidnappers away in the drunk wagon. Lucinda stared after them. Today when she started her shift she decided to do a little research on who had visited Talon Delgado in jail. After all, he could only speak to his legal representative so *someone* else must have put out the word about the bounty for him.

Sometimes The Bear Gets You

LUCINDA WAS going through the vid feeds from the Unique Leaf searching for the woman who had made the complaint about the Elven spell, when she spotted Jones on it talking to the two men who had tried to kidnap Azalure. Unfortunately, the bar was too noisy to catch the actual dialog.

She was frowning at it when Kalimari looked over her shoulder. "Hey that's Jones. Who is he talking to?"

"You might want to add this to your stuff to pass along," Lucinda suggested. "Those two men are the ones who tried to kidnap my sister the other day. I wish I knew how to make this thing isolate voices, then I could hear what is being said."

"Here, let me show you," Kalimari offered. "We already have Jones voice in our database from the interview. All you need to do is download the pattern and then set the comp to match it on this vid."

Following her directions, Lucinda was able to isolate the conversation. The vid clearly identified Jones' voice, but his image was fuzzy, as if another image had been superimposed over it.

Jones handed the two men a crystal. "Here are vid stills of the kids. It's worth two hundred credits a head if you can bring any of them undamaged to the address on here before the Festival ends."

"*Gotcha!*" Lucinda said softly.

Calling Mira over to show her the image with the voice recording, she asked, "What is wrong with his image? It's got a kind of halo around it."

"I've seen that kind of distortion before. He's using a holo imager," Mira said.

"So those two aren't going to be able to identify Jones as the man who put out the bounty on the kids?" Lucinda asked, frowning.

Mira shrugged. "They can testify as to the time and place, and we can tie Jones to that with his voice print on this vid. It should hold up in court. Sometimes that's all you can get."

"Oh, by the way, command has decided to transfer Exarch Tainte s'Maris out of the hospital to a holding cell downtown tonight. They're doing it tonight when there are fewer tourists around in case the rest of her team tries a rescue."

Microft looked up from his comp. "Is that likely?"

Everyone looked at Lucinda, who nodded. "Yes. They don't leave family behind if they can help it and the Soturi consider battle comrades family. I wonder..."

"What?" Mira asked.

"It might be possible to do a deal with the Magistra, just to get them off planet and out of our hair."

"Won't that encourage these Soturi to ignore our laws in the future?"

Lucinda shook her head. "It isn't the Hyati-Soturi themselves who are the problem; they do whatever they are ordered to do regardless of what laws they break. The issue is convincing the Magistra that any of their agents on Vensoog have to obey our laws."

As a precaution, Mira had ordered her operatives to patrol the hospital corridors during the time when the Exarch was supposed to be transferred. The hospital had cooperated by locking down the corridors along the route the prisoner would take.

There was one security operative outside the locked ward, and another inside with the prisoner. Command had sent over two additional officers to ride in the transpo with s'Maris. Everyone expected the Hyati-Soturi to try a sneak attack, but that wasn't the Soturi way.

The Hyati came in fast and hard, making quick silent kills of anyone who saw them. They were able to make their way to the locked infirmary before the alarm was given. The outside officer, a cadet on his first assignment, managed to get off one shot before the Soturi rushing him broke his neck. As he fell, he hit the alarm sounding the alert.

Inside the room, the other officer rushed to secure the door. He should have secured his prisoner first. The Exarch had been pretending for days to be in worse shape than she was. Now she threw off the sheet covering her, and thanks to her faster Trellyan reflexes, she was on him before he could turn, choking him into submission. When he dropped to the floor, she got his keys and opened the door, not neglecting to remove his weapon at the same time.

Protector Ferine nodded at her when she appeared in the doorway. "Can you walk?"

"Yes Protector," she replied, despite the sundry small burns from the Photon Equalizer explosion which thanks to her recent activity, were open and oozing blood.

"This way. I'll follow you," the Protector jerked her head toward the corridor leading into the spaceport.

The other two Soturi had been busy clearing a path marking the quickest way out onto the tarmac. The most direct route lay right through the combined PRS offices.

Twilya was the only officer left on the premises when Carrigor Hariko s'Tobin, the first Soturi to reach it entered the shared lobby. Twilya was not high caste like the Hyati-Soturi, (a Carrigor was equal to the rank of a private in the Confederation army.) On Trellya, Twilya's status as a half-blood meant she had no rank at all, but she didn't allow that to deter her. For the first time ever she felt the maxim 'Patrol ranks everyone' applied to her. Without hesitation, she tackled the Carrigor, and they ended up in a hand to hand, root-hog-or-die battle.

Confident of the outcome, Akron Semis s'Maris, the second in command, barely glanced at the roiling scuffle on the floor. As they had planned, he headed out to capture one of the parked shuttles.

Outside on the tarmac he encountered a setback; a joint clan security team with guns drawn was waiting for him. From behind a hastily erected barrier they ordered him to stand down.

Instead of complying, he fired at them, retreating into the lobby.

Twilya, with a bloody lip and a rapidly swelling black eye, was just finishing putting restraints on the Carrigor.

Climbing to her feet, she ordered, "Drop the weapon Akron."

When he started to turn, she fired her pulse pistol, catching him on the hip. His protective clothing kept the pulsar from doing any permanent damage, but the blow from it knocked him backward into the room.

"I said, drop it!" she snarled at him.

"No, you drop it," said the Protector from behind her.

Reacting swiftly, Twilya leaped through the open door. This allowed the outside team to provide cover fire until she could reach safety.

Retreating into the security offices, the Hyati-Soturi quickly secured them from outside attack. They were trapped, but so were the Clans. The Spaceport had been built to withstand an off-planet strike from a planet burner. The Soturi couldn't get out, but the Clans couldn't get in either.

For two days the Spaceport stayed on lockdown. Ships with cargo to sell and passengers eager to participate in the Festival stacked up in orbit around the Planet. Their complaints were caustic and getting more and more pointed.

At the request of Clan Yang, this year's head of Parliament, the Joint Clan Security Council met to discuss the situation at the Spaceport.

"This couldn't have happened at a more inopportune time," Nü-Huang Toshi Ishamara of Clan Yang, scowled at the Joint Clan Security Council. "Vensoog is just now beginning to recover from the economic slump caused by the war and taking in thousands of homeless refugees. A major break with one of our allies over this might give the Confederation an excuse to declare martial law and forbid opening the Festival to off-planet visitors. We need the revenue these visitors bring in."

The Duc d'Orleans, who was serving this year as the head of the Security Council, scowled back at her.

"You have a suggestion, Nü-Huang Toshi?"

She turned to Ispone who had accompanied her to the meeting. "From what Lady Ispone tells me, the Hyati-Soturi can't surrender without permission from a representative of the Magistra. We are in contact with them and they have diverted a ship that is now in orbit above us. As any agreement the Council makes with the Magistra will affect our security, we need your accord before we can move forward."

Shifu Mike Mullins of Clan Yang, and her consort, eyed his wife warily. "And just what is it you want us to agree to?"

She told him.

An hour later, a shuttle bearing Priestess Lomara s'Credence of the faction the Mothers of Water, landed at the Spaceport. She was met by Lady Katherine and Lady Ispone and escorted to where the task force had set up their headquarters.

"You may speak to the Hyati-Soturi from here my Lady," Lieutenant Margrove told her.

"I will speak to them in person, or not at all," the Priestess replied haughtily.

"With all due respect my Lady, we cannot guarantee your safety if you go in there," Mira protested.

"I need no guarantees from you. I assure you I am in no danger from my Soturi," the woman stated. She handed a crystal to the Lieutenant.

"Here is the authorization allowing your government to use an account set up to pay for damages to this facility."

She looked over at Ispone with acute dislike. "I am empowered also to tell you that you and yours are no longer members of the church. You are forbidden to set foot on Trellya."

Ispone drew herself up. "I withdrew from the church as is my right before I left Trellya. Under the law you may not deny me the right to visit my property," she countered.

The woman handed her a crystal. "You may name a deputy to act for you. The terms are set out here."

Ispone took the crystal with a wry smile and pocketed it.

The Priestess turned to Lieutenant Margrove. "Where are my Soturi?"

"Right through there," Jerusha told her, indicating the terminal entrance.

Ten minutes later, the Priestess came out, accompanied by four battered Soturi.

The Protector stopped in front of Lucinda who stood watching with the other officers. "You fight well. I could almost think you were one of us," she said.

Silently, Lucinda held up her fisted hands with the backs to the other woman and willed the tattoo to appear.

Ferine nodded. "It was an honor to fight you, Carrigor O'Teague."

"Thank you," Lucinda told her, "but I hold no rank in the Soturi. My loyalty is to Vensoog."

The Protector acknowledged this with a bob of her head. "None-the-less, you are entitled to claim that rank. I declare it."

Lucinda saluted her in the manner of the Soturi, arms crossed with closed fists. "It was an honor to match spears with you as well Protector."

Two days later when she joined Tom that evening for a meal at Fire & Ice, she found him frowning over his porta-tab.

"What's the matter?" she asked, leaning back as the server-bot put a plate of fried fish and chips in front of her. He set a Quirka special in front of Agra who was more interested in Lucinda's fish and potatoes. Sighing, she told him, "bring her a plate as well. I'll cut up the fish for her."

"I think I've found out how Jones managed to trick the imager in the data base," Tom said.

"Really? How did he do it?"

He turned the tab so she could see it. "Do you see this little bit of code here? Well it's on all of the images."

"Why don't you ask Roderick to take a look at it?" she suggested. "He's an ace code cracker."

He nodded. "I'll run that idea by the Duc. He will have to okay the expense. I hear that Soturi warrior tried to give you a field promotion."

"Yeah," she said. "It's flattering, but of course I told her my loyalty was to Vensoog." She made a face. "I just wish I had a handle on who put a bounty on my family. We caught a vid with Jones talking to the two would-be kidnappers in the bar, but he was using a holo imager so it may be tough to prove it was him."

"I heard about the attack when you took the girls shopping. Any follow up on that?"

She shook her head. "We have to find the head man here. The two we caught were hired in Delgado's name, but he couldn't have put out the bounty. He hasn't been allowed any visitors but his lawyer."

"The crew is probably afraid to come down; isn't there an arrest warrant out for them?"

"No, not on all of them; just Lorian Thayer. We don't have any indicators the others were involved in the murders, and even Thayer is only under suspicion."

"What about Jones' statement? Didn't he claim she threatened his family?"

"Not much good I'm afraid, especially since thanks to this little glutton here," she wiped grease off Agra's muzzle, "we know he lied during the interview."

When she got back from dinner, Lucinda discovered the comp had isolated a section of vid during the time the body had been dumped.

Scanning it, she found a segment immediately before the body appeared. Whoever rolled it off the cargo-bot was careful not to show a face to the cam, but the body shape was female, and that mane of red hair was unmistakable; it had to be Thayer. The cargo was clearly tagged as belonging to the Silver Samurai.

"We've got her!" Lucinda announced.

"Write it up," Mira told her, "and attach a copy of the vid with your report. I'll ask Lt. Margrove to get a warrant issued."

"That's the easy part," Microft said. "Getting the Samurai to allow us to come aboard to arrest her will be the hard part. A ship in space is considered a sovereign nation and they don't have to let us on board."

"If they don't allow it," Mira stated, "we can ask for the ship itself to be banned from Confederation ports. I doubt if they will risk that."

Hot Property

THE PRS team intensified their investigation of Lester Jones despite the many distractions caused by the rush of visitors to Vensoog. As soon as the debris from the fight with the Soturi had been cleared up the Vensoog Spaceport re-opened for the business of processing visitors and vendors.

The comp system worked in the background searching for bank accounts, deeds and leases with Jones' DNA signature while the officers worked cases.

Lucinda and Kalimari handled a complaint from a local cafe owner; two Lupuns had been brought in for starting a fight over a woman. The complaint had been brought by the Cafe Manager, who wanted them to pay the damages. After some negotiation, the pair agreed to pay for the broken tables and chairs in return for her dropping charges against them.

The fighting Lupuns and the Cafe Manager left the offices. As they exited, two taxi-sleds jostling for the best position to pick up fares, crashed into each other in the street out front. Neither driver was hurt, but both ended up covered by the safety foam that sprayed the interiors on impact. The two drivers hopped out of their cabs and proceeded to ineffectively punch each other; the slippery nature of the foam made their blows slide off. The remaining foam oozed out into the street making it slippery as well. The situation wasn't improved by several would-be passengers sliding around trying to load themselves and their luggage into the sleds.

Microft looked out the door at the mess in the street and sighed. "Hey!" he yelled, "A little help out here!"

"And I just cleaned this uniform," Mira lamented, as the team waded into the melee to separate the combatants and eject the passengers from the vehicles.

Sorting out the mess took a considerable amount of time, and it wasn't until everyone had been dealt with that Mira noticed Kalimari's search had results blinking.

Like Lucinda's earlier voice search however, the image connected to the deeds didn't look like Jones.

"Jones must have done something to the program for it to give that false image on all of these," Mira muttered.

"Hand the deeds over to Sipowitz and Gorsling," she told Kalimari. "Then see if you can figure out how the image was changed. If you can't, we'll need to call in a regular programmer."

"Will the budget pay for that?" Microft asked.

Mira shrugged. "It will if they want results. Did you get a trace on those shipments?"

"Most of the triangle consignments appear to have been siphoned off larger shipments of the same types, delivered by innocent businessmen or farmers to several warehouses. I see here that a discrepancy between the original amounts and the larger shipments was reported in the archives by Isiah Jorden, but nothing seems to have been done about it, and the smaller batches just *poof!* off into the ether. I'm attempting to contact this Isiah Jordan, but he hasn't been to work in a couple of days."

"He was roughed up by a couple of thugs for-hire at work and told to mind his own business. After that he was assigned to the Joint Security Council's investigative team," Lucinda told him. "Contact Tom Draycott out of L'Roux. He'll know where to find him."

"Would Draycott be the guy you eat lunch with every day?" inquired Microft with a grin.

Tom brought Isiah to breakfast the next morning.

"Don't tell me," Lucinda said resignedly. "You've both been up all night and you're hungry."

Tom set a data crystal down on the table. "Hey, I think you'll find this was worth it."

Lucinda picked it up before Agra could snatch it. "What is it?"

"Proof Jones is the one who put out the pick-up hit on the kids," Tom said nonchalantly.

"Really? That's wonderful!" Lucinda went to the robo-chef and programmed two of Martha's prize omelets with a side of bacon, orange juice, breadfruit pancakes and Cafka.

"We've also got a line on the two guys who tried to grab me," Isiah told her, his eyes widening at the size of the serving.

Agra landed on the table, sniffing at Tom's plate.

"You just ate you little glutton," Lucinda protested. "Oh alright," she went back to the cabinet and programed a Dactyl sized portion of what Tom and Isiah had been served.

Agra settled in to chowing down.

"Does she eat like that all the time?" Isiah asked.

Lucinda nodded. "Pretty much. I tease about it, but Dactyls use up a lot of energy flying around so I don't really worry about her gaining weight no matter how much she eats."

When she came into work the next afternoon, Lucinda found everyone was excited; Kalimari had discovered Jones's hidden bank accounts and Mira was in the process of getting warrants to search the accounts and the properties attached to them.

Lucinda handed the data to Mira. "I got this from my C.I.," she said. "We can charge Jones with the attempt to kidnap my sister and for putting a bounty out on minors."

When Gorsling and Sipowitz showed up for the morning meeting they had news as well. Sipowitz had found the house where Rachel had been attacked.

"Let me see that address," Kalimari said. She compared it with the updated list of Joneses properties.

"Look, it's here!" she told them.

"Okay," Mira nodded. "I take it you two want to be the ones to handle that search?"

"Absolutely," Gorsling told her.

"Well, that brings up a problem of manpower," Mira said. "We can't close the station while we all run off with search warrants. I've asked SSF to help cover in case the precinct gets swamped with complaints, but one of us is going to have to stay here and cover it."

She took out a packet of well-worn straws and shook them into a solid jar. Holding the jar over her head she had each of them draw a straw.

Lucinda opened her hand and looked at it in disgust. She had drawn the shortest straw. "I guess I get to stay here while you guys have all the fun," she said with a sigh.

"You never know," Kalimari told her. "Maybe someone on the most wanted list will come in here while we're gone and you'll get to make a sensational arrest."

"Oh, sure," Lucinda retorted.

Loose Ends

THOSE SILVER Samurai officers and crew directly involved with the Guild held a stealthy meeting in the wee hours of the morning. The meeting was secret because only Thayer, her husband, and three others were actually Guild members. Talon hadn't wanted an entire crew loyal to the Guild; he preferred to recruit Guild members who personally owed him loyalty.

With Talon in jail on Vensoog, Will Thayer, the Engineer had taken over as acting boss.

"It isn't good," he told the others. "I didn't get an answer from our sources on Vensoog. When I used Talon's private com to attempt to contact Jones, it had been blocked."

"He's written us off," said the Trellyan Trade Master, Kongrove s'Marin in dismay.

"It looks that way," Thayer admitted.

"We need to get Talon back," Lorian said.

"You mean grab him out of a planetary jail? The Patrol will outlaw us," protested the Trade Master.

She shrugged. "So? We won't be the first ship to go dark. We'll just change our name and our registry. The Guild's done it before."

"What about the rest of the crew?" asked Kongrove. "They'll never go along with us on this."

"They might if we can get the captain back," Will Thayer said. "Lorian, myself, Sovlong and Korgen," he pointed to the half-blood elf and human, "will take the shuttle and attempt to rescue the captain. While we are gone, Kongrove and Mislin will lock everyone else in their cabins."

"His hearing is tomorrow morning," Sovlong volunteered. "Hey," he exclaimed when everyone looked at him askance, "It was on the early vid broadcast."

"What else did the news say?"

He shrugged. "Apparently, it is normal practice to move prisoners over to the courthouse in the early morning so they don't draw a crowd."

Thayer frowned. "How early?"

"Around four in the morning, I think."

Lorian smiled. "How nice of the news to give us a plan. We need to be in place in the courthouse by midnight. The guards should be getting bored and sleepy by then."

"That means we need to get the crew locked into their cabins by eleven," Mislin said. "How will we make sure everyone is sleeping?"

Thayer nodded at Kongrove, "You and I will announce a crew meeting to discuss what we are going to do with the Captain gone," he said. "We simply drug the beverages. Everyone should be asleep in fifteen minutes."

"That means using up our profit on all the Payome we got from the temples," he said, making a face.

Everyone glared at him. "Oh, I know," he said, holding up his hands. "Just I don't want to hear any complaints when we have to tighten our belts later."

"Agreed?" Thayer said, and everyone nodded.

As a plan, it was workable, however, the Free Traders discovered their first obstacle was the guards were all awake and alert.

"Now what?" Solvang asked.

"Let me handle this," Lorian Thayer said. She made an adjustment on her belt and she disappeared before their eyes.

"When did you get a light bender?" her husband demanded.

A muffled laugh came out of the wall where she had been standing. If the crew stared really hard they could almost see the edges of her image as she moved in on the guard. When he suddenly stiffened and then collapsed, his companion turned to him in alarm.

"Hey!" he exclaimed. "Joe are you okay?"

A moment later, he too stiffened, collapsing as Lorian's knife bit into his spine and heart.

Finished, she straightened and turned off her light bender, motioning for the crew to join her.

Thayer looked down at the two dead guards with a moue of disgust. "Did you have to kill them?" he asked.

"Yes," she replied. "We don't want them awake when we come back this way with the Captain."

It was unfortunate for Thayer and company that the guard's superior was new and overly conscientious. Nervous about her new command, she ran spot checks every hour on all the guards to ensure they were all awake and alert. Her third screen of the exit doors showed her two dead men.

Cursing, she hit the quiet red alert button and began scanning the corridors for intruders.

When she found them, she quietly set up an ambush for the would-be rescue squad.

When the Samurai crew rounded the corner where they had decided to lie in wait, they found themselves confronted by several armed security officers with weapons drawn. A quick look behind them confirmed there were operatives waiting there as well. Everyone but Lorian raised their hands and surrendered.

She quickly turned her light bender back on, and stepped back into a doorway, waiting until her captured comrades had been marched away before she slipped outside.

Once out of the building, Lorian slithered along the streets headed toward the spaceport. Using the light bender for lengthy periods would deplete its battery, but she had no choice. By the time she reached the strangely deserted Spaceport, the light bender was flickering off and on.

Talon Delgado never knew his loyal crew had attempted a rescue until much later when he returned to his cell after being charged.

Sometimes You Get The Bear

THE NEWS about the failed rescue attempt came over the police com lines just after Mira and the rest of the team went out on their search warrants. Lucinda was just returning to the lobby from the locker room where she had taken Agra to clean lunch off her face and paws, when the dactyl suddenly screamed a warning. Reacting instinctively, Lucinda leapt away from the image the Dactyl had projected.

The handful of shuriken seemed to fly out of nowhere and several of them left bloody scratches when they nicked her face and clothes. She did a fast shoulder roll, coming to her feet gripping her force wand in the center. When the second set of shuriken flew at her, Lucinda already had her wand whirling like a buzz saw. The razor sharp stars bounced away from her spinning staff. The whirling action was a form of French Stick Fighting adapted for the shorter wand. Frantically she tried to locate the source of the attack.

Suddenly, Agra hissed and dived at what appeared to be a moving part of the wall. *Gotcha!* Lucinda thought. The attacker's image flickered as if the thrower was using a damaged light-bender. Light benders were designed to hide still objects, not moving people; if the object moved, the movement would cause the edges to blur. Once she had the focus, Lucinda could track whoever was throwing the stars at her.

The effect quit altogether as Lorian Thayer sprang at her with knives in both hands, striking with quick, sharp cuts. The silent, slashing attack was intended to frighten and disorient the victim. It seldom failed. But it did today. A tide of frustrated anger rose in Thayer. She had been so sure it would be a quick kill; she had many such assassinations to her name but this was the first time she had attacked a trained Soturi warrior whose fighting skills had been honed by a Recon Force Master.

Instead of being frightened and trying to escape, Lucinda jumped at Thayer, countering the knife strikes with the ends of her wand as if they were sword thrusts. Her earlier training against the faster reflexes of the Soturi in the brutal Kali-Targ techniques enabled her to easily counter Thayer's strikes, further infuriating the assassin.

Although Thayer's knife blades nicked the rainbow wood covering of the force wand, they couldn't penetrate it's titanium-steel core. Vensoog Force Wands were more than a staff. When fully extended, a wand was flexible enough to use as a quarterstaff or at half-length, a police truncheon. The Wands had been developed to be used primarily to control the huge water dragons, but in the hands of a skilled fighter they were a weapon of choice for close-in combat at either length.

Hovering over her embattled mistress, Agra watched for an opening to dart in and nip Lucinda's attacker. Although the little Dactyl couldn't do a lot of damage, her quick diving attacks distracted Thayer, allowing Lucinda to put her opponent on the defensive.

Thayer's lips drew back in a snarl as she was forced to back away from Lucinda's counterattack. She was shocked and furious; none of her other victims had been able to fight back this way. In her growing rage, Thayer began to confuse Lucinda with Darla Lister. The bitch wasn't better than she was. The idea made her angry and reckless. One of Lucinda's blows hit Thayer on the knuckles; her left hand numbed, she dropped a knife. The blow hadn't been without cost; Lucinda had acquired several more small cuts and nicks on her arms and wrists that were oozing blood.

Sensing Thayer was losing control, Lucinda rolled the stun control on her wand up to medium and began seriously trying to get in a solid hit behind her opponent's guard. Thayer continued to slash at her with her remaining knife, changing from the short stabs she had been using to wide, sweeping arcs.

Thayer was no mean opponent with a blade, but her fury at not being able to quickly crush Lucinda was rapidly causing bloodlust to overcome her skill as a Knife fighter. Her eyes acquired a feral light and her swings got wilder and more vicious with each swipe. Spittle began to form at the corners of her mouth. Finally she swung wide enough that Lucinda saw her chance. She pushed the wand's extension regulator, and the stunning end of the expanded wand shot forward and caught Lorian full in the belly. She folded like a broken flower stem and collapsed, hitting the floor with a sodden thud.

Panting, Lucinda yanked her restraints out and rolled the unconscious Thayer onto her belly so she could cuff her. Once she had Thayer under control, she collapsed beside her prisoner. Agra fluttered to her crooning encouragement. Lucinda petted her, projecting her pride and gratitude at her pet. Agra wiggled happily and licked her face

"Wow," said the young patrolman from the doorway, lowering the pulse gun he had been aiming at the battle. Lucinda recognized him from her cadet classes. His name was Joseph Hedrick. "I saw you fighting her, but I was afraid I'd get you if I shot at her. Who is that?"

"This little gem is Lorian Thayer, wanted on three planets as a person of interest in multiple murders, two of them right here on Vensoog."

He gestured to the couple with him to come inside, "It's okay folks, it's safe now."

Lucinda heaved herself to her feet. "Be right with you folks. Hedrick give me a hand getting her into the holding cell."

She grabbed Thayer's shoulders, "Get her feet, will you?"

Together they carried Thayer into the cell, propping her against the wall.

Lucinda checked her for hidden weapons, removing more knives, a metal garrote, and more martial arts shuriken stars before she took off the cuffs. As an afterthought, she also removed Thayer's belt and boots before she locked the cell.

She turned to the young patrolman. "What do we have here?"

"Um, this is Mr. and Mrs. Sorris. Mrs. Sorris had her purse snatched so I brought them here to fill out the complaint. How come you're the only one here?"

"Everyone else went out on search warrants. I drew the short straw. Someone had to man the office."

He studied Thayer's somnolent figure through the cell bars. "Not very smart of her to come through here even if there was only one cop on duty."

Lucinda shrugged. "She had to come through here to get to the shuttles on the tarmac. I've met her before. She's got a hair trigger. She lost our last encounter, so she might have thought finding me here alone was a bonus."

"Looks like she lost this one too. Why'd you take her boots and belt?"

She laughed, "Here I'll show you." Holding them by the heels, she smacked the boots together and a blade popped out of one of the toes.

He drew back startled. "Does the belt have stuff like that too?"

"Probably, but I took it because of this little gadget on the buckle. It's a light bender. A fiber optic cord runs around the back, picking up images from the background, and this projects them over her image. Makes her really hard to see. I'm betting that's how she got away when the others were caught trying to rescue Talon Delgado."

"I'm beginning to hate staff meetings—" Twilya announced as she came into the office. "Hey! What in the sweet Void happened to you? You're bleeding!"

Lucinda looked down at her arms and hands. She had left smears of blood on her desk. Now that the adrenaline rush was easing, the cuts were beginning to burn and sting. "Look over there," she gestured to the holding cell.

Her eyes widening, Twilya stared at the woman in holding, before she pulled a first aid kit out from under a cabinet. "Is that Thayer?"

"Yep. Ouch!"

"Sorry," Twilya said, "I know the disinfectant hurts a little. Look at it this way, at least you won't have scarring from these little nicks."

Agra whined in distress. "It's okay sweetie," Lucinda told her, *pushing* reassurance.

"Cohen's going to have a fit," Twilya chuckled as she ran the flesh knitter over Lucinda's forearms and hands, closing the cuts and putting a layer of plasta-flesh over the cuts. "Honestly, I don't know how he hears this stuff before it's officially announced, but Thayer, or rather the attack at the courthouse, was the subject of the staff meeting. The locals caught four others from the Samurai's crew when they tried to free Delgado. He says they left us a mess, and it's up to us to smooth things over with the Free Trade Registry."

Lucinda shrugged. "The news about the failed rescue attempt came over the police coms earlier. Maybe he has access to the police band."

"Maybe," Twilya said, putting down the healing wand. "I think that's all of them."

"Thanks," Lucinda examined her cuts. "Mom is going to be unhappy about me getting all cut up two days before the Introductory Ball," she remarked, handing the kit back to Twilya after wiping up the smeared blood off her desk.

"I don't see what there is to smooth over about us catching crooks, but you can tell me about it after I take a description from these folks. Mrs. Sorris here is a victim of a purse snatcher."

After she had taken the complaint and put out a bulletin with the snatcher's description, she returned to the original subject. "Twilya, why does Cohen think something needs smoothed over with the Free Trade Registry?"

They were alone since Hedrick had gone back out to finish his patrol. "Oh, the Trade Registry is in a snit about us keeping the Samurai in orbit and not returning their shuttle. Said we were impounding it without cause and it was vital to the ship's operation. We had to send it back up to them, remember?"

"Yes, I do and look what they did with it!"

"Well, look on the bright side; we probably couldn't have gotten hold of Thayer unless she came down here."

"Hey, I better com Jeness that we've got her. Now she can arrest her for the dockside murder."

Have We Met Before?

BECAUSE OF the number of girls, Katherine had selected a bedroom with an attached sitting room for her new daughters. She stripped the couch and chairs out of the sitting room and added two more bunk sets to the two in the bedroom. After dropping their makeup kits and shoes in their little sisters' rooms, Lucinda and Juliette made their way into the common room which had been converted to a spa for all the candidates. The spa idea had been created to pamper the new candidates, but all the women were welcome to participate. The men of the clan wisely escaped on a boat tour organized by Gideon and Zack. Katherine usually took advantage of the spa herself, but today she was more interested in introducing this female ritual to her new daughters, whose spartan existence on Brisai hadn't included such amenities. Most of the spa attendants were server bots brought by Nora Soames, who owned a spa in Port Recovery, or bot's belonging to the clan who had been picked for the service.

Nora saw Juliette and Lucinda approaching and immediately signaled a bot to attend them. "Katherine our candidates have arrived. What would you girls like to do first?"

"Hair," Juliette said immediately. "I would love a shampoo and head massage. I had to wash my hair in cold water this summer."

Nora gestured to the bot who took Juliette over to a chair in front of a bowl sink set up. She leaned the girl back in the chair, rested her neck on the rounded edge of the sink and began running warm water over Juliette's long curly hair.

Nora looked Lucinda over carefully. "Good heaven's child what have you done to yourself? Katherine look at these healed cuts!"

"Knife fight," Lucinda said defensively. "Hey, I won, the other woman's in jail."

Katherine sighed and took her daughters face between her hands. "My tomboy," she said resignedly, pressing a kiss to Lucinda's forehead. "Do what you can for the cuts," she told Nora.

Nora sat Lucinda next to Byrony, who had her feet in a vibrating pedicure tub. The girl's wide-eyed deep blue gaze turned to her. "Did you say you were in a knife fight?" She asked, fascinated.

"Yes. I'm a cop," Lucinda explained. "I had to arrest this woman..." Lucinda studied her younger sister. Brown hair, blue eyes. "Byrony, right?"

"Wow. You're good. Most everyone is still having trouble remembering who is who."

"Are you feeling you're getting lost in the crowd?"

The girl shrugged. "A little. I guess I'm pretty ordinary compared to the others. Hey, what is she doing now?" The bot had taken one of her feet out of the tub and began to clean around the toenails.

"Relax. She's going to trim your nails and paint them a pretty color."

"Oh." Byrony watched with interest as Nora came over with a hot towel and wrapped it around Lucinda's face. She leaned her back in the chair and began smoothing a cream down Lucinda's arms.

By the time everyone was done, it was time to dress for the ball. Nora dressed Lucinda's hair up in a sleek knot, applying a smoky eyeshadow that brought out the bright color of her eyes.

For Lucinda, Dame Teryl had come up with a sarong wrap dress in deep red silk. The silk of the dress gave the wraps a soft drape. The skirt flowed out from Lucinda's waist in waves of different shades of red. A matching red collar decorated with tiny opals was slipped over Agra's head.

To finish it off, Katherine took out an ornately carved wooden box. "On the occasion of your first ball, I present my daughter with Moonstones for the bringer of calm, peace and balance," she told Lucinda as she fastened the necklet of iridescent moonstones around her neck. Lucinda hung the tiny drop ear rings and slipped the matching bracelet over her wrist.

Dame Teryl had dressed Juliette in layers of filmy fabric made in a rich green that matched her eyes. The drape of the bodice made it look as if Juliette was as well-endowed as Lucinda in that area, and the skirt floated around her legs, alternately clinging and swaying free.

Katherine picked up another wooden box and opened it. "For my First Daughter on the occasion of her first ball, it is traditional for the next heir to Veiled Isle to wear these." She took out a pendant; a green stone nestling inside a seashell and hung it around Juliette's neck. The ear rings and bracelet matched. For Saura, there was a matching collar in the same setting.

Katherine took a deep breath and stepped back. "You are both so beautiful," she said, wiping her eyes. "C'mon girls, we will follow these two down the stairs. I don't want to miss Zack's face when he sees his daughters."

"You are both lovely," Zack said proudly. "Your mother and I expect you to have a good time, and remember, you don't have to make a choice tonight."

Upon arriving at Caldwalder Castle, Lucinda and Juliette waited with a group of nervous first-time candidates for a Maker to come forward to introduce them to their matches. Male candidates had already been separated and sent through another entrance. In contrast to the girls' colorful dresses, the Makers wore the drab grey and brown robes of their office. As was the correct order of precedence, the Makers collected the First Daughters and took them into the hall first.

Tonight Caldwalder was showing off its heritage. The Great Hall echoed with the sounds of feet on flagstones. Fake torches lit the room, and colorful tapestries picturing ancient hunting scenes draped the walls. In a corner on a raised dais, musicians dressed as 17th century bards played lilting dance tunes on flutes, lyres, small hand drums and tambourines. Pendeuic Dyue Angharad[1] and her consort Penteulu Owen Richards, sat watching the dancers from two raised chairs.

When Lucinda entered the Hall, she saw Juliette talking to a group of other First Daughters and some of the male candidates. She looked around for Tom, but didn't see him. She was disappointed, but not surprised. Generally the Makers liked to group all first time candidates at one ball. Tom was four years past his first List, so he probably wouldn't be here tonight. Smiling politely she danced with all the boys the Maker introduced her to.

It was much later in the evening when she noticed a few of the older candidates started showing up. Obviously they had fulfilled their obligations at the Ball they had been assigned and then began making the rounds of the others. She spotted Silas Crawford and Nels Ridenour and good grief, Gorsling as well. She made a mental note to try to avoid him.

Unfortunately, this proved impossible. He was waiting for her when Isiah returned her to the group around Juliette.

Surrendering to the inevitable, she smiled politely at him. "Hello Detective."

"Please, call me Jim. I'd like to talk to you for a few minutes if you don't mind."

"Sure, why not." Lucinda went over to one of the small tables and sat down, signaling one of the server-bots to bring her some Cafka.

She sipped her Cafka and watched him over the brim of the cup. "You have the floor."

---

1.   http://www.welshgirlsnames.co.uk/angharad/

"How much have you thought about advancing your career?"

"As much as anyone , I guess. Why?"

"Well, it's been my observation that a well-connected marriage can go a long way toward getting promotions."

Great Goddess, she thought, *is he actually going to make me a proposal on that basis?*

It seemed he was. Lucinda spent the rest of Gorsling's offer trying to figure out a way to decline without hurting his feelings. Katherine had told both her girls a marriage proposal should be turned down gently if possible. "No need to make an enemy if you don't have to," she had said.

When he finally ran down, she said, "I'm sorry, but even if I hadn't already made a choice I couldn't consider marrying anyone just to advance my career."

Gorsling stood up abruptly. "I see. You'd rather hook up with a cheap P.I."

Lucinda's scruples about not hurting his feelings disappeared in the blink of an eye.

"You're damn right," she said coldly.

"Nice to know I'm appreciated," Tom's voice came from behind her.

"Tom!" she exclaimed. "How long were you standing there?"

"Long enough to hear what he was up to. He's got his nerve coming to you with a half-assed proposition like that," he said. "Thanks for the vote of confidence by the way." He held out his hand. "Dance?"

The bards were playing a soft dreamy tune as Lucinda stepped into his arms.

"I wasn't sure you would come here tonight," she remarked after a few minutes.

"Why not?" he asked.

Lucinda hesitated, then decided to be honest. "All the time we've known each other, I've never been sure what you think of me," she admitted.

"What do you mean?" he asked.

"Well, I think we are friends and I know I've been useful in your investigations, but that's not the same as being attracted to each other."

He stared down at her in astonishment. "Woman you're crazy; even your dad knew how I felt about you."

"You never said anything," she said defensively.

He snorted. "I told you I don't play around with underage girls. When your dad warned me off, I knew he was right to do it."

"Oh."

"For the record, you've never said how you feel about me either, you know."

"Sometimes I'm not sure myself. You make me so mad—I don't want to inflate your ego, but somewhere along the line I started measuring all the men I met by you. Most of them didn't stand up."

He laughed. "Me too, I knew you were the one I want because I kept coming back, despite knowing I shouldn't. Going to be my girl for real?"

"Yes I want that too," she said softly.

He pulled her into a slow sensual swing around the floor and for the next hour Tom and Lucinda drifted, allowing the music to take them out of themselves. When Tom suggested it was time to say goodnight to their host and hostess, Lucinda agreed.

When they arrived back at the girls' apartment, Lucinda discovered Jayla had thoughtfully had Marta set up a snack tray under a stasis cube. Although she tried not to show it, Lucinda found herself getting more and more tense.

"Lucinda, look at me," Tom finally said.

When her eyes darted up to meet his, he said. "Relax, Nothing has to happen tonight."

She bit her lip. "I know you aren't pressuring me Tom, but—"

"Hey," he said, "if you aren't ready you aren't ready. There's no performance deadline here."

"I feel so silly," she said. "I know there isn't anything like that, I just—"

He stood up, pulling her to her feet. "C'mon, see me out. We can have lunch tomorrow during your shift."

Unmeasured Love

TWO DAYS after the Festival officially ended, Laird Genevieve announced there would be an adoption ceremony to welcome any new clan members in the outdoor pavilion. She had invited all the Clan heads and diplomats from Trellya, Oceana and Y'lelenor as well. The Pavilion was where O'Teague customarily held Clan-wide ceremonies. A buffet under stasis screens was set off to one side, and two rows of round, white covered tables with chairs had been placed around the edge. A special long table for Genevieve, the Clan heads and the diplomats ran along the Pavilion's perimeter across from the wharf.

Adoption ceremonies traditionally allowed new parents to announce the arrival of newly born children, but they also served as a method of introducing recently adopted Clan members. Everyone who intended to make an announcement was gathered next to the flower festooned alcove with a covered table holding boxes of the new clan coms for parents and sponsors to hand out.

Genevieve gave Ispone three bracelet coms. "These are for you and your elder daughters," she said. "The Clan coms permit you to get in touch with each other and also to notify us if for some reason you are separated from the Clan." She touched an engraving on Ispone's bracelet, "Empowering this will let you know if someone attempts to feed you drugs or poison. It will flash red."

"Thank you," Ispone said. She glanced down at Shalendra doubtfully. "What about her?"

Genevieve grinned at her and took out a much smaller bracelet which she slipped over Shalendra's ankle. "This one only has a locator. We tried to put one with everything in it on the babies, but the alarm kept going off when they chewed on it."

Ispone chuckled. "I can see that might be an issue," she admitted.

Katherine and Zack were giving their new sons and daughters instructions on how to use the coms.

"I put a rush order in for these after what almost happened to Azalure before the festival started," Katherine explained. "I couldn't see restricting you from going to your first Festival earlier which is why you were surrounded by guards when you went out in public. But Zack and I wanted you to have some extra protection. These weren't ready until today. Does anyone have any questions?"

Aymer raised a hand. "Does that mean if someone tries to grab us the Clan would come after us?"

"Absolutely," Zack told him. "In fact, I'm going to insist that all of you also carry a force wand, a knife, and a small pistol. I'm trusting you not to use it on each other."

Everyone laughed at this.

When Genevieve signaled for quiet, everyone who wasn't involved in making an announcement, went to sit at the tables provided.

Genevieve stepped forward. "Welcome Clan members and guests. We are honored to have you join us on this occasion." She gestured Ispone forward. "Please welcome Lady Ispone O'Teague *ni* s'Klam'y and her daughters, Eloyoni, Sesuna and Shalendra."

"Welcome," the Clan chorused. The diplomat from Trellya gave them a polite, if chilly smile and nodded acknowledgement.

Katherine and Zack were next. "Good morning all," Katherine said, "It is my privilege to introduce you to our new daughters and sons. Please make welcome, Lady Rachel O'Teague, Lady Patrice O'Teague, Lady Zahra O'Teague," As she introduced those first three, there was an audible gasp from some of the Clan at the resemblance to Zack and Katherine's older daughters. Katherine continued, "Lady Anita O'Teague *ni*Larkin, Lady Azalure O'Teague, Lord Mason O'Teague, Lord Tyson O'Teague, Lady Meredia O'Teague, Lord Aire O'Teague *ni*Philen, Lord Aymar O'Teague *ni*Eliven, Lady Selick O'Teague *ni*s'Rudin," here the Trellyan diplomat, sat up abruptly at the last name. Katherine shot her a look and the woman subsided. "Lady Byrony O'Teague *ni*Selman, Lord Taglen O'Teague *ni*Jorkinski, and Lord Kirt O'Teague *ni*VanHuron."

"Welcome," the Clan spoke in unison again, and the three older girls, Rupert and Roderick all rushed over to hug their new brothers and sisters.

Later, after the ceremonies had concluded, Lady Dulsia, the Syrene diplomat from Oceana, approached Katherine and Lord Zack as they stood watching their new family mingle with the clan.

"Lady Katherine," she said, "I have some questions about two of your new daughters. They appear to be of Syrene descent. I don't remember seeing an adoption request come through."

"That is because there wasn't one," Katherine told her. "You see, the place where we found our new children was an embryonic lab. Some of the records had been destroyed, but enough of them remained for us to discover that Azalure and Meredia, like Zahra, Patrice and Rachel were created there from egg, sperm and tissue samples."

The woman made a moue of distaste. "That is—unnatural. They should be destr—" she stopped when she met the dangerous sparkle in Katherine's eyes.

"I'm glad you thought better of finishing that sentence," Katherine said softly. "I also hope I don't hear any rumors of a cleansing bounty put on my children. Believe me, whoever set it would *deeply* regret it." She stared the Syrene down until the woman dropped her eyes.

"Of course. They are beautiful girls. I wish you joy of them."

"Thank you," Katherine stared after her as she walked away.

"That was certainly interesting," remarked the Trellyan diplomat. "I beg your pardon for listening, but I couldn't help but overhear some of that. Please rest assured that we have no intention of raising a like issue over Selick s'Rudin. I pledge to you that I will expedite the adoption consent from her family on Trellya."

Katherine studied her thoughtfully. "Thank you my Lady Siduri. The records I mentioned earlier show that Selick's relatives on Trellya *sold* her to a man named Grouter, who placed her in that camp. I doubt the s'Rudin family will want that to be known. You might mention that if they prove uncooperative."

"I will keep that in mind." She took a deep breath and went over to Ispone and her family who eyed her warily, relaxing when she congratulated them on joining their new family.

The Elven representative, Elric y'Louise bowed before Katherine and Zack. "My congratulations on enlarging your family, Lord Zack, Lady Katherine."

"Thanks," Zack said. He waited for the man to make the next move.

"You are aware that two of your new sons appear to have Elven blood?"

"Yes," Zack replied, giving him a smile that didn't reach his eyes.

The man hesitated, "They are considered halflings. That doesn't bother you?"

"Not a bit," Zack replied, still watching him.

Elric bowed again, "Very well, then. I will also expedite their adoption requests."

He turned and left. Zack exchanged a look with his wife. "Well, we brushed through that one with our skins intact and we didn't have to kill anybody," he said wryly, and Katherine laughed at him.

"How could we not with you to back me up?"

He threw an arm around her. "We make one Hell of a team," he agreed.

A Dactyls Romance

AFTER THE ceremony, Lucinda and Tom strolled into the fragrant gardens, holding hands and talking about the future.

"It was a beautiful ceremony," Tom told her. "We don't have anything like that at L'Roux. A crier walks around and reads the names of the new clan members. Your parents sure took on quite a houseful."

"They're up to it," she said confidently.

"Jake suggested I might like to move my P.I. office to the storefront below your apartment. Would you mind having it there?"

"Not a bit," she smiled. "It would be a relief to know *you* were down there instead of a stranger. Will you mind if Juliette lives with us part of the time? She won't be there a lot; only when Parliament is in session. The rest of the time she will be out on Veiled Isle."

"Of course I won't mind. Does that mean you agree to marry me?"

She nodded, smiling. "Yes I do."

He eyed her. "Forever And A Day?"

"Forever And A Day," she agreed. He lifted their clasped hands, and kissed hers before pulling her into a long slow kiss.

"Let's make it soon," he said when he finally raised his head.

By this time they had reached the orchards. A flock of wild Dactyls were messily feeding off the ripe fruit of a breadfruit tree.

"Oh look," Lucinda said. "I don't remember ever seeing them here before. I thought we were too far north."

"All the clans have them this year," he said. "The Princesse was having fits this morning over the mess they make."

Agra, who could be quite territorial, suddenly took offense and flew at the wild ones, whistling a challenge. To her shock, it was answered. She was immediately surrounded by a pack of male dactyls fighting with each other in an attempt to mate with her. Furious, she hissed and snapped at them, finally fleeing back to Lucinda crying piteously. All but one of the pack veered off when she neared the humans.

Lucinda received her pet and tried to sooth her. She judged Agra's emotions to be one-part fright, one-part anticipation and two parts sexual excitement. The remaining male dactyl was about Agra's age, with a blue-black sheen to his wings and body. He hovered, watching her gravely. Lucinda tested his emotions and found curiosity and interest. Agra peeked at him over Lucinda's arm.

"Hold out your hand," she told Tom softly. "Let's see if he'll come to you."

Obediently he did as she asked. The male dactyl sniffed his closed fist cautiously before alighting on it. Carefully, Tom moved his fist up to his shoulder, hoping the dactyl would change his perch. Agra chirped encouragement and the Dactyl delicately moved off Tom's fist to his shoulder.

"Are we adopting him?" he asked Lucinda.

"I hope so," she said soberly. "Dactyls mate for life. It would be hard on Agra if he leaves with the others. I wonder what his name is?"

"How did you choose Agra's name?"

"It just came to me. Let's go and sit at the outside tables on the terrace."

Juliette and Saura found them there a few minutes later. To everyone's astonishment, when Saura approached the male dactyl, Agra hissed at her littermate. Saura drew back in shock, ducking her head in submission.

"Who's he?" Juliette asked in surprise.

"Razuel, his name is Razuel," Tom said. "He joined us down by the orchards. "We're hoping he decides to follow Agra home."

"Better not take Saura down there," Lucinda warned her sister. "The males nearly gang raped Agra when we did."

"Good Goddess! I'll be sure to keep her with me," Juliette said. "Did you get everything settled?"

"Yes. We need to talk to Mom and Dad about the joining ceremony, and it's okay about you living in the apartment when you are in town. And Tom is moving his office into the storefront below us."

Moonlight Crusin'

U NBEKNOWN to Lucinda, Juliette dropped in on Tom when he was working in the Archives with Isiah.

"Isiah, can you give us a few minutes?" she asked him.

He looked disappointed but agreed. "Sure."

Tom eyed Lucinda's sister warily. "Am I in trouble?" he asked.

"No," she replied. "At least not yet. I just wanted you to know that I'll be spending the next few days out at Glass Manor, attempting to get to know my new sisters and brothers better. I'll be staying the night out there as well. Lucinda has tomorrow night off. It might be a good time for the pair of you to have a romantic evening."

"And if she isn't ready for a 'romantic evening' yet?"

Juliette shrugged. "Then you will have had a nice meal and a moonlit cruise." She handed him a pair of tickets.

He looked down at them. They were for a dinner and cruise on the paddleboat Sand Dragon and hard to come by. They also included a private room with a four-poster bed.

After a moment, he commed Lucinda. "Got a few minutes?" he asked.

"Yes, what's up?"

"Well, it occurred to me that we've been too busy to go on that date I promised you. If you aren't busy tomorrow night, how would you like to go out to dinner on a moonlit cruise? You can wear that dress you wore to Jayla and Jake's wedding."

"I'd love to."

"I'll pick you up about eight," he said. "If you can locate Agra's friend, bring him too."

Lucinda laughed. "I'll see what I can do."

Agra's friend, whom they had dubbed Razuel stayed around after his flock moved on. Not sure of the protocols with courting Dactyls, Lucinda invited him into the apartment and provided a bigger nest for Agra as well as a separate one for Razuel if he wanted it. However, it wasn't long before he was sharing Agra's nest. He also shared her love of shiny objects and allowed Lucinda to add several jeweled collars to his wardrobe. When he started joining them at work, she registered him as a special operative and got him an official collar for daytime work. She and Agra began patiently to teach him how to behave on the job. He was on probation until he passed the test but Mira allowed him to come to work with them for on the job training. Agra helped, scolding furiously if Razuel made an error.

The night of their date, Tom showed up in a luxury sled with a uniformed bot at the wheel. As requested, Lucinda was wearing the soft rose dress from Jayla's wedding. She added the moonstone necklace Lady Katherine had given her, and for the Dactyls, she added jeweled collars: red and gray for Agra and Black and red for Razuel. Both Dactyls were admiring themselves in the living room mirror when Tom entered.

"Wow," he said, and both Dactyls immediately demanded he appreciate their finery. "Yes, you look wonderful," he told them. When he turned his eyes back to Lucinda, she blushed at the heat in his gaze.

"No wonder Lord Zack warned me off that night," he said. "You are so beautiful—not that you don't look great all the time—" he added, ruining the effect of the compliment.

"I think I'm going to get you a little bronze shovel for your mouth," Lucinda told him grinning. "It was a beautiful compliment. Thank you. Now shut up."

"You're welcome," he said. "I don't know what it is about you, but I seem to always end up with my foot in my mouth around you."

"It must be my innate charm," she retorted.

The Sand Dragon was a luxury cruise ship. Ordinarily, it cruised the channel and made sight-seeing sweeps along the coasts of the two nearest continents. The Northern cruise made stops at Yang's main tourist city, where passengers could shop and enjoy a tour of the snow-capped mountain range. The Southern one stopped at DeMedici's Turbary Island, so the tourists could take advantage of the sunny beaches. The cruise ships had come back to Port Recovery for the Festival and were taking advantage of the locals desire to enjoy a few of their amenities in the short term before they re-started the longer cruises.

When Tom and Lucinda arrived, the hostess looked at the two dactyls fluttering around them and asked, "Are they with you?"

"Yes, they are," Tom replied. "I believe I notified you that there would be four of us when I made the reservation."

She made a note on her porta-tab. "Your table is this way. The bot mistakenly thought you were referring to children. Accommodations will be made."

The dining room glittered with faux candlelight. Lucinda and Tom were given a table close to the outer edge of the diners with a good view of the islands along the channel. As they approached, a server was hastily removing the children's plates and replacing them with smaller bowls used by the Quirka who accompanied their humans.

The bot poured wine into two glasses and then hesitated, looking doubtfully at the small, flat dishes that usually held water for Quirkas.

"Thank you," Tom told him. "The dactyls would prefer a light Cafka. A touch of milk for Agra and just sweetener for Razuel."

"Only about half full," Lucinda cautioned. "They are a little messy. We'll also need extra napkins for them."

The server put the wine bottle down on the serving tray and picked up the Cafka carafe.

Dinner was a colorful meal; a seafood specialty of Vensoog, Red-fish, whose flesh was orange-red when raw and a beautiful crimson when baked, wrapped in bacon strips. Combined with a pink bread-fruit loaf, rolled and fried, and large pods filled with tiny blue onion like bulbs. The dactyls were served essentially the same meal, but the fish and pods were raw.

After dinner, the band which had been playing softly while the diners ate, struck up a lively tune from Old Earth. When Tom offered Lucinda his hand to lead her out onto the floor, the two dactyls took off for a flight around the ship, coming back to keep time with the band while Tom and Lucinda performed a lively fox trot.

Lucinda laughed, remembering the first time she had danced.

"What is so funny?" he asked.

"I was just remembering the first dance I ever went to; it was on Fenris after Mom and Dad adopted us. The governor gave a ball in honor of his titled guests and Mom took us with her. None of us kids had ever danced before, and Rupert and I stepped all over each other. After that I danced once with Dad, who tried to teach me a few steps. When we got to Veiled Isle, Mom brought out a dance-bot to teach us all how to dance."

"Umm, Rupert is?"

"My foster brother. He and his twin Roderick are Dad's nephews by his blood brother Timon. They were the reason he was at the Placement Center. Van Doyle was trying to get us all for his kiddie porn stable, so Mom did some finagling with the Computers to make it look as if us girls were cousins of Dads. They got us out of the center just ahead of Van Doyle who was coming to grab us while Grouter was in the City."

The music slowed into a romantic waltz and Tom spun her around in a long slow turn. "That must have been scary."

"I suppose it was," she admitted, "but we were afraid all the time at the Center. It's funny, but I don't remember ever feeling safe until I came to Vensoog." She shook off the memory. "You dance well too. Where did you learn it?"

He laughed. "Learning to dance was a part of the 'refinement course' the Duc put all of us through when we got here. He made everyone take a course in court manners. Dancing was a part of it. L'Roux is a lot more formal as far as behavior goes than O'Teague."

When they returned to their table, the serve-bot told them dessert had been sent to their cabin. Each of the cabins had a view open to the sea. Privacy screens were set up so it was as if every couple was alone. Lucinda and Tom found their suite included a comfortable couch facing the channel. In front of the couch a low table set with an assortment of light pastries, creams, and their choice of a sweet dessert wine or Cafka. A discreet notice also said that a serving of Payome was available upon request.

When Lucinda showed it to him, Tom wadded it up and aimed it at a trash can. "I think we can do without that," he remarked."

"Oh yeah, I agree," Lucinda said with a shudder. "After being on that task force and seeing what it did to those children..."

Just then the privacy screen burped as Agra and Razuel flew through it. Agra landed on the table and began investigating the treats.

"Mind your manners," Lucinda scolded her pet. She set out two saucers and put an assortment out on each and tapped the plates, while Tom poured some Cafka into the two low flat cups for the dactyls. After stuffing themselves, the two dactyls snuggled into the nest created for them by the staff. Razuel laid his head across Agra's neck and his tail flipped over her, covering her protectively. Lucinda picked up a faint echo of sexual satisfaction from both of them.

Soft music began to pipe through the sound systems on the suites. Tom put an arm around Lucinda and she snuggled into his shoulder, relaxing as his hand caressed her arm. Gradually, she began to feel a slow heat built up in her groin and an ache as her nipples were suddenly sensitive. When he kissed her, she slid her arms around his neck, turning so they were facing each other.

"Are you sure?" he asked, his voice tense with the control he was exercising.

"Yes," she said.

Later, lying skin to skin against him in the soft bed, she felt the same relaxed satisfaction she had sensed from Agra.

"Tom," she asked, as a suspicion struck her, "how did you get the tickets? I thought these things were sold out for weeks after the festivals."

"Juliette got them for me," he said. "Why?"

Lucinda laughed, shaking her head. "Remind me to explain to you about accepting things from my sister sometime."

He lifted his head to frown at her. "Why? Is something going on I should know about?"

"Probably not," she said, and snuggled into his shoulder.

The next morning after Tom dropped her off, she changed into jeans and a tee shirt, and rode her sled out to the Isle.

She was going to have to get a bigger Dactyl seat, she realized. Agra and Razuel together were a tight fit in this one.

She ran Juliette to earth in the common room. Her sister was showing Patrice how to feed a baby dactyl.

"Where did you find it?" she asked.

Patrice looked up at her. "She was sick and her mom abandoned her. I think the other wild dactyls were going to kill her."

"What was wrong with her?"

"She had a partial blockage in her esophagus," Juliette answered. "Karen, our vet tech operated on it so she can swallow food now."

"Good thing you found her," Lucinda told Patrice.

"Yes, wasn't it," Juliette said.

Unwilling to be diverted from her purpose, Lucinda frowned at Juliette. "We need to talk," she told her, and her sister's expression told her she'd been right in her suspicions.

"Did you enjoy the cruise?" asked Juliette blandly, deciding to bluff it out.

"Yes, I did, but I don't know if I want to kiss you or slap you silly. Don't do that again."

"What are you talking about?" asked Patrice.

Several of the girls turned curious eyes to them.

Lucinda eyed them speculatively, debating how much to say in front of them. Juliette saw her quandary and gave her a smug smile.

"Just a little matter of some Payome added to some dessert wine," Lucinda said, deciding they might as well hear it.

"What?" demanded Rachel. "Are you alright?"

"Yes, I'm fine," Lucinda reassured her. "Payome isn't evil, with the correct dose, sexual urges are controllable, and there aren't any nasty after effects like what was done to you girls."

"You just needed to relax," Juliette told her unrepentantly. "Admit it—I was right to help you along a little."

Lucinda made a rude noise. "Tom and I would have muddled along just fine by ourselves. It just would have taken longer."

"I just want you to be happy," Juliette told her.

"Sis I love you anyway, but don't ever do that again, okay?"

"Yes ma'am," Juliette told her.

Lucinda's snort of derision was echoed by Agra. Razuel yawned.

A Historical Note

VENSOOG FOUNDERS considered themselves fortunate because their new planet was a semi-tropical paradise. Two ice-covered regions were found at each of the magnetic poles and five large continents were spread between the northern and southern hemispheres. Islands along the equator were strung between the large continents and provided an ideal base for starting a new colony. It was on these islands that the Clans first settled.

Like all planets though, Vensoog wasn't quite perfect. Every year the planet was subject to swarms of insects that pollinated the entire planet. The double moons in a close orbit created heavy tide surges during the hurricane strength gales that followed the invading bugs. The tempests killed off the hordes of insects, leaving dead bodies to decay and fertilize the land masses. Fortunately the fierce storm season was short, and the planet soon returned to its normal temperate weather patterns.

Vensoog had been blessed with abundant mammalian and avian life, and varieties of edible fish lived in the sea. Very few species of reptiles were discovered, although some of the larger mammals found resembled the legendary dragons and dinosaurs of Old Earth. Among them were several species of enormous herbivores the settlers dubbed Nessies or Water Dragons, and Sandies or Sand Dragons because of their resemblance to the fabled mythical beasts of old earth.

The oceans too had their unique species. Whale sized omnivores who fed on fish and kelp and resembled the fabled water horses of legend ("Ech-Ushkya" or as the "each-uisce" in Ireland) sometimes came close enough to the outer islands to trouble deep sea fishing boats.

The colonists found a fist-sized, empathic, chameleon-like vermin predator they named Quirkas. Because the Quirkas were small, cute, and bonded easily with humans, they were quickly adopted as pets proving adept at hunting vermin and insects that infested dwellings and animal enclosures. Quirkas adopted humans because humans provided a satisfying emotional bond and a readily available source of food.

Unique to Vensoog were mammalian flyers the settlers nick-named Dactyls because they brought to mind the Old Earth Legends of the Pterodactyls. Dactyls were found in three sizes: large enough to prey on the Nessies feeding along the channel. Seldom seen, although images appeared on the first-in scout vids was a petite variety of dactyl about the size of a spaniel. These were rare on the islands, usually they were only seen in the mountain areas on the continents. Flocks of a variety diminutive enough to fit in a human hand when fully grown were the sort most commonly found in human areas. Like Quirka, the very small dactyls were popular as pets, but they were shy and hard to catch. In the wild they competed for food with the avian population along the shores where most of the settlers had located.

Vensoog's temperate climate was hospitable to both man and the cattle, horses, goats and sheep the settlers brought with them to suit their agrarian lifestyle.

A spaceport was developed on an island central to a large chain of islands not too far from the northern continent of Kitingzen. Unfortunately, the settlers had copied other spaceport designs without taking into consideration Vensoog's fierce hurricanes. The high winds generated during the first of these gales toppled the Orbital control tower. The settlers were forced to rebuild, adopting a dome architecture style for the buildings; the new spaceport was renamed Port Recovery and became the capital city of the planet.

The Clans first settled on the eight Islands closest to the spaceport for convenient access to supplies brought in from the Confederated worlds and Free Traders. Each of the Clans was given possession of an Island to use as their main Clan embassy and the entire Clan lived there for the first five years, gradually moving to the Outer Islands which were intended as their Clan territories.

When a large deposit of Azorite was discovered on Kitingzen, they immediately began developing a joint Clan project to mine the crystals for sale to their space traveling visitors. Azorite crystals, used to power spaceship engines, were a valuable resource for the Clans. Income from this venture provided the new colony with funds to enable each Clan to move to the outer islands much sooner than projected. The profits from the mine also made possible many of the non-mechanical solutions to the difficulties facing the Clans.

Much of Vensoog's other continents remained unexplored except for a few adventurers whose journeys were sponsored by the joint Clans. The outbreak of the Karamine War cut these expeditions short.

The Confederation of Planets, of which Vensoog colony was a part, was a loose Amalgamation of human and humanoid worlds tied together by treaties which secured trade routes and provided for mutual protection. All member worlds contributed to the interplanetary organization IPP (Interplanetary Planet Patrol) charged with enforcing mutually agreed on laws and treaties.

The society created by the Vensoog colonists, like a number of other Confederation colonies came out of one of the social experiments designed on Old Earth after the last planetary war. Space colonization had become cheap because of the discovery of an efficient faster than light drive. Many Settlers colonized a planet to carry on their sociological theories undisturbed by conflicting viewpoints. All it took was enough money to register a claim to a planet with the Confederated Worlds and to buy ships and supplies to launch out into space with like-minded colonists.

Vensoog had been settled by a cadre of wealthy women whose leaders had concluded the patriarchal system controlling most of Old Earth was the cause of the majority of the power struggles producing conflict. They theorized that changing how political power was controlled, would in turn change how society reacted to resolving conflict. They also blamed the breakdown of the extended family on a lack of responsibility felt by both men and women for the children they created. To counter-act these influences, they designed a planetary government loosely based on Clan structures copied from Old Earth. Clan rule was entailed in female lines. Inheritance of titles, ruling offices and property would descend through daughters (although not necessarily blood related) instead of sons. Men could hold a lifetime interest in hereditary titles but only in trust for daughters or daughters-in-law if they had no girl children.

Since each of the women came from different ethnic groups and ancestry on Old Earth, they had different ideas of how their own Clan should be run. It was agreed that inside their own jurisdiction, each Clan was free to set up laws to reflect their ancestral traditions, providing those laws adhered to the principles set down by the colony designers.

The Clan based culture provided a stopgap when individuals fell through the cracks of society. The founders reasoned there would be less violence if everyone felt they had a place in the social order, and the loose makeup of a Clan would provide room for individuals who wanted to improve their lot in life or move up the social scale. A factor causing trouble in the past was the power holders on Old Earth (males) wanted to ensure their families kept what had been earned, but they had no real way of guaranteeing it. Without extensive testing there was no way to ensure their own sons inherited since they could not be sure if their progeny belonged to them. A woman would always know to whom she gave birth. Vensoog was not a true matriarchy (men were allowed hold positions of power but could not pass along those positions or property except through their daughters). Allowance was made for those individuals who didn't want to join a Clan; they fell under the authority of the Clan's joint Security Council.

A ruling parliamentary body of representatives from each Clan and Guild was created, with provisions for additional seats as the need occurred. Representatives met three times a year to make major decisions concerning planetary welfare or joint Clan enterprises such as the Azorite mine. This body regulated laws in areas outside of individual Clan control, such as Port Authority, River and Ocean navigation or joint Clan ventures like the Kitingzen mine on a yearly rotating basis. To ensure that no one Clan could dominate the government or planetary resources, a different Clan took responsibility for different areas of governance each year.

To suit planetary needs the Gene Makers Guild genetically enhanced some abilities already found in the domestic animals and plants brought from Old Earth. To insure inbreeding didn't damage the human gene pool, The Makers tracked all Clan members DNA and twice a year during the Harvest and Planting Festivals, suggested breeding partners to encourage biological diversity. When they reached the age of seventeen, all young men and women were issued "Match Lists" of ten or twelve suggested mates who would be a good genetic counterpart. It was for this same reason that the two types of marriages, the Year and a Day (a temporary marriage that could be ended at the end of one year) and the Forever and A Day Handfasting (a permanent life-time committment) were created.

Rigorous psychological testing had been given the original prospective colonists to certify they would be flexible enough to adapt to the new power structure. To help ease the transition, during the voyage the colonists were subjected to sleep training and mental manipulation to accustom them to accept the changes.

The prospective colonists, had also been tested for "special talents" (high aptitudes for psychic gifts). The overt reason was that greater empathy should encourage group consensus. A covert reason was several of the Clan bloodlines had always had the talent to perform what could have been termed "magic" by uninformed persons.

The founders erred on several assumptions. The theory that greater empathy would provide greater group harmony had not turned out as expected. While the Makers breeding program had produced high levels of certain types of psychic ability, it had *not* improved either communication or willingness to heal areas of disagreement. Human women were just as susceptible to jealousy, envy and downright cussedness as were human men.

The Vensoog colony had been settled for nearly three hundred years when The Karamine wars (another star-faring race with whom humans had come into conflict) started up again and wreaked havoc. Some planets were reduced to radioactive ruins, others devastated by Bio-genetic weapons. Economic disaster, starvation and anarchy now stared many planets in the face. After years of sustained warfare, the Confederation finally pieced together a truce of sorts with the Karamine Empire. The truce came about because both sides had used up so much resources they could barely feed their populations and maintain communication within their sphere of influence. In the Confederated Worlds, outlying planets like Vensoog now subsisted on meager alliances with the few Free Traders who had held aloof from the conflict and fought off onslaughts from the Jacks who preyed on them from space.

The Karamine policy was unless the planet was of strategic importance or had usable resources, to destroy a planet opposing them. On planets the Karamines intended to bring into the Empire, biogenetic weapons were used.

Vensoog had large deposits of the valuable mineral Azorite, so instead of trying to destroy it, they attacked with a devastating bio virus aimed at male humans. A study of human societies had convinced the Karamine Legion that in human society the males were the most aggressive, so the Bio-weapon used on Vensoog targeted males. All the men and boys on the planet who didn't die outright from the virus were rendered sterile. The Karamines customarily used conquered native populations as slaves. Since they planned on harvesting ova from conquored females and cloning more women slaves, the virus was engineered not to affect the female reproductive system.

Happily, the virus had a short life span and died off after a few months.

Although no more bio-genetic attacks came once the truce was declared, Vensoog was still in deep trouble. The reserves of viable sperm from the lower mammals brought along for colonization and periodically replenished by the colonists, had been protected in the sealed freezers at the original landing site and the native Vensoog mammals appeared to be immune to it. In the years after making landing all the frozen human eggs and sperm they had brought with them had been used up. With no prospect of new children being born, the colony faced extinction. Unless something could be done to re-introduce new viable human sperm, the colony would die out within three generations. Each of the Clans worked frantically to come up with a solution.

After studying the political and physical mess left by the war, Lady Katherine O'Teague came up with a plan to restore biological diversity among Vensoog's human population. Concluding new male colonists were needed, she decided the best candidates for new male colonists would be found among soldiers returning from the wars.

In theory, the Confederated Worlds military force was composed equally of men and women, but most of those choosing careers as soldiers were still male, and those soldiers whose planets had been destroyed were now homeless. While Vensoog wasn't the only planet to suffer from the bio-bomb virus, thousands of people, those who had been evacuated from their own colony when it was attacked by Karamine ground forces or destroyed needed new homes as well.

The Clans agreed to present proposals to adopt displaced soldiers in their sector of space to Confederation officials. Vensoog would accept the new immigrants providing those who applied could pass the immigration screening and were willing to either take part in a temporary Handfasting agreement with suitable Vensoog woman or provide genetic material. Clan representatives traveled to Fenris, Camelot, and Avalon where many of the returning soldiers were to be decommissioned to find their new Clan members.

After the first wave of new colonists left for Vensoog, the screening program remained went on automatic for potential new immigrants to use. The Confederated Worlds had many more displaced people than could be absorbed by Vensoog and the other undamaged planets. The Clans agreed to accept more relocated refugees providing the Confederated Worlds agreed to use Lady Katherine's screening program. A system of villages under joint Clan jurisdiction was built to handle the enormous numbers of homeless Confederation citizens.

UPDATE

Several years have passed since the Kitingzen Incident, and the O'Teague family children are growing up. Jayla and Jake are married. Drusilla and Lucas have a five-month-old girl named Caroline who promises to be as gifted as her parents. Due to her ill health because of the damage she suffered during the Kitingzen Incident, Reverend Mother Liana Caldwalder retired from the Dragon Talkers, naming Drusilla as her replacement. Lucinda is realizing her dream of becoming a police officer, and she and Juliette are sharing an apartment in Port Recovery City. Juliette is spending the summer with one of the Kitingzen exploration teams this year. Rupert and Roderick have started a company that builds security programs and Rupert is gaining a reputation as a creator of new medicines and cosmetics. The four of them are eagerly looking forward to the next Harvest Festival when they will receive their first Match Lists and become recognized as full adults in Vensoog society. Violet is immersed in the affairs on Talker's Isle, and although she has not formally been named as the First Daughter to the Reverend Mother Drusilla, she serves as Drusilla's right-hand woman.

Gail's Other Books

SPACE COLONY JOURNALS
Options Of Survival
Destiny Rising
Tomorrows Legacy
The Interstellar Jewel Heist
The Designer People
Alien Trails
Secrets Of The Stars (ETA* Fall 2020)
THE PORTAL WORLD TALES
ST. ANTONI SERIES
Warriors of St. Antoni
The Enforcers (ETA* Spring 2020)
MAGI SERIES
Spell Of The Magi
Magi Storm
NON-FICTION
The Complete Modern Artist's Handbook
PAMPHLETS
Introduction To The Internet #1
The Hard Stuff – Handbook #2
Art Show Basics – Handbook #3
Framing on a Budget – Handbook #4
Making Money At Arts & Craft Shows – Handbook #5
*ETA is subject to change

About The Author

Gail Daley is a self-taught artist and writer with a background in business. An omnivorous reader, she was inspired by her son, also a writer, to finish some of the incomplete novels she had begun over the years. She is heavily involved in local art groups and fills her time reading, writing, painting in acrylics, and spending time with her husband of 40 plus years. Currently her family is owned by two cats, a mischievous young cat called Mab (after the fairy queen of air and darkness) and a mellow Gray Princess named Moonstone. In the past, the family shared their home with many dogs, cats and a Guinea Pig, all of whom have passed over the rainbow bridge. A recent major surgery on her stomach and a bout with breast cancer has slowed her down a little, but she continues to write and paint.

A Note From Gail

This book was previously published under the title To Love & Honor as book 5 in the Handfasting Series. It had a few sales, but it wasn't selling as well as the quality of the book merited. After consultation I was told that the title read like a romance book which was off-putting to science fiction readers (the genre for which it was intended).I have re-titled both the books and the series to better fit in the Science Fiction genre.

I often get asked why I write and the answer is simple. I write stories I personally would like to read. Thank you for reading this book. It's always a joy to find readers who like stories that I like.

Reviews are bread and butter to Indie authors like me, so it would be much appreciated if you write a review and share it on the site where this book was purchased.

If you would like to know when my next books are coming out, please follow me on social media sites or sign up to receive E-mail notices:

https://books2read.com/author/gail-daley/subscribe/1/72820/

E-mail lists are never shared with 3rd parties under any circumstances. You will only receive notices about upcoming books.

Excerpt Of Spell Of The Magi

Rebecca was born to the Magi in a land where her abilities mean slavery or death. All her life she has hidden from the Shan's Proctors who control the enslaved Magi. To keep her family safe from them, she will risk anything, tell any lie, even trick an innocent man into a forbidden marriage. She never expected to fall in love with him, but it happened. Now she and Andre must defy the might of the Proctors with nothing but her untried magic and his skill with a blade.

In The Beginning

O N A PLANET called Earth in the Milky Way Galaxy, a way to open a Portal from world to world was discovered in the late 22nd Century. Were these new worlds simply other planets in the known galaxy or did the gateways lead to other dimensions with other physical laws? Or perhaps—both?

Earth itself was constantly beset by strife and wars. The Portals became simply another item to be fought over. It came to pass that a group on the losing side of one of these conflicts captured and held a Portal for a space of half a year, and seeing inevitable defeat in their future, sent their families ahead to another world. As the winning forces flooded the city, the last of the losers fled through the Portal, erasing their destination as they left so they couldn't be hunted down by their enemies.

Travel now to the world of Rulari, the new home of the escaping Terrans. Home also to refugees of a race descended from felines as men were descended from primates. Because of the Ley Lines, both groups arrived approximately in the same areas of Rulari and at roughly the same time. The laws and customs of the two societies were quite different, and although at first both groups were tolerant of these dissimilarities, disputes began to arise between them and gradually a kind of armed hostility became a way of life between the two populations.

Both peoples discovered that not only did time march differently on Rulari, but this new world answered to the rule of will, of heart, of mind and of magic as much as the laws science had governed earth.

Humans are adaptable and began to prize those families with the ingrained talent to use magic. Most Magi had the innate ability to learn magic but affinity for certain types of abilities usually manifested in those with strong magi talents.

In the years since man first came to Rulari, Places Of Power were searched out by both Terrans and Cat Men. The Terrans established new portals enclosed in keeps, and held by seven of the most powerfully gifted families. Formidable wards were created and set in place to ensure the keeps stayed in the control of the families, who were sworn to serve the best interest of the magic users or Magi as they came to be called. One of these ancient keeps was Ironlyn, on the northwestern sea of the country of Askela. It has been held by a family named Mabinogion for nearly two hundred years.

The Witchlings

Kathlea Mabinogion, heritary Draconi to the shire of Ironlyn, was a powerful, unregistered Magi. Her much loved husband Maxton was a great soldier, but he had no talent other than his swordplay. Magi were highly valued in the kingdom of Askela but only if they were a registered member of the Shan's Elite Magi Proctors. Unregistered Magi like Kathlea were hunted by the Magi Proctors and forced to join. When a Magi joined the Proctors, to ensure loyalty only to the Shan and the Proctors, the Proctors insisted all family ties be broken. To breed stronger Magi, the Proctors choose a mate for you. It mattered little to the Proctors if the Magi 'recruited' was already married, in a relationship or if they even liked their assigned partner. Had she been a registered Magi, Kathlea would never have been allowed to marry Maxton who had no Magi Talent. If the Proctors caught her now, they would try to force her to mate with a male Magi they had chosen, and her children would be tested for Magi talents. Any of her Magi gifted children would be separated from her and sent to a special school where they would be brainwashed in loyalty to the Proctors above all else. Maxton would be killed outright.

Not all Magi were in favor of being required to join the Proctors. Years ago, the rebellious unregistered Magi of Askela had formed a network called the Magi Cadre which was organized to enable Magi to escape the nets spread by the Proctors. Travelers like the Maginogion family picked up Magi hiding from the Proctors and aided them to escape to neighboring countries where the Magi Laws were different. For the truly desperate, there was Ironlyn Keep and a Gate

to another world. As the spymaster for the Cadre, Lewys Mabinogion, Kathlea's father, traveled around the kingdom eking out a living
selling spices, potions and medicine to various villages. While Lewys
and his family worked at overseeing the Cadre network, Lerrys Maginogion, a cousin with few Magi abilities held Ironlyn for them.

Magical in itself, for many years Ironlyn had defied attempts by
the Shan and the Magi Proctors to force their way into it. Unable to
break the wards or decipher the spell that created them, the Proctors
continually searched for members of the bloodline in the hope they
would be able use one of the blood to force a way into the Keep and
control the Gate.

Kathlea had born Maxton three children, Rebecca, age ten and
the twins Catrin and Owen, age four, all of whom were showing
signs of nascent Magi talent. There was also hope of a fourth child,
but on that fatal day when the Proctors found them, Kathlea hadn't
yet shared that with her family.

The Proctors found them on Rebecca's tenth birthday,. Her
grandparents had driven their wagon into a nearby village to meet
their contact and pick up a Magi hiding there. Kathlea and Maxton
had stayed behind because it was rumored the Proctors were in the
village, and Lewys Maginogion felt that two Traveler wagons would
draw too much attention.

Rebecca and the twins had been playing under the wagon when
Kathlea suddenly stood up and looked towards the town.

"What is it?" Maxton demanded.

"He's coming!" Kathlea gasped. "I feel him. He knows I'm here."

She turned to Rebecca. "Go! Hide where we found the berries.
Be quiet, and keep the twins quiet also. Don't come out whatever you
see or hear. Promise me!"

"I promise," Rebecca said. She grabbed Catrin and Owen's hands
and ran into the bushes. They barely made it before the Proctor and
his men thundered into camp.

Unknown to Rebecca, her mother cast a shadow spell on the children to keep them from being noticed. While her attention was diverted, the Proctor cast a Binding Spell on her to keep her from using her Rainbow Magic to help her husband as he fought the Proctor's guards. Rebecca could see the bubble of magic over her mother push outward as Kathlea tried to break through it. Hidden in a hollow in the brush with her hands covering the mouths of her brother and sister, she watched in terror as her father fought the guardsmen who came with the Proctor.

Catrin whimpered. "Hush!" Rebecca breathed and the children obediently stilled.

The Proctor had brought ten guards with him. Maxton fought like a demon to reach him, slaying all but four of his guards before an unlucky strike brought him down. Kathlea screamed.

"Shut up woman!" the Proctor yelled. "You are Magi and a strong one. I will let him live if you do not resist."

Sobbing, Kathlea allowed herself to be led away, the bubble binding her to the saddle. The remaining guards loaded up their dead and wounded comrades and followed their master.

Rebecca made the twins wait until the Proctor and his men had disappeared before they came out of hiding. Maxton was unconscious but alive. Anghard, Rebecca's grandmother had just begun to teach the girl healing, but she bathed and bound her father's wounds as well as she could, applying a poultice of crushed bayberry and skunkweed to stop the bleeding.

Lewys and Anghard had been forced to watch as the Proctor led their captive daughter through the village, arriving back at the camp to find Maxton alive but still unconscious.

As soon as he recovered, Maxton left to follow them and rescue his wife. The family packed up and left the area, traveling in a round-about way toward the Capitol city of Khios where the Proctors were headquartered, hoping to be able to help their daughter and her husband.

Lewys learned through his contacts that Kathlea had arrived there and been taken into the inner courts for training, but he could discover nothing more. Almost a year later, news came that Maxton and Kathlea were both dead.

"It is a tale of love and defiance to inspire rebels against the Proctors for generations," the woman, an escaped Magi, brought the news. "He fought his way in to her, and they defied the Chief Magi Proctor himself, but they were trapped on the highest tower of the castle above the ocean cliffs. They kissed each other and jumped into the ocean. It is believed they drowned."

Anghard sobbed. Lewys Maginogion's face was hard.

"Someday, I will kill them," he said. "All who support this cursed system that destroys families."

The woman telling the tale looked frightened. "There is more," she whispered. "It is rumor only, but they say before her husband found her your daughter birthed a babe who was smuggled out of the compound by a servant woman."

"What happened to the child?" Anghard asked, a desperate hope in her voice.

The woman shrugged. "Your daughter had been kind to her and she was well paid to smuggle her out of the nursery. That is all I know. I'm sorry."

"You are sure the babe was a girl?"

The woman hesitated. "That is what I was told, but—"

Anghard pressed her hand. "Thank you."

She turned to her husband. "We can't go back to Ironlyn until we find the child, Lewys."

Fire Magic

Thirteen years passed but the family never forgot their lost daughter or the child she might have born. The night the wasting fever took Rebecca's grandmother, spring was just starting to push up through ground that was frozen hard with winter. She and Catrin had been able to find only a few spring blooms to scatter on Anghard's body as they prepared it for the dawn service.

Rebecca stood under the funeral pyre looking up at the sky, feeling the weight of responsibility on her shoulders now that her grandmother was no longer there to share it. Anghard had fought the wasting sickness, and fought hard, but after months of agonizing illness, she succumbed. "You will be Draconi now," she told Rebecca. Holding her granddaughter's firm young hand in her wasted one. "Take care of your grandfather and your brother and sister. It will be up to you to find our lost one." She had pressed an amulet into Rebecca's hand. "Use this to help you skry for her."

"I'll find her grandmother," she vowed. "Mother is gone, but if her child lives, I'll find her. I promise."

Rebecca's straight, blue-black hair, plaited into a braid as thick as a man's arm, fell to her waist. Clear grey eyes below slanted eyebrows stood out against a porcelain complexion that never took a tan. The resemblance between her and the woman now resting on the funeral pyre had been uncanny.

"It's hopeless; we will never find our baby sister," Catrin said, wiping her eyes. She and Owen were sixteen now, a tall strapping pair, with curly dark hair, their father's green eyes, and sunny smiles. Just now their faces both showed evidence of grief.

Rebecca looked over at Lewys Maginogion's ravaged face. He would miss his beloved Anghard. She reached for her sibling's hands. "He will stay with her tonight, I think. Let's go back to camp."

Dinner that night was a simple stew which they ate in silence. Afterwards, Owen moved the rope corral around the unicorn herd to a fresh location. The herd consisted of twenty mares and half-grown colts. It was their Grandfather's pride and joy. Moving from village to village, Lewys would occasionally sell one of the younger ones if he decided an owner was worthy to own one, but they all knew the herd was destined for the pastures of Ironlyn when they finally took up residence there.

Anghard's funeral pyre would be set afire at dawn, as was the custom. Rebecca and Catrin were finishing up the supper dishes and setting out the bread to rise for breakfast the next morning, when they had unwelcome visitors—several men from the town outside the Trade Station where they camped.

The leader, John Thomas Lazarus was an important man in the nearby village of Joppa. He had expected these Travelers to be awed by his importance, and was displeased when they were not.

"What, no dancing around the fire? I was looking forward to that," he said jovially.

"I'm sorry, Mr. Lazarus," Rebecca replied quietly. "We are not entertaining visitors tonight. This is a camp of sorrow. Our grandmother Anghard passed into the great beyond this afternoon. Please excuse us."

She went back to wiping down the clean plates, ignoring him, hoping he would take the hint and go away.

Instead, he threw some coins down on the ground. "Here, I'll pay for my entertainment."

She made no move to pick up the coins. "No, Sir."

Lazarus frowned, but he hesitated. "Maybe I should ask the old man. Where is he?"

"Grandfather is sitting vigil with Grandmother," Owen, who had just returned to the camp, replied.

Lazarus looked at him in incredulity. "You mean someone really did die?"

The three just looked at him in silence.

"I see. Alright, I'll be back tomorrow then." He turned and left.

Owen spat on the ground at his back.

"Make sure he really leaves," Rebecca said. "I intend to skry for our lost sister tonight, and I don't want a witness."

"He and the others have left the Trade Station Circle and headed back into town," Owen reported. "Becca, are you sure this is a good idea? Grandmother always did it before."

Rebecca pulled out the bronze stone that had been Anghard's last gift to her. "Yes. I feel her spirit strongly tonight. She will help me before she passes on. I know it."

Catrin unrolled the ancient map of the kingdom, stretching it on the wooden folding worktable that served a variety of uses. She held down the map corners with four flat stones.

Rebecca pulled the necklace over her head and held the stone in one hand. She cut a small prick in her finger and rubbed it over the stone. Holding the stone over the map, she rubbed the blood on its surface.

"Bone of my bone, blood of my blood, flesh of my flesh, seek now she who is lost."

Catrin picked up the knife and did the same. Handing the knife to Owen, she too rubbed the stone and map with a bloody fingertip, and repeated the chant.

After a second's hesitation, he repeated the actions and joined in the chant.

At first, nothing happened, but finally, the stone began to swing gently. There was a surge of power and then the stone pulled strongly toward the west, finally coming to rest on the symbol for the village of Buttersea.

All three felt the soft caress as Anghard left them for the final time.

"What have you done?" Lewys demanded.

Catrin looked up at him with tears running down her face. "It was grandmamma. I felt her," she sobbed.

"We all felt her," Rebecca said coolly. "Look, we have a destination."

Lewys stared down at the map with the stone resting on it. "Yes," he sighed. "We will be going west in the morning. I heard from Cousin Lerrys. He needs to leave Ironlyn. The local Proctor is getting suspicious because so many Magi have disappeared in the area surrounding Ironlyn. We will go home. That village is on the way. If your sister is there, we will find her."

Rebecca nodded. "We will be ready."

"I need to go into Joppa tomorrow and pick up the supplies I ordered. You three will stay here and pack up so we can leave when I return," Lewys instructed.

At dawn, Lewys came to wake them. They stood quietly, while he lit the pyre, watching in silence as Anghard's earthly remains were consumed.

Breakfast was a subdued meal. Afterwards, Lewys put a pack saddle on one of the mares, saddled his stallion, Sunrise and left for Joppa, the village outside the Trade Station. His grandchildren began packing the two wagons for the journey. It was a complicated process. The limited space meant that everything had to be stowed in exactly the right place or it wouldn't all fit.

Packing took longer than it should have because Owen kept stuffing things in higgledy-piggledy. It was obvious he was in a hurry. After she had unloaded and re-packed the things he had already packed several times, Rebecca turned to him in exasperation. "What is wrong with you? This will take forever if you aren't more careful. Why are you in such a hurry?"

Catrin laughed. "He wants to get done so he can hurry over and say goodbye to Fiona," she said with a knowing look.

"The Station Master's daughter?" Rebecca inquired.

Owen nodded.

"Okay, take off then," his sister said. "The way you're working, we'll get on better without you. Scram!"

Her little brother kissed her cheek and loped off toward the Trade Station.

"Grandpa told us all to stay here," Catrin remarked.

"I know," Rebecca replied, "but he's only young once."

Catrin laughed and began repacking the pots and pans Owen had made a mess of.

"Leave a space for what Grandpa is bringing back," Rebecca reminded her.

"What is it, do you know?" Catrin asked.

"Not a clue," her sister replied. "He was very mysterious about it."

"Well, we've finished," Catrin said, a few minutes later. "I suppose we can harness the unicorns. Whose turn is it today?"

Lewys' prize unicorn herd were mostly draft animals and to keep from overusing any of them, the family rotated the ones used to pull the wagons.

"Let's rotate the teams," Rebecca suggested. She went to the rope corral and called four mares to her. She was about to lead them over to the front of the first wagon when they again had an unwelcome visitor; Lazarus was back.

"Not leaving already are you?" he asked Catrin, looking the girl up and down in a way that made her flush with embarrassment.

"Yes, we are," Rebecca answered him. She deliberately led the four large unicorns between him and Catrin, forcing him to move back out of the way.

"Really?" he sneered. "Leaving without allowing me to sample your wares? I don't think so."

Rebecca's eyes narrowed. She understood exactly what type of 'wares' he referred to, but pretended she didn't.

"I'm afraid we've already packed away our herbs and medicines, Mr. Lazarus," she said.

"I'm not talking about any piddly spices girl and you know it," he said.

"Catrin, get in the wagon and lock the door," Rebecca told her sister.

Catrin hesitated, but obeyed her.

"I'm sorry, Mr. Lazarus," Rebecca continued, "but we aren't receiving visitors, and my grandfather and brother will be back soon. I need to get our unicorns harnessed. Please excuse me."

She lined up the unicorns and was preparing to throw the first harness over one's back when Lazarus grabbed her.

Rebecca fought him, but he was stronger than she. When she landed a lucky kick on his knee, he slapped her hard across the face. The dizzying blow stunned her long enough for Lazarus to rip her blouse open. He yanked her to him and mashed his mouth down on hers.

When she tried to turn her head away, he grabbed a handful of her hair and forced her face back to his. With her arms pinned against his body, she was unable to move. Finally, she managed to free one of her arms and stabbed at his eyes with her fingers.

Lazarus hit her again, this time with his fist. She stumbled and fell to her knees, dizzy. He knocked her the rest of the way to the ground, following it up by falling on her body. He tore her blouse the rest of the way off, biting at her bared breast. The pain brought her awake, and she clawed at his face and head.

When she felt him fumbling at the buttons on her pants, she knew she wasn't going to be able to stop him unless she used her Magi talents. Rebecca was a fire Magi; fear and anger ignited her Magic. A fireball burst in his face, causing his greasy hair to catch fire. Lazarus screamed and drew back, slapping at his burning hair.

Suddenly, he was knocked off Rebecca by the solid *twack!* of a camp shovel wielded by Catrin, who had disobeyed her sister and come to help. He fell to the side, unconscious, with his hair still smoldering.

When Lewys and Owen arrived a few minutes later, they found Rebecca leaning on her sister's shoulder while Catrin applied one poultice to her swollen face and another to the vicious bite mark on her breast.

Lewys looked down at Lazarus in silence. He had checked the man for life signs and was disappointed to find him still alive. "You should have made sure he was dead," he informed his granddaughters.

"We can still do that," Rebecca said, half hysterically.

"No, child we can't. It would be murder. Owen, go and get Trade Master Jordan."

When Catrin started to take Rebecca inside the wagon, Lewys stopped her. "Better he sees her just like she is, so he knows this was justified," Lewys said.

The Trade Master arrived in Owen's wake, puffing. He was a round man, no longer made for running.

"Oh, no, Oh, no," he kept repeating, wringing his hands. "This is bad."

"It was self-defense," Lewys reminded him. "Look at my grand-daughter. Since when is it bad to stop a man from raping her?"

"Since the man is John Thomas Lazarus!" Jordan snapped. "You don't live here. He is the most powerful man in this county. He owns half the farms around here and at least a third owe him money. He pretty much does as he pleases."

"Including rape?" demanded Lewys.

"I've heard rumors," Jordan said. "Well, the first thing is to get you out of here. You boy," he pointed at Owen. "Get those unicorns harnessed. I'm going to the village to round up a few men to help me collect Lazarus and take him back into town to a healer. You need to be on the road by the time I return from town. I can give you about an hour. Who knows? Maybe he'll die in the meantime and solve both our problems."

While Lewys and Owen harnessed the unicorns to the wagons, Rebecca threw off her torn blouse and put on a loose comfortable shirt. She mounted the wagon box and took her place to drive.

"Are you able to do this, girl?" her grandfather looked up at her from the back of his golden unicorn.

She set her hat firmly on her head and nodded. "Yes, let's just go away from here."

They camped that night by a small creek deep in the black leaf forest, Lewys having decided that it would be wiser to avoid the Trade Stations until they were a long way from Joppa. Spring had brought out a few fresh grasses in the glade next to the stream for the animals to feed on.

Rebecca woke several times in the night, shaking with terror. After the third time, Catrin, whose skill lay in healing prepared a sleeping draught for her. Gradually the night terrors eased. To avoid thinking about it during the day, she kept herself as busy as possible.

The morning after they left Joppa Trade Station, Lewys ordered the sides of the wagons whitewashed, so they would appear a different color. Catrin was told to prepare a concoction he said would dye the unicorn's coats a different color. It turned Sunrise and the mares' golden coats to a dull brown.

To make Owen appear older, he brought out a fake beard for him to put on each morning, and told him to stop shaving. He would do the same.

It was while they were dyeing the unicorns that Rebecca found the three hungry kittens near the body of their mother. They were only a few weeks old, and hadn't yet grown the white manes they would have as adults. Gathering up the kits in her arms, she brought them back to camp. Milking one of the nursing unicorns, she mixed the rich milk into a feed for them.

For several weeks, the family continued to travel north and west avoiding any villages and Trade Stations. Spring was in full bloom when they camped in a clearing outside the village of Duranga. Duranga had no proper Trade Station, but the town had designated the clearing as common ground where Travelers or Trade Caravans could stop over.

A Spell Is Cast

HARRY SIMS, the proprietor of the Glass Slipper Tavern, was an unhappy man on this fine spring evening. He should have been happy. The Glass Slipper was full. The Spring Jamborees for local stock collection and sale had just finished, and all the holdings, small and large were in town and spending coin freely.

The chief cause of his unhappiness was not the rowdiness of the crowd; he was long accustomed to that. No, the cause of his worry was the five-man dice game going on in the corner. Harry knew four of the five players well. Leej Jonsyn, the rug merchant, was losing and was going to be in trouble with his wife. Ruddy Tyer, a long, skinny kid from Gryphon's Nest, was still reasonably sober but he would lose his Jamboree bonus before the end of the night. Charger French, a squatty rider from back in the badlands with, it was said—but *not* where he could hear it—a reputation for shady deals. The fourth player was Jajson Buttersnake the son of old 'Rock' Buttersnake, the biggest cattle breeder around. Jajson figured he was top dog in the town of Drycreek because no one dared challenge the son of old Rock. Rock ran a tough, salty crew of drovers. They didn't much like the boss's son, but they would take his side in a fight.

It was the fifth dice thrower who worried Harry. Harry had seen him ride into town earlier that day on the highbred, dapple war unicorn presently taking up space at Harry's hitching rail. The stranger wasn't a big man; he stood around five-eight with a short, neatly trimmed black beard and cold green eyes. To Harry, who as a young man had seen quite of few of his kind, the stranger had 'Merc' written all over him. His clothes were of too good quality and too clean, his thigh-high boots too new and shiny, and the saddle on that fancy unicorn stud was too pricey for a coin-a-day drover. His needle-gun was tied low on his leg in a well-worn holster, and unless Harry was mistaken, in addition to the knife on his belt, he had a blade down his back, one in his boot, and a second gun hidden in his other boot.

Absently, Harry polished a glass while he tried to place the man. He didn't look that familiar, but the blood feud over to the south between the RedBird and Smoker clans had just finished. Before he died, the Smoker Chief Hutchins had claimed Rupert RedBird was hiring paid Mercs, and the stranger had ridden in from the south.

The practice of hiring fighters from the Merc Guild in disputes wasn't against the law, but it was disapproved of by Shahen Tarragon. Since the Merc Guild was extremely powerful and used by many to settle disputes, his disapproval didn't mean much. The Guild was composed of hundreds of small and large bands of independent fighters and was reputed to have ties with the Wild Magi. The Mercs were completely independent of any government, and the Guild's influence stretched through all seven of the human kingdoms. Siding with the Shahen against the Guild might mean you couldn't hire their fighters in your next conflict. Few landholders wanted to chance angering the Guild by doing so. Rumor had it the Shahen was also trying to consolidate more power to the crown by discouraging the larger holders from keeping their own private armies. The Shahen wasn't having much luck with that either.

Because of his father's mental illness, the Shahen had been named Regent and virtually ruled Askela in his father's stead. Being aware that attempting to force the nobles to disband their large standing armies using his Magi Proctors might cause a rebellion against his already uneasy reign, Shahen Rupert didn't take any overt steps to accomplish his goal. It was common knowledge the neighboring Kingdom of Jacite would attack immediately if a war broke out between the Shahen and his nobles. Despite the Proctors' Magi talents, they were outnumbered by the Mercs who had the assistance of the Wild Magi. The Wild Magi were powerful, some said each of them was worth more in a fight than all the Kings Proctors combined. If the Shan tried to force them to disband their armies, the landowners would the Merc Guild for help who would in turn call upon the Wild Mages to defeat the Proctors.

Harry swore softly to himself. If he was correct about the identity of the fifth dice player, it meant he belonged to a troop he could call on if there was trouble. He was alone right now, but that didn't mean he didn't have allies nearby.

Harry was sure trouble was brewing because Jajson Buttersnake was drunk. When he was sober, he was a poor player and an even worse loser. Because he ran with the Buttersnake mob, he was usually safe when he had a tantrum; no one in his right mind wanted to start a fighting ruckus with Old Rock's crew.

Harry had a bad feeling the fifth dice player wouldn't give a damn how tough Old Rock Buttersnake's crew was. There was just something in that dark face that said, 'I don't care'. The fight would probably cause a lot of damage before things got settled. And it was going to happen in his place too, he thought bitterly.

Suddenly Buttersnake stood up, scattering dice and coins. "I want a new set of dice!" he cried. "You shouldn't have won that throw!"

The stranger came up out of his chair in one swift, clean movement. He slapped Jajson across the mouth, knocking him into the crowded bar.

The room exploded away from young Buttersnake. Leej Jonsyn, the rug merchant, dived away from the table so fast he knocked over his chair.

Jajson Buttersnake staggered to his feet, a trickle of blood dribbling from the corner of his mouth. He was white with fury. "You cheated!" he shrieked, pawing for his gun. He fumbled and almost dropped it in his rage.

The stranger waited until Buttersnake had his needlegun coming level before he drew and fired. His gun made a loud snapping noise as the puff of compressed air sent a fatal needle right down Buttersnake's throat.

In that instant, Harry recognized the fighter. Hammer Smith was the handle he went by, but Harry had come from the coast, and he knew Hammer Smith's real name was Andre Benoit. Benoit was a free-lance Merc. He joined the Mercs at the tender age of sixteen in the coastal area at the south end of Askela. He typically took on jobs that didn't require the services of an entire troop, but he held the Merc rank of a lieutenant. Hammer Smith was reputed to be in his twenties, but he was already known as a dangerous man. It was said that he never drew a weapon unless the man was armed and facing him but if you pushed him, you died. Jajson Buttersnake died.

In the stillness after the weapon fire, Hammer Smith calmly reloaded his weapon, scooped up his coins from the table and quietly walked through the swinging doors. Whispers started in his wake.

"Shot him in the mouth," someone said.

"Old Rock isn't going to like this," said another man.

A third voice spoke up, "He won't care. That's a hard man."

Hammer Smith mounted the dapple unicorn and set off at a brisk trot.

"So much for a warm bed for me and a soft stall for you, Blackfeather," he said. "Unless, I'm mistaken we're going to have a bunch of irate drovers on our tail soon. Why did I sit down at that game, anyway?"

Blackfeather's stride increased to a smooth, ground-eating lope. The double moons were full, making the road as clear as day, but Hammer Smith knew he was going to have to leave it soon. He started looking for a good place to leave the trail. Behind him, he could hear angry shouts and then the snap of needle gunfire.

"Okay, boy," he spoke softly to the unicorn, who cocked an attentive black ear, "let's ride some lightning."

Blackfeather was fast. Hammer Smith had traded him off a Cat Man who had used him for racing. The trouble was he had beaten every unicorn in the area so often that no one would race against him anymore, and the Cat Man was broke. Hammer Smith had traded him a half-broke unicorn with the disposition of a poison beetle crossed with a snapdragon, an extra needle rifle and twenty coins in eating money.

He knew if he could get a start on the impromptu mob forming behind him, he could make it across the line into Cat Man Territory. Not the safest place in the world to be, but safer than here, as it was unlikely any posse would follow him there. The Shahen had given orders that entering Cat Man territory was forbidden. No one wanted to re-start the raiding again, and the Cats would undoubtedly see any group of armed men as breaking the treaty. Single riders entered at their own risk, and with a little luck, might be ignored.

Suddenly ahead of him came the pound of running hooves and a wild screeching yell. Perhaps a mob coming in late off a Jamboree? If so, it suited Hammer Smith's needs just fine.

He checked the unicorn and faded off to the side, stopping under a kaleidoscope tree about twenty feet away from the road. The moon flecked through the shinny, semi-transparent leaves, causing light and dark shadows that blended with Blackfeather's coat, making the unicorn practically invisible.

A more cautious man would have taken the opportunity to scuttle out of there quick. But Hammer Smith was not a cautious man. Grinning, he watched as the mob from town ran full tilt into the celebrating drovers.

Chuckling, he started Blackfeather around the tree and to the north at an easy lope, heading into a forest of more kaleidoscope trees. In the melee behind him, he heard the snap of air guns as some fool started shooting; he knew everybody soon would be doing the same.

Karma has a way of catching up with a man. He paid a price for the inattention caused by his unholy amusement. In the darkness, he never saw the tree branch coming that dealt his head a smashing blow; stunned, he blacked out. Only his instinctive riding ability and Blackfeather's superb gait kept him from falling off. Several times, Blackfeather shifted stride and course to ensure his rider stayed in the saddle. Puzzled at being given no other signals, Blackfeather continued to travel west, taking the easiest route.

The sun was just coming up when Hammer Smith awoke. Blackfeather had slowed to a walk. Muzzily, Hammer Smith peered around. His head hurt and he was having trouble focusing his eyes. Blackfeather mounted the top of a small rise and started down toward a creek gurgling below.

Hammer Smith blinked harder to focus his eyes because he was sure he was seeing things. The loveliest girl he had ever seen knelt by the water washing her face. Straight black hair fell in a curtain to the ground around her, some of the strands floating in the water.

Blackfeather stopped at the edge of the creek and lowered his head to drink. The girl lifted her head to stare back at Hammer Smith out of the clearest gray eyes he'd ever seen. She stood, pulling her hair back over her shoulders. Her crimson night robe clung to the swell of her breasts and hips, making a bright splash of red against the green plants growing on the bank of the stream.

At that moment, Hammer Smith was beyond appreciating nature's decorating schemes. The whole world felt unreal. There was no one in it but him and the girl, and never would be. He nudged Blackfeather across the stream and stopped beside her.

She looked up at him with no sign of fear. He stared down at her. It seemed as if her eyes grew enormous and he was diving into a huge pool of gray water. This time, he did fall off his unicorn.

Rebecca tried to break his fall, but since he outweighed her, she ended up on the ground with him on top. Awkwardly, she sat up, wriggling out from under his weight. His head lolled back against her breast.

"Gosh!" exclaimed her sixteen-year-old brother Owen, "where did he come from?"

"Over the hill," Rebecca said absently, looking at the dark face. He wasn't bad looking; of course, you couldn't tell much with that beard...

"What's the matter with him?" demanded Owen's twin, Catrin. Like Rebecca, she was still in her nightclothes.

Rebecca had found the caked blood matted in his hair.

"He's been hurt," she said. "One of you go and get Grandpa."

"Gosh!" said Owen again. "That's a funny place to get hurt. Do you suppose somebody whacked him?"

"Maybe."

Blackfeather nudged Hammer Smith curiously with his soft grey nose. Why was he so still? Absently, Rebecca patted him.

"He'll be fine," she said to the unicorn. Blackfeather snorted gently and wandered off to crop some grass growing by the bank.

Pulling up the straps of his suspenders, Lewys Maginogion, awakened out of a sound sleep by Catrin, hurried up to them. His sharp old eyes took in the situation at a glance.

"Owen, unsaddle that unicorn and take care of it. Catrin, go fix up a bed in my wagon."

As the two hurried to obey, he knelt beside Rebecca.

"He's got blood on his head. Owen thought maybe he'd been whacked in a fight," she said.

Gingerly Maginogion turned Hammer Smith's head, running a finger in the gash on the top of his head and forehead.

"You'll make it bleed again," protested Rebecca.

"He's out like a candle. Doesn't feel a thing. We'd best get him in the wagon and that wound dressed before he wakes up."

Unobserved by Rebecca, Lewys Maginogion looked pensively down at the lovely visage of his eldest granddaughter, who was looking down at the face of the young man resting in her arms. It had been months since the incident at Joppa, and in all that time his beautiful Rebecca had not voluntarily let any man touch her, flinching even whenever Owen or her Grandfather came close to her accidentally. Yet she held this stranger against her with no sign of shrinking.

They put the unconscious man to bed in the wagon Owen shared with Lewys. As Lewys cleaned and dressed the wound, he thought about what he had learned in the village yesterday, and a plan began to form in his mind. Only if the young man proved worthy of course...

Twenty minutes later, dressed in a grey cotton shirt and trousers, Rebecca was sitting on a folding campstool, brushing her hair with the aid of a hand mirror.

A pan of sliced meat was sizzling on the fire, and Catrin, similarly dressed, with her long curly hair tied back was making sourdough wafers, her face flushed from the fire.

Owen was brushing the mud from the stranger's unicorn. Blackfeather seemed to enjoy it, one hip cocked as he sleepily munched a bag of grain.

Lewys Maginogion surveyed his brood proudly. They were good kids all of them. Owen was growing tall and straight as a young fire tree. He was gangly still, but his green eyes met a man head on.

His twin, Catrin, took after Lewys' mother, being tall and buxom with thick, curly dark hair. For all she was starting to draw the men's eyes like bees to nectar, she was still enough of a child not to notice their admiring stares.

His gaze dropped to his oldest granddaughter. With her hair drawn back, the resemblance to his dead wife was eerie. Rebecca wasn't the looker Catrin was; her red-lipped mouth was too wide, and those gray eyes under her slanted brows gave her heart-shaped face an unearthly beauty, but he knew from his own experience many years ago just how potent a spell that exotic loveliness could cast. He had been caught in just such a web years ago when he first laid eyes on his dead wife, Anghard.

"All of you, come here," he said. "I need to tell you what I learned in the village yesterday. Catrin, leave those biscuits alone. We won't starve in the next ten minutes.

Obediently, Catrin and Owen seated themselves on a nearby log. Rebecca turned to face him on the folding campstool, a thick black braid lying over her shoulder.

"John Thomas Lazarus has put out a reward for our arrest for unauthorized magic. I saw it posted on the wall outside the sheriff's office."

"But we haven't done anything!" Catrin cried, tears trembling on the ends of her lashes.

Rebecca said nothing, but she shut her eyes and clasped her hands in her lap. Magic users were regulated by the Shan. Powerful and mid-range users were recruited to serve in the Shan's Magi Proctors. Less powerful magic users were required to buy a license to use magic, or if proven to be of the right bloodlines, used as breeding stock. In either case, Magi were tested and licensed and paid a fee to the King to practice their arts. At least it worked so in theory. In practice, the rule of the Proctors over Askela's Magi gifted was absolute. Almost no licenses to practice magic were ever issued. Unauthorized users could be hung without trial if they committed crimes using magic. Their only choice to escape this fate would be to join the Wild Magi, if they could find them.

Owen started to curse, and was immediately called to order.

"Owen I'll not have you using words like that in front of your sisters," Lewys said sternly. "Besides, saying a thing like that about a man can get you killed in a challenge."

"Even when he deserves it?" asked Catrin wryly.

"Yes," her grandfather said flatly. "Especially if he deserves it. It's about how powerful he is, not if he deserves the name."

After a short struggle with himself, Owen said, "Yes sir. Sorry, girls."

"Never mind that," Catrin said. "What are we going to *do*?"

Her grandfather patted her hand. "I'll think of something," he said. In fact, he already had a plan in mind, but he wanted to talk to their guest before he came out with it.

"Now, how about breakfast? Am I to starve to death today?"

"Grandfather, what exactly does that notice say?" demanded Rebecca.

He took it out of his pocket and handed it to her. She frowned as she read it aloud. Travelers such as themselves always had a bad reputation in any new town, being automatically suspected of thievery and other less savory actions. Combined with hints of outlaw magic this spelled real trouble. Lewys and Owen were wanted for the assault and attempted murder of John Thomas Lazarus, Catrin and herself for a magical assault on Mrs. Charity Lazarus and for burning a wagon. All were hanging offenses, and the fact that most of it was a tapestry of lies wouldn't matter. In fact, only Rebecca had used any magic; Catrin had used a shovel, and Owen and Lewys had both arrived after the incident was over. Although defending herself hadn't been a crime, with the memory of the day the Proctor took her mother fresh in her mind, Rebecca didn't think being turned over to the Proctors was a better fate.

They had left Joppa quickly after the incident hoping to avoid notice by staying off the regular trade routes. They never gave their real names when plying their trade as sellers of herbs and medicines, but the descriptions of them on the flyer were good. Upon fleeing Joppa, they had turned the gaudy signs on the wagon's side inward and whitewashed the outside so the wagons looked more like ordinary travelling wagons. Unfortunately, Lewys' treasured herd of beautiful, golden draft unicorns were very noticeable. They had been forced to stop several times and reapply the dye that turned their golden coats to a muddy brown.

"Sorcery my foot!" Owen exclaimed. "That old hag probably died of spleen when she found out what her supposedly God-fearing husband was up to!"

"Look for the mote in your own eye," quoted Lewys, "before speaking of the one in your neighbors."

Owen made an angry noise. "I don't care! And don't quote that stuff at me! I'm sick to death of—"

"Stop it! Please!" Rebecca cried.

Everyone looked at her in astonishment. She was weeping. Rebecca never cried.

"This is all my fault," she sobbed. "I should have just done what he wanted—"

"Wash out your mouth of that filth girl!" Lewys roared. "No granddaughter of mine and Anghard's would make a whore of herself for any reason! You did just as you should have," he added more gently. "So did Catrin. What's done is done, and we live now, not in the past."

"Uh—breakfast is ready," Catrin inserted. "That is if anyone is interested."

They stayed another day by the creek finishing the laundry, tending to the wounded man and touching up the dye they applied to the unicorn herd. The man didn't really wake up, but Lewys was able to get a couple of spoons of broth down him.

The first night after everyone had gone to bed, Lewys sat up late. Another man might have been ashamed of himself for what he intended to do. Lewys Maginogion was not. He had a plan to protect his family but he needed more information about his patient before he could decide how much of it was workable. He opened the saddlebags Owen had taken off the unicorn. There wasn't much in them. One of the bags held a clean shirt, an extra needle gun, a small sleeve weapon, a package of kophie and a battered cup and pot. The other held tools for making needles and small containers of compressed air. The most interesting thing he found was a brass badge marked with three stars, a sword crossing an ax, bisected by a Magi wand etched on its face. It was a Merc Badge. The three stars meant the young man held the rank of lieutenant in the Guild. There were those in the Cadre who despised the Mercs, but Lewys wasn't among them. He had spent a little time as a young man with a Merc troop when he had considered becoming one of the Wild Magi. Wild Magi were a loose group of powerful Magi affiliated with the Mercs, but except in a few cases, not members of the Guild. The Guild actually preferred to use them rather than the Proctors, because they would take the loyalty oath to a Merc Commander, whereas the Proctors owed allegiance only to the Shan. The Proctors hated them, but only the most powerful of the Proctors dared to challenge one of them.

The saddle bags also held a gold pendant with a man and woman's image painted inside and a small packet of letters.

Most of the letters were addressed to Andre Benoit. The oldest of these was dated almost ten years ago and had been written to a schoolboy.

My dear son, Lewys read, *Mr. James, the head master from St. Anthony's visited us today and I am afraid your step-father is **very** angry with you. Dearest, you must learn to control that dreadful temper of yours or one day I fear it will lead to serious trouble. I am proud of you for standing up for that poor young man, but was it really necessary to half-drown his tormenter in the chamber pot? And did you really need to break a valuable urn over Jimmy Hendricks head? Not but what I do sympathize with your desire to hit him with something. A more horrid brat I've yet to meet, and his mother is just the same—but I hear your step-father coming. All my love dear and do <u>try</u> to stay out of trouble for a few days. Mama.*

There were several others, all in the same vein. The last one was not written by his mother. Instead, it was written by the Cleric at a church.

My Dear boy, my heart goes out to you at this time. I wish I could be with you to comfort you, but as I cannot, I can only tell you to call upon He who is our greatest comfort in our grief as well as in joy. Your mother did not suffer at all. Dr. Thomas tells us the fall killed her instantly. Your poor step-father is sorely stricken. I hope this mutual sorrow will heal the gulf between you. Call upon me if you should feel the need for my services and I will come. God be with you, Respected Vincent Mc-Cauley

There were two other letters. One was from someone named Marie. It was just a note thanking him for the money to get back home to her family and telling him of her upcoming marriage.

The last one was addressed to someone named Hammer Smith, desiring him to come a village named Cutterston and quoting a price of seven thousand silver coins for unnamed services. Lewys looked again at the dappled unicorn. It was a fine animal, obviously well-bred. A mount such as only a wealthy man or a highly paid mercenary might ride. The man's clothes were good quality, and his weapons well cared for. He was probably a successful Merc then.

Thoughtfully Lewys re-folded the letters and replaced them. A handful of letters wasn't much to base his plan on, but they were all he had. 'The Divinity helps those who helps themselves' he reminded himself. It had been one of Anghard's favorite sayings. Just the thought of her somehow made her seem closer. Would she have approved of what he intended? He thought so. Comforted, he turned into his bedroll and went to sleep.

The next morning dawned bright and clear. Looking into the wagon Lewys found his patient awake.

"Well," he said, "you scared us a mite son. How do you feel?"

Andre Benoit touched his head gingerly. "If I move will it fall off?"

"Headache? Well, I think that can be helped." Lewys rummaged around in Anghard's medicine box until he found a small leather packet filled with white powder. He poured a tiny amount of the powder into a tin cup, added water and swished it around.

"Here," he said, "handing Andre the cup. "This should do the trick."

Andre accepted the cup gingerly. "Who are you?" he asked.

Lewys looked at him in well-feigned surprise. "Why don't you know?"

There was a small silence as Andre finished his medicine. "No," he said at last, "I don't guess I do."

He paused, searching his memory and then he frowned. "As a matter of fact, I don't think I know who *I* am."

"Good Lord," exclaimed Lewys. "I've heard of such a thing, but—"

Andre took him up sharply. "What do you mean?"

"Why, memory loss after a blow to the head. When I worked on cattle station one summer, a fella got kicked in the head by a wild steer. He claimed he didn't know who he was either. Of course, we didn't believe him at first, but we came down to it in the end."

Lewys rubbed his chin. "As I recall, that fella never did get his right memory back."

Andre carefully set his cup down on the wooden chest next to him. "Do you know who I am? How I got here? How did I get hurt?"

"Whoa son," Lewys flung up a hand. "One thing at a time. First, your name is Andre Benoit and you're engaged to marry my eldest granddaughter Rebecca."

Lewys told that whopping lie without a blink. He rushed on before Andre could question him. "You're in bed because it looks like someone took a whack at you. We're not sure how it happened. You rode off hunting prong horn yesterday and your unicorn brought you back. I'm afraid there isn't a lot more I can tell you about yourself before you joined us a couple of weeks ago, because we only just met you, but your war bag is under the bed."

For once in his quick-tongued life, Andre was struck speechless. The story sounded fantastic and he wanted to hear more, but he was tired and found himself drifting back to sleep. Lewys watched him for a minute more, then rose and left the wagon.

That had been relatively easy compared to what was next—explaining to Rebecca, Catrin and Owen what he had done and getting them to go along with it.

The girls were down by the creek, washing clothes. Owen was making a fresh pot of kophie. He had heard what had gone on between Lewys and Andre. He scowled at his grandfather and opened his mouth to speak. Lewys shook his head at him.

"Where are Rebecca and Catrin?"

"Down at the creek doing laundry."

"Good. Come with me; we're going to have a family conference."

"We just did that yesterday," Owen grumbled under his breath as he followed Lewys. "Much good as it did us."

Arriving at the creek, Lewys said jovially, "You two girls look as lovely as flowers in springtime this morning."

Catrin and Rebecca exchanged glances over the bucket of dirty clothes. When their Grandfather started showering compliments, it generally meant he was up to something.

"Thank you," Rebecca said politely.

Both girls waited.

Lewys cleared his throat. "All of you read that wanted notice I brought back from town, didn't you?"

"We read it, Grandpa," Catrin replied.

"Well, then you know there weren't images of us, just a description of an old man, two girls and a younger man. We can't avoid the villages and trade stations forever and it occurred to me that what we need here is a bit of misdirection. Now we can't change our looks, but we can become a party of five instead of four. Ironlyn is still many weeks' travel from here and there are several villages between it and us, including Buttersea where we have to stop if we want to look for your sister. If we travel through those villages as a party of five, everyone who sees us will think of us a group of five people not four, even if the fifth member of the group doesn't stay around long."

Catrin was the first to speak. "You're talking about the man on the war unicorn. Has he agreed to this?"

Owen made a rude noise. "He'll probably stay. You should have heard that pack of lies Grandpa fed him!"

"What if he finds out about the wanted notice?" Rebecca asked. "He might decide to collect the two thousand coins by turning us in."

"He might not turn us in but not want to stay either—"

"Quiet!" Lewys glared them individually into silence.

"Our young friend—his name is Andre Benoit incidentally, has lost his memory because of that clout on the noggin he took."

"Permanently?" Owen asked. "What if he starts remembering?"

Lewys waved that aside. "Makes no difference. It'll stay lost long enough to suit us. Now stop interrupting me! Where was I?"

"Memory loss," Catrin supplied.

"Yes. Well I told him we met him a couple of weeks ago on the trail. He went hunting for meat and came back with a cut across his head. I also told him he was engaged to Rebecca so he'd have a reason to stay around."

Benignly he smiled at his offspring who stared back at him with varying degrees of exasperation, horror or amusement.

"Why you old reprobate!" Catrin exclaimed.

"You," said Owen forcefully, "are a sneaky, underhanded, unscrupulous old—I don't know what."

They both carefully did not look at Rebecca who had gone dead white. She raised stricken eyes to her grandfather.

"I'm sorry Grandpa, but I *can't*," she whispered. "He might want—I can't do it."

Lewys jerked his head at Owen and Catrin. "You two go back to camp. Rebecca and I need to talk. And mind, you remember what I told you if you talk to Andre."

Obediently they started back to the fire. Lewys put an arm around Rebecca and felt her involuntary stiffening.

"Child, you've *got* to do it. Ironlyn is the last hope of the Magi. You know we need a safe place to go—it's getting dangerous to keep up the traveling medicine wagon. We are beginning to be too recognizable. The Proctors were asking questions about us in the last town before Joppa. That flyer will give them the excuse to hunt us down. It takes one of the blood to hold Ironlyn and control the Gate. We can't allow it to fall into the any hands but ours. Besides the Magi Cadre is counting on us to take over at Ironlyn. You know how important that is to what we do."

She pulled away from him and covered her face with her hands.

"Don't you see, he's going to think it's *real*! I dread having even you or Owen touch me and I know you aren't going to—every time a man even touches my hand I remember—"

She broke into sobs.

Lewys' heart ached in pity, but he steeled himself against her tears. If she didn't overcome this fear, she would go maimed all her life.

"Rebecca, you know it isn't natural to feel that way. You must face your fear and overcome it. What is between a man and a woman is good, not evil."

"What happened to me was evil!" she flashed.

"The man is evil and what he did was bad," Lewys agreed. "I'm sorry your first experience was so ugly, but you cannot allow it to rule your life child. Do you want to end your days a sour old maid with no children to light your days as you light mine?"

Her eyes closed. "Grandpa, please!"

Lewys sighed. "Well, child I won't force you to do this for our benefit. The Magi Cadre will find someone else to handle Ironlyn. I can sell the unicorns—"

"Stop it!" she cried. She knew her grandfather loved his unicorn herd second only to his family. It would break his heart to let them go. Her refusal would bring hurt and destitution on everyone she loved and the innocents they were charged to protect. She lifted her chin and wiped her eyes.

"You're right. There is no other way," she took a deep breath and gave him a watery smile. "I'll try the best I can."

Lewys hugged her. "That's my brave girl. I knew I could count on you."

Rebecca deliberately forced her body to relax. Andre would be in bed for another day or so, she hoped. Perhaps by that time she could learn not to flinch.

Catrin and Owen both looked at her anxiously when she and Lewys returned to the fire.

"Are you alright, sis?" Owen asked, his eyes widening as he realize Lewys still had his arm around Rebecca's shoulder and she had not only walked all the way back to camp that way, but didn't move away.

"I'm fine Owen," she smiled at him, a rather strained smile, but a real one nonetheless. "I have agreed to Grandpa's plan."

Owen opened his mouth, thought better of what he had been going to say, and shut it again.

Lewys gave his granddaughter a last hug and moved toward the fire. "Catrin are you burning the biscuits?"

"No, Owen is. It's his turn to cook," she replied.

"*Aggh*!" Owen leaped toward the fire to rescue his mistreated breakfast.

Rebecca took a deep breath, poured a cup of kophie, and mounted the wagon steps. Andre was awake.

"I brought you a cup of kophie. Breakfast will be ready soon."

"I hope you're Rebecca, because if you aren't, I'm engaged to the wrong girl."

An involuntary laugh was surprised out of her. "What a thing to say! It would serve you right if I denied it!"

He smiled back at her, running his eyes over her possessively.

To cover her nervousness, she said hastily, "Here, let me help you sit up. You can't drink kophie lying down."

This was an error, she soon discovered. It brought her entirely too close to him, making her sharply aware of him as a man. He did nothing to ease her nervousness and when she attempted to help him sit up so she could place a pillow behind his back, he put both arms around her waist and leaned against her, inhaling her scent from her breast.

"Ummn—you smell good," he said.

"Your kophie will get cold," she said, pushing against him.

"Better cold kophie than a cold woman," Andre retorted teasingly. But he allowed her to settle him back against the pillow and hand him his cup.

"Where's yours?" he asked, lifting the cup to his mouth. Any doubts as to Lewys Maginogion's veracity had vanished the instant he set eyes on his supposed fiancée. It seemed the most natural thing in the world to him that he should have wanted to marry Rebecca. She was everything he had ever dreamed of in a woman. He was a little puzzled and hurt at her reaction to his embrace though. His dream woman wouldn't have pushed him back.

Rebecca retreated to perch on the foot of the blankets. "Grandpa says you don't remember us."

Andre almost laughed aloud at this simple explanation for her stiffness. She must feel extremely awkward to have him declare he was in love with her, ask her to marry him one day and then the next be told he didn't remember her. No wonder she hadn't responded.

He smiled warmly at her. "I plead guilty, but since I fell in love with you again on sight, I feel I deserve a suspended sentence, don't you?"

Rebecca's lips twitched. "Maybe I do and maybe I don't. There's your pack. Breakfast is in ten minutes." Shaking her head, she left the wagon. A few minutes later, she heard Andre's boots hit the floor.

<u>FIND OUR MORE</u>[1]

Don't miss out!

Visit the website below and you can sign up to receive emails whenever Gail Daley publishes a new book. There's no charge and no obligation.

https://books2read.com/r/B-A-USDE-TJOBB

BOOKS 2 READ

Connecting independent readers to independent writers.

Did you love *The Designer People*? Then you should read *The Interstellar Jewel Heist*[2] by Gail Daley!

[3]

When she finds the body of a retired shopkeeper on the beach, a series of mysterious events draws Lady Jayla into a web of passion, terror and murder. She finally realizes that if she wants to stay alive, she must figure out who the killer is before she becomes the next target.

While dealing with this crises, she also needs to control her dysfunctional house-bot who thinks he's a sex-bot, cope with Jake, her nosy boyfriend and her overprotective family, come to grips with the interplanetary jewel thieves who keep breaking into her shop looking for their missing loot. And then there are the local and interplanetary detectives who think *she* either stole the jewels or that she makes excellent bait for the real thieves. Take your pick.

2. https://books2read.com/u/47Eveg

3. https://books2read.com/u/47Eveg

Read more at www.gaildaleysfineart.com.